WHEN JOSS MET MATT

To Joe, for everything

WHEN JOSS MET MATT

It took me weeks to work up the courage, but on a sunny Friday in May, I was finally ready to tell Matt that we couldn't go on like this anymore. But, of course, I was stuck at work. I spent the afternoon feeling like I was standing with my toes curled around the end of the high dive. The anticipation was killing me. When I finished with the last patient of the day—a rabbit named Bugs—I rushed Nellie through the narcotic count and sterilizing the instruments. I wanted to get on the phone with Matt. Like yesterday.

When I snatched up my bag and dug for my phone, I came up empty. *Oh, please let it be in the car, please let it be in the car* . . . It would just figure if I'd lost my phone on the day I finally got up the nerve to talk to him. My heart pounded as I jogged across the parking lot.

"Come on, come on, come on . . ." I cupped my hands to the window and peered inside. There, on the floor of the passenger side, my phone was waiting. "Oh, thank you!" I didn't know who I was talking to. The words just fell out of my mouth and a tide of relief made my knees weak.

I scooped up the phone and, clasping it to my chest, took a deep breath. I could do this.

"Just call him. All you have to do is call him. Figure out the rest later."

But when I looked down at the screen there was already a text message from Matt himself waiting for me.

Joss, I need you tonight. Call me.

My heart shot into my throat. He only said he needed me for one reason, and one reason alone. It was only supposed to be after a breakup. *He'd been seeing someone?* The thought was like having a bucket of ice water dumped over my head.

All the time I spent figuring out how to tell him how I felt, and he was busy going out with someone? He'd never said a word.

"Oh God, I'm an idiot." I let my head come down on the steering wheel, a little harder than I expected. "Ow."

Maybe I'd misunderstood. Maybe he'd said it by accident. Maybe his autocorrect had done one of those weird things . . . maybe I was grasping at straws.

A knock on the window made me jump. It was my best work friend, Nellie, and she was laughing hard enough to make her ponytail bob up and down wildly. I turned the engine over and let the window down.

"That was hilarious," she said.

"You scared the crap out of me."

"Yeah, yeah. Call him." The laughter was gone from her voice now.

"But he—"

"Ah-ah!" She held up a cautionary finger. "I don't care. You were ready five minutes ago and I'm not going to let you weasel your way out of this."

"But I think—"

"Stop."

"Nel—"

"Shhh!" she snapped. "Call. Now." And when I didn't move she made as if to reach through the window to do it for me.

I yanked my phone out of reach, smacking the plastic Mardi Gras beads dangling from the rearview mirror with the back of my hand. They chittered gaily together. "I will."

She rested her elbows on the window ledge and gestured with one hand for me to go ahead.

"I'm not going to do it in front of you."

"Make the call, and I'll walk away."

I glared at her, but she just made that Nellie face that said, "Go ahead and try to change my mind. See how that goes for you."

"I hate you," I told her, but pressed the speed dial button for Matt. I turned the display so she could see his name and number.

"Thank you!" Her voice was perky now. "Now you better tell him, or I'll have to hit you with my shoe on Monday, mmmkay? 'Kay." And with that, she was gone, fingers waggling.

"You're a terrible frie—" I started to call after her, but Matt cut me off.

"Hello?"

Instant butterflies. "I got your message."

He got right to the point. "Are you busy?"

"No. I'm not." I hoped he couldn't hear how nervous I felt.

"Do you want to have dinner?"

"Huh?" I blinked.

"Dinner? You know, where you eat?"

I couldn't help smiling, even while my stomach churned. "Yeah, I know dinner."

"So, do you want some?"

Maybe I'd misinterpreted his text. Maybe it really had been one of those autocorrect disasters. "Um, sure. I guess."

"Seven?"

"Okay."

We said our goodbyes and disconnected. I stared at the blank phone for a moment. He would never suggest dinner if all he wanted was Sorbet. So maybe tonight was my night after all. The thought made my stomach go into a full-on Olympic gymnastics floor routine, my heart pounding and cold sweat making my skin prickle. I was going to need some serious courage, and I couldn't think of a store that sold it on my way home from work.

Damn.

Seven years had led up to this. It was something of a miracle we were still on speaking terms after all we'd been through, and I was about to put it all on the line.

To think it had all started over my inability to drink beer.

CHAPTER TWO

SEVEN YEARS EARLIER . . . FIRST SEMESTER FRESHMAN YEAR OF COLLEGE

Matt Lehrer's college roommate was a politician above all else. I figured that out halfway through his obviously-not-spontaneous visit to my dorm room—coincidentally located directly above his. He'd come to invite us to a party, just a couple of hours before he planned to haul a quarter-barrel of Coors Light through the window. All he wanted was to make sure my roommate, Rachel, and I wouldn't narc on him for all the noise. We wouldn't have, but he didn't know that, and I wasn't going to turn down the invitation. I was out on my own—well, as on my own as a double-occupancy dorm room at the University of Wisconsin–Madison would allow anyway—and determined to have my first taste of freedom. Or Coors Light, in this case.

Rachel was a lot like me—a good girl from a good home with a boyfriend who'd just become long distance. She wasn't sure about the party, but she was willing to come along for the ride. I didn't know anybody in the room, which was expected but still made me hyperaware of everything I did. I felt even shorter than my usual five-foot-two and my curly—let's be honest, frizzy at that point in my hair-wrangling history—strawberry-blond hair felt like an advertisement for not blending in. The only place left for Rachel and me to sit was on the short end of one of the twin beds, wedged between a big guy from central Wisconsin and the cinder-block wall. The position made it hard to lift my plastic cup of beer to my mouth, which was okay with me. I'd figured out pretty quickly that (a) I didn't like the taste of beer, and (b) it was getting worse the longer it warmed in my hand.

Our host was also playing bouncer, shuttling people through the door in small groups like some half-baked Harriet Tubman. A dark-haired guy perched on the wall-mounted desk just a few inches from Rachel's bare knees. He glanced down at my cup, still half-full, and met my eyes. I took a self-conscious sip.

"What's your name again?" he asked me.

"Jocelyn Kiel," I said, then quickly amended it to, "Joss." The only people who used my full name were teachers, doctors, and my parents when I was in trouble.

"Matt Lehrer." He held out his hand, which I had to shake awkwardly with my left. I wasn't used to shaking hands, but I would have felt even more stupid leaving him hanging. His hands were warm, and his grip firmer than I expected.

"Do you live in the dorm, too?" I asked.

"I live here." He pointed down to the floor. "You're sitting on my bed."

"Oh!" I felt like I should get up, even though he'd been watching me sit there for over an hour. Instead I looked down at the bedspread for clues to its owner. It was subtle, brown and blue stripes, and entirely too neutral to say anything about anyone. "That's cool."

"You're the girls upstairs, right?" he asked, indicating Rachel and me.

"Yeah. How'd you know?"

He grinned, making dimples appear around his mouth. "Chris said I was supposed to be nice to you." His eyes went automatically to the door, where his roommate was still holding court. Then he spotted something across the room and slid off the desk with an irritated look. "'Scuse me."

Rachel had wandered off to talk to a girl she recognized from orientation and my beer was almost body temperature by the time Matt came back to his perch on the desk. He looked down at my cup, sighed, and got off the desk again. He bent to whisper in my ear. "Come with me for a second."

"Excuse me?"

"Just come with me."

I narrowed my eyes at him. "Why?"

"Relax, I've got something for you."

"What is it?"

He glanced around to see who was in earshot. "Something I'm not willing to share with everyone here, okay?"

"Like, what? Herpes?"

His eyes widened and he laughed. "Just come on."

I gave him a once-over. He seemed harmless—in fact, he practically oozed non-threatening nice guy. Besides, he'd laughed at my herpes comment, how bad could he be? I squeezed out of my seat, and followed him out of the room.

"Where are we going?" I asked as we walked down the hall.

"You're a very suspicious person."

"Wouldn't you be?"

"Relax," he replied, smiling over his shoulder with an eye roll.

We left the building by a side door and walked into the cloud of smoke that constantly lingered in the area. It was the only designated smoking area and it was almost never empty. A small clutch of smokers loitered there, leaning on the bike racks nearby. Matt led the way around the corner of the building. It was dark there, away from the lighted sidewalks. Despite his nice guy aura, I knew I shouldn't be alone outside in the dark with a guy, any guy. I'd even be willing to suck in lungfuls of secondhand smoke for the safety in numbers. I slowed my pace and looked back at the smokers.

"Jocelyn, would you relax?" Matt laughed. "I'm not gonna hurt you."

"It's Joss. And what are we doing out here?"

He reached into his back pocket and produced a small, flat bottle of something clear. "I don't have much of this, but you looked like you could use something a little . . . sweeter."

I hesitated, feeling like an After School Special waiting to happen. Wasn't drinking from a stranger's open container, like, number two on the *Do's and Don'ts of Avoiding Date Rape* pamphlets that had been in the welcome folder we'd all gotten?

"It's not even open, promise," he said, holding up his other hand in surrender.

"You read the date rape pamphlet, too?" I said, smiling.

" 'No means no,' " he quoted, then made the bottle dance. "Peach schnapps, now roofie-free!"

I laughed and took the bottle from him. He was telling the truth, it was still sealed. I cracked the plastic cap and took a sniff. It smelled like candy. Couldn't be any worse than beer, I figured, so I took a healthy swig. It did taste like candy, until the heat hit my throat.

I choked. "It's good."

His laugh wasn't mean, but my cheeks got hot anyway.

"Good." He took a drink himself and pulled a face.

"What?" I laughed.

"Kind of girly."

I smiled and took another sip. "So, why are you sharing with me?"

"Watching you torture that beer for the last hour was depressing me."

The blush spread from my cheeks to my ears. "I've never really drank much." *Drunk much?* I could never decide.

"Me either."

I wondered if that was true, but it hardly mattered. We leaned against the wall together, passing the bottle back and forth. Matt, true to his word, kept his hands to himself. Ahead of us, the wide grassy space optimistically called The Riviera sparkled with fireflies. There was almost no traffic at this end of campus after dark. Just the occasional bus and one car headed toward the university hospital.

"Can I tell you something?" he asked.

"I guess."

He sipped from the bottle then handed it to me before speaking. "I'm just waiting for someone to figure out I have no idea what I'm doing here."

I knew exactly what he meant. It was nice to know I wasn't alone.

He turned his head to look at me and the corner of his mouth twitched down. "Can you not tell everyone I said that?"

I laughed. "So why are you telling me?"

"I don't know." He squinted at me and accepted my offering of the bottle. "You seem like you won't hold it against me."

"Shows what you know. I could be downright evil."

"Are you?"

I shrugged. "Still deciding."

"Well then, I guess I'll have to buy you off with peach schnapps."

"Where are you from?" I asked.

"Mequon."

About forty minutes from my hometown. I knew the area a little. "Mmm, rich boy."

He smiled lazily. "Why, where are you from?"

"Milwaukee," I said.

"Liar." He handed me the bottle.

"Elm Grove," I corrected.

"Rich girl."

"Yeah, right." But to be honest we were both from affluent suburbs. Not exactly where the Hiltons and the Trumps would live, but comfortable.

He didn't answer so I just looked out at the dark Riviera and let the peach schnapps warm my insides. After a few minutes, heat washed up the back of my neck, and tingled in my brain as a wave of dizziness came over me. "Whoa."

"Did it hit you?" he said.

"I think so." I turned my head in his direction and got a faint sensation of spinning. "Yeah."

"You're a lightweight." He laughed again.

"I guess so." I took another drink of the sweet liquor and handed it to Matt. "I should probably stop for a while."

He shifted his weight to return the bottle to his pocket and leaned into my personal space. He smelled like clean laundry.

"You okay?" he asked.

"Yeah."

He inspected me for a second. "Sure?"

I nodded, making my vision swim. "I think I'm drunk."

He laughed. "Just buzzed, probably." He ran his knuckles along my arm. "You're all red."

"How can you tell? It's dark out here."

He leaned closer, inches from my face. "You're still red."

My heart jumped into high gear. He showed no interest in backing away. I thought of my boyfriend from home. Ben, who loved me and promised me we would make it long distance. What would he think about me standing out here in the dark with this dark-eyed stranger? I needed an escape.

"Was Cole Hall your first choice?" I asked. The question was practically obligatory among freshmen. Everyone wanted to know where you *meant* to live, the ultimate clue to how you identified yourself.

He shrugged. "I wanted somewhere in Lakeshore." Housing on campus was divided into two major sections, Southeast and Lakeshore. Southeast was more centrally located, more urban and newer. Lakeshore was traditionally collegiate, with smaller buildings nestled around quads of green space and the lake in view from about half the rooms. "It's nicer over here, don't you think?"

"Nice and low," I said without thinking. In spite of their many convenient features, the Southeast dorms were high-rises, while the tallest building in Lakeshore was four stories.

"What does that mean?"

"Oh. I don't like heights very much." *Or, you know, I have a paralyzing fear of being more than a few stories above the ground.* It wasn't the sort of information I liked to share the first time I met someone. Or ever, if I could help it. People feel obligated to cure others of their phobias, and I didn't want curing. I was perfectly comfortable with avoidance.

"That's funny," he said, smiling and leaning close again.

"It's nicer over here anyway," I added, knowing it sounded like the lame afterthought it was.

Matt's hand lighted on my waist and I struggled to swallow. When his mouth was just a breath away from mine, my brain sent up flares and I remembered Ben. "I have a boyfriend."

He paused. "Really?" He was close enough that I felt his words as much as I heard them.

"Yeah. Ben," I said.

"Okay." He backed away and I caught my breath.

"Oh." I'd sort of expected him to say "So what?" and kiss me anyway. Apparently he really was as nice as he seemed. Or maybe he had memorized the date rape pamphlet. Either way, he was clearly not the romantic "So what?" type. Not that I wanted him to be, I reminded myself. I had a boyfriend.

"You wanna go back in?" he asked. I nodded and fell in step behind him.

I was late for my first chem lab. I didn't even like the subject, I was only taking the stupid class because I'd made the mistake of telling my advisor I wanted to be a vet when I was a kid, and now I was lost. I felt like the biggest dork of a freshman in the history of the world. My eyes were red with unshed tears of frustration as a result of my frenzied search through the basement of the monolithic chemistry building. In short, I wasn't looking my best when I was confronted with Matt Lehrer for the first time since we'd stood in the shadows of our dorm and almost kissed. Well, we'd thought about kissing, I guess. Or, at least, I had. I was sure he'd thought the same thing, but he grinned at me when I came through the door and tipped his head at the empty seat at the table beside him. Apparently, he wasn't bothered by my rebuff of his advance.

I took the last empty seat at the four-person table. One of the legs on my stool was short, and it tipped far enough to make me flail my arms a bit. Matt was across the aisle, but he smirked at my suave move, and held up one finger in the signal for "Wait a second." After listening to the teaching assistant introduce herself, Matt tapped the guy next to him on the shoulder. He whispered, "Hey, would you mind switching with my friend?"

I must have looked skeptical about the title, because Matt dropped a wink at me. The guy was willing to switch, and I didn't want to cause any more of a scene than my late arrival already had, so I took his seat.

Matt leaned sideways on his lab stool, close enough to stir my curls with his breath when he spoke. "Thanks, that guy hates me."

I turned my head to give him a confused look. "Why was he sitting with you?"

"He doesn't know he hates me yet."

"What?"

"I fully intended to let him do all the work."

I laughed loud enough to get everyone looking at me, which made my cheeks burn. Matt laughed softly and whispered, "Sorry."

"You should be."

"I'll make it up to you."

"How?"

"See the two people on the other side of our table?"

"Yeah."

"Pre-med. Honors types. We'll pass this class for sure."

I twisted in my seat to look at him. "I think you're my kind of evil."

"Evil? You?" His expression was incredulous and amused at the same time.

I nodded at the pre-med types facing us from the other side of the lab table. "I can read upside down."

He grinned and held up a curled hand for a fist-bump.

And that was how I found myself partners and friends with Matt.

At the beginning of October, my boyfriend, Ben, called to tell me he was coming up for the weekend. I was so excited, I could barely think. It was the first weekend Ben and I were going to spend together, alone. I felt like a grown-up, although I wouldn't have admitted that to anyone.

Rachel knew how happy I was. It would have been hard not to notice; I was practically climbing the walls. On Friday afternoon, she kindly made herself scarce.

At four o'clock I'd already vacuumed, changed my sheets, showered, and done my hair. There was nothing left to do except sit on my bed pretending to watch TV, but really watching the clock. Each minute dragged into eternity. It was nearly unbearable not knowing when he would arrive.

Finally, at 4:52, a knock at the door sent me flying to my feet and my heart into my throat. I opened the door to Ben's smiling face.

"Hi!" I squeaked, throwing my arms around him.

"Hi," he answered, hugging me tight. I kissed him, hard. He walked me backward into the room, mouth covering mine without a break.

"It's so good to see you," I breathed, trying to put my hands on every inch of him at once.

"It's good to see you."

I helped him take off his coat and drop his backpack on the floor. We fell onto my bed, kissing, and his hands were under my shirt in a heartbeat, clawing at my bra.

In a matter of minutes, my careful hair and makeup job was ruined. We were under the sheets and naked before I could catch my breath. It felt so good to be in Ben's arms again.

"Make love to me," I whispered, feeling cheesy even though I really meant it.

He did. Over and over again for two days. We holed up like criminals in my room, eating delivered pizza and making up for the long weeks apart. Ben was my first everything. First real boyfriend, first love, first *first* . . . and talking on the phone had not been enough. I had never been so happy to see another person in my life. It was incredible.

Sunday morning, Ben was up early—eight o'clock. He had a long drive ahead of him, and he needed to leave soon. I started to cry as soon as he began packing his things.

"Jossie," he said, sitting beside me on the bed, "don't cry."

"I don't want you to go," I bawled.

"Come on, now. You know I have to."

I nodded, miserable.

"Please don't cry. I wanted to talk to you before I go anyway; come on."

I sniffled a few minutes before getting myself under control.

His face was stiff and strange.

"What's wrong?"

"I—I—" he stammered.

"What?" I repeated.

"Joss, I—uh, sort of, um . . . met someone."

I blinked at him. He might as well have been speaking Mandarin. I didn't feel anything—yet. "I don't understand."

"I met someone. At school." He couldn't meet my eyes, looking instead at something over my shoulder.

"What do you mean?" Anger lit a flame within me, but it was just at a simmer so far. I needed more information.

"Her name is Kate."

Her name stoked the flames, and I was rapidly moving from simmering to boiling. I stared at him, silent.

"I didn't want to break up with you over the phone."

Finally, I could move. I got off the bed, dragging the sheet with me and snatched my jeans off the floor. My hands were thick and clumsy, but anger kept my grip tight.

"You're breaking up with me?"

"I'm sorry."

I had to get dressed. I had to protect myself from his eyes. I had to be ready in case I decided to kick him where it hurt. I shoved my legs into my jeans, mindless of my lack of underwear, and pulled a sweatshirt out of my closet. I held it to my chest while fury rattled through my limbs.

"You're breaking up with me *now*?" My voice rose with every word.

"It didn't seem right over the phone."

"It didn't seem *right*?" I repeated. "You thought it was *better* to come up here and—and *fuck* me for two days?" I shouted. He winced. "You—you *asshole!*"

In the silence that followed, I ducked into the sweatshirt and wadded up the sheet. When I saw it in my hands, I threw it at him. It dropped on the floor without impact and I growled in fury.

"Calm down," he implored.

"Calm down? Fuck you!" Moving quickly, I seized the sheet and balled it up again. I wanted to hit him this time. Inside my chest my heart thrashed, sending blood so hard and fast to my body that my vision seemed to pulse with each beat. I wanted to hit him. I needed something that would *hurt*. My fingers wouldn't ease from their grip on the sheet but my eyes looked for something with substance.

"Joss, I'm sorry."

"How could you?" The unbridled anger made me shake and tears breached my lids.

"I didn't mean to—for this to happen. I didn't want to do it . . . over the phone." He stood, letting his hands hang loose at his sides.

A sob escaped my chest. It was like breaking the dam that held

back the floodwaters; I wailed like a baby, humiliated an
let the sheet drop and used my hands to cover my face.

"Jossie." He approached and reached for me. I cracked
forearms down on his with enough force to hurt us both.

"Don't you touch me," I snapped.

"I didn't mean . . ."

A horrifying thought struck me. "Did you sleep with her?"

He didn't answer, but his face told me he had.

I made a senseless noise, rubbing the heels of my hands down
my body. I wanted to wipe him away, get the feel of his hands
off me.

"I'm sorry," Ben said.

"Get out," I moaned. "Get out now." He didn't move, so I
scrambled for the doorknob and threw the door wide. He still
didn't move. "Get out!" I shoved him, but he only had to take a
half-step to save himself. I hated that I couldn't hurt him.

"Jossie, please . . ."

"Get away from me!"

"Joss," he said, but I looked away. He stepped into the hall
and I took resounding pleasure in slamming the door in his face.

Then I crumpled to the floor and cried.

CHAPTER THREE

SEVEN YEARS EARLIER . . . FIRST SEMESTER FRESHMAN YEAR

It took a week of three-times-a-day showers and hysterical crying before I formulated my idiotic plan. It was this: the best way to get over my first love was clearly to have meaningless sex with someone I knew only by his first name. Brilliant, right?

So, the following Friday, I recruited some girls from my floor and sought out info on a frat party.

I wore my tightest jeans, a shirt that showed off my midriff, and no coat. Even at the time, I knew going coatless marked me as a freshman, but I couldn't figure out what older students did with their coats when they went out. All I knew was that I didn't want mine to end up stuffed in a corner getting God knows what on it. Armed with five dollars for my keg cup and a condom, I led the charge into the frat house.

I tried out several guys before I found one who seemed drunk enough to be used and who would then forget me. Just what I wanted. His name was Jeff and he was big and not the sharpest crayon in the box. The kind of guy that gives athletic scholarships a bad reputation.

Around one A.M., I made several vows to be careful and sent my friends packing. Jeff took me up to his room. It wasn't just messy, it was actually dirty. The rug was ground down and stained, the walls marked and the furniture nearly buried under empty soda and beer cans. The whole place smelled like dirty socks. I swallowed my urge to flee and tried on a sassy smile.

He shoved the blankets back to reveal sheets decorated with a sweat ring and collapsed onto the bed with a grin.

"Come here, cutie," he said. I straddled his lap, fully clothed. I was honestly afraid to take my shoes off, but I knew it would have to happen eventually.

His breath smelled like cheap beer and his kisses were sloppy. The longer we fooled around, the looser Jeff's hands were getting on my body, but I persisted. When I sat up to take my shirt off, I realized he had passed out.

Well that's just fucking great.

In my desperation, I actually checked the crotch of his pants. Soft. I dismounted my unconscious frat boy and stood back to survey the situation. To proceed or not to proceed?

It was depressing. Not to mention humiliating. I couldn't believe I was even considering the possibilities. Did I really want to perpetrate a sexual assault? Me? No. *Get out now,* I decided. My nose itched with the telltale warning sign of tears. This was a low point, for sure. Probably the lowest of my life.

I closed the button on my jeans and slipped out of the room. The party was still in full swing when I went downstairs, but I found the door. I was ready to go home.

Outside, the air was still and cold. The sky was clear and starry, but I didn't have time to waste looking at it. I was shivering without my coat, and cursing my choice to leave it back in my nice warm room. Cursing my whole stupid plan, actually. Frat Row was loud with music, laughter, and the sound of girls' heels clicking on the sidewalk. I passed couples, trios of sorority sisters with their arms linked, groups of guys who had reached the play-fighting stage of drunkenness. No one was alone. I picked up the pace.

At the end of Langdon Street, I found the bus line that would take me back to my dorm, and waited for the next pick up. My breath made clouds before me, and my nose was starting to run. I used the edge of my sleeve to wipe it, and realized my shirt smelled like cheap beer and cigarettes. Thank God I didn't smell like Jeff's room anyway. I blinked, expecting my eyes to be running as well, but I seemed to be out of tears.

I wrapped my arms around my exposed middle, questioning my judgment for the millionth time that night. My dorm was across campus, and the only paths there were over a huge hill or down a dark, isolated path along the lake. I was just contemplating walking the lake path back to my dorm when the bus turned the corner.

We called it the Drunk Bus, and for good reason. After dark, the university ran four bus lines in the city for free. It was the best way to move large groups of inebriated students around, and everybody knew it. The bus chugged to a stop in front of me. I could see through the windows that it was already full of students.

When the doors opened, drunken singing poured out like theme music. I climbed the steps and used the handrails to pull myself through the crowded aisle. Since the passengers weren't paying, the drivers had no compunction about filling the buses well beyond capacity. The pink-cheeked drunks on board were launching into a rousing chorus of "You've Lost That Loving Feeling" when the bus pulled away from the stop.

I managed to squeeze my way into a bit of space near the rear door, and found Matt Lehrer sitting in one of the side-facing seats.

"Hey, Joss," he said, blurry-eyed.

"Matt, what's up?" I mustered a smile.

"Are you alone?" he asked.

"Yeah." I shrugged.

"I didn't think you guys did that." He smirked.

"Who's that?"

"Girls. I thought you were pack animals."

"I'm a rebel." I wanted to dissuade him from asking me more about my night. It was too pathetic. "You alone?"

"Yeah, I met some guys from high school while I was out, but they live in Southeast."

The bus lurched around the hairpin turn next to the library and I had to wrap my arms around the nearest pole.

"You wanna sit?" Matt offered.

"No, I'm good."

The Drunken Choral Singers moved on to the opening strains of "Hooked on a Feeling," really relishing the ooga-chakas. I smiled.

"Whereju go tonight?" he asked.

"Frat party."

"Awesome." Matt made a face and turned his hands into the international symbol for "Rock On."

"Shut up. What did you do?"

"I checked out some of the bars on State Street."

"How did you get in?" I demanded.

Matt pulled out his wallet and flashed me a very passable Utah driver's license that listed his age as twenty-one years old.

I took the wallet from him. "Utah?"

"Yeah, I figured they don't see a lot of Utah IDs around here because of all the Mormons. Don't drink much."

I laughed. "Interesting theory. Where did you get this? How could you not tell me about this?"

"There's a guy in Chadbourne selling them for seventy-five bucks," he said, naming the so-called "honors" dorm.

"Seventy-five?" I echoed. "That's a lot."

"It's worked at every place I've tried."

I twisted my mouth, considering. "You got his name?"

"Email. In my room."

"Sweet."

The bus jerked to a halt at the Lakeshore stop, and the Drunken Chorale Singers poured into the quiet of the street, still howling the chorus of "Hooked on a Feeling." I followed the crowd off, Matt falling in step beside me.

"So, seriously, why are you alone tonight?" he asked.

"I was with a bunch of girls from my floor, but they took off."

"Ooh, you get in a fight?" He grinned.

"No, I was talking to this guy . . ." I pressed one palm against my bare stomach. Without even mentioning his name, the thought of Jeff made me feel a mixture of embarrassment and nausea.

"What about The Boyfriend?" he asked.

"Um . . ." I didn't want to talk about Ben so I shifted my gaze away.

"Ah."

I shrugged "Whatever."

He stood back to let me precede him down the narrow stairs leading from the cafeteria parking lot to the lower elevation where our dorm was. I crossed my arms for warmth, waiting for him. He tripped on the last step and stumbled into me. I grabbed him and we staggered into a wall together. I cracked my head, hard enough to make an awful noise, but not hard enough to hurt . . . much.

Matt burst into laughter before he could stop himself. "Oh, ouch! Are you okay?" He cupped the back of my head.

"Yeah, I'm fine." I covered his hand with mine.

"That sounded really bad," he said with muffled laughter.

"What's a little brain damage among friends, right?" I tried to laugh it off, but it did smart.

He squinted at me, like he could somehow check my pupils like a doctor instead of a drunk college freshman. We were once again alone in a dark corner, nearly nose to nose. I thought he was going to kiss me. I wanted him to kiss me. Ben would have kissed me. Before we were dating, I mean.

A gust of wind rounded the corner of the building and I shivered.

Matt eased back and said, "Come on. You're freezing. Let's go inside and I'll give you the guy's email address."

It was the nice guy thing to do, and I have to admit, it frustrated the hell out of me. I wanted a guy who would do what I wanted without me having to ask. Someone who would have rescued me from the clutches of my evil frat guy and swept me off on his white horse. Or at the very least, would have seen that I was ripe for kissing, pressed up against the wall as I was. Matt was either Mr. Rogers nice, didn't find me attractive enough to kiss, or didn't have a romantic bone in his body.

Whatever the reason, it wasn't going to happen. And that meant he wasn't my type.

But he was a friend, the only thing that made chemistry bearable, and he had the goods on a fake ID connection. I didn't need him to be my type.

We hurried across the grass to the entrance of Cole. Matt fitted his key in the door and let us in. I followed him down the hall to his room. The halls had the musty, damp smell of weekends. There was a dark patch of something wet on the mottled blue carpet outside one of the rooms we passed and I wrinkled my nose. Down the hall, someone's stereo was throbbing bass. The frequency was low enough to rattle my chest even though it wasn't very loud.

He unlocked his room and I followed him into the dark.

"Where's your roommate?" I asked.

"Dunno."

"Oh." I sat on the missing roommate's futon, watching Matt go through his arrival routine. He hung up his coat and tossed his keys on the dresser before powering up his computer. It was dim in the room, with only the desk lamp and one wall sconce on, but I could see that he and Chris had changed the room a bit since I'd last been in there. The futon was a new addition, for example. And there were some posters on the wall. Above his bed, Matt had mounted a large black-and-white poster of a brunet pinup from the 1940s or '50s, I wasn't sure. The rest of the wall was a mishmash of photos, a German and an Irish flag, and a UW pennant.

"Who's that?" I pointed to the poster.

"Rita Hayworth," he said. "I'm digging an escape tunnel through the wall behind it."

I grinned at him. "Nice."

He dropped into his desk chair and looked back at me.

"So, who were you with tonight?" he asked.

"Jessie, Geena, um . . . Kerry and Megan."

"I know Jessie," he said, for no apparent reason. I didn't answer.

Matt logged into his email account and scrolled through the messages. "Here it is," he murmured. "What's your address?"

I gave it to him and he forwarded the message to me. "Thanks."

"Let me know when you get one. We can go out."

"Cool." I stood up.

"Are you okay?" he asked.

"Yeah." I nodded. "I think so." I swallowed hard and tried a smile. "Probably drunk."

"You must be building up a tolerance." He turned to the small refrigerator and pulled out an open bottle of blue Powerade. "Want some?"

"I don't drink anything blue," I said.

He laughed. "Why not?"

"I make it a rule not to drink anything that's an unnatural color."

"Blue is natural, the sky is blue," he said.

"You can't drink the sky."

He laughed again. "That's a weird rule."

I shrugged. "It just freaks me out."

"You're a weird girl, Jocelyn."

"I just don't like blue drinks or food."

He took a long drink. "What about blueberries?"

"They're not blue inside."

"So . . . do you peel them?"

"Okay fine, I don't eat electric blue food."

He laughed again, but let the subject drop. "By the way, thanks for ditching me in lab this week. Must have been a hell of a weekend with The Boyfriend." I'd still been wallowing when chem lab came around and skipped.

Apparently, my supply of tears was not out yet. I turned away when my eyes welled up, but I guess I wasn't fast enough.

"Whoa, what'd I say?" Matt asked, standing.

"No, it's nothing. I'm sorry." I blinked hard.

"Are you sure?"

I took a few deep breaths, trying to control my voice before I spoke, but I failed miserably. "He broke up with me."

"Oh."

"He met someone else."

"Oh," was all Matt had to offer.

I covered my face with both hands.

"He's a jerk," Matt added after a moment.

I gave out a choked laugh, looking up at him. "Yeah, you're right." My eyes stung and I covered my face again, swallowing my sobs.

He put his arms around me. I melted into his embrace and tried not to get snot on his shirt.

"It's okay, Joss," he said into my hair.

"I'm sorry." I tried to pull away, but he kept me close.

"Don't. It's okay."

I let him hold me, rubbing my back and swaying slightly, but after a while I seemed to run out of steam. I turned my head, resting my cheek on his chest, and sighed.

"I'm so sorry. I didn't mean to . . . whatever. I'm sorry."

"It's okay." He loosened his arms, letting me lean back.

I wiped at my face. "God, I must look awful."

"Not awful." He squinted at me. "Sit down."

We sat on his bed and he wrapped his arm around my shoulders.

"How long did you guys go out?"

"Since sophomore year."

"Wow."

"Yeah, I know." I dropped my head onto his shoulder.

"So, you've, like, never dated anyone else, have you?"

"Pretty much not."

He laughed quietly.

"It's not funny," I protested.

"It's kind of funny," he said.

"No, it's not." I swatted him in the leg. He didn't answer, but squeezed my shoulder.

I wiped the makeup out of my eyes with the corner of one sleeve. My shirt still smelled like a frat party.

"God, do you know what I did tonight?" I sighed.

"No."

I slumped forward and covered my head with my arms. "I tried to get a frat guy named Jeff to sleep with me," I said to my lap.

Matt's hand landed on my back and he drummed his fingers in thought. "I'm not sure if it's more pathetic that you thought that was a good idea or that you actually failed to get a frat guy to sleep with you."

I sat up. "Hey! He passed out. It wasn't my fault."

He grinned at me. "That's sad."

"Ugh, he was so nasty. Thank God he passed out!"

"Why did you want to sleep with him anyway?"

"It wasn't him! I just . . . I just wanted to . . . I don't know."

"Get your boyfriend out of your system?"

"Yeah." I felt deflated, hearing it out loud like that. "I didn't want him to be the last person I slept with anymore."

"Like sorbet."

I must have looked confused because he elaborated. "You know, at a fancy restaurant, you get sorbet between courses. To cleanse your palate."

"That's exactly it!" I slapped his thigh with both hands.

He laughed.

"I need to 'cleanse my palate.'" I made finger quotes. "Sorbet Sex."

"There's a problem, though," Matt said.

"What?"

"If you have Sorbet Sex with the wrong person, you'll just have to find another person to sleep with after that. It could go on and on . . . years."

I thought about that. "Jeff definitely would have been the wrong person."

"Good thing he passed out."

I smiled. "Thank God for binge drinking."

We fell quiet, looking at each other. I licked my lips, willing him to make the first move. Scoop me up and press me into his bed like a bodice-challenged romance cover girl. It would be so much easier if he just took the lead—I wouldn't have to think. But, he didn't. He didn't look away though, and the corner of his mouth turned up in a tiny smile. I didn't know what to make of him. What I did know was that I was running out of time before the moment went from awkward to creepy.

Just get this over with. The hell with it, I thought, and leaned in. Our lips had just met when the sound of metal scraping on wood startled us and I turned to the door. The key finally sank home, and Matt's roommate, Chris, opened the door.

"'Sup," he mumbled.

"Hey," Matt replied.

Chris peeled off his jacket and stepped out of his shoes before falling into bed, face-first. We watched him breathe for a while, afraid to move or speak. After a few minutes, Chris struggled on the bed until the blankets were more on top of his body than below it. A few minutes after that, he let out a loud snore.

"I should go," I said.

Matt nodded slowly, looking at Chris's motionless form. "Yeah. I guess so."

Matt followed me to the door and held it open for me. I turned in the hall and looked at him in the dim light. He was too nice to ask if he could come back to my room with me, I was pretty certain. I wasn't entirely sure he wanted to, for that matter. I knew I could do the asking, but I had no idea where Rachel might be, and I sort of felt the moment had passed. Matt and I were meant to be friends, probably. I decided to take the high road.

"Thanks for letting me freak out."

"No problem."

Impulsively I hugged him. "You're a good guy."

He gave me a look that said he thought I was crazy as clearly as the words would have.

"Good night."

"Good night, Joss."

I made it home after only a mild battle against the traffic. My cat, Dewey, greeted me at the door with his usual loudmouthed bid for attention. I bent to scratch his head, but it was never enough for him and he pursued me through the house, winding between my ankles and meowing.

"All right, all right," I said, hunkering down to give him a more thorough petting. He flopped onto his side and started doing all his best yoga stretches for me. I rubbed his belly and lied to him that he was a good boy. He ate it up.

Partially satisfied, Dewey let me get back to the business of coming home. I let my laptop cycle on while I divested myself of the crap I toted to work. There were an impressive number of junk emails. The only items of interest were a random hello from my friend Deanna, and the notice that my order from Gap.com had shipped. But I couldn't concentrate well enough to read Deanna's message thoroughly, let alone respond to it.

Dewey jumped onto my lap and put his paws on the keyboard sending the computer into fits. I knocked him away, but he was like a feline bungee jumper and popped immediately back into the same position. The computer went into a restart cycle, thanks to Dewey's lucky paw placement. Taking it as a sign, I decided to go through my snail mail instead.

Again, a remarkable collection of junk with only a few gems.

New issue of *Glamour*, funny card from my sister, Darcy, and the unmistakable calligraphy of a wedding invitation. I slit it open and extracted the inner envelope. It was a square one. Expensive. Usually means an expensive wedding to go with it. The invitation was for Jessie's wedding.

I carried the card to the bulletin board where I kept invitations and announcements pinned. This year was shaping up to be a wedding extravaganza already. I had four Save the Date cards on the board, two invitations and a bridal shower invitation. As luck would have it, Jessie's wedding was on a different day than any other event so far. God forbid I should miss an opportunity to wear uncomfortable shoes and eat lukewarm chicken cordon bleu. I tapped the date into my phone's calendar and made a mental note to find out if Matt was invited.

He probably would be. Jessie had adored Matt since freshman year. She always said he was the nicest boy in the world, even now that he hardly qualified as a boy. All because of Halloween.

CHAPTER FIVE

SEVEN YEARS EARLIER . . . FIRST SEMESTER FRESHMAN YEAR

Halloween is practically a religion in Madison. Not dressing up is strictly a faux pas, and everyone goes out on Saturday night to see and be seen on State Street. The street is closed to traffic and the costumed masses take over. The more creative your costume, the better. At least, for the seasoned pros. As a freshman girl, I followed the unwritten rule: wear something cliché and skimpy. I opted for the angel version. My friends Jessie, Geena, Kerry, and Megan went as a belly dancer, a nurse, a pirate, and a butterfly. We pretty much looked like five exotic dancers on break from the club, but so did most of the other girls on the street.

Matt's roommate, the infamous Chris, had a disreputable older brother. He was having a house party, and he had given Chris the go-ahead to invite anyone who could come up with five-dollars for a cup. I made the list.

Geena brought a bottle of Malibu rum to my room and the five of us spent a couple hours getting ready for our Halloween debut and drinking.

Around nine, the girls convinced me to call Ben and leave him a nasty message on his machine. He picked up. I hung up.

At nine-thirty I called again, and got his answering machine. My extremely mature message went something like this:

"Hi, Ben, it's Jocelyn. Um, if—what's her name?—Kate isn't

with you, I think you should save this message for her later. Did you tell her you slept with me when you came up here? Like, a hundred times? Does she know that? Just checking."

It was totally immature and stupid, but it felt great. To this day, I hope that he brought Kate back to his room and she heard it.

We hit the street parade right after that, teetering down the street with the rest of the costumed masses. It was crowded and freezing, but the costumes we saw made it worth the trip. One group of about ten guys ran up and down the street wearing nothing but Speedos and water polo helmets. Not very creative, but ballsy.

With Kerry navigating, we found our way to the house party. Wielding five-dollar bills, we gained entrance and found an apartment filled with black lights and fluorescent paint. The walls were covered with some kind of plastic and painted with slogans like "Happy Halloween" and "Go Badgers." Also a lot of silly doodles, many of which were undecipherable. The black lights filled the room with an eerie glow, and a fog machine added to the gloom. The only incandescent light came from the kitchen, where I knew the keg would be. We made our way to the light like moths. I spotted Chris loitering in the door to the kitchen.

"'Sup, ladies?" he greeted us, checking us out like cuts of meat. "You guys look good."

He was our benefactor for the evening, so all I said was, "Thanks," despite the fact that he made my skin crawl.

We took our turns at the keg, filling plastic cups, then moved back into the dark living room. The music was loud and it was hard to talk, so we mostly stood in a rough circle and bobbed to the music, draining our beers. I still hated the taste, but my tongue was pretty numb from the Malibu we'd had earlier in the night, so it wasn't as bad as usual.

I got nudged in the back and turned. Matt, disguised as a devil, was behind me.

"Hey." I smiled. "Nice costume."

"What costume?" he shouted over the music.

I laughed.

"You're drinking beer," he noted.

"Trying." I nodded.

He leaned in to my ear and asked, "You doin' okay tonight?" He'd been sweet about the whole Ben thing, asking how I was doing every time I saw him.

"Yeah." I nodded again. "Thanks."

"Good."

Chris appeared at Matt's shoulder and shouted something about "Boat Races."

Matt looked at us. "Wanna play?"

"What?"

He inclined his head toward the kitchen and I followed, curious. Jessie and Geena followed me. There was a drinking game in progress, involving chugging a beer and trying to flip the cup over on the edge of the table. It seemed pretty stupid, but it was amusing to watch.

"You in?" Chris asked me and the other girls.

I shook my head, but Jessie and Geena were ready to play. I watched for a while before I got pulled into a couple of rounds. I lost both times due to my poor chugging skills, and declared myself incapable. I settled for cheering on Jessie and Geena, who showed surprising skill at the game. At first.

It was only one-thirty when Geena started to look a little green. "I don't feel so good."

Chris showed her to the bathroom and I followed with a couple cups of water. I hunkered down behind her while she puked, but I was careful to avoid sitting on the floor. Already sticky and patterned with footprints, I couldn't imagine putting anything but my shoes on it. Geena wasn't so picky, and I couldn't blame her. People kept hammering on the door, but she'd a lot to drink—her stomach seemed bottomless. As soon as she slowed down, I talked her into going outside. She could use the fresh air, and I figured it was better to have her vomit out there than start a riot over the bathroom.

She made it as far as the living room before she sagged against the wall.

"I need to sit down," she said.

"No, come on, let's just get outside."

She didn't answer, but slumped down the wall, eyes closed.

I looked for Jessie, Kerry, and Megan, but I could only find Jessie. She was tucked into a corner of the couch nearly asleep. I shook her awake and demanded, "Where are Kerry and Megan?"

"They left," she mumbled.

"Geena's puking," I informed her.

She didn't reply, but made a face.

"We gotta take her home."

Jessie nodded slowly. "Right behind you."

I forced my way through the crowd to the spot where I'd left Geena. When I got there, I'd lost Jessie again. It was like herding cats. I growled to myself and hunkered down in front of Geena, giving her a full up-skirt view if she'd cared to look. She didn't, of course. She didn't want to see anything but the inside of her own eyelids.

"Are you better now?" I asked.

"No," she groaned.

"Come on, let's go outside." I pulled her to her feet and dragged her toward the door. Outside, I found a dry spot on the steps and directed Geena onto it. "Stay," I told her, then waded back into the party to retrieve Jessie. She was just where I'd left her, and nearly asleep again. I frowned, wondering how I was going to get them both home.

Leaving Jessie for a few minutes, I looked for Chris and asked him where his brother's phone was. "I need to call a cab," I explained.

A guy in earshot started laughing. "Yeah right. You'll never get a cab on Halloween, honey."

"I won't?"

He shook his head. "No way."

"Shit." I'd have to take my chances on the street. Hopefully getting Jessie into the cool air would wake her up a little.

I got Jessie to her feet and pulled her arm over my shoulders. She was always taller than me, and in her stacked heels she towered. I took a staggering step toward the door and earned a few less-than-helpful comments on the way out.

"Dead man walkin'!"

"Tim-ber!"

Chris's brother spotted me and shoved a few people out of the way. "Make a hole, people!" I had a feeling he was more interested in avoiding a spectacular display of bodily fluids in his living room than he was in helping out the little curly-haired angel trying to shove the taller, less steady belly dancer out the door.

Matt was near the door and he rushed to pull Jessie's other arm across his own shoulders. "Let me help you."

I was in no position to protest, or even thank him.

"She okay?" he asked when we got outside.

"Hope so. I've got to get Geena home, too."

Geena at least, was on her feet, but hanging over the railing, heaving.

"I'll help you," Matt said.

"You don't have to," I said.

"I know." He shrugged.

"Seriously, Matt, you don't have to leave. I'll be fine." Jessie unfurled from my shoulders and slumped against the door.

"Yeah, totally fine," Matt agreed.

Geena made a particularly guttural sound and Jessie whined, "Gross."

"Shut up," Geena said, and then gagged.

"Last chance," Matt offered.

I sighed. It was no use fighting the inevitable. "I need help."

"No problem."

The walk to the dorm, which should have taken ten or fifteen minutes, took half an hour. Jessie kept sitting down and Geena was practically dead weight. Matt did most of the work hefting Geena, which left me with the task of directing the aimless Jessie. She begged to stop walking, to sleep anywhere we would leave her.

"At least she's not as useless as Geena," I said, tugging Jessie away from the concrete cover to one of the steam tunnels.

"Hey!" Geena protested.

"I'd rather be Geena tomorrow," Matt said.

"Why?"

"At least she got it all out of her stomach. Jessie's got to sleep it off."

"I think I might—" Geena hiccupped, and Matt rushed her onto the grass, keeping one hand on her elbow, but stepping back to avoid the splash zone.

Jessie took the opportunity to lie down on the sidewalk.

"No, Jess, come on!" I nudged her thigh with my foot. "You gotta get up."

"I'll get her in a second," Matt said.

"Why are you so nice?" I asked. "Don't you get tired of it?"

"What do you mean?"

"You're, like, the nicest guy in the world. You'll help anyone."

He gave me his "you're crazy" look. "No, I won't."

"Why are you helping me?"

"We're friends, dumbass." He patted Geena on the back. "Done?" She nodded and he led her back to the sidewalk. "Why are you helping them?"

"They're my friends."

"So why is it okay for you, but not me?" he asked, bending over Jessie to grab her hands.

"I'm cold," Jessie announced.

"You need to get off the ground," Matt said.

"Because you're a guy," I said as if Jessie hadn't spoken.

"So?"

"So most of the guys I know wouldn't leave a party to help a friend get a couple of drunks home."

"You don't know many nice guys, do you?" He got Jessie up and set her adrift down the sidewalk, so he could retrieve Geena.

"Ben was nice," I said. "Before, I mean."

"Right."

"He was!"

"Nice guys don't—" He cut himself off. "Do what he did."

I winced, but it wasn't Matt's fault. I was the one who brought Ben up. "Yeah. I guess not."

Matt didn't answer, but he exhaled sharply.

He was right, of course, a nice guy wouldn't have led me on for the whole weekend, cheated on me with Kate, then cheated on Kate with me, and then acted like I was irrational for being pissed. But, he'd said he didn't plan it that way, and only two weeks after the breakup, I had to believe he wasn't a monster. I wouldn't have wasted my entire high school dating career and my virginity on a monster, would I?

Jessie had gotten ahead of us by half a block, and as we watched, she chose a spot between two bushes beside the agricultural library and curled up for a nap.

"If she won't get up this time, I'm going to let her sleep there," I told Matt.

He laughed. "Do you think she realizes that our dorm is right there?"

"Jessie!" I shouted. "We're almost home! Get up!"

She stirred, surveyed the area, then jumped up. "Home!" Her heels clip-clopped as she broke into a run. I wondered if she had a key with her.

It took us a few more minutes to guide Geena home, and definitely not at a run. We found Jessie sitting in front of the main entrance to Cole Hall when we rounded the building.

"Did you lose your key?" Matt asked.

"No, Geena has it!" she moaned.

Matt used his own key to open the exterior door and the two of us hustled our drunk charges into the ancient elevator. There was no way Geena could navigate the stairs.

"Where's the key?" I asked Jessie when we were standing in front of Room 213.

"Mmm . . ." She looked befuddled for a moment, then patted Geena's hips. "Here!" She pulled up Geena's skirt on one side, revealing the key safety-pinned to her underwear.

"Smart," Matt observed, while I unclipped the key and opened the door.

"Oh, bed, bed, bed, bed, bed!" Jessie hummed, climbing up the ladder to her loft. Her clod-hopper shoes dropped off the side after a moment.

I looked up at Geena's matching loft, and decided she'd be

better off on the couch below it. We lowered her onto it and I pulled some bedding down from the loft. Matt put a wastebasket by Geena's head and looked in the tiny refrigerator. The only available liquid was a Diet Coke, so he left that next to her as well. I unzipped her boots and pulled them off her feet and then we left them to sleep.

"Thanks," I said when we were in the hall.

"No problem."

My room was across the hall and two doors down. "You wanna come in?" I asked.

"Where's Rachel?" he asked.

"Oh God, she's so lame. She went home for the weekend."

"On Halloween?" He made a face.

"I know, right?" I rolled my eyes as I turned my back slightly to retrieve my key from my bra, and let us into the room. Rachel had her bed lofted with a love seat underneath, but my bed remained on the floor—being on the second floor was all the height I could handle. Lofts scared me. The bed seemed small as I looked at it, and I was strangely embarrassed. "You want something to drink?" I asked. "I don't know what I have."

"I think I need to lay off for a while. I've got some serious gut rot."

I turned from the refrigerator and offered, "Tums?"

"No thanks." He sat on my bed.

I stood for a moment, unsure of where I wanted to settle. Finally I slid into my desk chair and picked at the clasp on my high heels. "My feet are killing me."

"Yeah, but you look good," Matt said.

I rolled my eyes with a smile.

"You don't have to sit over there," he said. "I won't, like, assault you or anything."

"I know." I hesitated a moment, then stood and crossed to

the bed. I sat beside Matt and let one foot slide over to rest against his. "Thanks for helping me get them home."

"Sure." He rubbed at his hairline where devil horns protruded. I could see the spirit gum was ready to give up its hold.

"Your horns are coming loose."

He smirked. "Is that some kind of pick-up line?"

"Not on Halloween." I smiled, flicking at his horns with one hand.

He reached up and set my halo bobbling. When he lowered his hand, he brushed it down my arm, reminding me of the time he'd almost kissed me outside the dorm.

"It's weird to be alone with a guy and not wonder if Ben is going to get jealous," I said. Alcohol always brought out the spirit of confession in me.

"Kind of ironic that he's the one who cheated on you, don't you think?"

"Yeah, I guess it is." I frowned down at a scab on my knee. I'd nicked myself shaving. "Asshat."

Matt let out a surprised bark of laughter. "My great-grandmother was from Ireland, and when she really wanted to insult someone she called them a muppet."

I squinted at him. "Did she mean, like . . . ?" I made my hand into a poor imitation of a puppet in action.

"No, but when I was a kid, I thought she did, and it made me wonder what she had against Kermit."

I laughed. "Then Ben's a muppet."

"I take it you haven't found a conscious frat guy yet?" he asked.

"Shut up." I shoved at him and he laughed. "I haven't. Not that it's any of your business."

"So, you're still looking for a Sorbet Guy?"

My cheeks flushed and I looked away. "Yeah."

He shifted to scratch at the peeling adhesive of his horns, and his fingers brushed my arm again on the way down, so I turned to look at him.

"It shouldn't be someone I know, should it? I mean, shouldn't it be . . . ?" *What? A cheap one-night stand?*

"I still say you run the risk of needing more Sorbet Sex if you go with a stranger. You don't know what you're going to get."

"But if it's someone I know, there's bound to be weirdness between us afterward." My heart downshifted and revved its engines.

He shrugged. "Maybe. But maybe not if he knows what you're after from the beginning."

"And what would he get out of this arrangement?"

"A chance to sleep with a cute girl, no strings attached."

"That sounds a little cheap." My stomach got in on the act, stirring with guilt and nerves. I tried to settle it with nothing but will. After all, I hadn't done anything.

"I may be a nice guy, but I'm still a guy. Trust me, sex is its own reward."

I laughed, looking up at his horns again before letting myself look into his eyes. He met my gaze without hesitation.

"So . . . are you volunteering?" I asked.

His eyebrows lifted. "I am merely discussing a hypothetical situation with you."

My heart did a Tokyo drift maneuver into my throat, making it hard to swallow. Was I seriously considering this? Was he really offering, or was it truly a hypothetical situation? On the other hand, what did I have to lose? I could probably get back my original, wobbly lab stool from that guy if I wanted to. I licked my lips. "Are you sure it won't be weird?"

"It won't be weird. We need each other to pass chem."

Relief quelled my stomach, but my pulse was happy to have a

reason to stay in overdrive. "I thought you were merely discussing a hypothetical situation."

"Oops." He grinned. "Right."

The date rape pamphlets didn't have any information about how to get a guy *into* your pants. Damn him and his keep-your-hands-where-I-can-see-'em nice guy ways. He was going to make me do all the hard work, wasn't he?

"Would . . . what . . ." I paused. It was harder than I thought.

He smiled and looked down at my hands.

"I don't know how . . ." I tried to catch my breath, suddenly absent, ". . . how to ask . . ."

"It's okay," he said. "You don't have to."

CHAPTER SIX

SEVEN YEARS EARLIER . . . FIRST SEMESTER FRESHMAN YEAR

He rested his hand on my leg, tracing a circle around my kneecap with one finger. My skin was so cold from the walk home I could barely feel him touching me. The beer may have contributed to the numbness, for that matter. I concentrated on his hand until I could feel every cell that connected us. Nearly hypnotized, I raised my head and looked at him.

He leaned in and kissed me.

Matt was the third person I'd kissed since my sophomore year of high school. It felt strange, and so exciting. A shiver ran through my back, and a giggle escaped my throat.

"What's so funny?" he asked.

"I'm sorry. I'll stop."

He kissed me again, and my mouth twitched toward another smile.

"What?" He pulled back.

"I don't know. I'm sorry." I tried to sober my face, but the giggles bubbled up again.

"You're crazy," Matt said with a slight smirk. I clapped a hand over my mouth, snickering. "You wanna stop?" he offered.

"No," I said immediately.

"Then shut up," he teased in a low voice, making the insult sound sexy.

I let myself smile through the next kiss, but I managed to keep the nervous laughter at bay.

"You okay?" he asked.

"Yeah. Good."

"Good." He flashed a smile of his own at me, but it was brief. He had better things to do with his mouth.

We kissed for a long time, easing closer and closer. When Matt put his arms around me, he bumped into the wings of my costume. I pulled back and slid my arms out of the straps. Swinging the wings off, I smacked Matt in the head with one.

He flinched. "This must be why angels and devils don't mix."

I laughed. "It's totally the wings," I agreed.

He smiled and kissed me again. Without the wings in the way, he managed to pull the zipper on my dress down. I wanted to keep things fair, so I started in on his clothes. He winced when I pulled the devil horns off, but didn't stop me. Soon we were down to our underwear and I pulled away.

"Wait," I gasped.

"Okay, okay." Matt put his hands up like I was robbing him.

"No, that's not what I meant." I smiled. "I'm cold."

"Oh." He looked lost.

"The blankets," I supplied. The light dawned in his eyes and we stripped back the comforter. Under the sheets we resumed exploring each other's bodies. He was built like a soccer player with muscles long and hard, but not bulging like a weight lifter. I was amazed; to think he'd been hiding that body under his clothes all that time I'd sat beside him in lab. His skin smooth and warm—almost hot. If he'd been flushed, I'd have thought he had a fever. To my cold hands, he felt amazing. He was stronger than Ben; he almost took my breath away when he held me close to rearrange our position.

Matt kissed every part of my body that crossed his path: a shoulder, my chin, the palm of my hand. He was equal opportunity when it came to kissing. It was a new experience for me, and it turned me on like crazy.

Nervousness kept me pleasantly on edge. I wanted this—I wanted it more with every second. But, it was scary at the same time. I'd never been with anyone but Ben. I wondered if I was any good in bed. How could I know that with only one person to ask? A person who was obviously a lying jerk.

Never mind Ben, focus on Matt.

That wasn't hard. He'd found his way into my panties and was doing his best to get every last drop of my attention. I bit my lip and squeezed my eyes shut. If I let him, he could put me over the edge in the space of two breaths.

"I want you." I pulled at his hips, trying to strip off his boxer shorts. He did the job for me, tossing his boxers to the floor and reaching for me.

"Joss," he whispered in my ear, "are you sure?"

I made an affirmative sound and dug my fingers into his back. Physically, I was two hundred percent sure. Mentally, I didn't think I'd ever be completely sure this was the right decision, though. But, I was sure enough.

"Is that a yes?"

"Yes. Please, you're driving me crazy." I reached for him, but he twisted away. "What's wrong?" I asked.

"Just a second," he said, rummaging on the floor.

He returned with a condom and I kicked myself for considering going without. After putting it on, he looked at me. "Are you sure?" he repeated.

"Oh my God, stop asking! I'm sure." He had to stop. I was as sure about such an obviously shaky plan as I was ever going to be. He laughed. When he kissed me, I let the last bit of doubt melt away. He was a damn good kisser. He was damn good at every-thing.

When it was over, Matt leaned on his forearms and propped his forehead against mine, breathing heavily into my face. I scrunched up my nose, knowing my breath probably wasn't any cooler or sweeter than his. After a moment, he seemed to have his wind back enough to lift his head.

"You okay?" he asked.

"Yeah. You?"

He chuckled, the sound abbreviated by his panted breaths. "I'm exhausted," he confessed. "I should get up."

When he got out of bed, my skin stiffened with goose bumps. He'd left cold in his wake, cold that didn't stop at the surface. I gnawed on the inside of my cheek while I watched him move around the dim room, putting on boxer shorts and messing with some of his belongings on the floor. I figured he would get dressed and leave me alone for the rest of the night. A night which seemed very long and quiet to face alone. I'd known what was at risk by asking for a one-night stand—even if it was with a friend. But Matt returned to the bed and slid in with me. My heart rate slowed instantly. He wrapped his arms around me and kissed my face all over.

"Are you okay?" he asked again.

I was, I realized on consideration. "Yeah," I said. An itch in my nose made me think I might let my relief spill down my cheeks. I stifled the tears with a pinch.

"Do you feel better?" he asked. "Palate clear?"

"Yes." It really was.

"Good."

"Thank you," I said into his chest.

"Thank *you*."

"For what?" I asked, looking up.

"You don't seriously have to ask, do you?"

"That wasn't your first time, was it?" I hadn't considered the possibility before.

He laughed. "Uh, no, sorry."

"No it's—I don't know, I figured I should ask."

"No, that questionable honor went to a girl named Sarah a few years ago."

"A few?"

"Don't make me do math, Joss, I'm too tired."

I didn't answer, turning to fit our bodies together like spoons. Matt's arm rested along my thigh, hip to elbow. He squeezed my leg lightly and squirmed into a comfortable position.

"Good night."

I woke up stiff and uncomfortable. Matt had sprawled onto his stomach, pushing me toward the wall. My right arm was pinned beneath me and my legs were cold from pressing against the cinder-block wall. I grunted and pushed back against Matt. He gasped into consciousness and rolled away from me, nearly falling off the bed. Tangled in the sheets as we were, he didn't fall, but we both slid closer to the edge.

"Matt, wake up!" I hissed.

"Oh shit," he gasped. "Shit."

"What's wrong?" I turned toward him. "Are you all right?"

He scrubbed a hand over his face. "Sorry." He blinked at me like an owl. "Sorry. I was having this dream . . ."

"It's okay," I repeated.

"Sorry. I didn't mean to scare you."

"That's okay." I pressed one hand to the side of his face, trying to center him. "What were you dreaming about?"

"I don't remember it all. Something about a cliff. God."

"You almost fell out of bed," I told him.

"Yeah." He rubbed his eyes and blinked at me for a few more minutes. "We slept together last night."

I couldn't help a small laugh. "Uh, yeah."

"That's what I thought."

"Thanks for remembering."

"I didn't mean . . . I didn't forget," he protested. "It just seemed kind of like a dream."

"I'm not *that* good," I said.

He considered me for a second. "There's no way I can answer that."

"Sure, you just say, 'yeah, you are.'"

"Would you believe me?"

"No."

"See?" He smiled and rolled over to kiss me. I cupped the back of his neck and held him there for a while, kissing him several more times.

He propped himself on his elbows, looking down at me. "My head is fucking pounding," he said.

"Mine, too," I agreed.

"You hungry?" he asked.

"A little."

He curled onto his side, facing me, and touched the tip of his nose to my shoulder. "Let's get some breakfast."

"Okay."

Rolling out of bed, he poked around on the floor for his clothes. "Oh man, I am not doing the walk of shame in this," he muttered, holding up his devil horns.

I laughed. "Can you hand me my robe?" I pointed toward the hook on the wall.

He looked at me, paused with one leg of his pants on. "No, I don't think so."

"What?" I said.

"Just get dressed."

"Not in front of you!" I protested.

"I am," he reasoned.

"It's not the same," I said.

"Yes, it is."

"I take it all back. You are not nice."

"Nice has nothing to do with it."

"Matt!" I had to resort to whining. I didn't know what else to do.

"Oh, fine, but hurry up." He tossed my robe at me and sat on Rachel's love seat to put on his shoes.

I managed to slither out of bed without revealing an inch of skin between my neck and my knees. Underwear and yoga pants were easy enough to put on, but I couldn't figure out how to get a shirt on without losing the robe first. I glanced over my shoulder and positioned myself at just the right angle to show Matt nothing but spine. In a swift move, I dropped the robe and ducked into the shirt. I turned to him and made a little ta-da gesture.

"I saw them last night, you know," he advised.

"You were drunk."

"Not *that* drunk."

I crossed my arms over my chest, self-conscious.

"Come on." He opened the door and gestured for me to go first. The hall was deserted. We walked together to the dining hall and found it nearly as empty.

"I guess we're up early," I said.

Matt glanced at his watch. "Everyone else is late."

I surveyed the hot food line, but my stomach turned at the thought of the cafeteria's eggs. I opted for cereal instead. I checked out before Matt and found a booth with a good view of the television in the corner.

Matt slid in across from me and tucked into a plateful of eggs covered in ketchup. I had to look away from his food to even get the first spoonful of cereal into my mouth.

"You okay?" he asked after glancing at me.

"Your food is making me ill."

He nodded. "You're hungover."

"No, it's the ketchup."

"What's wrong with it?"

"Besides the fact that it's on your eggs?"

"I thought your rule was about blue food."

"New rule: ketchup goes on burgers, fries, and hot dogs." I ticked off the list on my fingers.

"You have a lot of rules."

"Just about disgusting stuff."

"Have you ever tried ketchup on eggs? It's good."

"No, and no."

He responded with the mature gesture of showing me a mouthful.

I squeezed my eyes shut and concentrated on swallowing.

"Wimp." Matt laughed.

I kicked him under the table, and he responded in kind.

"Ouch!" I pulled my leg up and rubbed my shin. He grinned at me and I pulled the other leg up preventatively. "This is not very romantic, you know," I said.

"Yeah?" His fork hovered in midair.

"Yeah! This is not exactly what a girl has in mind for breakfast the morning after . . ."

The forkful disappeared into his mouth and he shook his head. "Romance is overrated. Besides, it's different with Sorbet Sex," he said.

"Oh, really?"

He nodded.

"And you're an expert?" I crossed my arms and leaned back in the booth.

"You'd never even heard of it before you met me."

"So, picking on me is just part of the deal?"

"Part of the deal."

"So, you get sex with no strings attached *and* you get to abuse me the next day?"

"I never said there were no strings attached."

"You used those exact words."

He narrowed his eyes in thought. "Never mind that."

"Never mind?"

He stabbed another forkful of ketchuppy eggs and waved it at me. "New rule, okay?"

"There are rules?" My heart was beating hard, although I couldn't be sure if I was nervous about the future of my friendship with Matt, or if my stomach was giving me an early warning sign of an oncoming revolt.

"If you can have rules about food, I can have rules about sex."

I couldn't resist a quick survey of the area to see if our conversation was drawing any attention. We were alone for a two-table radius in all directions.

"Fine. What's the rule?"

He laid his hand, palm up, on the table. "Now, we have to be friends." I gave him a confused look, so he continued. "See, if we never have anything to do with each other after this, then this was just a one-night stand, and you might need to find someone else to sleep with to get rid of that." I nodded, and he went on. "But, if we stay friends, then last night was just a good way to get your ex out of your system. Sorbet."

"I see." And I did. Matt made sense to me, in his own weird way.

I laid my hand in his. We had a deal.

And now we were on the verge of another round of Sorbet, or so it seemed. I looked down at myself. My scrub top was covered in black and gray fur. There was also a water ring across my belly where a guinea pig had peed on me early in the morning. *Yuck.* I peeled it off as I went upstairs, and dropped it, followed by my pants, into the washer in the bathroom closet.

Dewey wandered into the room. He always got concerned when I spent any time in the bathroom. I think he was impressed with my ability to immerse myself in water. Maybe he was waiting for the day when I finally realized how horrible it was to be wet. I don't know, but he settled himself on the rug with his paws tucked in, and looked up at me with feline interest. I scratched his head with my toes and turned on the shower.

I had learned in my first month as a veterinary tech that there was no point in showering before a shift. Well, I guess I could shower before, but I'd just have to do it again at the end of the day.

"*Mow,*" Dewey advised me.

"I'll be fine," I told him and stepped into the shower.

It felt great to get the guinea pig pee off my torso and the smell of animal fear out of my hair. It was kind of ironic that animals were so scared of going to the vet, when all vets and vet techs are animal lovers. No exceptions. You don't get into the field if you don't love animals. In my case, that love extends only to the furry varieties. Luckily, a lot of vets don't do exotic animals. Reptiles and birds need not apply, thank you very much.

I heard my phone ringing on the bathroom counter, but I knew I'd never dry my hands off quickly enough to get it. Besides, not everyone enjoys talking to someone in the shower.

Finishing up, I pushed open the sliding door. Dewey jumped to his feet and began pacing in a circle, yowling and mewing.

"I'm all right, you idiot," I said, stepping onto the bath mat. He reassured himself by rubbing against my wet ankles. "Yuck," I admonished him, nudging him away. I didn't need a fresh coating of cat hair.

Checking the phone, I saw that the call had come from Nellie. She never left messages, so I just called her back.

"So how'd it go?" she answered the phone without a greeting.

She was going to be disappointed in me. "It didn't."

"Why not?" she shouted, loud enough to make me jerk away from the phone.

"He said he needs me."

Nellie was one of the few people in my life who knew all about my Sorbet arrangement with Matt. To say she did not approve would be putting it mildly.

"You are *not* going to sleep with him!"

"I don't know," I lied.

"You are so dysfunctional with him!" she protested. "You promised me—no, forget that—you promised *yourself* you were going to stop with this bullshit."

"Nellie." I sighed. "You don't understand."

"Oh, I understand plenty. You just sit around waiting for Matt to break up with his latest hootchie so you can scrape up the sloppy seconds."

I pressed my fingers to my temple. We'd had this conversation ad nauseam. "It's not like that. He does the same for me. It's mutually beneficial."

"It's mutually sick."

"Nellie," I whined.

"I like Matt, you know that." Everybody did. He was just one of those guys. "But you two are like an episode of *Jerry Springer* waiting to happen. Seriously, what are you going to do when he gets married?"

The thought made me ill. "He's not getting married."

"Do not argue semantics with me, Joss. You have to end this. Now."

"I'm not doing it over the phone," I said.

"Fine. But do it. Tonight. You are worth more than these booty calls."

"Nellie," I said again, but without the whining tone.

She sighed into the phone. "Joss, I love you. You know that. Just fix this."

"I know."

"Call me later."

But even with Nellie's scolding in my ears, and my own resolve from earlier in the day, I still found myself going through the usual post-shower rituals that I always did for Matt.

I have to confess to a unique level of primping before a night with Matt. I guess it's easier to maintain the illusion of perfection when you only go to bed with someone a couple times a year at the most. I shaved my legs to baby-smoothness, exfoliated my entire body until it was beet red, then soothed my skin with handfuls of expensive lotion. I even put a dab of perfume behind each knee and in my cleavage.

I devoted some time to choosing an outfit, starting with the frilliest, prettiest underwear I owned. Silk, lace, and bows, what more can a girl ask for? I've always been a huge fan of lingerie.

Passing Victoria's Secret, I hear a siren song that I simply cannot refuse. Wearing it makes me feel pretty. Even when I have guinea pig pee on my scrubs, I feel pretty wearing lingerie. Matt has always been fond of my collection, and I found myself picking out some new things he hadn't seen even though I told myself it was coincidence.

I really was pathetic.

Dewey hopped up on the bed and started batting around my panties.

"Stop it!" I yelped, all too aware of what his claws could do to silk.

He took them in his mouth and jumped off the bed, headed for one of his secret hideaways. I pursued, catching him at the top of the stairs, and carefully extracted his prize from his teeth. No damage.

"You're lucky you didn't rip these! I would have . . ." I shook my fist at the cat, who was unimpressed with my idle threat.

Back in the bedroom, my phone started ringing again. It was Matt this time.

"Hey, Joss, it's me."

"What's up, Matt?"

"Instead of going out for dinner, do you want to come over? I can make something."

I did a double take at the phone. This was completely unprecedented. It took a second to find a normal tone to reply. "Wow, you're spoiling me rotten today. I can't wait to hear this story."

"I'll tell you over dinner," he said. "Pasta okay?"

"Yeah, sounds fine. Do you want me to bring anything?"

"Just yourself. Be here at seven."

A glance at the clock told me it was a few minutes after six. I would have enough time to control my hair and make it to Matt's right on time. We said goodbye and disconnected. Dewey was on the threshold of the bedroom, eyeing me with no small amount of contempt.

"What is going on in your boyfriend's head?" I asked him. The cat loved Matt with slavish devotion.

"Yeah, I don't know either."

He yawned and eyed the silk underwear still in my hand.

"You're too late," I told him, shaking them in his direction. "I'm putting them on."

I stepped into my underwear and headed back to the bathroom to do battle with my hair. Curls are nothing to be trifled with—if you can master them, you'll have good hair for life, if you can't . . . you might as well start amassing your hat collection now. There is no hope.

Three products and a light diffusing later, I was satisfied with the result. The last step was a little makeup, and then it was back to the closet. I couldn't help hesitating. Normally, I'd pick something and call it a day, but Matt had thrown a wrench in the system with this whole dinner thing.

Am I misinterpreting this? I wondered. *Maybe he didn't mean he needed me.*

I drummed my fingers on the edge of the closet, considering. There was something distinctly unusual about the evening and I couldn't put my finger on it. I could call Matt back and demand answers, I knew. That was part of the deal. We were friends. Good friends.

He would probably laugh it off and tell me I was thinking too hard.

I sighed and chose a trusted black top. It was one of those go-to shirts that I put on when nothing else seemed right. It would be fine for dinner, and it would be fine for my walk—er, drive—of shame tomorrow. I supposed I could bring a change of clothes for the morning, but that was never part of the deal. I don't exactly know why, other than the fact that we established the rules during college.

Written rules. Now that I thought about it, I couldn't remember which one of us had them last, though I remembered clearly when Matt had started the list . . .

CHAPTER EIGHT

SEVEN YEARS EARLIER . . . SECOND SEMESTER FRESHMAN YEAR

There is an art and a science to staying friends with someone you've slept with. Matt and I were blazing new territory in the field, however, as we'd never had a relationship prior to having sex. Since he'd come up with the concept of Sorbet Sex, it was tempting to defer entirely to him for protocol. But he didn't know what to do any more than I did. We never talked about it, but the casual touching was the hardest part.

When I'd get to chem lab, he'd be waiting in his seat and I never quite knew what to do. Act like he hadn't seen me naked and keep my distance? Embrace it and kiss him on the cheek? High five? Fist bump? Perhaps just a thumbs-up. Eventually, we settled on a high tolerance for incidental touching. Like when I slipped into class late, he leaned in and put his hand on my thigh to ask if everything was all right. But we never went beyond that, which was good, because another guy in our lab section asked me out just before finals.

He was my first First Date since my First Date with Ben. No lie, I was nervous. But I knew I would have been more nervous if it hadn't been for the magic of Sorbet Sex. I was no longer the girl who gave it up to her high school boyfriend and got summarily dumped. Chem Lab Guy got to be just someone I went on a date with. Turned out, I liked dating.

By my second semester as a college student, I'd gone out with, or had study dates with, three guys. I kissed them all—even the one who had spent the evening talking about his ex-girlfriend—because I wanted to. There was a time I'd imagined myself to be one of those girls who got lucky, found love early, and made it last forever. Now that Ben had proved me wrong, I found that I didn't want to be a girl who waited around for Mr. Right. Don't get me wrong, I wanted to find him, but I was okay with finding a few Mr. Right Nows along the way. So I kissed them all, and let one of them get me out of my pants. I didn't sleep with him, but he got to see my polka dot panties. I also committed two party crimes of opportunity with guys I couldn't recall the names of later. Not my proudest moments, but I didn't regret any of it. I could live with being a kissing slut for a little while. It was fun not to be a good girl.

Matt and I were in the same ethnic studies class second semester, and that's where he met Her Highness. She had a name, Courtney, but I never called her that. At first, it was because I didn't know who she was. Then, it was because I did.

She was pretty, I'll give her that. More like beautiful. Long dark hair, olive skin, and perfectly straight, white teeth. She was one of those people I could hardly believe existed. Especially being a member of the much more average group of humans: I had curly hair that I had not yet learned to control. At that point, I was still a frequent victim of frizz and a frequent ponytailer. Add to that a build like a fourteen-year-old boy, and a loud laugh that made me show off all of my teeth, including my fillings. Her Highness had no fillings.

It took Matt a few weeks to get her to talk to him. I was sitting next to him at the time, with Geena to my left. Their conversation was whispered, since we were in class, but I could hear it well enough.

"I've been trying to figure out how to get you to talk to me," he said. "And I can't think of anything."

She looked at him suspiciously. "And?"

He shrugged. "I just think you're beautiful, and I want to get to know you."

She smiled—just a little—and whispered, "I'm Courtney."

"Matt," he said, and offered his right hand to her, just as he'd done to me the first time we met.

She raised an eyebrow, but shook his hand.

At the end of class, Her Highness slipped Matt a piece of paper with her number on it. We let her walk away before we spoke.

"Well, well . . . the ice queen thaws," Geena joked.

"Nicely done, Matt." I raised my palm and he gave me a high five. It was a testament to how well we'd learned to be platonic friends that I really was excited for him.

"Thanks." He grinned at us.

"I can't believe you just told her the truth and she went for it," I said as I threaded my arms into my coat.

"It was worth a shot." He smiled. "I guess it worked."

"Hey, you guys, I gotta get to the M.E. building," Geena said, looking at the clock on the wall. "I'll see you later."

Matt and I said goodbye to her and walked out onto the crowded sidewalks.

"So what are you gonna do now that you've got her number?" I asked.

"Call her." He gave me a look that filled in the unspoken *"obviously."*

"And what are you going to do to impress . . . what's her name again?"

"Courtney."

"Yeah, her."

He stepped back to let me precede him down a short flight of steps. "I have no idea."

"Sticking with the honesty thing, huh?" I teased.

"Yeah, I'm sure she'll be really impressed when I call her and say, 'I want to take you out, but I don't know where.'"

"Oh, for sure, girls love that."

He smiled at me. "I'll figure it out."

He must have done something right, because the next week when I got to class, Courtney was sitting next to Matt with the full force of her white smile shining on him. I sat beside Geena in the row behind them.

"I think she has extra teeth," Geena said in a low voice when I was settled.

"I think they just reflect light and *look* like more," I said.

"Like diamonds?"

"Yeah." I leaned forward and whispered in Matt's ear. "I take it you did well on the phone."

He didn't speak but nodded slowly.

In a matter of weeks, Matt and Courtney were officially dating. Or at least it seemed that way to me. He took her out a few times, and they always sat together in class. When she ran out at the end of class, she always gave him a kiss on the cheek and a million-watt smile. Matt said she had a class to get to right after, so I never really got a chance to talk to her until Matt invited her to a study session for the mid-term.

Geena and I arrived at the library together, and found Matt holding down the fort at a table in the crowded group study area.

"Hey! Where's Her Highn—Courtney?" I asked.

He narrowed his eyes at me, but ignored the slip. "She should be here any second."

"I'm glad we finally get to talk to her," I said. "I feel like you've been keeping her a secret or something."

Matt shook his head. "Nah, she just doesn't really come to our side of campus ever."

"Still, you should bring her around. We need a chance to give you our approval," Geena agreed.

"Yeah, okay," he scoffed with an eye roll.

"Afraid of what we'll think?" I raised my eyebrows, which is not all that impressive since they're strawberry blond and practically invisible against my freckled forehead.

"No. She's great."

"Afraid of what *she'll* think?" Geena asked.

"That's more likely," I agreed.

"Yeah, so behave yourselves," he said, standing up to flag down Courtney from across the room.

Geena rolled her eyes at me, but was all smiles by the time Her Highness joined us at the table. We did the typical exchanging of names, and Courtney dropped her leather bag in the middle of the table.

"So you guys are friends with Matt?" she asked.

"We live in the same dorm," Geena supplied.

"Oh." She was digging through her backpack when she spoke, and emerged with her cell phone. She checked the display and turned her mouth into a pretty pout before stashing it again.

We studied for a bit, but it was hard to focus. Her Highness seemed to know half the people in the library, and everyone kept coming by to talk to her. It took me a few interruptions to realize what was wrong: she wasn't introducing Matt as anything but a guy from her class.

After an hour, Geena let out a frustrated sigh. "Look, you guys, I have a lot of work to do for my physics class. I'm gonna head out."

We said goodbye while she packed up, and once she was gone, I was the official third wheel.

"Hey, you wanna get some dinner?" Matt asked, looking at Her Highness, then me.

"Yeah, sure," she agreed.

"Joss, you in?"

I hesitated. I didn't really want to be on a date with them, but I was hungry. "If that's okay with you guys."

Her Highness shrugged. "Whatever."

As unwelcome as I obviously was, I wanted to go anyway. Her icy bitch routine was fascinating in the way that a car accident is. I needed more time to stare at her. I wanted to see her thaw and get a glimpse of whatever it was that attracted Matt to her. Apart from the obvious facts of her face and those damn teeth.

We packed up and hit the street. Courtney wanted to go back to the Southeast side of campus, closer to her dorm. It would mean a long walk home later, but I hadn't eaten at that cafeteria, so I thought it would be worth the adventure.

Sitting at dinner with Her Highness was a lot like sitting in the library. She seemed to know everyone. Or at least everyone who had come from the East Coast. The girls all shared a similar look—dark hair, tanned skin, a lot of white teeth. It was like they'd been discharged from a cloning facility. I felt very out of place with my orangey curls and Norwegian looks.

Courtney was engaged in a conversation with a particularly loud pair of girls when I decided not to hold my tongue anymore. I leaned closer to Matt and whispered, "Are you sure we can sit here? I don't have a Prada bag."

"So much for being a rich girl, huh?" He cocked an eyebrow, as if he was enjoying me coming down a peg or two.

"I never said I was a rich girl." I reminded him, enjoying throwing it back in his face.

He grinned. "Oh, that's right, I said it."

"You wanna revise that statement?" I asked.

"Nah."

I whacked him in the leg with the side of my foot and he laughed.

"Um, Matt?" Her Highness directed her attention to Matt for the first time in a while. "I've gotta get going, okay?"

"Oh." He blinked. "I guess I'll talk to you later."

"Great." She gave him her big, beautiful smile and I was struck again by how pretty she truly was. "Sounds good." She leaned over and gave him a kiss on the cheek. "Bye."

She disappeared with her friends, leaving us staring after her. Matt seemed considerably more impressed than me.

"Where's she going?" I asked.

"I'm not sure."

"Doesn't that bother you?"

He redirected his attention to me. "Why?"

"I thought you guys were, like, a thing."

"We've gone out a few times," he said with a shrug. "I guess that's a thing."

"You talk about her like you're a thing."

He shrugged and popped his last French fry into his mouth.

I studied his face, and couldn't get anything out of it. He seemed . . . impassive. "She always kisses you on the cheek," I said. "Has she ever done more than that?"

He laughed. "Uh, yeah."

"Oh?"

He grinned at me. "I'm not going to tell you."

"Why not?"

"'Cause that would be rude."

I raised an eyebrow. "There's nothing to tell?"

He shrugged. "Not much."

"You haven't slept with her?"

"Um . . . ." He drummed his fingers on the melamine cafeteria tray. "Yeah. I did."

My eyes widened. "Really?"

"You sound surprised."

"Well, no . . . I mean, I . . . you just seem so . . . unsure of yourself."

"What do you mean?"

I searched the ceiling for the right words, and of course, found nothing. "Matt . . . you got me to sleep with you like that"—I snapped my fingers—"how can this princess be making you act all weird?"

He laughed. "Okay, first of all, it was not like that." He did his own snap. "We had a deal. There were rules . . ."

"Oh, that's right." I nodded, as if I was just now remembering. "Rules. Did I sign a contract that I'm not aware of?"

"Yeah." He nodded. "In blood."

"Wow. When did that happen?"

"That night you were all over that frat boy. You seriously don't remember this? I faxed a copy to your office . . ."

"Remind me to fire my assistant." I laughed.

He slid his tray out of the way and produced a pen and notebook from his backpack. "I'll just give you the bullet points."

"Great, thanks."

A few minutes later, Matt slid the notebook across to me.

His handwriting was a testosterone-induced scrawl, but I could read it.

Rules for Sorbet Sex

1. *You must spend the night with your Sorbet partner after Sorbet Sex occurs.*
2. *You must remain friends afterward.*
3. *You must harass your Sorbet partner the next day.*

"That's it?" I asked.

He rolled his eyes. "Well, I can't remember all the details off the top of my head."

"Is there anything in the contract about wearing devil horns?"

"Strictly optional."

I laughed.

"You can keep this." He tore the page out and handed it to me.

"Great. I'll have my assistant laminate it." I tucked it into my own backpack.

"You ready to get out of here?"

"Yeah, let's go." I collected my tray and followed Matt to the return conveyor. "So, wait—what was your second of all?"

"What are you talking about?"

"You said 'first of all, it was not like that.'" I snapped again. "What's the second of all? Why is Princess Courtney making you all weird?"

He dropped his tray onto the conveyor belt and sighed. "Never mind."

"Oh, come on, what is it?"

"You're not going to like it."

I felt my eyes light up. "Now you have to tell me."

He frowned, but still held the door for me as we headed for the wintery quad of the Southeast dorms. "Jeez, it's cold," he hissed. "Wanna get the bus?"

"Hell yeah. But you still have to tell me."

"She's hot, okay?" He kept his eyes down toward the pavement. "She's really fucking hot."

It was true, but I couldn't help cringing internally. Her Highness was hotter than I could ever hope to be, and she turned Matt into a shy, awkward mess. I, on the other hand, had never made anyone stammer, or even go for a second, slow look. You try and try to tell yourself that guys are interested in more than a pretty face. It's never true.

When I didn't reply, he said, "I told you you weren't going to like it."

"Hey, the heart wants what it wants, right?" I paused. "Well, maybe it's not your heart in this case, but you get what I'm saying."

"Oh come on, give me a little more credit than that."

"I'm not the one thinking with my—" At the last moment I cut myself off. "My libido."

He laughed. "Nice recovery."

"Thanks."

"And you can't tell me that you're not just as biased *against* her for the way she looks as I'm biased *toward* her."

I sighed. "I'm sure she's delightful, Matty. I just wish she was a smidge nicer to you."

"Matty?" he echoed. I'd never called him by a nickname.

"Don't change the subject."

"Yeah." He sighed. "All right. I wish she was, too."

"You sound like a battered wife."

He frowned at me. "You've made your point."

"I'm just saying—you've given your penis what it wants, maybe it's time to give your soul a little TLC now."

He choked on a laugh. "You just kinda say whatever you're thinking, don't you?"

"I guess I do."

"Can you maybe not? About this?"

"All right." I held up my mittened hands in surrender. "But if you change your mind, I'm available for a reality check any time you'd like."

"I'll have my secretary make a note."

CHAPTER NINE

SEVEN YEARS EARLIER . . . SECOND SEMESTER FRESHMAN YEAR

Rachel and I were watching *Grey's Anatomy* the next day when Matt tapped on our open door.

"Hey, it's Nacho Bar, you guys in?" he asked.

"I already ate," Rachel said.

"But it's Nacho Bar," he protested.

"I'm in," I said, standing up.

"You're gonna miss the end," Rachel warned.

"It's *Grey's*," I said. "They'll save one person, one person will die, and all the main characters will have angst. Fill me in if anything interesting happens."

Rachel frowned at me. She was into pretty much all the nighttime dramas on television. I could take or leave them.

"I'll be back later," I told her.

"'Kay." The commercial break had ended and her attention was back on the screen.

Matt led the way down the stairs and out across the cold quad to the cafeteria entrance. Neither of us had bothered with coats, and the icy wind found every hole in my sweater. I shivered once from the top down when we were safe in the warm entrance.

"You remind me of my dog when you do that," he told me.

"You remind me of my dog all the time," I replied. It was kind of true. Matt's eyes were the same shade of brown as Maxine's, my golden retriever.

"Great." He shook his head and started up the steps to the serving line.

"Nobody else wanted nachos?"

"Guess not."

"Weird." I loved Nacho Bar. We got in the short line and waited for our turn to pile our trays high with beans, cheese, olives, and jalapeños.

"Nice work, Joss," Matt said when we were ready to pay. He was eyeing my heap of food appreciatively.

"I think I would eat nachos every day if I could."

"I think your guts would rot if you did that."

I popped a jalapeño in my mouth and shrugged in response.

"What if they were blue?" he asked. "Would you still eat them every day?"

"Nope. But, I wouldn't know what I was missing because I never would have tasted them in the first place."

He grinned. "I can't believe you'd let your weird prejudice get between you and nachos."

"Blue food is gross."

He laughed. "You're so weird."

The dining hall was sparsely populated, with most of the people seated conveniently next to the TV, where *Grey's Anatomy* was playing. Matt led us to a less crowded area and slid into a booth. I sat across from him and propped my feet against the edge of his seat.

"I have to tell you something," he said.

"What?" I was intent on my pile of chips, rearranging peppers so that I'd have an adequate taste of heat with each bite.

"Do you remember when you asked me if I'd slept with Courtney?"

"Yeah, and you were all weird about it," I said and shoveled a well-dressed chip into my mouth.

"Yeah. That's kind of my point. I don't think she remembers it."

Instantly, I regretted the chip in my mouth. It was hard not to choke as I gasped, "What?"

"She acts like it never happened."

"You only did it once?"

He looked irritated, but answered, "Yeah. The first time I took her out."

"So, wait . . . you've just been . . . what? Waiting this whole time?"

"Well, we haven't really been alone much since then."

"What about when you go out?"

"That's it." He shrugged. "We never even go back to her room, or anything."

I sat back in amazement. "Wow, Matt . . ."

He sighed. "I don't think she likes me very much."

I paused and considered my next move. I didn't think she did either, but I couldn't decide if he was looking for confirmation or reassurance. "Um . . . why do you say that?"

"Well, my first clue was that I saw her out with some guy named Chuck today."

"How do you know his name is Chuck?" I asked.

He sighed and looked past me as he answered. I had a feeling this whole thing was pretty embarrassing for him. "She introduced him."

I wanted to scoot around the table and hug him and try not to laugh at the same time. *Poor guy.* "Wait, just tell me what happened."

"I went to the Nat to work out after my last class. I was just walking in when I saw her coming out of the locker room. I stopped to say hi, and this guy came out of the men's locker room and stopped by her, too. I was just kind of looking at him, and she goes, 'Oh, sorry this is Chuck. Chuck this is Matt, he's in my African Studies class.' And I'm like, 'Hey what's up?' and he just looks at her and says, 'You ready to go, babe?'" He repeated what Chuck had said in moron-voice.

"Maybe he's just one of those people who calls people by nicknames," I tried.

He gave me a pointed look. "I'm not done yet." He went on to tell me that he'd asked Courtney to talk for a second, and she'd sent Chuck on ahead. "I asked her if she wanted to hang out this weekend, and she just looked at me like I was speaking ancient Greek or something. Then, all she said was, 'My boyfriend's waiting, Matt. Can we talk about this later?'"

"Ouch," I said, feeling a sympathy pain in my heart.

"Yeah. That was the biggest clue."

"No kidding."

"Do you think I should call her or something?"

"I think you should probably just find another place to sit in African Studies."

He sighed.

"What a bitch."

A slight smile lit his eyes for a moment.

"Seriously, Matt, she's not even worth the effort. All she is is beautiful."

He sighed again and looked past me, not focusing on anything. "It would have been nice if she just wanted me a little," he said.

My instinct was to say "Aww," like he was an awkward puppy, but I thought that might hurt his feelings. "She's just too stupid to know any better."

He brought his focus back to me and smiled. "Thanks."

"Now are you gonna eat your nachos or are you just gonna stare at them?"

"Eat 'em." To demonstrate, he stuffed a heavily weighted chip in his mouth. When he cleared enough to speak, he asked, "So, what's going on with you? You seeing anybody?"

I laughed. "Not since the guy who told me my boobs were too small."

"Who was that?"

"That guy from Bradley. Jonas."

"He actually said they were too small?"

"No, it was more like, 'I usually go for girls with bigger chests, but you're pretty cute.'"

"On behalf of my gender, I'd like to apologize."

I rolled my eyes. "Don't. He wasn't sober at the time."

"Doesn't being drunk usually make people more honest?"

"Yes. And less likeable."

"For what it's worth, I thought they were very nice." Matt dropped his gaze to my chest for a second.

There was no way to avoid blushing after that remark. *When in doubt, deflect.* "You're so nice, you're even nice to my tiny little tits."

He laughed. "Did you seriously just say that?"

"What?" I looked down at my own chest. "I think we can both agree that if I hope to have a future in porn I'm going to need a boob job."

"I'm just not used to girls who talk like you."

I shrugged. "What can I say? You bring out the crude in me."

He shook his head. "You're nothing like I expected when I first saw you, I can tell you that."

"What did you expect?"

"I don't know. Maybe someone who volunteers at a day camp and leads the youth group at church."

I burst into startled laughter. "Sorry to disappoint you."

"Don't be sorry. I like who you are. There's just not a lot of youth group in you."

"I've been washing dogs at my sister's grooming parlor for three years. You can only wash so many dog butts before you get a little crude."

He held up two hands. "I don't want to know."

I grinned. "A little too much youth group in you, perhaps?"

"Hey, I'm the one who taught you about Sorbet Sex. I'm pretty far from Bible study."

"I guess." I looked at him through narrowed eyes. "The nice guy bit is just to cover up your black soul, huh?"

He laughed. "I knew you were the right person to bring to Nacho Bar."

"I always am." I plucked a jalapeño from the pile and laid it on my tongue with a smile.

When I got back to my room that night, I dug the *Rules for Sorbet Sex* out of my backpack, and added a new item to the list.

4. You must hate your Sorbet partner's ex.

I considered taking it downstairs to him right then, but I couldn't decide if he was looking for a reciprocal offer. I tapped my pen on the paper for a moment, and ultimately decided to put it back where I'd found it.

"Any word from Courtney?" I asked him a few days later, as we paused to collect our mail after dinner.

"Nope." He emphasized the P with a popping sound, and snapped his mailbox shut with unnecessary force.

I tried to organize my face into something neutral. "Are you mad yet?"

"Getting there."

"Good."

"You don't like her very much, do you?" he said, looking up from his small pile of mail.

In response, I dropped my backpack from one shoulder and rooted for the rules. When I found it, I offered it to Matt. "I added a new rule."

He read the list and laughed. "Nice."

"So, I'm just following the rules."

"Are you . . . offering?" He wasn't even looking at me when he asked, stepping out of the way of a group of people coming into the commons.

"I'm . . . available. Just so you know." My ears grew hot, even sticking to this non-language. Even with all the dating I'd caught up on in the last few months, I'd never propositioned a guy before. It was kind of exhilarating.

He smiled. "Thanks."

We fell in step as we crossed the concrete quad to Cole Hall.

"I wish I was way hotter," I said.

"What? Why?"

"So I could make Her Highness jealous for you."

Matt laughed again. "You know, Joss, you hide quite a little vindictive side in that cute exterior."

I tipped my head and gave him a wide-eyed smile. "I'm only thinking of you."

"Well, I appreciate it."

"And cute is exactly the problem I'm talking about. I'm like a little chipmunk or something. You'd need a fucking unicorn to make Her Highness jealous."

"A chipmunk?" he repeated.

"Oh, come on. I've got curly red hair and freckles. Little Orphan Annie never made anyone jealous."

"It's more reddish-blond," he countered.

"My mother always said *strawberry*-blond." I drew out the word and gave an eye roll.

"Whatever." He opened the door to our dorm building and waved me through. "You don't look like Little Orphan Annie."

"Thanks."

"Or a chipmunk."

I laughed. "Well, that's a relief."

We paused in the vestibule and Matt met my eyes. "I should probably . . . finish my Shakespeare paper."

"By which you mean start it?"

"Right."

I nodded. "That's what I thought."

He held up the rules, now folded between two fingers. "Thanks."

"Anytime."

The next week, when I got to African Studies class, I was sur-prised to find Matt in our usual area of the auditorium. It meant Her Highness would be sitting nearby.

"I thought you were gonna find a new place to sit," I said.

He shrugged. "She's gonna pretend like nothing happened, I can pretend like nothing happened," he said.

"Bold."

It was mid-term day. We were instructed to sit only in the desks with odd numbers so there would be spaces between us, and the T.A. passed out the test. The questions were easy—multiple choice—and I was done well before the end of class. I turned in my paper and went to the hall to wait. I had nowhere to be and I was curious about Geena's and Matt's impressions of the exam.

Geena was out soon after me and she agreed that the test was easy. She took the chance to get to her next exam site early for a last-minute review and left me to wait alone again. Courtney came out a few minutes later, and I decided to be the bigger person.

"Hey, Courtney!" I waved to her. "How'd it go?"

"Fine." She shrugged. "Not too hard."

"Cool. Do you have any other mid-terms today?"

"No, I just have to turn in a paper." Her accent wasn't as strong as some of the East Coasters, but she still had a trace of it. To me, it always sounded like they were all trying to hold a couple of marbles in their cheeks and not swallow them.

"Lucky." I spotted Matt coming out of the auditorium and called his name.

"Hey, Joss." He approached and nodded at Her Highness. "What's up, Courtney?"

"What'd you think?" I asked him.

"No biggie." He shrugged.

"Great, then let's get the hell out of here," I said.

"You got it." He slipped the second strap of his backpack on and smiled at Her Highness. "See ya, Court."

We were only a few steps away when she jogged after him and stopped Matt with a perfectly manicured hand on his sleeve. "Look, Matt, I'm sorry about the other day . . ."

"No biggie," Matt repeated.

"It's just that Chuck can be kind of jealous . . ." She made a pretty pout.

"Nothing to be jealous of, right?" he asked with an expression that said she was a little confused, if not nuts.

"Oh . . ." She didn't hide her surprise well. "I guess not."

"Cool. See you later." He turned his back on her and I threaded my hand through his arm.

When I was confident we were out of earshot, I whispered, "That was awesome! I'm so proud of you!"

"Thanks."

"Are you really this cool, or was that just a case of right place, right time?"

"Obviously, I'm really this cool." He glanced at me to see if I was buying that. I wasn't. "Okay, fine. I'm sweating fuckin' bullets."

"Well, I think you should send your deodorant company a letter of appreciation, because you, my friend, look calm, cool, and collected."

He laughed. "I'll have my assistant draft something."

That night I was sucked into a riveting game of Candy Crush when my phone rang, and totally ruined my score. I scowled at the picture displayed on the caller ID before answering.

"I was about to beat level 235, Matt!"

"You've got to quit that game."

I huffed out a sigh. "What's up?"

"Um . . . I . . . I need to see you. Could you come down to my room?"

Electricity sparkled down my back, and my frustration was instantly gone. I was pretty sure I knew what he wanted. "Can you give me a few minutes?" I asked.

"Okay." He took a few experimental breaths. "Chris is gone tonight."

"Oh." My voice cracked and I cleared my throat. "Okay."

"I'll see you in a bit."

"Bye."

I tossed my phone on the bed and grabbed my shower caddy.

If Matt intended to collect on my Sorbet offer, I intended to deliver something worthwhile.

My preparations took about twenty minutes, and then I had to make a wardrobe decision.

Rachel had retired to her loft for one of her marathon phone calls to the long-distance boyfriend and paid no attention while I sorted through my underwear. I'd always had a love of pretty underwear. It's the girliest thing about me by far. My collection wasn't huge or well funded at nineteen, but I took some time picking out some choice pieces. What I wore over my lingerie didn't matter so much to me, as long as I had something silky or lacy underneath, like a superhero costume waiting for the big reveal.

"Good night, Rach," I said as I opened the door.

"What?" She glanced at me. "Oh . . . bye."

"You'll probably be asleep when I get back."

"Okay." She waved distractedly and I closed the door.

Taking a deep breath, I passed through the varied clouds of noise and air pollution that marked the hall of my dorm as I headed for the stairs.

On the first floor, I retraced my steps until I was at Matt's door. It wasn't latched, so I gave it a gentle push.

"Matt?" I asked.

"Hey, Joss. Come in." He was sitting at his desk.

"Should I close the door?"

"Yeah, probably."

"Okay." I leaned against the door until it clicked and reached back to throw the lock. "Is everything all right?"

"Yeah." He stood and came into the center of the room.

"What's up?" I took a few steps closer.

"I got a 'fuck you' email from Courtney."

"Are you serious? Who the hell does she think she is?" I demanded.

He smiled slowly. "I was hoping you'd say that."

"Well seriously, Matt, what did you think I'd say?"

"What is it you call her?"

"Her Highness?" I asked.

"That's it . . ." He nodded. "What a bitch."

"Did you want to show me the email?" I took another few steps.

He sighed. "No, I think you got the take-home message from my description."

I couldn't restrain making a sympathetic face.

"So. Does . . . the offer still stand?" he asked, closing the last few feet between us.

With a smile, I assured him, "Absolutely." I stood on tiptoe to kiss him, resting my fingertips lightly on his shoulders for balance. He grasped my hips and pulled me closer, making me stumble a bit in surprise. His greater size prevented me from doing anything but falling into him, which seemed just fine by his way of thinking, judging by the way he hiked me halfway up his body. I hooked one leg around his waist and did my best to hold on.

My body responded quickly—there was undeniable thrill in knowing I wouldn't have to decide how far to let things get. I wound my arms around Matt's neck and kissed him hard. He made an awkward move toward the futon, and I broke away.

"Isn't that Chris's?"

"The sheets are clean," was all he said.

"Okay, good." I went back to his mouth, loving the feel of his lips and tongue against mine. He was still a really good kisser, even with my larger sample size to compare it to now, and I intended to take advantage of that.

He sat on the futon, taking me down with him and knocking our teeth together.

"Ow!" I gasped and checked my lip for blood.

"Oh, sorry, you okay?"

I silenced further questions with my mouth and he seemed to take that as a good enough answer. We fell back on the mattress and I used my feet to pry off my shoes. They hit the floor with a slap, and I drew my knees up to sit back for a moment. I peeled off my sweater and went back for the shirt beneath.

"You want me to turn off the lights?" Matt asked.

"No, fuck it," I mumbled as I yanked my shirt off. I full-on wanted him, and I didn't care about the ambience.

He laughed, but spread his hands over my bared stomach and ran his thumbs along the lace of my bra. "Nice."

"Thanks." I was glad I'd taken the time to choose carefully.

It was a team effort to take off the rest of our Wisconsin winter layers, but we got it done, and then we were under a sheet together. Matt's hands roamed over my body with enthusiasm while I kept my efforts focused on his mouth. I have always loved kissing, and it was what I missed most about having a steady relationship. I'd collected a lot of kisses since my breakup with Ben, but no one kissed like Matt. I was going to get my fill if I had anything to say about it.

"You're never still, are you?" Matt murmured when I rubbed one foot down his shin.

"Why would I be still?" I asked with a smile. Quite frankly, I was enjoying the hell out of myself.

"No reason." He shifted me until we were facing each other and slipped a hand down between us. My breath caught when he touched just the right spot and I shifted closer.

"You don't have to . . ." I said, even as my movements were insisting that he most certainly did. "This is for you."

"Uh-uh, both of us get something out of this. It's in the rules."

"Mmm . . ." It was getting hard to focus, but I made the effort. "Have your assistant get me an updated copy."

"I'll send out a memo."

I couldn't speak anymore at that point, although my mouth continued to move as I gasped for breath. With my last ounce of control, I grasped his wrist and opened my eyes. To my complete embarrassment, he was grinning at me. I squeezed my eyes shut and said, "Please. Now."

"But—" He started to protest, but I dug my fingers into his shoulder. "Okay. Hang on."

"Hurry."

I dragged him close with every limb I could spare. He pressed into me and we both moaned at the contact, which then made both of us laugh.

"Sorry, it's been a while," I said.

"For me, too." He pressed an openmouthed kiss to my jaw.

"What about Her Highness?"

"A while since anything good," he amended and I felt an unexpected thrill of victory. I celebrated by shifting to the top and pulling my knees up to bracket his ribs.

It wasn't long after that. He was sweating by the time I was done with him, and I only hesitated for a moment before stretching out on top of him. "Is that okay?" I asked. "Am I too heavy?"

"Don't be such a girl," he admonished.

"What's that supposed to mean?"

"You're not too heavy for anyone over the age of twelve."

"Are we going back to the harassment part of the deal already?"

"Yes." Matt pulled me in by the back of my neck and kissed me.

"I thought this part stopped when the harassment started," I said, running one fingertip across his lips.

"This doesn't stop until you have your clothes back on."

"But the harassment starts immediately?"

"Now you've got it." He grunted as we separated.

"This is quite a complicated contract I signed."

He slipped out of bed and stepped into his boxers. "Yeah. I probably would have read it more thoroughly if I were you."

I sat up, covering myself with the sheet. "I'll have my lawyer review any future contracts you offer me."

"Smart move." He pulled on a T-shirt. "I'll be back in a minute. Don't go anywhere."

I smiled. "I'm contractually obligated not to."

"Oh, that's right . . ." He sounded downright delighted.

We spent the night together, talking about everything and nothing. It was barely ten o'clock, unlike on Halloween, and we weren't exhausted. It was nice to just hang out together. I put one of Matt's T-shirts on, but kept my pants off to keep my window for kisses open. I knew it was a silly formality, but I kind of loved that. Our arrangement depended on observing the rules, and without them, we wouldn't be able to function as friends after tonight. Too messy.

In the morning, I had to go back to my room to get my coat and backpack for my first class.

"Hang on a second," Matt said, bending over his desk.

"What?"

He held up a finger and continued scribbling. At last, he handed me the very wrinkled loose-leaf paper that contained the *Rules for Sorbet Sex.* He'd made a few additions:

5. *Both Sorbet partners must get pleasure from the encounter.*

6. *The harassment period begins immediately after the Sorbet encounter.*
7. *The Sorbet encounter is not officially over until both partners are fully clothed.*
8. *The encounter must be followed by the walk of shame. No change of clothes is permitted for the visiting partner.*

"What's with the last rule?" I raised one eyebrow.

He shrugged. "I thought it was funny."

"Fair enough."

He slid one arm around my waist and gave me a friendly kiss on the corner of my mouth. "Thanks, Joss."

"Anytime."

CHAPTER TEN

NOW

I ran a last-minute check through the house, knowing I wouldn't be back until morning. Dewey was happy to get an extra-large serving of food, but after a moment's introspection, gave me a baleful look. He knew what the super-size dinner meant—he'd be on his own tonight.

"Sorry, puss," I said, stooping down to scratch him behind the ears. "Matt predates you. It's a seniority thing—you understand."

He did not.

I went down on all fours and shook my head to make my curls bounce for him. He swatted at one half-heartedly and then turned his back, tail up to show off his butt.

"Gross."

"Mrow."

"Have a good night, buddy."

I threw on my coat and grabbed the huge shoulder bag I was disguising as a purse for the night. It was full of things that were just the other side of forbidden by the silly walk of shame requirement: clean underwear, some toiletries, and my phone charger. My phone would be dead as a doornail if I didn't plug it in at night.

"You're in charge, Dewey. No wild parties," I called to the empty living room. The cat was conspicuously absent. "Fine. Pout. I'll see you tomorrow."

I tossed my bag in the car and dug my phone out for a last-minute text to Matt: *On my way. Sure you don't need anything?*

I was out of the garage and navigating toward the complex's exit when the reply came. *All set. See you in a few.*

Tuning my phone to a playlist from college, I aimed my car for the freeway. The first song that came on, however, nearly made me run off the road. Well, not the song, but the fact that I had to rush to skip it. It reminded me way too much of an ex-boyfriend who was much better forgotten . . .

SEVEN YEARS EARLIER . . . SECOND SEMESTER FRESHMAN YEAR

For a few weeks after the Courtney Sorbet incident, I thought entirely too much about the feel of Matt's lips on mine, and his hands on my body. I knew I needed to find a distraction, because Matt was so clearly not boyfriend material. He was too nice, too even-tempered—he made a great friend, but I liked guys with a little more passion. It was weird that I could be simultaneously proud of Matt for the way he handled Courtney, and know in my heart that I would have wanted him to make some kind of grand gesture to win me back if I were her. That was the real issue—he was completely unromantic. I wanted romance in my life. Hell, Courtney probably wanted it in hers, too, and Matt wasn't that guy. A great guy, yes, but not her guy. Or mine. We weren't meant for each other, and I needed to find someone more my type.

And then I met Alex.

He saw me in my pajamas and my glasses—which I hardly ever wore except when I wanted to see the scrolling headlines on TV at the cafeteria—on a Sunday morning. I should have been repellant. But as we stood waiting for the toaster to free up, he laughed.

"What are you doing?" he asked.

I looked up from my bowl of Trix. "Um . . . taking out all the blue ones?"

"Why?"

Something told me not to be completely honest. "I just don't like them."

He laughed again. "That's pretty weird. I'm Alex."

"Jocelyn."

The guy monopolizing the toaster finished up, and Alex stepped snappily to one side. "Ladies first."

Right away I wanted to throw my glasses in the nearest trash can and yank my ponytail down. Chivalry makes me want to be the kind of lady who deserves it. "Thank you," I said, and laid my wheat bread on the metal conveyor.

"Would you like to have breakfast with me?"

That time, I couldn't restrain one hand from flying up to my glasses. So embarrassing. "I, uh, I—"

"Please?" he asked with an adorable puppy-dog face.

"Okay." I had to give myself an internal pep talk the entire time we were toasting our bread and looking for a seat. I wanted to tell him I'd be right back, run to my room, get dressed and bury my glasses in the quad, but I couldn't figure out how to do that with any subtlety.

It didn't seem to matter to him, though.

Breakfast was just the beginning for Alex and me. We started with study dates at the library. A total pretense, since we weren't in any classes together and he was actually two years ahead of me. Soon it was movies and concerts at the student union, and walks through the arboretum. He had a single room in one of the upperclassmen dorms and the privacy felt like heaven.

By the time summer break arrived, I didn't want to go home.

* * *

On the last day the cafeteria was open, one of the R.A.s came through the hall looking for anyone who wanted to go to the cafeteria. She had a ton of money left on her food card and wanted to use it up. I was in Matt's room at the time, ripping one of his CDs onto my computer. We decided to take her offer.

"So, are you coming up to the cottage or what?" he asked as we trailed the dozen or so people headed for the cafeteria. Matt's parents had a timeshare in a resort town on Lake Michigan. Matt was organizing a trip up there for July Fourth and I hadn't given him a solid answer yet.

"Um . . ."

"Oh, come on, I'm sure Darcy will let you take a Friday off. She's your sister."

"That won't be a problem. It's just—" I pinched my lips shut.

"Alex," he finished the sentence for me, jaw set forward.

We did not see eye to eye on my boyfriend. "He just worries."

"About what?" Matt spread his hands to indicate himself, me, the general area—I wasn't sure what he meant to include in his assessment.

"Well, he can't be there. Can you blame him for wondering what might happen?"

"Yes."

"Matt—"

He put his hands up in surrender. "Okay, whatever you need to do . . . The invitation stands, okay? It's gonna be fun. Everybody's coming."

"Jocelyn!" Alex's voice caught my attention from across the quad.

"Speak of the devil . . ." Matt muttered.

"Stop," I said, giving him a sour look.

Alex jogged the short distance between us and slipped his arm around my waist. "Hey, pumpkin." Then, he spared a nod for Matt. "Hey, man."

Matt nodded back. "I was just telling Joss she really should try to come up to my parents' place for the Fourth of July. It's gonna be a lot of fun."

Alex's hand tightened on my waist. We'd officially dropped away from the group of people going for food. "Yeah, she told me about that. I wish we could make it." He tugged me close and kissed my temple. "I was trying to call you, Jocelyn."

"Sorry."

"Good thing I know where to find you." He laughed a little.

"Hmm. I guess I'll see you later, Joss." Matt waved and took a few steps before he turned and looked at me again. "Please try, it'll be fun."

"I'll try," I said.

He turned again and Alex rubbed my lower back as we watched him walk away. "You're not really thinking of going, are you?" he asked.

I shrugged. "I don't know. It would be really nice. A lot of my friends are going."

"But you know I have to stay in Madison for classes this summer, pumpkin." He made the puppy-dog face I always found adorable. "It's already going to be awful to be away from you so much. You wouldn't want to go without me, right?"

"Well, no . . ." I stuffed my hands in my pockets. "Couldn't you come home just for the holiday? We could go up together."

He smiled and kissed my forehead. "I'm sure we could come up with better things to do for the holiday."

"It'll be a lot of fun. Matt says his parents' place is great."

Alex looked in the direction of the cafeteria. "That guy wants to get in your pants so bad he can taste it." He frowned. "I just don't like the way he looks at you."

Guilt clutched in my gut. I had never, and obviously could never, tell Alex about Matt being my Sorbet Guy. "It's not like that. Matt's my friend."

Alex's frown deepened, then he let out a breath and wrapped me in his arms. "Can you blame me for wanting to keep you all to myself? You're so beautiful. Who wouldn't want you?"

I let the pleasure shiver through me, even as a small part of me answered him in silence, *Anyone but you?* He adored me, and seemed to have no idea that I was just . . . me. "You're so sweet," I said.

He kissed my forehead again. "So, what were you doing? I called your phone three times before I finally came to look for you."

I'd left it in my room, actually, but I knew I had to lie. "I was helping Jessie with her loft. I didn't hear it ring."

He smiled. "I wish you weren't going home this summer. I hate not knowing where you are, what you're doing . . ."

"I'll be locked up like Rapunzel in my parents' house, no worries. Just washing dogs and hanging out with my high school friends, I'm sure."

"And coming up here to see me. Every weekend. Because you can't bear to be away from me."

I laughed. "Right. And that. Aren't you going to come visit me at all?"

"You really want me to take the bus? You can just drive up here."

"No, you're right. I should."

"That's my girl." He smiled. "Now, I have an idea. What do you say I take my gorgeous girlfriend down to the Union and get something better to eat than this cafeteria crap?"

"I say okay." I smiled and he squeezed me with a deep sigh of contentment. I didn't want to go home either. I wanted to stay with Alex. He made me feel like a rare diamond, and I loved that he thought I was a grand prize he'd won. He was so convinced that every guy I knew wanted to steal me away from him. I knew he was dead wrong, but that was part of what made it so endearing. He reminded me of Ben with his protectiveness, except, you know, not a cheating asshole.

Jessie and I drove up to Door County together for the holiday. She'd come through Milwaukee on her way up from Illinois, and we were both delighted not to make the trek alone. Three hours, ending in a feverish search for small, unmarked roads, was not something to take on solo.

"I just cannot believe this is the same lake that I've seen down in Chicago," Jessie said, face pressed to the passenger window.

"Well, it is," I said. "And it's the same lake over in Michigan and all the way up to the Upper Peninsula."

Jessie stuck her tongue out at me, but grinned. She hadn't stopped marveling at the lake since it had come into view.

"I'm so glad you're here!" she squealed. "It would have sucked to drive up here alone!"

"I just wish Alex was coming."

"You see him all the time, this will be good for you."

"Weekends are not all the time."

She rolled her eyes. "Whatever. He's the one being a dork about this."

I kept my mouth shut. I was pretty mad at Alex myself, but I didn't want to talk about it. Saying it out loud would mean admitting that, and for reasons I couldn't fully explain, I didn't want to admit anything was wrong with my relationship with Alex. There were sides to be taken, and being surrounded by friends who would gladly take mine made it harder to remember that Alex was sweet, adoring, and wonderful. He was really stressed out by his summer classes was all. And being apart was harder than we'd expected. I was sure he hadn't meant to upset me. He probably didn't even realize I was upset.

Not that he'd know—he was going camping for the holiday with "some buddies." He wanted me to promise not to go up to Matt's place even though he was gone, but I'd sidestepped the issue. He thought I wasn't going, and I knew I was. We'd deal with it when he was back in range of a cell tower.

"So, um, does Matt have a girl coming up for the weekend?" Jessie asked.

I laughed. "Besides you, me, Geena, and Annemarie, you mean?"

"Yeah." She leaned forward and turned the volume on the radio down to almost nothing. "Like, is he seeing anyone?"

"Oh. Not that I know of. He wasn't seeing anyone last time I talked to him."

"Hm."

Her efforts to sound disinterested were pathetic. "Are you into Matt?" I asked.

"No, I—" she gasped. "He just—he's just really nice is all, and I thought—"

My foot eased up on the gas and the car slowed.

"What? What did I say?"

"Jess. . . ." What the hell was I going to tell her? The truth? Something completely made up that would put her off the trail?

"You think it's a bad idea, don't you?" she asked.

"It's not that—"

"Does he not like me? Did he say something?"

"No! Of course not." I forced myself to bring the car back up to the speed limit. "I, um . . . it's just that I kind of . . ."

"*You* don't like him, do you?" she asked. "You're with Alex!"

"I know that! God! And Alex is madly in love with me, and we are perfectly happy together, by the way—"

She snorted.

"I slept with him."

"No shit."

"Not Alex. Matt."

"*What?*" she shrieked.

I ended up telling her everything, leaving out the irrelevant details, like the fact that he was still the best kisser I'd ever encountered. When I was done, all she wanted to know was, "Does Alex know?"

"Do you think I'm insane?" I demanded.

"God." She slipped one sandal off and propped her foot on the dashboard. "Well, never mind *that* plan."

"Sorry."

She shrugged. "Hey, it's not your fault you got there first."

"I didn't know you were interested in him."

She shrugged again. "Not enough to pick up your sloppy seconds."

I let go of the wheel long enough to give her a shove.

She laughed. "So, wait—what the hell are you doing with Alex if you could have Matt?"

"It's not like that with us. He's a good friend, but he's so not my type."

"You know that makes you sound like a big tramp, right?" she asked.

I gave her another shove.

"I'm just saying . . ." She grinned. "Would you cheat on Alex if Matt wanted to hook up this weekend?"

"No! Jeez! What do you take me for?"

"Hey, I think that's our turn up ahead." Jessie pointed and squinted at the map. I slowed again, and took the right as she confirmed the name of the road. We left my question unanswered as we both started looking for the sign for the next turn.

After we'd found it, Jessie propped her foot on the dashboard again and turned to look at me. "Would it piss you off if I said I think you should date Matt instead of Alex?"

"Why don't you like Alex? Why doesn't anyone?"

"Why doesn't that tell you something?" she retorted.

I scowled at her. "You guys just don't get to see what he's like when we're alone. He's so sweet and he thinks I'm like the greatest thing since sliced bread. Do you know what that's like?"

"Sounds pretty standard to me."

"How so?"

"Isn't that the point of boyfriends? They're supposed to think you walk on water, aren't they?"

"I guess so."

"Well, that's the kind I want." Her other bare foot joined the first on the dash. "Except, you know, I want him to trust me." She gave me a pointed look.

"He's protective. I think it's cute."

"Protective is cute. Freaky jealous—" She sucked air through her teeth. "It gets old. Fast."

We fought. For the remaining six weeks of summer, we fought. I did a lot of apologizing. Enough to make me sick of it, frankly, because I hadn't done anything wrong. I'd done exactly what he'd done, in fact, but that didn't seem to matter to him. Jessie was right, jealousy gets tiring in a big hurry. Sure, it was cute that he thought I was such a catch that other guys were clearly out to snatch me from him at every turn, but there's a little thing called trust, and Alex didn't seem to have any of it in me.

Even after I moved back to Madison in August, it didn't stop. I had hoped our proximity might ease his mind, but nothing changed. Every time I went out with friends, he thought I was cheating on him. Every time a guy smiled at me in public, he got irritated. If I'd breathed a word of our ongoing struggle to my friends, they would have told me to break up with him, so I didn't. I let it all collect in my core, wound tight and tense.

The problem was, aside from the jealousy, I liked him, I couldn't believe that things wouldn't change. For six months, I convinced myself he would change, relax, or finally trust me. Then, it was another three months of telling myself it was time to get the hell out and stop being lazy. See, it turned out that I'm something of an addict for being someone's girlfriend. It took a lot for me to admit that to myself. I like having a boyfriend. I like having someone to count on for a weekend's entertainment. Someone who will come to my apartment and move furniture for me. Someone to spoon with. And Alex was the first long-term boyfriend I had after Ben. It was hard to think of cutting all of that comfort out of my life.

So, I waited. And, yes, maybe I pushed a few buttons in the hopes of bringing myself out of the comfort coma. Ultimately, however, the decision was his. The first time.

I had plans with Jessie, Annemarie, and Kerry for the night. It was just going to be a girls' night out. Nothing exciting. We planned to drink champagne, get strangers to buy us drinks, and give them nothing in return. Our typical definition of fun.

Alex had plans for the night as well. It seemed perfect.

"Do you want to meet up with us after the game?" he asked when we spoke on the phone before he left for the hockey arena.

"I'm not sure. I think the girls are planning on just us for the night."

"Why? Are you trying to meet other guys?"

"No!" I said, feeling my patience stretch to the breaking point. "God, Alex, when are you going to trust me?"

"I do trust you. I just don't trust other guys."

"Which is stupid. If you trust me, you have nothing to worry about."

"At least tell me where you're going to be."

"I don't know." It was true, I didn't know.

"You just don't want to tell me."

"No," I drawled, working hard at not getting mad. "I seriously don't know." Each word got individual enunciation and emphasis as my temper threatened to explode.

"Fine." He hung up the phone.

I stared at it for a moment, stunned at his outburst. He'd never hung up on me before. I considered calling him back just to hang up on him, but there is nothing satisfying about hanging up a cell phone anyway. I decided it wasn't worth the effort.

When we hit the bars that night, it was with a vengeance. I was pissed, and I needed the girls to help me work up a full head of steam to break my relationship inertia. It was the first time I was completely honest about my relationship, and it was like opening a floodgate. I was caffeine-jittery by the time I let it all out, spewing language that would have made a nun faint. To be fair, the girls were not surprised. And they were more than willing to help, offering the classic girlfriend gems:

"You're too good for him."

"You could do so much better."

"Who does he think he is?"

"You should call him up right now and dump his ass."

I probably would have done it anyway, but Alex sealed the deal before I had the chance. He left me a voice mail. I hadn't even heard my phone ring in the crowded bar. I got the message when we were in transit to our next location.

"Jocelyn, it's Alex. I don't know if I can take much more of this. I just can't stand it when I don't know what you're doing. And you don't seem to care. I'm not sure this is working." The message was hard to hear over the background noises. I realized he must be at the arena and that, more than anything, pissed me off.

"That fucker just dumped me during halftime!" I shouted to the girls.

"What?!" was the general reaction. They all insisted on listening to the message and then launched into a five-minute diatribe about Alex's character that involved language far worse than anything I'd come up with.

"Come on," Annemarie said, "let's go find some guys for you to really make him jealous."

"No way," I protested. "I'm not hooking up with some stranger to make a point."

"Oh, come on," Jessie reasoned. "It would serve him right."

"I've got a better idea," I said, already searching my new phone's directory to find Matt's number. He should have been in my favorites, but I was always afraid Alex would see it there and freak out.

"Hello?" he shouted when he picked up.

"Matty, it's Joss."

"Hey, Joss, what's up?"

"Where are you?"

"I'm at the hockey game," he shouted. "Why?"

"I need you tonight."

There was a long pause.

"Matt?"

"My place or yours?" he shouted.

I grinned. "Mine."

"I can be there in an hour."

CHAPTER ELEVEN

SIX YEARS EARLIER . . . FIRST SEMESTER SOPHOMORE YEAR

My nose was still red from my chilly walk home when Matt showed up at my front door. I let him in and told him to have a seat on the couch while I took off my boots. Instead, he followed me into my bedroom and sat on the bed.

"So, what happened?" he asked.

"Huh!" I snorted, and tossed him my cell phone. "Listen to the message." He tapped into my voice mail and held the phone up to his ear, his expression unreadable.

"When did you get this?" he asked.

"Just before I called you. He was at the hockey game. The jerk actually called me from the Kohl Center at fucking halftime!" I yanked my boot off.

"There's no halftime in hockey," Matt said.

I shot him a look. "Whatever." The boot hit the back wall of the closet when I tossed it.

"I'm just saying . . ."

"Well, just don't," I said, throwing my other boot to meet its mate.

He gave me a naughty grin. "Hockey has three periods."

"Matt, I swear to God—" I let the threat hang in the air.

"Man, you are really pissed."

"Wouldn't you be?" I snapped.

"Well, yeah . . ."

"I got dumped on voice mail on a fucking Saturday night!" I ranted. "This is a new one for me, that's for sure!"

"At least it wasn't an email."

"Oh, yeah, there's a fucking silver lining." I pulled my earrings out quickly enough to hurt a little and winced.

"I think this is too fresh," he said. "Are you sure you want to . . . ?"

"Absolutely." I peeled off the hideous white tube socks I'd worn to keep my feet warm inside my boots. "I am so done with him, I don't even want to talk about it."

"Are you sure?" he repeated. "'Cause you're talking about it an awful lot."

"Matt. Seriously. Shut up." I yanked my shirt over my head and shoved my skirt to the floor.

"You really know how to get a guy in the mood," he teased.

"I'm taking my clothes off, aren't I?"

"That's supposed to be enough?"

Now clad only in a black satin bra and lace panties, I put my hands on my hips. "Isn't it?"

"Joss . . ." he hedged.

His hesitancy started to wear through my red haze of rage and I saw the scene for what it was at last. "Dammit." I pressed the heel of one hand against my left eyebrow and squeezed my eyes shut. "I'm just . . . so pissed!"

"I know."

"He's such a . . . jerk."

"Come here."

"Why?"

He rolled his eyes and gestured for me to come closer. I sat beside him on the bed and let him put his arm around me. "Are you okay?"

"Yes. No. I don't know."

"Okay." He pulled me tighter and kissed my head. I turned and kissed him on the lips, cupping his jaw to hold him in place. "Still hot for me, huh?" he teased.

"Just . . . please?"

"Yeah, okay." He sighed.

I looked up at him, surprised. "Really? You're giving in?"

"Well, Jesus, Joss, it's a little hard to say no when you're sitting there in your bad girl underwear."

I let out a surprised laugh and closed my eyes for a moment. "Yeah?"

"You really do have great taste in lingerie."

"Thanks. I'm glad you like it."

"I like it a lot." He nudged me with his shoulder.

"So, are we doing this?" I asked.

"We're doing this." In a remarkably fluid move, he turned and pressed me back on the bed, his body covering mine. The screen print of his T-shirt was cold against my skin so I made short work of pulling it off. He was smaller than Alex, but firmer, and I liked the way his back felt under my hands. I liked a lot of things about being naked with him, for that matter. He was the perfect antidote to a stale relationship. Being with Matt was such a strange combination of familiar and new. The first-time anxiety was gone, but the long gaps between our encounters made each time something exciting.

Even though it wasn't our best work, it was still exactly what I wanted. Matt distracted me from my anger; made me feel good. He actually worked really hard at making me feel good.

"It's okay . . ." I panted, stilling his hands against my body. "I don't know if I can tonight . . ."

"The rules," was his only answer.

I let out a breath, feeling intimidated.

"Relax," he said. "I'm just here for you."

I nodded, and he went back to touching me in all the right ways. I closed my eyes and focused my attention on his hands, his mouth, and his soft breathing. At last the tightening began somewhere between my hips. My hands grasped at the sheet and came up empty. My back arched and my toes curled tight. A thin gasp escaped my lips once, twice, and on the third time stretched into a sound that only comes from one thing . . .

As soon as I could speak, I grabbed at Matt and got downright demanding. "Now, now, now."

He complied eagerly and sighed against my ear when we were joined. I wrapped my legs around his waist and pulled his mouth to mine. Pleasure was still rippling through my body and I wanted to make it last.

An unformed thought flickered through my mind as we moved together. Something about the contrast between Matt and my short list of other lovers. I let it go in favor of an empty mind and a very occupied body.

After, it was hard to breathe with his weight on me, but I didn't mind. He felt warm and familiar. I used my fingertips to follow the shape of his shoulder blades beneath his skin and found the slight hollow over his spine near the middle of his back. He wriggled away from my touch with a soft laugh.

"That tickles."

"Sorry," I said.

"Are your roommates home?" he asked.

"I'm not sure."

"So, walking naked to the bathroom would not be recommended?"

I laughed. "Uh, no."

"That's a shame." He sighed. "I'll be back in a minute."

I slipped on pajama pants and a sweatshirt when he was gone and went to the kitchen to get something to drink. I'd had nothing but champagne and a vodka cranberry all night, and I was parched. Matt found me halfway through my second glass of water.

"You got dressed," he observed.

"Remember that whole not-walking-naked-through-the-house thing?" I said, offering him my glass.

He took a grateful drink and refilled it from the pitcher in the refrigerator. "You know, technically, you've put an end to this . . . session by getting dressed."

I lowered the waistband of my pants enough to show bare hip. "No underwear."

He grinned. "Nice."

We emptied the glass a few more times without talking, then Matt said, "I'm starving."

"Pizza?" I suggested.

"Genius."

We ordered a pizza and went back to my room to wait for it. I picked up my discarded clothes while Matt stretched out on the bed and flipped through the channels on my TV.

"How can you even see the screen on this TV, Joss?" He shaded his eyes and squinted at the small screen.

"It's six feet away. Maybe you need to get your eyes checked."

He fluttered his lashes at me and went back to channel surfing.

I scooped my bra off the floor and returned it carefully to my underwear drawer.

"So, seriously, do you always have sexy underwear on?" he asked.

"Yes," I lied.

He looked dubious, but said, "I knew there was a reason I liked you."

I put my lacy panties into a lingerie bag hanging in the closet and climbed onto the bed next to him. "Oh, yeah, it's sexy twenty-four-seven around here. I mean, look at me." I gestured to my oversized sweatshirt and plaid flannel pants.

"There's something to be said for easy access," he countered, putting one hand inside the cavernous interior of the shirt.

A tap on the door was the only warning before it opened and my roommate Laurel looked in. "Hey, Joss, you ordered a pizza?" She did a double take. "What's going on?"

I sat up, and Matt let his hand slide out of my shirt. "Alex and I broke up."

"Oh, no!" she said. "Are you okay?"

"I'm fine." I shook my head. "Actually, I'm pissed."

Laurel's face vacillated between curiosity, concern, and confusion. "So . . . what . . . ?" She couldn't seem to figure out which question to ask.

"Is the pizza guy here?" I asked.

"Oh, yeah. Sorry."

"I got it," Matt said, climbing over me to get off the bed.

"Wait, lemme give you some cash—" I started to follow him, but he stopped me with an upraised hand.

"You get the next one." He squeezed past Laurel to go to the front door.

"Joss, what's going on?" she hissed as soon as he was out of earshot. "Are you okay?"

"I'm really fine. I'm just hangin' out with Matt. He . . . he's distracting me." That was as good a description as any, I figured. I had only successfully explained Sorbet to two people, and Laurel was not one of them. I had unsuccessfully explained it to a handful of others. The usual reaction was an assumption that I'd had a one-night stand with a friend, or that I'd slept with a guy I barely knew, then realized we were better off as friends. Only my friends Kerry and Geena seemed to embrace the concept. Geena was, in fact, looking for a Sorbet Guy of her very own. Kerry had her doubts about how long we could sustain the agreement, but understood where it had come from.

Laurel squinted at me for a moment. "Is there anything I can do?" she asked.

"I'm okay, Laur. Thanks."

She nodded. "Okay, well . . . let me know if you need anything." She disappeared from the doorway without further comment. Laurel and I were at opposite ends of the chain reaction that formed my house of four. I was friends with Kerry, who was friends with Lisa, who was friends with Laurel. I'd ended up in the place as a last-minute addition when another girl had backed out of the agreement. I didn't really mind; sometimes it's easier to live with people who aren't friends. The business-y aspect of sharing bills is less emotional.

Matt returned with the pizza, and we settled on the floor for our midnight snack. Kerry came home in the middle of it, and followed the smell of hot cheese and sauce to my door. When she saw who I was with, her eyes widened.

"You broke up with Alex?" she said.

"Listen to this." I got the voice mail queued up and handed her the phone.

Her face went from calm to disgusted. "He broke up with you over voice mail?"

"Yeah."

"I see why you're here," she said to Matt.

"At your service." He gave her a two-fingered salute.

"At her service," Kerry corrected, nodding toward me.

I smiled and leaned close enough to Matt to rest my head on his shoulder. He gave me an affectionate scratch.

"Okay, this is officially the weirdest third-wheel position I've ever been in," Kerry declared. "I'm going to bed."

"Good night, Kerr," I said.

"Good night," Matt echoed.

"So, I guess I'll see you both in the morning," she said with a look of amusement.

"Yep."

She closed my bedroom door behind her as she left and we were alone again.

"You're taking this remarkably well," Matt told me.

"I'm pretending it's not happening."

"Do you want me to go?"

"No. Please stay."

"It's in my contract." He grinned. "Come on, let's go to bed."

Sometime after four A.M. my cell phone rang. I figured it was either Alex or a wrong number. I wasn't interested either way. I stuffed the ringing phone under my pillow to muffle it, but Matt was already awake. He shifted and rolled, gathering most of the blankets around his body like a tortilla.

"Hey!" I protested quietly, pulling on the covers.

"Mmm, sorry . . ." he mumbled, rolling again to free up some real estate. "Who was on the phone?" In his half-asleep state, it came out, "Whosonnafnn?"

"Dunno." I sighed.

"Okay?" he asked, stretching an arm across my stomach.

"Yeah." I wiggled closer, landing myself in a cold section of previously unoccupied sheets. "Just . . . thinking."

"That's not a good idea in the middle of the night."

"I know."

"What can I do?"

I moved closer and rested my palm against his chest, over his heart, then kissed him. "Is that okay?" I asked.

"Mmm hmm."

Hours later, the sun finally penetrated my consciousness and I gave in to the waking world. Matt was still asleep beside me, mouth hanging open and a dried line of drool on his cheek. I couldn't help laughing, my voice a morning croak. His eyelids fluttered and he caught sight of me.

"What are you laughing at?"

"You were drooling." I tapped his cheek.

"Oh, great." He backhanded the offending mark and blinked at me. "Better?" I made a so-so gesture. He sighed and curled into a sitting position. "I'll be back."

While Matt went to the bathroom to clean up, I dug out my cell phone to check for a message from the middle-of-the-night phone call. There was only one, and it was from Alex.

"Jocelyn, I'm sorry. I shouldn't have left you that message. I don't even know what I was talking about. Can we just start over? Please call me. Please. I'm sorry I'm such an asshole sometimes. I don't want to mess this up. Call me, okay?"

I chewed on my lip, wondering what to do.

"What's wrong?" Matt asked when he came back to the room.

"I got a message from Alex."

"Oh." His expression was thoughtful and almost neutral. Almost. There was a touch of . . . something. Something negative.

"Just listen." I set the message to replay and handed him the phone.

"What were you fighting about anyway?" he asked.

I blew out a sigh and fell back on the bed. "The same thing we always fight about. He just gets crazy jealous all the time. He always thinks I'm cheating on him."

Matt couldn't hide a quick smirk. "Yeah, go figure."

I pinched the bridge of my nose as a wave of guilt washed over me. "Well, I guess I proved him right after all."

"It's not cheating after you break up."

"I'm not sure he knew we broke up."

"Well . . ." Matt hesitated. "Yeah, that could be a problem. But not if you tell him you broke up."

"Oh God, I don't know."

He frowned. "Joss, come on. You can't get back together with a guy that pisses you off as much as you were pissed off last night."

"You're right." I sat up, nodding. "You're right, you're right, you're right."

He gave me an appraising look. "You believe it yet?"

"Um . . ."

He shook his head. "You are gonna owe me big time for this one."

I made an embarrassed "I know" face.

"Just do me a favor."

"Anything."

"Don't wait too long before you call me again."

"What do you mean?"

"Call me when you're done with him for real, okay? And it better not be long."

"Matt, come on. You know me better than that."

"So, you're not getting back together with him?"

"I—I don't know."

He sighed and bent over the bed to kiss me softly. "Just call me when it's over."

"Matt . . ." I protested. "You're making me feel like a horrible person. I thought this was supposed to be about making each other feel better."

"I felt better last night. How 'bout you?"

There was a tight ache in my chest. My reliable Matt, my Sorbet Guy, had succeeded in making me feel like a complete jerk. "I'm sorry."

"Me, too."

"Can you please just tell me you don't hate me?"

His eyes widened. "I don't hate you, Joss. That's not the problem."

"Then why are you acting like this?"

"I just can't believe you're going back to him."

"I didn't say I was."

"You didn't have to."

"Matt—"

"Whatever, Joss. It's your call. I'm not gonna stop you if you want to waste your time."

"It sure sounds like you'd like to try." I was starting to feel the familiar boil of my temper just out of reach.

He bit off his words a few times before he finally made eye contact. "Remember how you felt about Courtney?"

"Yes."

"That's how I feel about Alex." He rubbed one hand over the back of his head and made a frustrated sound. "I'm just gonna go. I'll talk to you later, okay?"

"Matt . . ." I tried one more time. He looked at me, and I was at a loss for words. I settled on, "I'm sorry."

"Yeah, me, too."

CHAPTER TWELVE

SIX YEARS EARLIER . . . FIRST SEMESTER SOPHOMORE YEAR

My life was a study in guilt after that. Guilt over cheating on Alex, guilt over taking him back without telling him, guilt for disappointing Matt. I could hardly separate one source from the other. Every time I saw Alex, my stomach felt like it was full of lead shot.

After he fell all over himself apologizing for acting like a jerk, he knew something was bothering me. He assumed it was him. He said he'd never felt so strongly about anyone before, and it was hard for him to believe that I liked him as much. He said that he'd been cheated on before, and hadn't found out about it for a long time, so he was always suspicious after that. He said that he wanted to work on his jealousy, and be the boyfriend I wanted. I felt so awful for cheating on him—even though I'd assumed we were broken up—that I accepted his apologies and his promises to do better. I made myself a mental promise to do the same.

We lasted two more weeks.

The last straw was an argument about holiday plans. Christmas was coming up, with my birthday not far behind. Alex was from St. Louis, and I wasn't willing to change my family plans to go down to Missouri with him, even though he said that I was making life difficult for him with his family. This particular fight happened over the phone, which always made it easier for me to speak my mind. Seeing his puppy-dog eyes made me lose my resolve.

"Jocelyn, they're counting on meeting you. We've been together for nine months. It's not only appropriate, it's necessary."

"Why?"

"I shouldn't have to explain this to you. I'm sure your family will understand if you come down to St. Louis for the holidays."

"Would yours?" I challenged.

"My parents invited you," he said. His tone made it plain: he didn't appreciate that I hadn't extended an invitation to him from my family. The thought of bringing him around my parents and my sister, Darcy, made me cringe. I knew what Darcy would think of him, and I didn't want to see that look in her eyes. All of it added up to a great, big, flashing, red neon sign in my head: WARNING! THIS RELATIONSHIP IS OVER! GET OUT NOW!

"Alex, I'm not coming to St. Louis. End of story."

"Where is all this hostility coming from? This isn't like you at all."

Yes, it is, I thought. *I haven't been myself since I met you.* "I'm just tired of having the same argument over and over again. I want to go home to see my family for Christmas. Not yours."

"You're going to meet up with some guy, aren't you?" he said. "That's why you don't want me there. You've got some guy waiting for you back home."

"No!" I shouted, twisting a handful of my hair hard enough to hurt. "There. Is. No. One. Else." Even though it was technically true, I couldn't prevent an image of Matt from entering my mind. I squeezed my eyes shut as if that would block him.

"What am I supposed to think when you're being like this?"

"Oh, I don't know, maybe you could just believe me?"

"Then tell me who you're going to see."

"No."

"Why not?"

"Because you won't believe me anyway." My head pounded with my heartbeat.

"Or maybe you're just trying to hide something from me."

"Friends!" I ground the inside of my wrist into the pulse point on my right temple. "I'm going to see some friends from high school."

"Which friends?"

"No one you know, Alex." I said his name with the same intonation I would have given the much-less-flattering names I *wanted* to call him.

"Who?"

"My friend Lila and her boyfriend, Tom, my other friend Danielle . . . I don't know yet!"

"Who else?"

"I don't know! Stop accusing me of cheating on you in the future!" It was hard to say the words, knowing that in fact, I had.

"I'm not saying that."

"Yes, you are."

"I hate it when you tell me what I'm thinking!" he snapped, and I let the phone drift away from my ear in annoyance.

"It's just that you always think I'm up to something!" I retorted. "You don't trust me."

"Yes, I do."

"Obviously, you don't."

"Jocelyn, I'm working really hard at this. But you're not helping me. You don't tell me what you're doing, who you're seeing . . . it's like you're intentionally hiding shit from me."

"Maybe I am," I said and hung up the phone. The moment I did it, I felt like a heel. A real pillar of maturity. So, I dialed his number right away, and told a big fat lie. "Sorry, I dropped the phone."

"Why would you say that? You know that's gonna drive me crazy."

I sighed. "Maybe that's the point."

"What are you hiding?"

"Alex, just drop it."

"No, tell me!"

"There's nothing to tell." Although my conscience protested, *Yes there is, you big fat liar.*

"Jocelyn, I hate it when you do this shit."

"This shit?" I repeated. "When have I ever done this before? Why are you so fucking suspicious of me all the time? What have I ever done to make you think I'm such a horrible person?"

"I'm sorry. I know." He sighed. "You're not a horrible person."

"I just don't think this is working."

"What do you mean?"

"I can't be this stressed all this time. You're too intense for me."

"What are you saying?"

"I'm saying . . . I think we should not see each other anymore." The nervous fluttering in my stomach settled the moment the words were out of my mouth. "I think we're just not meant to be."

"Don't say that. We can work on this. I swear."

"It's not just that," I said.

"Whatever you say. I'll work on it. Just tell me."

"You can't work on it, Alex. It's not like that."

"Why not? We can get through this. Just talk to me."

I squeezed my eyes shut and covered them with one hand to block out any possible light. "I—I cheated on you."

There was dead silence from the other end.

"Did you hear me?" I asked.

"Who was it?"

"It doesn't matter."

"Who *was* it?" he growled.

"No." I swallowed hard around the tears that threatened to choke me. "It doesn't matter."

"It matters to me," he snapped.

"I'm not going to tell you."

The click and silence in my ear told me he was on his way over.

I could have broken up with him without telling him I'd cheated. I don't know why I did it. Maybe some misplaced idea about confession being good for the soul. Maybe I was small enough that I wanted to hurt him. I don't know, but now that I'd said the words, I had to follow through.

It was an ugly, drawn-out breakup fight of epic proportions. It could have had a music montage if it had been a movie. It would have been done in high speed, with the two of us pacing around my living room. I refused to give up the name of my partner in crime, even more stridently when it became clear that Alex only wanted to know so he could find the guy and beat the crap out of him. He started in the What-did-I-do-to-make-you-cheat? camp and slowly moved through How-could-you-do-this-to-me? on his way to You-filthy-whore.

After my throat was sore from talking, my shoulders were hunched up around my ears with tension and my head was pounding with exhaustion, I finally found my last words. The ones that put an end to the fight and removed Alex from my life.

"I knew I had to break up with you when I realized I felt like I was cheating on *him* by staying with you."

"Do you love this guy?" Alex asked, head resting in his hands. All the fight was out of him. His voice was hoarse and quiet. I felt evil.

"In a way . . ." I said, too tired to explain what that meant.

"And you don't love me?"

"Apparently not the same way."

He winced. "Okay. That's fine." He stood up from the couch and looked at me. "I hope you're happy together."

"We're not together," I said without thinking.

He winced again. "Then I hope he fucking breaks your empty fucking heart."

"Thanks, Alex," I said tonelessly.

"You're a bitch."

My temper flickered back to life and I leveled a glare at him. "You can go now."

"I'm not done yet."

"Yeah, you are." I hopped to my feet, applied both palms to his back, and propelled him toward the door. I think it was sheer surprise that allowed me to move him—he was much bigger than me, and at least seven inches taller. "You're completely. Utterly. Beyond. Fucking. Done!" I ripped the door open and gave him a final shove. He could have stopped me that time; he had to see it coming, but he went out the door and didn't turn back when I slammed it behind him.

The very next thing I did was go to my computer and send an email to Matt. *It's over. It's exhaustingly, humiliatingly, humblingly over and I am the world's biggest idiot. I'm sorry.*

I didn't get an answer right away, but he called me the next day.

"Hey, Joss."

"Hi."

"I got your message."

"I'm so sorry."

"It's okay."

"No, really. I shouldn't have done that to you. You didn't need to be involved in that."

"It's okay," he repeated.

"You were totally right. He was just a jerk."

"I have to hate him, remember? It's in the rules."

I felt relief at the mention of the rules. It gave me hope that I hadn't broken our relationship beyond repair. "Right."

"So, you're sure this time?"

I thought of the hours of soul-crushing arguing the night before. If I never saw Alex again, it would be too soon. "Oh, I'm sure."

"Sounds like an interesting story."

"Completely uninteresting, actually," I said. "It was just this horrid, drawn out argument that ended with him calling me a bitch and me throwing him out of the house."

"Now that I would have liked to see." His grin was audible.

The spark of hope in my chest caught fire as we found our footing. I let myself smile as I answered him. "I was magnificent."

"I'm sure." He laughed.

"Does that mean you're not mad at me anymore?"

"I was never mad. Disappointed, maybe."

"Ugh! That's worse! My mother is always disappointed in me."

He laughed. "Good, then that's exactly the word I'm looking for."

"Matt . . ." I couldn't stand the thought that he was actually *disappointed*. I wanted to curl up in the fetal position and rock myself.

"I'm kidding."

"Why do I not believe that?"

"That's on you, Joss." I could picture him shrugging as he spoke.

"I did mention I'm sorry, right?" I chewed on the inside of my cheek.

"You did."

"And you're not forgiving me. Is that about it?"

He inhaled loudly through the phone. "I wouldn't say that."

"Is there something I need to do to make this up to you? Three Hail Marys, that sort of thing?"

"Definitely not that."

"Okay, well . . . what?"

He hummed for a moment. "I'm not sure. But I'd like to keep my options open for the future."

It was a lighthearted enough response that I felt a little better. "You're like a goddamn mafia don, I swear."

He laughed.

"So . . . am I allowed to be in the same room with you again?"

"Joss, it was never like that . . ."

"Okay, but your . . . *disappointment* was a wicked third wheel to have around."

He chuckled softly, seeming pleased with that idea.

I sprung my last test. "Are you free tonight?"

"I can be, why?"

"I'd like to see you."

"Do you *need* to see me?"

"That's not what I'm saying . . ." It was what I meant, but not what I was saying. I wasn't sure how far through the apology process we'd gotten. I didn't want to snap the first fragile supports of a rebuilt bridge between us. "I haven't seen you in *days*."

"All right, all right." He laughed. "It'll be late, though, I have to work."

* * *

Matt's late shift at the restaurant gave me plenty of time to go through the usual preparations. I had no idea what the night would bring, but if there was even the slightest chance of him seeing what was under my clothes, I wanted to be ready. I wanted to be more than ready. By the time he showed up at eleven, I was smooth, dressed to kill—against my skin anyway—with clean sheets and minty-fresh breath. Nothing I couldn't account for on a regular night, but I knew my intentions. They were not pure.

"Wait, before you say anything, I have something for you," I said after I'd let him in. I crooked my finger at him to lead him to the bedroom and retrieved the tattered sheet of loose-leaf from my desk. It was the rules, and I had a new addition. I handed it to Matt.

"Number nine. The relationship requiring Sorbet must be over for Sorbet to take place," he read aloud, then laughed. "Good call."

"Did I mention that I'm sorry?"

"Two or three hundred times."

"I actually felt worse that I made you mad than I did for breaking up with Alex."

"I wasn't mad, Joss." Matt rolled his eyes.

"I know, I know. You get what I mean."

"Yeah, I get it."

"So . . . I broke the rules, and I'm sorry." When his expression made a move toward annoyance, I held up my hands. "Last time."

"It better be." He studied the contract. "According to your own addition . . . yeah, you broke the rules."

In that moment, the thought occurred to me that no one else

I knew would be able to play this ridiculous game. It wasn't just that Matt had originated it—he was the only person I knew who would be so dedicated to an arbitrary list that was one step shy of being written on a cocktail napkin. We'd always had a deep appreciation of the absurd in common.

"Maybe . . ." he murmured before searching my desk for a pen. He bent over the rules for a moment. "There."

I took the paper from his hand and read:

10. *The Sorbet partners are allowed one violation of these rules without penalty.*
11. *Any conflict between the partners should be considered eligible for a Sorbet resolution.*

"So I'm not banned for life?" I asked.

"Nope."

"How do you figure rule eleven?" I asked.

"Well, why do you need Sorbet Sex?"

I folded my hands at my waist like a good pupil. "To get rid of the bad feelings left from the last guy."

"So, there can't be any bad feelings between us or it won't work, right?"

The whole thing smacked of rationalizing, but I wanted to agree. "So, we have to Sorbet our way back into Sorbetability."

He laughed. "Wow, that's a hell of a word."

"I made it up just for you." I smiled.

"Thanks."

"So . . . ?"

"Yeah, I'm in."

I smiled and put my arms around his neck. "Thank you."

"It's okay. I think we both need this one."

I kissed him, happy to get an equal response. "I picked out some really nice underwear for you."

"You were pretty confident you'd get your way, weren't you?"

"I was willing to take my clothes off again, if I had to," I said in all seriousness.

He laughed. "That's your go-to move, huh?"

"It worked last time."

"True."

"So . . . do you want to see?" I asked.

"Absolutely."

Snow fell overnight, and the temperature in my bedroom dropped dramatically. December had been unseasonably warm, although a few nights had already alerted me to the crappy insulation in my bedroom. It had northern and eastern exposure, which combined to create a chilling effect during the winter months.

I knew it was cold when I woke up with a drippy nose. I snuck an experimental arm out from beneath the blankets and immediately regretted it. I shivered and buried myself deeper in the comforter, scooting closer to Matt to borrow some body heat.

"Hey," he greeted me, reaching back to pull me tight against his body.

"You're awake?" I asked.

"Yeah, I have been for a while. I'm afraid to get out of bed."

"Why?"

"It's freezing in here!"

"I know!" I agreed.

"Look at this." He turned his head so I could see and blew a plume of frosted breath into the air. "I can see my breath. Inside."

"I know, it's awful."

"Is it always like this?"

"Only when the temperature drops."

"Jeez." He twisted to face me and hugged me close. "Does your landlord know about this?"

"Ha!" I scoffed. Our landlord was not prone to answering his residents' complaints. Nor did he have to be, I supposed. We'd all be moving on at the end of one year, and he could wait for the next tenants to notice that the front two bedrooms didn't heat. All over Madison, the property owners who rented to students were an immoral, unsavory bunch. By the time anyone realized it, it was always too late—contracts signed, deposits made.

"I guess you're right," he said.

"I'm glad you came over last night," I said. "It's way warmer with you in here."

He laughed. "You're just using me for my metabolic rate."

"No, no, no. I'm using you for lots of things."

He laughed again, and I kissed him.

"I'm glad you came over. For real," I said.

"Me, too."

"I guess I'm ahead now, huh?"

"Two to one."

"Not that you're keeping track, right?"

"Of course not." He grinned.

"Well, I guess you better get yourself out there," I said.

"I'm out there, trust me."

"Okay, so you need to get out there and find someone you actually want to see more than once." I slipped a foot between his shins and wiggled my toes.

"I'm doing just fine, thank you."

"I'm serious, Matt, you're a great guy, you should find yourself a new girl."

He hooked one of my rogue curls away from my lips. "You realize this is a completely fucked up conversation, right?"

"How can you say that?" I slung my thigh over his waist and gave him a wicked grin.

He covered my face with one hand and sighed. "Okay, I have a question."

"Shoot."

"Why don't *you* want me?"

Fear darted through my stomach. "Matty, I—I—"

"Relax." He rolled his eyes. "I'm asking out of pure curiosity. You're sort of in a unique position, you know."

"You're just . . ." I shrugged. "You're not my type, I guess."

"That type thing is bullshit."

"Oh, really? So why don't you want me?" I challenged him.

"No way, I'm not telling you that."

I lifted my head and narrowed my eyes at him. "Why not?"

"I'd have to be an idiot to tell a girl I'm in bed with why she's not girlfriend material."

I considered pursuing the line of questioning, but he was probably right. I didn't want to lose my Sorbet Guy, or more important my friend. Honesty is not necessarily the best policy. Alex would probably agree with that one. "It's because I won't eat anything blue, isn't it?"

He laughed.

"Never mind, don't tell me."

He freed one hand and held it out to me. "I'll never tell if you don't."

"Deal." We shook on it, and I unhooked my leg from his waist.

"I guess I should get up." Matt sighed.

I groaned. "If you move, it's gonna get all cold under the covers."

"I thought you wanted me to get out and meet a new girl."

"I do! But I also don't want you to take away your warmth."

"You are a complicated woman."

"What can I say? You're very warm."

"Using me again." He shook his head and gave me sad eyes.

"Guilty." I pulled the blankets up higher around our shoulders. "Who knows? This could be the last time we do this, you know. You could meet the love of your life on the way home this morning."

"I'd never recognize her in this weather," he said. "Too many layers."

"True."

"And that would require me getting out of your bed."

"Also true."

"It's frickin' cold out there."

"So, maybe not today." I shrugged. "Maybe you'll meet her tomorrow."

"Yeah, I'll wait."

Matt's apartment wasn't far away as the crow flies, but it took a while to get there. He lived on the east side of the city, in one of the strangest digs I'd ever seen. His apartment was the former servants' quarters of one of the large mansions on Lake Drive. It had been converted into a rental space by the owners of the house, who also had a condo in Florida, a ski chalet in Aspen, and a yacht, inexplicably in Virginia. They liked to have a tenant who would take in their mail and presumably scare off potential thieves with his four meager windows lit in the northwestern corner of the property. The place was gorgeous, though, and Matt was alone on the gated lot most of the year. Apparently, the servants had lived well when they were there: hardwood floors, a natural fireplace in the living room, and high plastered ceilings. My own apartment was a pre-fab nightmare in comparison.

I parked in the short drive that served the back of the house and walked around the ivy-covered corner to the side entrance that was all Matt's. I hit the buzzer and had to wait for him to come down the stairs to let me in. The owners had updated the place to the hilt when they'd converted it, but had stopped short of installing an actual mechanism to open the door from the second floor.

It took him a long time to answer, which made me more nervous. I swallowed hard, and shifted my shoulders. It seemed that my light cardigan had somehow shrunk two sizes. It felt so tight—like it was trying to crush me. Hastily, I unbuttoned it and shrugged out of it. Then it was my hair that seemed determined to wrap around my neck and squeeze out the air. I used my hands to gather it back into a ponytail for a moment of reprieve. It was then I realized I'd left my glasses on in my distraction. I took them off and stuffed them into my purse. I knew it would be a miracle if I remembered where I'd put them, but at least I'd de-nerded.

Then suddenly, Matt was pounding down the stairs in his socks, nearly slipping on the third-from-the-bottom and flinging his arms out to gain his balance. I watched the whole thing through the mullioned door and couldn't help laughing.

"Hey, come on in," he said, turning his back to run back up the stairs without further greeting.

"Nice to see you, too!" I shouted after him, stopping to take off my shoes.

"Sorry!" he called back. "My timer just went off!"

I wouldn't exactly call what Matt had at the bottom of the stairs a foyer, but there were a few hooks on the wall for coats and a small collection of shoes he left there. I always took mine off when I arrived, though he'd never asked me to. It just seemed like the thing to do.

When I went to hang up my coat, the usual hook I used was already occupied by a dirty baseball cap. I burst out laughing when I saw it. Matt wasn't the kind of guy who wore hats all the time, like so many of the guys I'd known in college. But there was one summer where he always seemed to have a hat on. Like he was in disguise. And it had been this sad, filthy cap. I hadn't seen it since then, now that I thought about it. I thought he'd lost it.

For that matter, I thought I'd thrown it into Lake Mendota.

CHAPTER FOURTEEN

FIVE YEARS EARLIER . . . SUMMER BEFORE JUNIOR YEAR

I was twenty when I fell in love.

Unfortunately, it wasn't with another human being. After two years of fumbling through a biology major with no clear idea what I wanted to do, I fell in love with a class. It was animal biology.

I'd always been an animal lover. There was no other reason to spend my working hours soaking wet in my sister's grooming parlor, cooing to terrified dogs and getting clawed for my trouble. Dogs made me smile, sucked away my stress at first sight, and gave me a reason to look forward to the wet work of washing them.

So, in my second semester of my sophomore year of college, on track to graduating in four years, I realized I wanted to be a veterinary tech. All the joy of working with animals without the pesky doctorate in veterinary medicine I didn't want to get. This epiphany required me to become a voluntary nerd, however. I enrolled at the local technical college and began collecting credits from two schools simultaneously. If I planned carefully, I could still get out in four years, I'd just have to do summer sessions.

Meanwhile, my love life sank to an all-time low. At first I thought it was related to my increased class load and decreased fun time. But, there had to be some kind of bad luck involved. Or karma coming back to bite me in the ass.

First came John, who set the standard for romance in college. He swept me off my feet with amazing plans for our first three dates. We picnicked and went for a long walk, we went to the art museum and drank wine in the middle of the afternoon, we took a tour of the capitol building, and when he wanted to go up to the dome's observation deck and I had a complete fear-of-heights freak-out, he acquiesced without a second thought. John stood alone in my college dating history as the sole example of classic romance. I thought he was my very own handsome prince come to life.

But after our fifth date, he took a phone call while he was still in my bed. When he glanced at the display, he smiled. Then, he put a finger to my lips as he answered.

"Hey, sweetie, I was just thinking about you," he said into the phone.

The first trickle of doubt ran down my insides.

". . . Not too much. Just hangin' out with the guys." He gave me a half-smile, like we were in on a great joke together. . . . "I miss you, too, babe."

That was the point at which I got out of bed. My hands shook as I grabbed my bathrobe off a hook.

". . . Of course I am," he continued as if I weren't there. ". . . Yeah, I know. I wouldn't miss it."

If there is such a thing as karma, then John was my punishment for cheating on Alex. Or sort of cheating on him. Either way, I'd clearly done something to earn such a karmic kick in the pants.

My lungs ached with the strain of holding in a sob as I stooped down to gather John's clothes off the floor. He wasn't paying attention to me. So, when I carried the load to my window, he didn't try to stop me. Then, I went back for his shoes.

"Hey! What are you—?" John said when I chucked the first shoe out the window. "Sweetie, I'm gonna have to call you back."

He disconnected his call as I sent the second shoe after its mate. "What the fuck are you doing?"

"You have a *girlfriend*?" I said. "What the fuck are *you* doing?" My vision was blurry with tears of rage, unshed.

"She lives in Portland!" he shouted. "Are you insane?"

"Just get out."

"What is your problem?" he said, sliding to the edge of the bed to look for his clothes on the floor. He didn't seem to realize I'd defenestrated them.

"Me? You cheating asshole! Get the fuck out of my house!" I pointed at the door.

"Oh, believe me, I'm going."

"Not fast enough." I stomped across the room and threw open the bedroom door. "Get out!"

"Where are my clothes?"

"Well, the dumpster's right below my window, so I'd start looking there."

"You crazy bitch." He stood, holding his cell phone in front of his genitals like a tiny shield.

"Go!" I stamped my foot once, blinking hard and fast to stay in control.

"Joss?" The voice came from the bottom of the stairs. Jessie's voice. "Are you okay?"

"I'm fine!" My tone had gone nasal and I knew it was a matter of seconds before I started to cry.

"I'm not going down there like this," John hissed.

"The hell you aren't."

"Fuck you!" he said.

"You already did, asshole." I raised my voice. "Jessie, are you alone?"

"No, Evan's here." Jessie's boyfriend. A hockey player. Perfect.

"You okay, Joss?" Evan called up.

"Can you come up here?" I called back.

John's face went dark. "You gonna get your friend to beat me up? You get off on that kind of shit?"

I squeezed my eyes shut for a moment. "I just want you to go."

Evan's heavy footsteps thumped up the stairs.

John stared at me with narrowed eyes, his jaw set tight.

"You might want to hurry," I said. "Someone might be running off with your shoes right now." It was an idle threat, but not outside the realm of possibility in Madison. College students are not renowned for their lawful behavior and good judgment.

"Crazy bitch," John mumbled his parting shot and walked past me just as Evan reached the top of the stairs.

"Whoa, sorry, buddy!" Evan said, holding up a hand to block the sight of naked John.

John didn't say a word, but hurried down the stairs with his phone still held in fig leaf position. Jessie screamed when he came into sight, but didn't stop him from going out the front door. My angry tears were stunned into a hiatus, and I ran down the stairs in my bathrobe to watch John's progress through the front window.

"What the hell is going on?" Jessie demanded.

I didn't answer, pressing my face to the glass until he was out of sight. Then, I ran to the back of the house and climbed gracelessly onto the kitchen counter to look out the window over the sink. That was the ultimate sign of how pissed I was. Normally, I considered even climbing on counters to be too high for my taste. But, with my head at just the right angle I could make out John's naked form as he circled the building, looking for his clothes on the pavement.

"Joss, what happened?" Evan startled me and I knocked my head into the glass.

"Ouch!" I rubbed my temple. John moved out of my narrow view. "Damn."

"Joss!" Jessie said loudly.

I turned and eased myself off the counter. "Do I have some kind of sign on my forehead that says, 'Assholes only'?" I asked.

"Not that I can see," she said.

"Me either," Evan agreed.

I shuddered. "I have to go shower. For about nine hours."

So much for princes and white steeds and all that.

Two days before I put Naked John out into the street, Matt met Shelby, a Southern girl who'd lived in the north for most of her life, but clung to her identity and her accent with a tenacity that reminded me of one of my sister's clients, a rat terrier named Buster. He used to bare his teeth the entire time I scrubbed his fur. Shelby was like that, except with subtle sniping.

She had real skill in the area. The first time I met her, she said, "Oh my, you pull off red hair better than most people, don't you?" It took me a moment to determine the intent of her comment, that's how good she was. I would have taken it personally, but she did it to everyone.

"It's so refreshing that people around here don't follow fashion."

"I just think it's adorable the way you still hang out with the first people you met in college."

"My daddy drove a BMW before he got his promotion. It was all right until he got his Mercedes."

She was pretty, of course. Matt could never pass up a chance with a pretty girl, no matter how vicious her venom. It was his greatest weakness as a male, and one of the top three reasons why I would never date him. She was smart enough to keep most of her honey-coated barbs out of his earshot, which only confirmed that she knew exactly what she was doing.

I liked to call her Miss Alabama.

She lasted three weeks.

That was our first case of mutually needed Sorbet. In later years, we referred to it as the "What the Hell Were We Thinking? Time."

Then came Ryan, Brian, and Bryan, in that order and so unremarkable, I felt like I was caught in an alternate universe where I went on the same first date nine times.

Next, I decided to put Jessie in charge of finding me some candidates. She was a little smug after finding Evan, but I was reaching burnout stage with my summer classes at the time and I felt like delegating the task was better than giving up entirely. What ensued was a series of blind dates, or uncomfortable double dates between Jessie, Evan, me, and the Guy du Jour.

Note: Blind dates are the work of the devil and no caring friend should ever submit a friend to one, no matter how great she thinks the match would be. There is nothing less romantic than being forced to share time with someone you don't know. It's like sitting next to a stranger on an airplane and expecting to fall in love.

Double dates, on the other hand, have the added bonus of making the potential mates play the part of fourth wheel on an alternating basis.

JESSIE: Evan and Tim used to live with this guy named Brooks— tell her about that thing with the fish . . .

EVAN and TIM laugh and tell a story about the ex-roommate.

JOSS laughs politely.

EVAN: Tim is from North Carolina. Didn't Jessie say you have some cousins in North Carolina?

JOSS: South Carolina.

EVAN: Oh, right.

JESSIE: [*laughs*] Oh my God, that reminds me of that Final Four party we went to last year, remember?

JOSS and EVAN: [*together*] This pizza tastes like pretzels!

JESSIE: Hoo doggie!

JOSS: [*laughing*] Hoo doggie!

EVAN: [*to Tim*] You shoulda been there, man.

TIM: Guess so.

I went through three versions of the Tim date and two blind dates before I told Jessie to stop setting me up.

Left to my own devices, I came up with a new plan: try something completely different. My so-called type was obviously not working out. I didn't really have a physical type; it was more a personality style that I went for. Someone who would do things like plan a romantic picnic, bring me flowers, and yes—get a little jealous. I hated to admit it, even to myself, but I'd always kind of enjoyed that protected feeling that a jealous type gave me. I knew it was stupid and immature—my most jealous boyfriend was unbearable, and my mildly jealous ones had been cheaters themselves. Any Psych 101 student could see they'd been projecting, but that was hardly a consolation. No matter. One thing was clear: romance does not equal trust, caring, and a healthy relationship. So, it seemed to me the next step was to find someone who was none of those things.

Kevin was that guy. There was nothing princely about him, which is exactly why I decided to flirt with him. He was the kind of awkward bookish type that always turned out to be a great guy in teen movies. In reality, they are every bit as nice as the movies indicate, but never actually end up with the dream girl. I wasn't the dream girl anyway, so I'd always secretly feared I would end up with a guy like that, until Ben asked me out. Saying yes to Kevin's proposal of meeting at Memorial Union made me feel shallow. Because prior to accepting, I could convince myself I wasn't interested in him because he was an intellectual snob, or that he rubbed his nose too much. After, when I learned that he was smart, genuine, and interesting to talk to, I had to admit I just wasn't physically attracted to him.

Still, I was determined to break my own bad habits, so I kept seeing him. And while he did grow on me—he was even nice enough *not* to invite me to his place on the ninth floor of a new apartment building when he learned about my height phobia—still, I never felt the spark I wanted to feel. Ultimately I broke up with him. I'd like to say that I felt worse about it than he did, but from the look on his face, I guessed that was unlikely.

"You have to stop beating yourself up about Kevin," Jessie advised me as I entered my second week of guilt. We were lounging on the couch with Popsicles while we waited for the landlord to arrive and unchain the air conditioner. It was nearly July and he'd finally answered my tenth plea to save me from melting to death in my place. "You can't force chemistry with someone."

"I just feel like a bitch for dumping this perfectly decent guy. There was nothing wrong with him."

"But there was also nothing right with him," she said.

"I swear, dating karma is going to get me for this one. I'm never going on another date because I dumped poor Kevin."

She gave her orange Popsicle a healthy slurp. "The universe is not out to get you."

"You can't know that."

"Neither can you."

"Look, it's not like you left him at the altar. It just wasn't meant to be. Get over yourself."

My Popsicle—cherry—was melting fast, and I chased a rivulet of red juice with my tongue as it ran down my wrist. "I still feel bad," I said.

"What, did you take his virginity or something?" She laughed.

"No. We never even had sex."

"Then you're extra-lame for freaking out about this guy. What about Tim and Rob and Carlos?" Three of the guys she'd forced on me in one way or another—at my request, yes, but that was hardly the point. "You didn't even go out with any of them. Where are the tears for them?"

I narrowed my eyes at her and gave my Popsicle an aggressive suck. The end fell off in my mouth and I got instant brain freeze. "Ah, dammit!" I clapped my palm over my forehead and groaned.

Jessie laughed.

"See? I told you. Karma." Except that I was talking around the cherry-flavored iceberg in my mouth, so it sounded more like "Suh? I toe yah. Kah-uh." I worked the chunk around until I could swallow it and repeated, "Karma."

"Yeah, yeah," she said. "Straighten out your chi already and forget about Kevin."

"Way to mix your Eastern philosophies there, Jess."

She waved a hand. "Chi, karma, getting right with Jesus—whatever you want to call it, do it."

I wanted to call it Sorbet.

Luckily, Matt was a free agent at the time, and conveniently staying in Madison for his job that summer. We called that one The Chi Straightening.

Dating is not a logic problem, but I was slowly compiling a list of constants.

1. Romance does not equal love.
2. Princes are usually spoiled brats.
3. Chemistry is a requirement.
4. Guilt is no reason to stay with anyone.
5. If a minor flaw feels like a deal-breaker early on, it's only going to get worse.

The Duck Painter taught me the last lesson. His name was Seth, and he painted duck decoys for fun. I thought he was joking when he told me on our first date. I laughed.

It wasn't a joke.

And Seth, despite being attractive, smart, and willing to watch a chick flick with me, was a non-option as soon as I saw his apartment. Because it was full of duck decoys in various stages of his artistic attentions. One might have been okay. Five would have been pushing it. The fifty-six that he had lined up on every flat surface was too much for me.

I didn't answer when he called the next day. Or ever again.

* * *

Matt, meanwhile, was in the middle of a streak of girls I liked to call The Squad. Four blondes and a brunette. They were a peppy collection: one former gymnast, two former cheerleaders, a show choir girl, and the one who wanted to audition for *American Idol.* To be fair, they were nicer than a lot of Matt's previous girl-friends. A couple of them practically sweated good cheer. Good matches for the always amiable Matt, I supposed, although his laissez-faire brand of nice was a far cry from the pep squad.

They were all younger than us. The last, a blonde named Kelly, was the youngest at eighteen. Her lack of a fake ID was only tolerable because it was summer, and they could spend time at the Memorial Union Terrace. Although a lot of the student population left for the summer, enough people had crappy leases that didn't end until mid-August that I could always count on having a few friends around for the summer. And Matt was always one of them, so I ended up spending a lot of time with Kelly. Enough that one evening, while Matt was winding his way through the crowd with a pair of beers, Kelly turned to me and blurted out a confession.

"I'm a virgin. Do you think that's a problem?"

After gagging on my own saliva, I managed to squeak out, "What do you mean by 'problem'?"

"Well, Matt's not." She looked at me with palpable hope. "Is he?"

My lips quivered as I fought hard against the impulse to laugh. "Um, no. Not exactly."

Across the wide outdoor terrace, Matt had stopped to talk to someone. There would be no rescue from this conversation.

"So, do you think that would bother him?"

There were two possible paths she meant to take. I bought

myself a moment of thought by taking a sip of my drink and looking at Matt from a distance. He was only a year older than her but
he might as well have been forty for the gap in their innocence.

"Are you waiting? For—marriage?" I asked.

"No." Kelly shrugged. "Just the right guy."

I went noncommittal. "Mmm."

"Don't tell him, okay?" she said. "If I think he's the right guy,
I don't want him to get all weird about it."

"Sure," I said, affirming her last sentence, and letting her believe I meant her question instead. Underhanded? Yes, but I
wasn't going to honor a request like that.

I snagged Matt away from her as soon as I could. "You cannot
sleep with this girl."

"Why not?"

"She's a virgin."

His eyes lit up beneath the brim of his hat. "Are you serious?"

"Yes. She doesn't want you to know. She thinks you might be
The One."

He glanced over his shoulder in the direction she'd gone to
find a bathroom. "Really?"

"Matt!" I pinched his forearm. "You cannot do this."

"Why not?"

My mouth fell open. "Are you kidding me? You are *not* The
One."

"I could be." He smirked, and I knew he was just playing with
me at that point. "Sooner or later it comes down to fate . . ."

"Don't you dare quote Billy Joel to me." I popped him in the
shoulder with the heel of my hand. "You are not The One."

"Why?"

I cocked my head. "Are you planning to marry this girl?"

"No," he said with no hesitation.

"Then don't ruin her first time by being the guy who dumped her."

"It's not that big a deal," he said. "Why do girls always make it such a big deal? You didn't seriously think you were going to marry Ben, did you?"

"Kind of." Completely, but I wasn't going to admit that to him.

His eyebrows drew together over a half smile. "Oh, come on, you're cooler than that, Joss."

"Just don't do it, okay? Don't ruin it—she's too sweet."

"Sweet?"

I stuck my tongue out at him. "Like Bambi. Like a kicked puppy."

He sucked air through his teeth and groaned. "Do you have any idea what you're asking me to give up?" This was Razzie-worthy martyrdom.

"If it's not supposed to be a big deal to her, why is it a big deal for you to pass on it?" I arched my eyebrows at him.

"Come on, who doesn't want to be someone's first? It's like being the first person to walk in new snow."

"Don't be gross."

He laughed. "That's rich, coming from you."

"Matt, I am serious!"

"About me being gross?"

I caught sight of Kelly making her way back to us over his shoulder. "She's coming."

"Ah, I don't know about this, Joss. How often do you have someone offer you their virginity on a silver platter?"

"God, do I even know you?"

"What if she begs?"

"That ugly-ass hat is infecting your brain. You've become dis-

gusting! I should take it off your head and throw it in the lake."
I took a swipe at his head in a fake attempt to grab his hat, but he
ducked away, laughing.

He clamped one hand over his hat. "I'm just messing with
you—come on, you know me better than that. And leave my hat
out of it."

Kelly was about twenty feet away now.

"Tell me you're not going to deflower that poor girl, Matt, or
I'll never forgive you."

"Deflower?" he repeated as if the word had a sour taste.

I nodded, eyes fixed on Kelly.

He twisted to look at her—a petite, fresh-scrubbed, blond,
country girl—then back to me with disappointed puppy eyes.
"You know my conscience would have been sufficient. You're just
beating a dead horse."

I made another move for the hat, but he dodged me again.
"Very big of you not to be scummy."

"Don't push your luck, Alvin." He'd taken to calling me Alvin
after I'd made the mistake of comparing myself to a chipmunk.

"I'll tell her about us," I threatened with arched brows.

"That's just low."

"What is?" Kelly asked, arriving at the table.

"Nothing," Matt said, accepting her kiss on his cheek. "I was
just reminding Joss that she owes me a favor."

"As soon as you finish your part, Matty." I darted my eyes to
Kelly for a second.

He glared at me. "I got it."

Kelly looked confused, but after a moment she faked a yawn.
"I'm getting tired! You wanna walk me home?" Her eyes glis-
tened in the light of the nearby lamppost. She was excited and
nervous. She'd made up her mind.

"Sure," Matt said.

I kicked him under the table as he stood.

"Hope you don't mind, Joss. It was cool to hang out with you tonight." Kelly smiled at me.

"No problem. Have a good night."

She bounced on her toes as Matt paused to take a final swig from his cup. "I'll talk to you soon, Joss. You owe me."

"You know I'm good for it."

He grinned. "Always."

He called the next day. We named that one The Payback.

CHAPTER FIFTEEN

NOW

I shook my head free of the memories of that summer, and pursued him into the apartment. I was surprised to find the new addition of a grand piano in the living room.

"Whoa! When did you get the piano?" It hadn't been here the last time I was over.

"It was my dad's."

"Oh." That stopped me short. Matt's dad had died unexpectedly of a heart attack just six weeks earlier. I dropped my oversized bag onto the couch and went closer to inspect the instrument. It was clearly well cared for, although a few of the keys were chipped. A thought struck me, and I wandered toward the kitchen to avoid shouting. "How did you get it up here?"

Matt grinned at me. "Very carefully."

"I'm serious."

"We had to have professionals do it," he said. "My mom wanted it out of the house. She's selling, did I tell you?"

"No. Where's she moving to?"

"Arizona."

"Why?"

He shrugged. "Her sister is down there. My brother is in Nevada. Apparently, I'm not enough of a draw to stay here." He smiled to show me he was joking.

"My mom moved to Arizona, and all I got was this lousy piano," I said.

"Something like that." He pulled a pot off the stove and dumped its contents into a waiting colander.

"Can I help you?"

"Nope."

"So, what should I do?"

"Amuse yourself." He waved me off, eyes focused on his task. It was a familiar gesture, but I'd been thinking so much about the first few years we'd known each other that it struck me how much older he looked now.

I went back to the living room. As always, I was drawn to the bulletin board that hung above his desk in the corner of the room. He'd had it in every apartment he'd lived in since sophomore year. Over the years, the pictures had piled up, to the point that some of the older ones were totally obscured, but he never took them down. It was a miracle that ordinary pushpins could still penetrate to the cork. I peered behind some of the looser photos, seeing a montage of my own life as it intertwined with Matt's. In one corner, barely visible, I found the unmistakable Caribbean blue of Meghan Lowry's eye.

Jesus . . . Meghan . . .

THREE YEARS EARLIER . . . FIRST YEAR AFTER GRADUATING FROM COLLEGE

The first date I got after I became a reasonable facsimile of an adult—a college graduate, with a real job, and my own apartment—was thanks to my cat. I'd sort of forgotten what it was like to live with a cat, and I left the door open as I carried a few boxes from the spot where I'd left them by the elevator. When I went out for the last box, I saw Dewey's feather boa tail disappearing down the stairwell at the end of the hall.

For a moment, I did an unintentional slapstick comedy routine, going for the box, then the stairs, then my door, then the stairs, and back again all without accomplishing anything. Finally, I shoved the box through my front door, slammed it, and ran after the cat. He was only one flight down, pawing and yowling at the door of apartment 207. His objective was clearly the source of the intoxicating smell coming from within. I reached him just as the door opened. A guy with a warm smile and the ugliest pants I'd ever seen was on the other side.

I froze with the marmalade puffball that was Dewey dangling from my arms. "Sorry, my cat—"

"I heard—" he started.

"I'm sorry," I said.

"Mmrrrowr!" Dewey did a full body twist, slipped from my grasp, and headed straight for the stranger's kitchen.

"Dewey!" I rose on my toes, looking for him, but hesitant to follow.

"My chicken," Ugly Pants murmured, rushing after the cat.

I bobbled on my toes in the doorway. "Do you want me to come get him?" I called in.

"Yeah, please. Come in." His voice was a soft tenor, incongruous with his buzz cut hair and the tattoo I could see poking out of the sleeve of his T-shirt.

I left the door open and stepped into the full force of the cooking smells. "Oh my God, what is that?" His apartment was basic, but nicely furnished. A stark contrast to the world of student housing I'd just left, and the still-moving-in chaos of my own place. When I turned the corner to the kitchen Ugly Pants was holding a plate aloft like he was considering it for a hat.

Meanwhile, Dewey was on the kitchen counter, standing on his back feet and pawing the air below the plate. "Dewey!" I snatched him off the counter. He tried another escape maneuver, but I clamped one elbow tightly to his ribs and wrapped my other hand around his back feet.

He protested with a pitiful mewl.

"Oh hush, you big boor."

"You got him?" Ugly Pants asked, still levitating the chicken out of the cat's reach.

"Yes, I'm sorry. Really. He just got away from me."

"It's okay. It happens a lot."

"He's been down here before?" I asked, eyes wide.

"No, but whenever anybody loses a pet in the building, they almost always end up at my door." He looked at me, smiling easily for the first time, now that his plate was safe. He was actually quite nice-looking, I realized. Light coloring and faded blue eyes. He was older than me, I could tell. Probably over thirty, if the bare imprints of lines around his eyes were any indication.

Dewey wrenched his body again, and almost got loose, but I shifted him to a cradle hold with all four feet trapped in one fist. I didn't want to get clawed.

"It's the smell of the chicken," I said. "He's a food whore."

Ugly Pants laughed. "I've never really heard it described that way before."

I grimaced as I realized I'd probably gone a little crass for a first conversation. "Oh. I . . . What are you making? It smells incredible."

"Chicken with shallots, prunes, and Armagnac."

"Oh!" The hideousness of his pants clicked into place. "Are you a chef?"

"Yeah."

"Oh wow. That's—" I stopped before I said "hot." Because

I'd already worked "whore" into our first conversation, I didn't need to embarrass myself any further.

Dewey made another bid for freedom, this time getting enough momentum to make me take a few steps before I got control again. "I guess I should get him away from here. Sorry, again."

"It's all right."

I was at the open door when he spoke again. "Where do you live? In case . . . Dewey? . . . comes back."

I turned to look at him. "Three-oh-five."

His lips shaped the words as he repeated my apartment number to himself. He smiled. "It was nice to meet you . . ."

For some reason, I gave him my full name. "Jocelyn. And you're . . ." I found myself caught in his gaze while warmth spread through me from my stomach outward.

"Martin."

Dewey squirmed once more, pulling me back to reality. This was no time to make goo-goo eyes at the neighbor—even if he was a handsome, tattooed chef who seemed to be smiling at me in just the same way. "I'll see you around, I guess . . . Martin." I made my exit, while the cat redoubled his efforts to stay by the source of the heady scent of chicken with shallots, prunes, and whatever it was he'd said.

A few minutes after I'd given Dewey a stern talking to and poured him some cat kibble, I heard a knock at the door. I opened it to find Martin.

"Hi," he said.

A flock of butterflies took off from my stomach and filled my chest. "Hi."

"Would you like to have dinner with me?" he asked. "I always make too much."

I smiled. "I'd like that."

"My place?" he offered.

"If that chicken is still there—yes."

Martin was eleven years older than me. I'd never dated someone younger than me, but the biggest age gap I'd ever dealt with before was two years. Eleven was a whole new ball game. When I was graduating from high school, he was getting ready to celebrate his thirtieth birthday. When he was going to prom, I still had training wheels on my bike.

We spent our first dinner finding all the most extreme examples of our age difference and laughing over it together, but it seemed to be a subject Martin never tired of. The second time he asked me down to his apartment for dinner, he started in again.

"First concert," he challenged.

I smiled. "I don't want to tell you."

"Oh, come on, everyone's first concert is a little embarrassing," he said. "Mine was Iron Maiden."

I laughed. "Then you really don't want to hear mine."

"It wasn't *NSync, was it?" he asked, nose wrinkled.

Cheeks pink with wine and embarrassment, I confessed. "Britney Spears—but it wasn't my idea."

He dropped his head onto his arms. "You're so young."

I grinned at him. "Oh, come on, you're not exactly dying of old age here."

He sighed and stood to clear the table. I gathered up what he couldn't carry and followed him to the kitchen. He loaded everything into the sink and ran the tap hot.

"I'll dry if you want," I offered, sliding next to him. He was taller than me—everyone was—and built strong. If I hadn't seen the hideous pants, I would have guessed he worked in construction, or ran with a biker gang in his spare time.

"I'll do it all later," he said, taking the dish towel from my hands.

We looked at each other for the length of three breaths. The corners of his eyes crinkled, then smoothed as he contemplated me.

"How old were you the first time you had sex?" I asked, because why not just get it all out there?

He licked his lips. "Eighteen."

I popped one eyebrow at him. "I was—"

"Seven, I know." He broke his gaze from mine and rubbed one of his earlobes between two fingers for a few seconds.

"Do you want to know how old I was?" I offered.

"Not in the slightest." He caught me by the waist and crushed his lips to mine.

Martin had stories, furniture that he'd bought himself, and patience in bed that made me feel like a kindergartner. *He* never made me feel that way, but there was just no avoiding the contrast.

There were times he seemed to love the gap—he went on about my relaxed attitude and willingness to try almost anything. Luckily, as a chef, he didn't cook any blue food. He loved and contributed to my lingerie collection. He had great taste in underwear. Yet, other times, like when I didn't know a movie or song he referred to or when he found out that I'd been in grade school during September 11, he would just close his eyes and rub his temples in a my-head-is-going-to-explode way.

We both knew we were doomed as a couple from the start—we even talked about it on our first date. Still, two days before New Year's Eve, I was surprised when the age gap made another appearance. I wanted him to come to Madison with me, where I had invitations to three parties. He didn't want to go.

"Come on, it'll be fun!" I waggled my nearly invisible eyebrows and nodded.

"Sweetie, I know you're going to have a great time, but I'm too old for that crowd." He was cleaning up after cooking me yet another to-die-for dinner. He was very particular about his pans, so I was sitting on a stool in the doorway to keep out of his way.

"No one will care." I crossed my heart. "They're all really nice. You'll love it."

"I'll care." He crossed the small kitchen to wrap his arms around me and rest his chin on my head. "Just call me at midnight."

"No, it's okay. We don't have to go."

"Just go, Joss. These are your friends."

"You're my friend, too."

"I see you a lot more than they do." He released me from the bear hug and smiled. "Please go."

I frowned, but I really wanted to go. I missed my college friends horribly.

Martin could see my hesitation. "I thought you were all gung ho to meet Matt's new girlfriend."

I was. "Well, yeah, but . . ."

"Go." His soft smile took the sting out of the implication that he might not want to be with me on New Year's Eve. "Meet the girl. Drink champagne. Have fun."

I tried a final enticement. "Geena's party is a James Bond theme."

"You said." He went back to his soapy sink.

I took a sip from my wineglass while my thoughts formed two distinct factions: those in favor of staying home with Martin and those who wanted to go back to my old stomping grounds and have a blast. The only thought on Martin's side with any real merit was a sense of guilt. Ironic, since he was all but forcing me to go.

"I really want to meet Meghan," I said, knowing how much I sounded like I was making excuses. "Matt says I'm going to like her, but he has the worst taste in women."

"Not the worst." Martin tilted his head to one side and gave me the once-over. "Not by a long shot." In a moment of wine-induced honesty, I'd told him about my strange arrangement with Matt. He found the whole thing amusing.

"Thank you." I flushed. "I like to think I'm the best thing that's ever happened to him." Nothing like a little false bravado to deflect a compliment.

"I'm pretty sure you are." He stopped sudsing for a moment to kiss my forehead. "And I think we need to talk."

We need to talk. Four words that are as informative as any of the words that follow them. I knew I had to stop him, save him the trouble. But, there's always that flicker of curiosity: What would his reason be? What would the real, unspoken reason be? In Martin's rare case, those would the same—the age gap. We were at completely different stages of our lives, blah, blah, blah, *et cetera, et cetera, ad nauseam.*

"I know." I curled my hands into his shirt and forced him to look at me. "You don't have to say it."

He smiled sadly. "If it was even five years . . ."

I shook my head. "Please don't."

"I'm sorry, sweetie." He kissed me. "It was never going to work."

He was right, but that didn't stop me from feeling like a cup of spilled milk. I wasn't heartbroken, nor did I have the overwhelming feeling of ickiness that some of my ex-boyfriends had left behind. I was . . . empty. It was like entering a contest, knowing in your head you're never going to win, but hoping in your heart that you might. There is no cure for disappointment that comes from false expectations.

Geena greeted me at the door with a *Hello My Name Is* tag in one hand. Without asking, she slapped it on my hip. I glanced down.

"Solitaire?"

"*Live and Let Die*," Geena said. "Jane Seymour played her. You got a good one."

"And this isn't some kind of dig about me showing up dateless?"

Her eyes widened. "No! I'm sorry, I'll get you another one!" She reached for my tag, but I put my hand over it.

"It was a joke, Geena-Beana. I'll be Solitaire."

"Yay!" She grinned and thrust one finger in the air. "To the champagne!"

I mimicked her gesture. "To the champagne!"

Being at the party, surrounded by my old life, was a welcome distraction from my breakup with Martin. It was as though my life back in Milwaukee was a dream, and I'd awakened on New Year's Eve. The illusion would have been perfect if everyone hadn't greeted me like the prodigal daughter. Hugs, kisses, and the traditional UW-Madison greeting of "Let's do a shot!" I was out of practice—and probably healthier for it—and had to start declining offers early in the night. Still, I was more than a little blurry-eyed and hot-cheeked when Matt showed up with the new girl in tow.

I was shocked when I saw her. Not at all his usual, too-pretty-for-her-own-good type. She was more cute than pretty, something I could relate to. If I were a chipmunk, Meghan might have been a puppy. Dirty blond hair and freckles, a smile that was just a few teeth too wide for classic beauty, and the most shocking blue eyes I'd ever seen. An electric blue like a postcard from a tropical island. But it was the warmth in them that made her so different from all the Courtneys, Shelbys, and Pep Squad Wannabes he'd dated before.

"Joss, Meghan; Meghan, Joss."

"Joss!" She threw her arms around me. "I've heard so much about you! I was starting to think Matty made you up!"

I gave Matt a look over her shoulder, all wide eyes and the unspoken question: *Does she know about us?* He shook his head just slightly. Meghan released me.

"Okay, sorry." She stuck her hand out. "I'm Meghan."

I grinned and knocked her hand away. "Forget that. We're not going backward now."

By midnight, Meghan and I were like old friends. She was smart, funny, and one of the most fun people I ever met. She had me standing on Geena's coffee table with a long string of beads around both of our necks, belting out the chorus to a song she'd requested when someone cut the power to the stereo and shouted, "Five minutes to midnight!"

Everyone scrambled to get a glass of champagne—a bottle in some cases—and to get close to whoever they wanted to kiss at the first moment of the New Year. That slapped me back to my freshly single status. My old life felt a little less comfortable when the room paired off in preparation for midnight. There were new couples everywhere I looked. Old friends with new flames, and me on my own. I watched Meghan and Matt find each other, and cheat the New Year by a good thirty seconds.

I pressed my lips into a thin line, unable to prevent myself from remembering the feel of Matt's mouth on mine. He was a good kisser anytime; alone and lonely on New Year's Eve, he might as well have been a glass of water just out of reach while I died of thirst. I pulled my eyes from the scene and received Geena's friendly kiss on the cheek.

Moving through the room, and away from Matt and Meghan, I collected hugs and kisses that ranged from dry and on the cheek to wet and a little too friendly. Ultimately, it was Meghan who grabbed me from behind and pulled me into a hug.

"Happy New Year!" she shouted, before planting a noisy kiss on my temple. Then, she shoved me at Matt who caught me by the waist.

"Happy New Year, Joss."

"Happy New Year." I put one hand on his chest to regain my balance and stared at his mouth.

He smiled a little, then leaned in to kiss the corner of my lips. I scrounged up a smile for him. "I like her."

"Yeah, I can tell."

"Your taste is improving."

"You're just saying that because she's almost as little as you."

I eased back from him and twisted to look at Meghan. We weren't twins by any means, but she was close to my height and also built light and small. "Like I said—improving."

The night wore on, as New Year's Eve so often does, until the inevitable bad idea happened. So, at five in the morning, I found myself in the backyard of Geena's boyfriend's house, huddled around a charcoal grill with a marshmallow on a stick. January in Wisconsin is cold. Especially in the predawn morning. But we'd all been drinking long enough to think the unseasonably warm temperature of forty-two degrees was obvious s'more weather. Within five minutes, it was obvious what a horrible idea this was, but we had the kind of dedication that only the drunk and exhausted can give to a bad plan.

"I need some kind of rotisserie." Meghan put her back to the fire, then immediately shifted to face the tiny pyre. "I'm burning up in front, and literally freezing my ass off in the back."

Matt leaned over to check her out. "Nope, still there."

She twisted to check for herself. "Huh, look at that."

I laughed and dropped my marshmallow into the flames. I groaned.

"There're more inside," one of the guys who lived there offered.

I knew there was a distinct possibility I wouldn't return if I got a taste of the warm interior, but a s'more sounded good. I went back to the house then grabbed the whole bag of marshmallows and a fuzzy blanket from the back of the couch. When I came back, Meghan was in the middle of a story about her half-hearted attempt to rush the sororities first semester. She'd been talked into it by a group of girls who lived in her dorm, who convinced her that it was the way to make lifelong friends and do something important on campus.

"I don't know what I was thinking," she said.

"No shit, Meghan," someone else agreed. "You're not the sorority type at all."

"Well, I know that now," she agreed with a theatrical eye roll. "I quit on day three."

"Thank God," I said.

She turned to smile at me and noticed the blanket. "No fair!"

"I'll share, but I'm not giving it up," I said.

"Yay!" She wobbled through the trampled area of snow

around the grill and grabbed one end of the blanket. We squeezed together and succeeded in cutting off the wind.

"Ahhh . . ." Meghan sighed and wiggled fractionally closer.

"Speaking of Greeks . . . did I ever tell you about the time I almost sexually assaulted a frat guy?" That got the laugh I was expecting, and I launched into the story of my pathetic attempt to seduce the useless Jeff. I skimmed over the rationale for the attempt, feeling remote from the heartbreak of Ben's cheating.

"So, did you ever find a more helpful volunteer?" Meghan asked.

I found Matt's eyes on the other side of the fire and he gave me a pleading look. It was what I'd expected, and I dropped a wink at him. "Not for a while. It's just as well . . . I think Jeff would have made me feel dirtier than Ben."

I stayed in Madison for the weekend, sleeping on couches and borrowed beds wherever I could. I'd dropped Dewey off with my fellow vet tech, Nellie, so I didn't have anything pressing me to get back to Milwaukee. Avoiding home seemed like a better plan anyway. Geena tolerated my dissection of the Martin breakup better than I expected. I guessed not seeing me for a while made her more willing to listen to my dating drama.

Matt was the last person I saw. We had a breakfast on Sunday that by all rights should have been called lunch. Meghan always worked in the call center for the university hospital on Sunday mornings, so it was just the two of us. It reminded me of dozens of times when I'd sat across from him in the four years we'd known each other. Even the setting was familiar—Mickie's Dairy Bar, a Madison institution in the field of breakfast. The place was noisy, crowded, and usually required a long wait, but we got a seat after only twenty minutes. The city still seemed to be nursing its collective hangover. I always liked sitting on the red stools near the windows at Mickie's. It made me feel almost normal height, though I kicked my feet like a kid the whole time.

We talked about my job, about his decision not to walk in the December graduation ceremony, about my cat, where Matt should live when he moved to Milwaukee for law school, about Martin and Meghan. There was a lot of talk about Meghan.

"What made you stray so far from the Barbie aisle?" I asked, and poked at my half of the scrambler we were sharing. I had pressed a butter knife through the center of the obscene mountain of breakfast food and wiggled it until there was a moat between our halves. Matt's half had ketchup on top of it. Demonstrating enormous personal growth and maturity, I hadn't thrown up at the sight, and even managed to eat a good portion of my half. The food was going to emerge victorious, I knew, but I intended to give it a good fight.

He narrowed his eyes. "Cute. You've been saving that one up, haven't you?"

I didn't answer, but grinned at him.

"Honestly? You."

My insides whirled and I had to reach for my coffee for distraction. "Why me?"

"You were dating a thirty-three-year-old." He shook his head. "I figured I should try something new."

"It's not a contest," I said.

"Yeah, it's just . . ." He shrugged. "I don't know. I just saw her at the Nat, and she was cute and funny, and I thought, why wouldn't I ask her out?"

"Do you hear that?" I cupped my hand behind one ear. "I think that's the sound of Matt Lehrer maturing."

"Bite me."

"Oh, no. I was wrong." I grinned at him.

"Just do me a favor and don't go rambling on about all the girls I've dated when you see her, okay?"

"I would never—" I started to say.

"Not even if you've had too much wine?" he interrupted.

"So, she doesn't know you're a man slut?"

"I really hate that you came up with that."

"What? It's not my fault you can't keep it in your pants." I was smiling, because I was teasing, but there was a strange feeling of nervousness in my stomach. Like I was at the top of a slippery slope and one false step would send me down the path of saying mean things just to make him feel bad. Apparently, I was taking the breakup harder than I was willing to let on. Harder than I even realized. I tossed out a belated, "You know I'm teasing."

Matt picked up the ketchup bottle and tilted it over my half of the plate, cap on. "You sure about that?"

I wrinkled my nose and sat back fast enough to almost slip off my stool. "You wouldn't."

He grinned and set the bottle back on the table. "So, what were you saying?"

"I take it she hasn't been enlightened to the concept of Sorbet . . ." I said.

"Um . . . no."

"I get why you're not telling her, but at the same time, I have to ask: What are you worried about? You hadn't even met her the last time we . . ." I crossed my legs and pressed my knees tight together. We were experts at compartmentalizing the two parts of our relationship, but nothing could stop liquid heat from dripping through me when we spoke about our intermittent sex life in the light of day.

"I know." He nodded. "But, I'm not sure she'd be thrilled that we're still friends."

"It's in the rules," I reminded him.

"True."

"Maybe you should just show her the contract." I nudged his foot with mine.

"Do you still have that? The rules, I mean."

In a box in my front hall closet. "Probably somewhere."

"That's good."

I considered all the possible meanings of his uninterpretable tone while I busied myself with a forkful of hash browns and eggs—sans ketchup. Of course, the right words came to me when I was still chewing. "Planning to invoke them anytime soon?"

He looked down at his coffee, smiling a little. "I hope not."

"Ooo-ooh!" I smirked. "Matty's in loo-ooove." *Ah, sarcasm . . . balm for any unmentionable wounds to the soul,* I thought. There was just too much irony in Matt Lehrer finding a long-term girlfriend while I was breaking up with yet another inappropriate man. *Ugh.*

He laughed. "Screw you, Joss."

"Apparently not."

"Oh, right."

I drummed my fingers against my thigh. It would be so much easier if I could just have been with Matt one more time. If he could have met Meghan next week, or just stayed my Sorbet Guy forever. Taking risks was easier with a safety net. Without Matt around, I might have to stop careening through the dating world like a toddler on a sugar high. Unless . . . "So, anyone else you'd recommend since you're bowing out as my Sorbet Guy?" Not that I could imagine having a contract with anyone but Matt.

"I think Jay would be more than happy to step in."

"Okay, I like Jay, but gross." Jay was an acquaintance who had asked me out once. I was seeing . . . someone at the time, and had been grateful for the excuse to say no. He was fine enough to have a chat with if I ran into him, but he was self-important for no good reason, and frankly, a bit lacking in personal hygiene.

"Gross?"

"Oh, come on, Matt."

He let out the smirk he'd been trying to hold back. "Yeah . . . gross."

"Thank you." I sighed.

"Look, I'm sorry I can't help you out with the Martin thing . . ." Matt started.

I laughed. It wasn't funny, but there was just something so absurd about an apology for failing to provide sex. "No, it's okay. I don't really need it." Partially true. I wasn't distraught over Martin, but I definitely wouldn't have turned down the offer if he'd been able to make it.

"Really?" He raised his eyebrows. "I thought you liked this guy."

"I do. Did." I shook my head. "It was doomed from the start. I'm just being stupid."

"Well, anyway, I'm sorry."

"Don't be." I looked out the window at the light traffic on Regent Street. "You don't belong to me."

"I know. I just—" He shrugged and reached for his coffee cup.

I looked back at him and smiled. "End of an era, right? We're big important college graduates now." Maybe it was time to grow up and stop playing our silly game. If we left Sorbet Sex in Madison, it could be just a part of my college years.

Matt tapped one knuckle against my hand. "Still friends, right?"

"Sure. It's in the contract."

He laughed. "Seriously, though. We're cool, right?"

I rolled my eyes. "Come on, Matty, you're not *that* good in bed." Liar, liar, liar.

He tossed a wadded up napkin at me. "Gone for one semester, and I already forgot what a complete pain in the ass you are."

"I'll have to teach Meghan all of my tricks before I go home."

"She knows plenty without your help, trust me."

"I knew I liked her."

"She likes you, too. God help me."

"Good, then I want a good seat at the wedding."

He blanched. "Not funny."

"I guess little Matty's not all grown up after all." I laughed. "Fine, then just try not to screw this up, okay?"

He laid one hand over his heart. "Believe me, I have no intention of screwing anything up."

CHAPTER SIXTEEN

THREE YEARS EARLIER . . . FIRST YEAR AFTER GRADUATING FROM COLLEGE

Dewey was in the living room when I arrived at Nellie's to pick him up, but the minute he saw me, he hightailed it to parts unknown. Nellie tilted her head, listening, then grimaced.

"That would be the sound of a fat cat squeezing behind the washing machine," she said. "We'll have to wait him out."

"He's mad at me." I sighed and sank onto Nellie's couch, arching my back to dig out a rogue dog toy from the crease.

"Cats are such divas," Nellie agreed, scooping up one of her own cats before taking his place on the armchair. "So, how was your weekend?"

"Good. Mostly good." I rubbed my wrist over my forehead. "I think I have a headache."

"Still hungover?" she teased.

I ticked off my reasons on my fingers. "Drank too much, slept on couches, stayed up too late every night, feeling like a loser after brunch today."

"Why are you a loser?"

I laughed softly. Classic Nellie to phrase it that way. "My friend Matt has a new girlfriend." I shook my head. "It's . . . complicated."

"You want him for yourself," she said.

"No! It's not like that. I'm happy for him. And her. She's great." I slumped farther into the couch and pressed the heels of my hands into my eyes just hard enough to see fireworks. "It's a long story."

"I got time."

Nellie absorbed the Sorbet story without much comment, but at the end, after a few considering breaths, she said, "That's fucked up."

"Oh, come on, you've never heard of friends with benefits?"

"Yeah, and that always works out so well." Nellie rolled her eyes. "Seriously, did you think you could keep something like that up?"

"It's been four years," I said. "We're pretty good at it."

"Well, something had to happen. One of you was going to get serious with someone else, or you were going to start dating each other."

"No way. He's not my type at all."

She opened her mouth, considered, then closed it. She repeated the process a few times until she found her voice. "I'm not even gonna touch that." She put one finger up as if I'd interrupted her. "So if he's not your type, what are you all drama-ed up about the new girlfriend for?"

"I just—It's just that—" I bit the inside of my right cheek as I considered how far to tread into honesty. "I always figured it would be me who found my perfect guy first. Matt wouldn't have cared if I cancelled the arrangement, but it makes me feel like a loser that he has Meghan, and I just broke up with Martin."

"How old are you again?" Nellie asked.

"Twenty-three."

She made a sound from somewhere near the intersection of derisive snort and disbelieving non-word. "Please. You're not collecting Social Security yet, Joss. You'll find someone. Trust me."

"I know." I didn't really doubt that. But it didn't stop me from wanting a little Sorbet Sex to soothe my ego. Bruised by Martin, bruised by being alone for New Year's Eve, bruised by the loss of my Sorbet partner—and the only cure I knew for these injuries was exactly what I couldn't have. I was downright petulant. At least no one knew.

"Just don't put pressure on every relationship to be *the* relationship," Nellie said.

If only that was my problem. "I think that's part of why I'm feeling like such a loser. I keep dating these guys I know there's no future with."

"There's nothing wrong with that. It's called having fun."

"Yeah, but . . ." I searched for the right words. "If dating is like doing the crossword, I've been writing in pencil and Matt was my eraser. Now, all of a sudden, I've got *The New York Times* Sunday edition and a permanent marker."

"Okay, first of all, don't be such a drama queen. Second, that just means you're in the ring with everyone else. It's called being normal."

"Well, whoop-de-freakin'-doo for being normal. So far, being a grown-up sucks."

She laughed. "That's the secret, you know. Being a grown-up sucks."

"I should have stayed in college."

Martin moved out of the building in February, which made life easier. I hardly ever saw him, but I still caught a whiff of whatever he was cooking if I took the back stairs. He knocked on my door the day before he moved to break the news. I thanked him for telling me, hugged him, and wished him luck in his new place.

He kissed me, just enough to make me consider the merits of hauling him into my bedroom one last time, but it would have been a mistake. Judging from the look in his eyes, he'd been debating the same thing. In the end, we parted ways at my door, and he became the last person I kissed for a very long time.

I took a break from dating. To my surprise, it wasn't that hard. I spent time with my friends, my sister, and her husband, and embraced the incomparable comfort of sprawling out on my couch in the evenings in the same ugly cutoff shorts night after night. Dewey was in favor of my new lifestyle; quickly finding all the most inconvenient places to wedge himself when I settled in for the night.

Matt started splitting his time between Milwaukee and Madison in April. He'd gotten an internship at a local law firm, which meant he had to be in town Monday through Friday. Meghan meant he had to go back to Madison as often as he could. She was still in school, and would be for the duration of Matt's time in law school. He was confident they could make it long distance, and I couldn't disagree.

The internship came on short notice, and he spent the first two weeks sleeping on my couch four nights a week while he handled his living arrangements in both cities. He'd never slept at my place without sleeping in my bed before. Saying good night to him the first night was foreign and embarrassing for some reason. He gave me a sweet smile and a hug, then hesitated twice before kissing me on the cheek.

"Don't worry, I'm not going to molest you in your sleep or anything," I promised.

He laughed. "Damn."

I *tsk'd* at him. "Calm yourself. Your man-slutting days are supposed to be over, remember?"

He rolled his eyes. "I can't help feeling a little guilty."

"We haven't done anything." Although I knew exactly what he meant. "And we're not going to."

"I know. It's just that she doesn't know . . ."

I propped one hand on my hip. "You wanna call and tell her right now?"

"Very funny."

Dewey yowled at Matt's feet and started making figure eights around his ankles. The cat had fallen in love with Matt at first sight, and didn't like it when he couldn't have his full attention. Matt shifted to free one foot and rubbed his arch on Dewey's head.

"Look, Matty, we can't un-have sex. It happened. It happened before Meghan happened. We have to figure out how to do this, or we can't be friends."

He nodded. "I feel like I've missed my window. I should have told her about you already."

"You don't have to tell her anything," I said. "I promise I will never say a word to her."

"I know you won't."

"But, if you keep acting weird about me, she's probably going to think something is up anyway."

He blew out a breath. "Good point."

"I don't know what the etiquette is in this situation." I shrugged.

"Me either." He chuckled. "I'm not sure anyone does."

"We'll figure it out."

"I want you both in my life," he said. "You're one of my best friends."

Warm tingles bloomed in my chest. "Thanks, Matty." I stood on tiptoe to hug him again and he gave me a breath-stealing squeeze. When I could talk, I said, "We'll figure this out. You can have both of us."

His eyes glinted for a microsecond before he smiled. "Yeah?"

I crossed my arms. "No way, pal."

"What?" His eyes went puppy-wide. "What did I say?"

"You didn't have to say anything. I know how your mind works, you big perv."

"What?" he tried again, lips betraying him with a grin. "I didn't say anything."

"Uh-huh." I gave him a shove. "I'm going to bed."

He laughed. "I didn't say a word."

"You didn't have to."

He kept laughing as I headed for the bedroom.

"Men."

"You brought it up!" he called after me.

I turned. "Okay, fine. But, you're still a pervert."

"Is that a definite 'no'?" he called after me, still laughing.

"Tell you what, call Meghan. Run this by her, and then we'll talk."

He stopped laughing out loud, but his shoulders still shook. "Don't think I won't."

"I *know* you won't."

"Good night, Joss." He grinned.

"Good night." I managed to get my door closed before I let my own amusement show. It felt good to be making absurd jokes with him again. I felt like we were getting back to solid ground. We could actually be friends.

Everything fell apart in June.

The annual Fourth of July trip to Matt parents' cottage was already planned. I couldn't wait to spend some time with old friends again. Matt was living in Milwaukee by that time, still visiting Meghan like a devout churchgoer. I was still single and happy with it, though I was finally starting to consider a lift on the man embargo. Life was good.

Then, Matt called me on a Thursday night and I could tell he was stressed.

"I think I'm in trouble, Joss."

"What's wrong?"

He blew out a long sigh. "It's Meghan . . . she's acting a little strange."

"How so?"

"She . . . I don't know. She was supposed to come down this weekend, and she just told me she can't. She won't say why."

"I'm sure it's nothing, Matty. A girl's allowed to have a few secrets."

"She sounded upset."

I pursed my lips, thinking. Over the last six months, I'd gotten to know Meghan pretty well. Our connection was through Matt, of course, but we had enough of a relationship, that I could make an offer to help. "Why don't I just call her?"

"Would you?" He sounded so relieved I almost changed my mind. More than likely, I wasn't going to learn anything from Meghan if she wasn't going to talk to her own boyfriend.

"Yeah, I'll call."

"Thanks, Joss. I owe you."

"Don't worry, I'll collect on the debt sometime."

He laughed a little, and I felt a small relief that he hadn't lost his sense of humor.

"I'll call her now."

We said our goodbyes and I found Meghan's number. I dialed, feeling a sense of dread. I knew I shouldn't be interfering.

"Meghan, it's Joss."

"Oh my God, how are you?" She sounded pleased to hear from me.

"I'm good. How are you?" My tone sounded overly pleasant, even to my own ears. She must have known this was not a social call.

"I'm good. What's going on?"

"Are you coming up to Matt's place for the Fourth?" This was the pretense I'd constructed for my call. It seemed legitimate, if a little forced.

"I'm supposed to," she answered, which was really not an answer.

"Why do I sense a 'but' here?"

There was a quiet sigh from her end of the line. "I don't know if I'm gonna make it."

"Is something wrong?" I twirled one of my curls around one finger until it was tight to my scalp. I was nervous on Matt's behalf.

This time there was a long silence.

"Meghan?" I asked, wondering if we'd become disconnected.

"I shouldn't be talking to you about this."

My heart fluttered into a rapid tattoo. "It's okay. You don't have to."

"No . . . I—" Her voice broke and I heard a thick intake of breath. "Oh God, I'm the worst person in the world!"

It was my turn to be quiet. I couldn't imagine what she meant.

"See, I was late, but it was all a mistake, but it made me realize—oh God . . ."

"I don't understand."

"It's just not enough," she said and sniffed loudly.

"Meg, I don't know what you're talking about. What can I do? Do you need help?" Curl twirling was no longer enough. Time to fit my thumbnail between my teeth.

"He asked you to call, didn't he?"

"No." That was true, but I couldn't leave out the rest. "I offered."

"Shit," she said, to herself I think. And then she told me the truth. It was all a terrible misunderstanding. She had counted the days on her calendar wrong, and for a moment—just a long, terrifying moment—thought that her period was late. That she was pregnant. But that moment was all it took for her to realize something awful: she didn't love Matt enough to ruin her life.

"It would have been over, Joss. Completely over. I'm not ready to have a kid. I don't even know if I want to, and the thing is, I know—I know—that Matt would have been okay with it. He would have married me. I know he would have. And you know what? I don't want that. I love Matt so much. So, so much. But I can't give it all up for him, and that means he's not The One."

"But it was just a mistake," I said. "Nothing happened." Even though I wanted to reassure her, inside, I was dying for her. In all the times I'd taken the risk of sex, I'd never had a pregnancy scare of any kind. I could only begin to imagine the terror she'd felt as she stared at the calendar. My stomach clenched in sympathy.

"But it all came to me like that. I would have gotten rid of it. I wouldn't have even told Matt. Isn't that sick? God, what's wrong with me?"

"Nothing's wrong with you," I promised. I could imagine myself curled up in the fetal position and bawling if I'd been in her shoes. But I forced myself into confidence. "You just had a scare. Why don't you tell Matt what happened?"

"No, I can't. I'm just gonna break his heart someday. I know I don't want the same things he wants."

"How do you know? You have to talk to him."

"Do you know that I gave up study abroad for him?"

"What?" I was confused by the sudden change in subject.

"I was supposed to go to Italy. In the fall. And I just—dropped out. I never even told him."

"He would have wanted you to go," I said. "He would do anything for you, Meg."

"I know. That's the problem." She sighed. "He would have wanted me to go, and I would have gone, and the whole time he would have been missing me, and I would have been happy, but at the same time, I wouldn't have enjoyed myself. I would have known he was home, waiting for me, and I would have felt guilty if anything had happened while I was over there. I mean, what if I met someone? How could I break his heart? I mean, it's Matt. I love him so much. How could I forgive myself if I ever did that to him?"

"But you're thinking about doing it now," I reasoned.

"Because now I know I have to," she said. "I don't think I love him as much as I should."

"But maybe you love him enough for now."

"Enough for now is not enough," she said, and the words rang in my ears like bells.

"Meg . . ." I was at a loss.

"I know," she said. "I'm sorry. I have to go." She disconnected.

The call from Matt came the next morning.

"You know why I'm calling," he said as a greeting.

"Yeah."

"What am I gonna do?"

"I . . . I don't know."

"Fuck me . . ." He sighed. "You still coming up to Door County next week?"

"That's still on?"

"Yeah, I guess."

"Matty, you don't have to do this."

"Why not?"

"Maybe you should just skip it."

"No, I need this. Really. You coming?"

"Yeah, I'll be there."

"Thank you."

Matt did a good job of pretending to be fine when we were all up at the cottage the following weekend. Everyone knew about Meghan, of course, but he was willing to make us all feel better about it. There was something in his eyes, though—I could see it.

The cottage was crowded and noisy, and everyone had a fantastic time. Except, of course, for Matt.

On the second day, we took a paddleboat out, just Matt and me, and when we were far enough from the shore, he finally let down his guard.

"I couldn't talk her out of it," he said.

"I guessed that."

"She just kept saying she loved me too much. What the fuck does that even mean?"

"She told me she knew she'd break your heart one day," I said.

"Yeah, well, apparently today's the day." He gave the edge of the boat a solid kick.

"Oh, Matty . . ." I tried to stand, but the boat wobbled in a terrifying way and I had to drop back to my seat abruptly. "Sorry."

Matt threw his head back and let out a loud bellow. There were no words, just a giant sound of frustration. Then he slumped down in the molded seat and sighed. "I want to hate her."

"You don't?"

"Nope." He plucked a dried leaf from the bottom of the boat and tried to throw it, but it just fluttered toward the water.

"Do you want me to start hating her?" I offered.

"I just want her back."

"I'm sorry."

"What can I do to get her back?"

I stretched out a hand to rub his head. "I'm afraid this might be one of those awful situations where you have to let her go. If it's meant to be . . ."

"I don't want to let her go."

"I know that. But if you chase her, she'll just run."

"What if that's all bullshit? Why should I let go of something I love? It doesn't even make sense."

I didn't have an answer for that.

"This sucks," he said.

We bobbed on the lake in silence for a while.

"Just let me know if you want me to start hating her," I offered at last.

He winced. "I don't want anyone to hate her. It's Meghan. I love Meghan. You love Meghan."

I did. She was wonderful, and I would have thought she was The One for him. But, I was willing to at least say I hated her if it would help him feel the tiniest bit better. "Well, you know my offer stands."

"I know."

I hesitated, but added, "All of the offer." All my self-coaching about outgrowing Sorbet Sex was out the window. If there was anything I could do to soothe his broken heart, I would do it. Though, the offer felt shallow once I'd said it aloud.

He nodded and looked away from me. "I don't think I want that right now."

"Okay." My stomach turned. It was as trivial as I'd imagined.

"You know it's not you, right?"

"You don't have to make me feel better, Matt. This is about you."

"But it's not you."

"I know."

"Okay."

I focused on the shore, and realized we'd drifted quite a ways. "I think I'm getting a little seasick."

"We can go back."

"Thanks."

We paddled our way toward the dock and my queasy feeling started to lift. I don't know if I was really seasick or if the conversation was making me uncomfortable. Either way, I was glad to head for shore.

Matt seemed reluctant to go to bed that night. He stayed at the fire pit until his eyes were glazed and his focus had drifted to somewhere near the rocks that surrounded the fire. One by one, the others left the fire with, "I'm tired, man, I'm going to bed," or "Okay, that's it for me." I was nearly asleep myself, curled up on the chaise I'd claimed as my own over the years. I even had the same fleece blanket. It was plaid and smelled like a wood-burning fire with a tinge of lake.

"Joss, come on, let's go to bed," Kerry said, hauling herself up from a canvas chair.

"I'm coming," I promised. I was cozy and drowsy, and I knew that pulling the blanket off would invite in the night air. I wasn't eager to do that.

"I'm too tired to wait," she said. We were sharing a room, being the two single girls on the trip.

"Go," I told her.

Matt stood and reached for the bucket of sand near the fire. He poured it over the glowing embers, plunging us into a deeper dark. "Come on, Joss," he said softly.

I got to my feet and swathed myself in the blanket as best I could. The loss of firelight gave me pause before I was willing to negotiate the path back to the cottage. "I can't see."

He came around the pit and found my shoulder with a fumbling hand. "There you are."

"I'm here." I yawned.

Matt's hand navigated up to rest at the back of my neck. Then, he kissed me in the dark with the sound of the crickets all around us. It was a hard, closed-mouth kiss.

"What are you doing?" I asked when he stopped.

"I don't know."

"You're not ready for this," I said.

"Maybe not."

"I'm not gonna be something you regret, Matt. That's not how it works."

He let out a soft laugh. "The student has become the teacher."

"You bet your ass."

He pulled me close again, but just gave me a hug that time.

"Come on, let's get you to bed," I said, charitably opening my blanket cocoon to put an arm around his back.

"Thanks."

"This is not an entirely selfless act, you know. I'm exhausted."

He laughed softly again and squeezed my arm. "Me, too."

"Good."

We made our way to the cottage, stumbling a few times in the pitch black.

"I'm sorry I kissed you," he said just before opening the door.

"It's okay. You've done worse things to me."

When he laughed that time, it was an authentic one. "Great, thanks."

"I'm here for you, Matty."

Six weeks. Matt's devastation took six weeks to ease. It was mid-August, and I'd gone on my first date in months just days before he called me. It was a fine enough date, but there was no spark and he didn't call me again. I didn't mind. I was just happy to have gotten a date under my belt after the long hiatus.

After the trip to the cottage, Matt had made a few failed attempts to win Meghan back. It had ended in tears for both of them. In the end, she'd decided to do her semester abroad after all. I don't know how she managed to get in the program so late, but she did. It seemed that an ocean and half a continent would finally be enough to give her the distance she needed. When Matt asked her if there was a chance for them after she'd had her time alone, she finally found the words to drive it home for him: "I don't know what I want, Matt, but I know that I can't stay with you. You love me too much. You make me want to give things up for you, and I hate that about myself. I couldn't live with it if I started to resent you in a few years. I'm walking away while I still love you. That way, this will always be a wonderful memory."

By then, I actually was starting to hate her a little. Just a little. It wasn't anything about her personally, it was about the way she had taken his heart and crushed it between her fingers. He was devastated. Even when he finally understood her twisted logic, he was miserable.

Watching him suffer through that breakup was like watching an educational video on the Kübler-Ross model of grief. Shock and denial gave way to bargaining and anger. Depression lasted longer than the rest, but in its place came resolve. He wasn't going to let her be the only one to walk away with good memories. Once he came to accept that she was a closed chapter in his life, he could even talk about her without looking like a kicked puppy.

When the phone call came, I was surprised. I knew he was getting over Meghan. I had seen it with my own eyes, but I thought Sorbet was over, too. I'd assumed he thought it was too tawdry to follow Meghan. But then he called.

"I need you tonight, Joss."

"Oh. Really?"

"She can't be the last one anymore."

"I'll be there."

The sex was somber, if such a thing is possible. More about comfort than vindication. The last step in letting go. I kissed his face the whole time, fighting the urge to apologize for not being Meghan.

After, we lay together in the slanted light of the streetlamp that was entirely too close to his window. The apartment was a summer sublet near the campus of his law school. The day he moved in he started looking for a new place. Preferably away from the squalor of the campus. Four-and-a-half years of student housing was enough—no real adult would be expected to put up with the nonsense that plagues the rental properties filled each year by college students. I've seen toilets at the top of the basement stairs, rooms so small that a hanging rod suspended across the room served as a closet and left the clothes dangling above the bed, and a kitchen with no sink. Matt's proximity to the streetlight was minor in comparison to some of those, but it didn't seem minor when the light gave the room an orange glow like a sunrise.

"How do you sleep at night?" I asked.

"Here—" His voice was strained as he hauled to his feet and

crossed the room to the windows. After a bit of fumbling, he brought the shades down and the room was dimmed to a late evening glimmer. "Better?"

"Yeah, thanks."

He came back to the bed and slid under the sheets with me, kissing the exposed underside of my upraised arm.

"Do you feel better?" I asked.

"You know, I kind of do."

"Just kind of?" I was disappointed.

"I was only expecting to feel nothing. No change. That would have been enough."

"But you feel better?"

"Yeah, I do." He kissed me, and I seized the chance to catch my fingers in his short hair and keep him close for longer. My self-imposed exile from the dating world had left me hungry for the contact of another person's lips on mine. And Matt was still the best kisser I'd ever known. Something about the way he moved—I could never put my finger on it, nor did it matter when I had free rein to collect evidence from the source.

"Well, then I guess I kept up my end of the deal," I said when I finally let him go.

"And then some," he agreed.

"Good." I stretched one foot across to rub against his shin.

"I'm sorry about Martin," he said.

"It's okay. I didn't really need you after . . ." And while I'd learned I could get through a breakup without Matt, I still wished he'd been available at the time. But he didn't need to know that.

"I guess that's good."

"Yeah."

Matt rolled onto his side to look at me. "Are you gonna stay tonight?"

"Of course," I said. "I thought that was part of the deal."

"Just asking."

I let a short silence stretch out before I spoke again. "Can you do something for me?"

"Yeah, sure. What do you need?"

"Look . . . it's been a while since I shared a bed with anyone—can you just . . . spoon me?"

He laughed, but moved closer and let me fit my body into the shape left by his. "Like that?"

"Yeah, thanks."

He shifted a few times and made some sniffing sounds. "Your hair is in my face."

"Sorry." I twisted my hair and pinned it under my head.

"Thanks." He put a hand on my hip and I felt his body settle into the mattress.

I sighed, enjoying the feeling of a warm body at my back. "We might need to work this into the contract."

"Yeah, I don't know about that. I might be able to get it excluded on grounds of curly hair."

I reached down to pinch his leg and he laughed, knocking my hand away. "You don't have to do it for long," I promised.

"I'll deal." He kissed my shoulder. "Thanks for being here."

"Of course. What are friends for?"

"Not too many of them are for this."

"True." I slipped my fingers through his where they rested on my waist. "I guess it's a good thing we met."

"And a good thing we both suck at relationships."

"No kidding." I laughed. "Is it so much to ask that I meet a nice guy and just have a nice, normal relationship? No eleven-year age difference, no cheating, no . . . wooden ducks."

Matt burst into laughter. "No ducks? Now you're asking too much."

"Okay, then, how about someone whose weirdness doesn't bother me?"

"Now you're thinking. Everyone's a little weird, right?"

"God knows *you* are." I pushed my elbow into his stomach.

"Don't make me get dressed, Joss."

I twisted in his arms and pressed my mouth against his. "Not yet."

Matt found me browsing the picture board and came up beside me to take a look for himself. "What's got your attention?" he asked.

"Meghan, actually," I confessed.

"Wow, where did that come from?"

I tapped the barely visible photo of her electric blue eye.

"Oh." He leaned closer and inspected it. "Sure enough."

Something unpleasant pinched in my stomach. Some blend of my lingering negativity toward Meghan and an ugly trace of jealousy that he still kept her photo around. There was so much of my past swirling through my head tonight. I had to change the subject.

"So, is dinner ready or what?" I asked, poking him in the ribs.

Matt inhaled, his eyes seeming to snap back to the present. "Yeah, just about. Do you want something to drink?"

"What are you offering?"

"I think I have the bottle of wine you opened last time you were here . . ." He looked thoughtful.

I raised my eyebrow at him. "Did you put the cork back in?"

"Yes." He rolled his eyes.

"Then, yes, I'd be delighted to have some." I gave him a winning smile and batted my eyes.

"Come and get it, then."

I trailed him to the kitchen and accepted the glass of wine that he poured.

"What happened, Matty? I didn't even know you were seeing anyone."

"What do you mean?"

"You said you *needed* me."

"Oh. I guess I did. Right."

"And . . . ?" I asked.

"Gimme a minute," he said, gathering plates to serve our dinner. I kept my peace as he spooned out pasta and sauce, then handed me the plates. "Can you take these to the table?"

I carried them to his small dining table and returned for my glass of wine. Matt carried out bread and the rest of the bottle of wine and we settled into the chairs.

"So, now are you going to tell me?" I asked.

He twirled a forkful of spaghetti while he thought. "Can I just tell you after we eat?"

This was torture. "Oh. I guess."

He smiled and went back to his food, but didn't eat much more. Neither did I. Silence, usually comfortable and short with Matt and me, felt strange. I had to get out of my own head. Sifting through topics, quickly, I seized on something neutral.

"Hey, you going to Jessie's wedding?" I asked.

"I don't see why not."

"Wanna ride down together?" I asked with a nod to show him the right answer.

He laughed. "Doesn't sound like you're giving me a choice."

"I mean, unless you're bringing a date or something."

"Not planning to."

These short answers were killing me. Everything about this night was too damn strange. I had to confront him.

"Matty, what's up with you?" I asked. "You're so quiet."

He pushed his plate to the side and took a moment to arrange his fork before looking at me. "I've been thinking more about leaving school."

"Oh. And?"

"And . . ." He shrugged. "I think I should."

"What are you going to do?" I propped both elbows on the table, lowered one hand to the table as if to touch him, but brought it back up to my chin. I didn't know what he was feeling—I didn't know what to do for him.

He shrugged again. "I've been really thinking a lot about . . . things . . . everything, I guess. I feel like I should start doing what I *want* to do with my life, instead of what I should do. I need to stop just . . . marking time."

"So, what does that mean?"

"It means I need to make some changes." He pressed a fingertip against one tine of his fork, making it seesaw off the table. "My lease is up in June. I think maybe I should try somewhere else for a while."

Butterflies took wing in my chest. "Like?"

"Somewhere different. San Diego . . . North Carolina . . . Portland . . . I don't know yet."

"But . . ." I wanted to say "what about me?" but I didn't. "You don't know anyone in any of those places, do you?"

"Nope."

Dinner, which had been difficult to get down in the first place, made a determined effort to ascend my throat. I pressed my teeth together and focused on the reflection on the outside of his glass.

"I don't even want to be a lawyer. Why am I wasting my time?" He picked up the glass I'd been staring at and took a drink. "How much would it suck if I got in a car accident or something and the last thing I'd done was go to a class on real estate law?"

I flinched at the thought, not of the class, but the accident. "So what do you want to do?"

He hesitated, then looked over his shoulder toward the living room. "Come on, let's go sit down where it's comfortable." Without waiting for an answer, he led the way to the couch. I followed, a little slower, and tucked myself into the opposite corner of the couch, feet extended toward him.

"Okay." He stretched one arm along the back of the couch, looked at me for a second, but ultimately refocused across the room when he started speaking. "So . . . there's a girl—a woman, I guess, when the hell do I have to stop calling them girls?"

"When they're old enough to be somebody's mother?" I suggested, and he laughed a little. This was familiar territory, and my nerves untangled a bit.

"Anyway, her name is Tara, and she's in my class," he continued.

"A lawyer? I thought you didn't date lawyers."

He smiled weakly. "Right. Well . . ." He shifted and hooked the fingers of one hand on the back of his neck. He was nervous, I realized. Why? "You know I haven't really been seeing anyone since my dad's funeral. And I wasn't really seeing anyone before it either . . ."

I was trying to be patient, but I couldn't see where he was going with all of this. "Okay, so you met Tara. What happened?"

"I've been thinking about how we've sort of been . . . less rigid with the whole Sorbet thing. Since . . . well, I'm not sure, exactly. But, the stuff after my dad died . . . that wasn't what we started out doing."

"That wasn't exactly normal circumstances."

He closed his eyes briefly. "I don't know if I would have made it through that week without you."

My heart hurt, remembering the way he'd been. We'd

stretched Sorbet to the limits back then, and although I wouldn't have changed a single thing I'd done for him, it had been rough. On both of us.

I put on a smile for him, though it felt a little out of place. "You know I'd do it again."

"I know." The squint he angled at me was unreadable. "Anyway. So the Sorbet thing has been getting kind of gray. Since . . ." His eyes rolled up in thought. "Since . . . God, Alex? Maybe that was when."

"Blech," I said automatically. "But that was so long ago. And Meghan was a clear-cut case."

"But what about junior year when you went out with all those random guys? The duck decoy guy?"

I crossed my arms. "How about The Squad? And you almost deflowering Kelly?"

"But I didn't," he said instantly. "And that's exactly my point. None of those were even breakups and we *still* had an awful lot of Sorbet Sex that summer."

For all intents and purposes, it had been a series of booty calls, and I knew it. "Okay, so maybe that was a stretch."

"Which time?" He smirked, and I was so happy to see some reaction out of him I almost didn't mind the smugness.

"That was some of our best work." The flush in my cheeks gave away my complete lack of cool.

He sucked air through clenched teeth. "Yeah, it really was."

"But, I digress . . ." I made a rolling gesture. "You were saying?"

"Well, my point is, that was the first time that we really just threw the rules away."

"Actually, I'd say it was with Alex. The second time."

He nodded. "Yeah, okay. The point is that we've been pretty lax about the whole thing since then."

"I don't know, the whole T.J. thing was pretty straightfor-ward."

He made a whatever-you-say face. "T.J. was just a mistake, and you know it."

"That's my point," I protested. "He was a mistake and I to-tally needed you afterward."

"It's not like you were all distraught over him," Matt rea-soned.

"Well, no. It was just the ick factor." I shuddered.

"Still . . ."

"That's what Sorbet is all about. Getting rid of the bad mojo, right?"

"How long ago was that?" he wondered.

"A few years, I guess."

"Jesus." He dropped his head onto the back of the couch and focused on the ceiling for a moment. "When did time start going so quickly?"

I snickered. "You sound like an old man."

"Sorry." He lifted his head and looked at me. "I'm just . . . thinking."

"So wait a minute, you were gonna tell me about Tara."

"No, it's fine. T.J. is relevant to this whole thing."

"T.J. isn't relevant to anything," I said, shuddering again.

Matt grinned. "You're never gonna let that go, are you?"

CHAPTER EIGHTEEN

SECOND YEAR OUT OF COLLEGE

"To being single."

"To Constitutional Law."

"To the new season of *The Bachelor*."

It was Sunday, and in my world, that meant it was brunch time.

Within a few weeks of Matt starting law school, we'd established a loose tradition of having Sunday brunch. It was a casual affair with a constantly fluctuating membership. Sometimes there were as many as a dozen people—law school friends, Nellie and her boyfriend, Jason, siblings in town, or friends both local and visiting. The smallest ones were just Matt and me. Part of the tradition of our brunches was the toast. Everyone at the table had to offer one as we lifted glasses—sometimes mimosas and Bloody Marys, sometimes the more pedestrian coffee or juice. Even when it was just the two of us, we toasted.

That particular Sunday, we had a larger group. Nellie, sans Jason for once, Matt's brother, Tom, and a couple of his law school classmates. The brunch spot was new—to us and to the city. It was brightly lit, with a decor that reminded me of a Pottery Barn catalog.

The tables were wooden, with hand-painted phrases scattered across the tops in painstakingly random fashion. The phrases were meant to be conversation starters, and damned if they didn't do just that.

"Here's a good one," Tom spoke up after the toasting. "What's the longest you've ever gone without sleep?"

That one was still making the rounds when the food arrived.

When Nellie came back from the bathroom, she was giggling.

"What's so funny?" I asked.

"When I walked past that table" she pointed in the direction of the ladies' room—"I glanced down and saw one of their questions." She paused for a fit of laughter. "I have no idea what the question was *supposed* to say, but a packet of sugar was lying *just right* and all I could see was *Who was the best . . . you ever had?*" She giggled again.

I glanced down the table to Matt's classmates, Laura and Gavin. They were still an unknown quantity on the Sophomoric Humor Appreciation Scale, although Tom, Matt, Nellie, and I were already laughing. Laura cracked a smile, followed by Gavin and then all of us were snickering like a sixth-grade lunch table.

"Somehow, I don't think that's the image they're trying to promote here," Laura said.

"No shit," Nellie agreed.

"Do you think that sugar packet was placed intentionally?" I asked. Two middle-aged women occupied the table in question.

"Definitely," Nellie said. "Look at 'em over there. Clearly sex fiends."

That started a fresh round of choking giggles from the group, until enough glances from other tables encouraged us to calm down. We tucked into our plates again, trying to avoid eye contact with each other.

Laura started it. "Dan Smith."

"Huh?" Matt asked.

"Best I ever had," she explained. She nodded, then shuddered. "Yeah. The best."

"So, what happened?" I said.

She smiled ruefully. "Don't know. I met him on spring break. Lost his number."

"Oh, ouch!" Nellie said. "You couldn't track him down?"

"His last name is Smith." Laura shook her head. "I didn't even know what school he went to. I don't even know if that was his real name. It was not possible to track him down, trust me."

"Bummer."

"Tell me about it."

"Angela Herrera," Gavin said and scrunched up his face in remembered pleasure.

"My wife, Ally," Tom said, earning a matched set of "Isn't that Sweet?" awwws from Nellie and Laura.

Matt's mouth quirked and one eyebrow went up. "She's not here, you know. I won't tell on you."

Tom nodded. "I know. I'm telling you the truth."

"Ooh, lucky man." I grinned.

"Damn straight," he agreed.

Nellie spoke next, holding one hand up as if she was giving testimony. "Terrence Johnson."

"Who's that?" I asked. I hadn't heard his name before in all the hours I'd spent talking to Nellie over anesthetized animals.

She shook her head slowly. "Just an ex. He was a shitty boyfriend, but—damn." She turned it into three syllables *duh-a-amn*.

"Does Jason know about this guy?" I asked, truly curious.

"Hell no. Are you crazy?"

Everyone laughed.

"How about you, Matt?" Laura asked, and my heart took the express elevator into my throat.

He shrugged. "I don't know."

"Sure you do, someone has to be the best," Laura prodded.

"Yeah, even if they all suck, one has to suck less than the others," Nellie said. I lashed out with my foot under the table, but struck wood.

Matt stabbed a chunk of waffle on the end of his fork and surveyed everyone at the table. "I'm not gonna answer, so you can all just go back to your eating."

I tried to catch his eye, but he wouldn't look at me. I wanted to give him a telepathic message, *It's okay, you won't offend me.* Though I knew in my heart it would sting if he said someone else's name. Ridiculous.

"All right, if you're going be a douche about it . . ." Nellie rolled her eyes. She was the only other person at the table who knew why he wasn't answering, and she always enjoyed the hell out of a good secret. She was the definition of smug when she turned her attention to me. "What about you, Joss? Who gets the title?"

I was prepared. "No one."

That knocked the smug right off Nellie's face. "Why not?"

"Because I firmly believe that I haven't had the greatest sex of my life yet. There is always room for improvement."

A collective sigh of disappointed disgust came up from the group, except for Matt, who smirked. "That's not the point," Laura said. "We're just asking who was the best up to this point."

I had to scrunch my toes tight inside my shoes to keep from looking at Matt. I had a feeling he'd read my telepathy loud and clear now. *Figures.* "All right, all right. I confess—it was Nellie." I dropped my head onto my crossed arms and faked some sobbing. A few people started to laugh. Something bounced off my head—a napkin judging by the harmlessness of it.

I chanced a look up and found Nellie laughing along with the rest of the group.

"I smell a conspiracy," Gavin said.

"Okay, Erin Brockovich," Matt said and, when no one was looking, winked at me.

I smiled, glad not to know his answer and glad he didn't know mine. I'd been honest about one thing: I didn't believe I'd had the best sex of my life yet. I never wanted to achieve that mark, because everything after would pale in comparison. I wanted someone who would set a personal best as often as possible, and constantly compete to outdo himself.

And it was with those high aspirations that I met T.J.

I would like to say I had a clue that T.J. was not right, but I didn't. I don't mean he wasn't right for me, although he wasn't. I mean, he was not right in the call-the-nice-men-in-the-long-white-coats sense. Okay, that might be exaggerating a bit, but he definitely wasn't your run-of-the-mill guy.

He seemed so normal. Average, even. Then again, isn't that what the neighbors always say about serial killers?

I met him on Halloween, while I was dressed like Strawberry Shortcake. He was a Jedi, which was fine by me. I'm not a crazy *Star Wars* fan or anything, but I'd dutifully gone to the movies and I could appreciate a good pop culture reference, as evidenced by my own selection. He struck up a conversation about all the '70s and '80s icons come back for treatment in the new millennium, and we ended up in a lively debate about the worth of Hollywood remakes. I was in the "sure, why not?" camp, as I so often am in arguments, while he was vehemently opposed.

These were all clear signs that he was a geek, but I think everyone is a geek in their own way. I used to be on a synchronized swimming team, and it doesn't get much geekier than that. Pretty much, if you're willing to let your freak flag fly the first time I meet you, I'm probably gonna want to get to know you a little better.

So it was with T.J., and I willingly handed over my phone number at the end of the night. He surprised me by calling two days later, and I agreed to go out for sushi with him.

As first dates go, T.J. was a good one. He was as funny as I remembered, which was delightful. He reminded me of Martin in that respect, and Matt, for that matter. I'd always loved funny, but I'd only dated a few guys who truly were. Score one for personal growth—I was ready to trade in a handful of fairy-tale romance for a good belly laugh.

In addition to being funny, T.J. took me to a decent restaurant, paid the bill, and let me take the lead when he dropped me off at the end of the night. I kissed him, but that was it. Like I said before, I'm a huge fan of kissing and I rarely see a reason not to try it out with someone new.

The next week, we went out again, this time to see his friend's band play. It was hard to talk much with the loud music playing, but it was a decent enough time, and I was friendlier when he came into my apartment that night. We stayed in the living room, as if some unseen parents were watching. It felt safe there, and too dangerous to take off any clothing with the balcony doors showing everything to anyone who had enough ambition to watch. All of that meant I had the dreaded third date horizon ahead of me.

Nellie was a tireless cheerleader in this process—she always wanted me to find someone to date long-term so she could have a "couple's friend" with her boyfriend, Jason. Part of me wanted to resist her just to avoid the gag-inducing title, but I also knew she wanted me to be happy, so I let it slide.

I know there's nothing magical about the third date. I didn't have to sleep with him. I never actually had to sleep with him. But, I liked him, and it had been a long time again—not counting Matt, of course, which I didn't. Not really. It seemed reasonable to give T.J. a chance.

We did the classic dinner-and-a-movie date, and then T.J. invited me back to his place for drinks. I'd driven that night, since we went to a restaurant on his end of town. I figured, *What the hell?*

T.J. let me into his house and gave me a tour. It was a nice place, even if it was a typical bachelor pad. He had a pool table in the dining room and a huge TV. Predictably, he saved the bedroom for last. It seemed a little bare bones—hardly end-of-the-tour worthy, but we both knew why he'd ordered it that way, and I wasn't going to complain.

I did my part to make my intentions known, sitting on the edge of the bed and leaning back on my hands. I must have succeeded in looking at least a little seductive, because T.J. joined me on the bed and kissed me. I rested one hand on his shoulder and put the other on his waist. He was heavier set than anyone I'd been with before, and for a moment, I thought longingly of Matt. Everything was just a little softer than I was used to. He was very gentle though, and I liked that. He also seemed to like a lot of things about me.

"You have such beautiful eyes," he said.

"Thank you." Compliments always make me too aware of whatever has been complimented, and suddenly I was conscious of every blink and shift in my gaze.

"And such soft lips." T.J. kissed me again, resting one hand against my jaw. That is hands down my favorite kissing move and I knew right then I was going to let him get a good long look at my lingerie choices for the evening. I'd gone sort of middle of the road on the sexiness scale—nothing that wouldn't impress, but a girl has to save a few things for later. You don't bring your best stuff out the first time.

Slowly, in that heart-fluttering way of the first time, we took off our clothes and moved up onto the bed. When I was down to my skivvies, he pulled back to look at me. It was at this point that I won or lost a man's attraction. Some guys like the small-breasted, narrow-hipped end of the feminine spectrum. I've been called everything from nymph-like to delicate. Others are afraid they're going to break me. They call me miniature or frail.

"Wow, you look amazing," T.J. said, eyes undeniably drawn to my lacy bra. A tiny voice in my mind wanted to know if he was reading from a prepared list of compliments, but I ignored it in favor of believing he might actually like me. At least he appreciated the effort I put into my underwear.

His hands roved over my skin and I arched into each move, following the sensations. T.J. knew what he was doing, that was obvious. I was impressed by how much attention he paid to me. To the extent that he rebuffed my attempts to return the attention. He was very gentlemanly about it, but still firm.

"Just lay back," he instructed, "I want you to feel good."

"Okay," I mumbled, put a little off balance by his focus. I closed my eyes and concentrated on my other senses. The room was quiet, except for the rustling of sheets and my own irregular breath. My skin was hyper-alert, awaiting his next move, the next sensation. His fingers and lips painted my body. It was hard to lie still. I wanted to sink my fingers into his hair, twist my legs through his, and taste his mouth again.

After a while, I couldn't be passive any longer. "We can . . ." I suggested, slipping my thumbs under the elastic of my thong. "If you want."

"If you'd like," he said.

"I've got a condom in my purse," I said. He probably had them, but I was never willing to count on someone else to protect me. I always figured two people with condoms was better than one. "I hope that's not a problem."

"No, of course not."

Good answer.

I got the condom out and handed it to T.J. He did his part while I slipped off my underwear.

"Come here," he said with a soft smile.

I swung a leg over his hips and bent low to kiss him. My heart trembled in my chest. It had been a long time since I'd been with someone new.

My eyes slipped shut as we found our rhythm. His hands never seemed to rest and the constant flood of sensory input had me panting for air in no time. I forced my eyes open and looked down at T.J. who was staring at me with intent.

"What?" I asked, feeling self-conscious.

He shook his head and grunted "Just watching you."

Pleasure ebbed and flowed through my body as T.J. tried several different paces. He just couldn't seem to find one he liked. I stopped trying to help and let him take complete control. I could see frustration in his eyes.

"Is everything all right?" I asked.

"Fine," he said through clenched teeth.

I was coming out of the pleasure haze as I watched him. The concentration was obvious. Sweat began to bead on his forehead.

"Is there something . . . ?" I trailed off, not sure if I should end with "wrong," or "I can do."

He slowed to a crawl and looked up in my eyes. "I'm sorry, I . . . I'm having a little trouble."

Not words a girl wants to hear. "Do you need to change positions or something?" I asked.

"Um, yeah, maybe."

I slid away and waited for him to make a decision.

He appeared to be considering options, shifting his weight and looking very serious. "Could you, uh . . . do something for me?"

My pulse ratcheted up a notch. The question felt . . . loaded. "What?"

"Okay, this might sound kind of weird . . ."

Oh God.

"But, uh . . . sometimes when I'm . . . having trouble . . . it helps if you use your hands."

Phew. "What would you like?" I asked, tucking my legs under me to lean forward.

"Here . . ." He guided my hands to his erection, still in the condom.

"Um . . ." I kept a loose grip and did my best to help him get closer to the big moment.

"Can you squeeze a little tighter?"

I didn't answer, but tried.

"A little harder . . ."

My eyebrows pulled together in confusion, but I followed his instruction.

"A little harder . . ."

My arms strained with effort. I wouldn't be able to keep it up for long. "I'm sorry, my arms are getting tired," I said when the rhythm faltered.

T.J.'s eyes opened, but he didn't look at me. "Then, can you just hit it?"

What? "What?"

"Hit it."

I shook my head. "I don't know what you mean."

"Sometimes it helps. Hit me. Really hard."

"Excuse me?" I could feel the weird look I had on my face.

"Just . . . you know, punch me."

"What are you talking about? Where?"

"Right here." He pointed at his crotch.

"What?!" I pulled my hands back, curling them tightly against my chest.

"It really helps me. You could use your knee if you want."

"N—no . . . no . . . ." I shook my head. "No, I'm not gonna do that. No."

"I know it's a little weird . . ." he said.

"It's a lot weird!" I scooted backward on the bed. As soon as my feet hit the ground, I looked for my clothes.

"It's actually not that uncommon . . ."

"I've never heard of it," I said.

"It's no worse than people who like biting."

"Ha!" I slid on my bra so fast one of the straps twisted.

"Jocelyn, I'm sorry. Don't leave like this . . ."

"No, really, it's okay. I'm just gonna go."

"I didn't want to say anything. It's just something I need to get excited sometimes. I know it's weird."

I shook my head as I reached back to hook my bra. "I don't think you do. I gotta go."

"Dammit," he muttered, getting out of bed himself. "Well, then, can we just forget what I said?"

"No." I yanked my shirt on and shoved my feet in my shoes. "No, we really can't."

T.J. sighed. "Well, could I call you again?"

That stopped me in my tracks. I looked at him with wide eyes. "Are you kidding me?"

"No, then?"

"Please don't."

He called my name as I hurried down the hall, looking for my coat. I ignored him, and snatched up my coat and purse. I didn't even bother putting it on, just ran out the door and to my car, frantically thumbing the UNLOCK button on my key fob.

CHAPTER NINETEEN

TWO YEARS EARLIER . . . SECOND YEAR OUT OF COLLEGE

I had Nellie on the phone before I even had my seat belt on. "I hate dating, I hate it, I hate it, I hate it!" I shouted at her.

"What happened?" she drawled, her words dripping with reluctant tolerance.

"You are never going to believe this one." All of my body nerves buzzed with adrenaline. To think that he'd touched me—I shuddered.

"Try me," she said.

I told her what T.J. had asked me to do and had to hold the phone away from my ear when she shrieked, "WHAT?!"

"I know! The *first* time he asks me to punch him in the fucking balls? What the fuck is wrong with him?"

"Oh my God, I've never heard anything like that!"

"I know! He's some kind of pervert or something."

"Hang on, I have to tell Jason—"

I tried to stop her. "No! Don't tell Jason! My God!" But it was too late. I could hear her murmuring in the background.

"Nellie!" I shouted, trying to get her attention.

"Jason said he saw something about that online once. He said some guys can't get off without it."

"Oh my God! How the hell do you even think of that?!" I demanded. "Who decides to try out getting punched in the balls?"

"I know!"

"God, what a twisted bastard! I just—ugh!"

"No kidding."

"I want to take a shower. I want to take twenty showers!" I shuddered again, making my car wiggle in the lane as I sped away from the scene of the perversion.

"I don't blame you! That is so weird."

"I'm never dating again."

"Well, maybe if you work it into conversation real early on, you could screen out the weird ones."

"How the hell am I supposed to work that into conversation?" I demanded. I visualized myself sitting at dinner with a first date. "Mmm, this pâté is delicious! By the way, do you require physical violence against your genitals to get aroused?"

Nellie burst into laughter. "There, see? Totally natural!"

"I am not doing that!"

"You didn't actually do it, did you?" she asked. "Punch him, I mean."

"No! Of course I didn't! What do you take me for? I just got dressed and ran out of the house."

"You got up and left in the middle of everything?" she asked.

"Yes! What did you think I was gonna do?"

Nellie snickered. "So, poor ol' T.J. is all alone with no one to punch him in the balls . . ."

"For all I know he could be slamming them in a drawer this very second. I don't know and I don't care!"

She started laughing even harder. "Oh my God, can you imagine . . . ?"

"I don't want to." I glanced in the side mirror as if I could see T.J. back there.

"Where are you now?" she asked.

"In my car. I'm going home."

"Ooh! Jason just pulled up a website about this!"

"Oh Jesus. I gotta go," I told her.

"Come on, it's funny!"

"It might be funny after my twentieth shower. I'll let you know."

"Suit yourself."

"I'll talk to you later, Nell."

"Bye, Joss."

We disconnected and I decided to call Matt. When he answered the phone, I could hear voices in the background.

"Hey, Joss. What's going on?"

"Where are you?"

"Home. I've got a few guys over to play *Call of Duty*."

"Oh. Sorry, I'll let you go."

"No, that's okay. We just took a break. I've got a couple minutes."

"I was just on the worst date in the history of the world."

"With T.J.? I thought you liked him."

"I did. But then he got weird."

"How so?"

I repeated the story and earned a bellow of laughter from Matt.

"No fucking way!" he exclaimed. "Man, I always thought that was just made up."

"You've heard of this?"

"Yeah, but . . . I've never heard of anyone actually doing it."

"I didn't do it!" I protested.

"Yeah, I know that." He paused and I could imagine the eye roll. "Man, that was a ballsy move."

"No pun intended?"

"No, that was totally intentional."

"Great."

"Seriously, though . . . I almost have to admire him." His voice was painted with laughter.

I made an "ew!" face even though he couldn't see it. "Why?"

"You gotta have some big brass ones to whip that out the first time you sleep with someone."

"Or a serious lack of brain cells."

"Hey, listen, are you gonna be okay? They want me back in the game."

I sighed. "Yeah, I'll be fine. I'm just gonna go home and shower twenty-seven times."

"Make sure you don't scrub your skin off."

I hesitated for a moment. "Um, how long are the guys gonna be there?"

"I'm not sure. Why?"

"Just . . . curious."

"I'm around tomorrow. If you need something. If you need me."

Nellie spent the rest of that night and most of the following day sending me definitions of different kinds of fetishes. She accompanied each message with the words, *See? It could have been worse!* I could just imagine her cackling wildly over her own joke. Each time, I replied with something along the lines of, *I hate you and you are the worst friend in the world*.

A small selection of the things Nellie came up with:

Formicophilia: deriving sexual pleasure from insects crawling on the skin.

Klismaphilia: deriving sexual pleasure from receiving an enema.

Autonepiophilia: deriving sexual arousal from diapers.

> *Phalloorchoalgolagnia: deriving sexual pleasure from a painful blow to the male genitals.*

The last one was accompanied with the note, *I guess T.J.'s not alone!*

I had dinner with my family the following night and I studiously avoided all discussion of my love life. Conveniently, my sister, Darcy, had big news—one of her dogs was going to have puppies. The way she was going on about it, I would have thought she was pregnant. I love her, but she's a little nuts.

Nevertheless, impending puppydom gave me plenty of time inside my own head. There, a sham debate was under way—should I call on Matt after last night, or go at it alone? I knew I wanted to call him. I even knew I would. But for reasons I couldn't articulate, I needed to spend a little time coming up with reasons why I might not. After a salad course, the main course, and dessert, my list was this:

> *1. I only sort of had sex with T.J., so it barely counts.*
> *2. I want this too much.*

The second one was the problem. I wanted Matt. I'd been on my self-imposed dating hiatus for too long, I guess. Three dates with T.J. had reminded me of what I loved about dating, and then smashed it all flat with his shocking request. I wanted so badly to feel the way I'd felt earlier in the date. And I knew I'd get just that with Matt. The problem was he was only one night. I wanted a more permanent solution. I knew I should be a big girl and turn down a temporary, if certain, dose of gratification. But on the other hand . . .

As soon as I had finished helping my mom with the dishes, I excused myself, explaining that I had plans with Matt.

"You should have brought him to dinner," my mom said.

"He had plans already." This was a bald-faced lie. I had no idea what Matt was doing for dinner. But it was hard to imagine bringing him to my parents' house for a family meal before we headed back to my place to have sex.

"Too bad. Invite him next week if you want."

"Yeah, okay."

I phoned Matt when I left, and he was already at my apartment complex by the time I got home.

"That was fast!" I said when he got out of his car.

"Maybe you were just slow." The tip of his nose was cold when he kissed me in greeting.

"Come on, let's go inside."

He followed me into the building without saying much. I let us into my apartment, and before he could even get his coat off, Dewey was weaving around his ankles and purring.

"Yes, Dewey, I've missed you, too," he said in all insincerity.

"Mrow."

"You might as well pet him now, you know he's not going to leave you alone until you do."

Matt sighed, but hunkered down to scratch behind the cat's ears. "There, are you happy, you big hairball?"

Dewey flopped on his back and stretched, purring happily.

"I swear, you should just take him with you when you go. When you're around it's like I don't even exist." I hung our jackets in the closet and tossed my bag onto the table.

"No pets allowed in my apartment," he informed Dewey. "We've been over this."

"He thinks you should move somewhere else, then."

"Sorry, cat. No deal." He straightened up and stepped on the backs of his shoes to remove them.

"Did you eat dinner?" I asked.

"Yeah, I'm fine. Thanks."

"My mom said I should have invited you. Sorry." I retrieved my cell phone from my bag and tucked it in my back pocket.

He squinted at me. "That would have been kind of weird."

"That's what I thought. She said you should come next week."

"Maybe I will."

"And that won't be weird?" I asked, pausing with one hand on the light switch for the living room.

"For some reason . . . no."

"Something in the rules I'm not aware of?" I teased.

"Yeah, 'Never dine with your Sorbet partner's parents on the day of Sorbet.'"

I laughed. "What number would that be?"

"Hmm . . ." He looked thoughtful. "Who knows? Don't you have the rules?"

"Do I?"

"I think so . . ."

"I bet it's in that box of crap from college in my office . . ."

"Your office." Matt snorted. He found my name for my spare room amusing. The apartment was technically a one-bedroom, with a "bonus room," little more than a glorified closet. I certainly didn't do any work in there, but I had my desk and a filing cabinet in it, so as far as I was concerned, it was an office.

"Shut up." I went into the so-called office and pulled a plaid banker's box from the corner. It was full of odds and ends from college, including—as it turned out—the computer printout of my last semester class schedule, some cardboard Blue Moon beer coasters, and a picture of me and Jessie with our faces painted red and white for a football game.

Matt hunkered down behind me, covering my shoulder with one of his hands for balance. When I came across a picture from freshman year of all of the girls on Halloween, he leaned forward for a better look.

"Hmm, I remember that costume . . ."

I smiled and tilted my head against his. "Yeah, me, too."

The picture slipped from my fingers. I let it go and picked through interlaced stacks of papers, pictures, pamphlets, magazine clippings, half-finished crosswords, and an expired prescription for codeine cough syrup.

"Why the hell are you keeping this stuff?" he asked, extracting another water-stained coaster from The Pub.

"I don't know." I shrugged, and Matt swept my hair around to my right shoulder to get the clingy curls away from his face.

"Aha!" I produced the *Rules for Sorbet Sex* with triumph. "Rule twelve."

"Twelve it is," he agreed, plucking the paper from my hand. "Where's a pen?"

"There's probably one in here . . ." I rummaged in the bottom of the box and came up with a red pen.

"Give it here."

"No way, you wrote the last three rules." I took the paper back and bent down to write on the floor.

12. *Never dine with your Sorbet partner's parents on the day of Sorbet.*
13. *You may dine with your Sorbet partner's parents on any other day.*
14. *The female Sorbet partner is entitled to spooning.*

"Hey! You totally snuck that last one in!" Matt protested, taking the worn list from me.

"No way, I brokered that deal from you last time."

"But now it's in writing." He sank to sit, one knee still raised behind me.

"Exactly." I grinned at him and tapped the pen on the tip of his nose.

He snatched the pen and leaned on one elbow to add another rule.

15. *The male partner may never ask the female partner to punch him in the nuts.*

I burst into laughter when I saw the addition. "That should just be a rule in general. Like, for life. It should be posted on signs in public places. Like 'No Smoking.'"

"What do you suppose the little signs would look like?" We grinned at each other.

I let the rules fall into their familiar fold-lines and handed the small square to Matt. "Here. You can study up on rule fifteen—make sure you understand it."

"I'll do that." He leaned over to tuck the paper into the pocket of his jeans. When he straightened up, we nearly knocked our heads together. He laughed and kissed the corner of my mouth.

"You know what makes me so mad?" I said when he pulled back.

"What?"

"He officially ruined my favorite make-out move of all time."

"Who, T.J.? What are you talking about?"

"This—" I demonstrated the hand-on-the-jaw move that T.J. had earned so many points with the night before. "I used to love that. Now . . . everything he did just feels . . . gross. Dirty . . . I don't know." I sighed.

"We'll fix it all," Matt promised, moving his hands to cradle my face and kissing me softly. I edged closer, and pressed my fingers into the tight muscles at the crest of his shoulder. "What else?" he murmured against my mouth as I tried to continue the kiss.

"He . . . touched me . . . and kissed me . . . all over."

"Okay . . ." Matt's hands left my face, drifted over my shoulders, and down to the edge of my sweater. He lifted it slowly, knuckles grazing against my skin until I had to lift my arms to let him pull it free. Goose bumps followed in the wake of his fingers and I couldn't help a shiver.

"Nice," he said, riding his fingertips along the edge of my bra. It was black, with textured embroidery that made it impossible to wear under anything form-fitting. Under a sweater though, it was a girly dream come true. The fact that I paired it with the matching lace panties should have been all the information my subconscious needed to tell me how this day was going to end long before I called Matt.

"We could go . . ." I glanced at the door where Dewey sat, watching the proceedings with feline boredom.

"Later." He brushed my hair away from my shoulder and kissed the hollow made by my collarbone. I shivered again. "Like this?" he asked.

I shook my head. "No." He stilled, and I rushed to explain. "You do it better."

His soft laugh tickled my throat. "Okay, good."

Bit by bit, Matt erased all the false hope that I'd had the night before. His hands smoothed across my skin, taking away the counterfeit affection T.J. had given me. His lips, tongue, and teeth were persistent reminders that I didn't have to settle; that there was more. Best of all, he gave me free rein to return the attention.

We were still on the floor of my little office when he lifted the back of my bra, looking for the closure.

"It's a little stiff," I breathed against his cheek, "but, don't—let's go to the bedroom."

"Okay," he agreed.

I got to my feet, leaving most of my clothing on the floor. Matt was right behind me and scooped me up as soon as we crossed the threshold to my bedroom.

"Oh!" I startled, but he had me firmly as he put one knee on the bed.

"Are we doing okay so far?" he whispered.

"Yeah, we're doing just fine." I smiled.

We found our way under the covers and out of our last bits of clothing and then it was nothing but the delicious feeling of skin on skin and wet kisses and his much more satisfying body under my hands. He smelled like the cold air of November, and the same laundry detergent I'd smelled the first time we met. His mouth tasted like Crest with an undercurrent of coffee, his skin like . . . Matt, just Matt.

He eased my knees apart with one of his own then flattened his palms against my inner thighs, pressing upward. I recalled the motion from our other times together. It was something only he did and it made my pulse go wild. I arched off the bed when he reached the end of his path and he gave me a lazy smile. Reaching out with both hands, I beckoned him down to kiss me. He complied, but tortured me by bracing his weight to prevent any contact except for our lips. So, I slipped my hands between us and scratched my nails lightly over his abs. Already tensed for the position, he couldn't help laughing, breath rushing out against my cheek. He caved, dropping into the waiting cradle of my raised knees and pushing his fingers into my hair.

We rocked our hips together in a familiar rhythm, and I let my hands go on exploratory missions across his back. He had unfairly smooth skin back there and I loved the feel of it on my fingertips.

He tipped my head to kiss my throat, which urged a moan from my lips. He laughed again, softly against my skin.

"Is that a good sound?"

"Yes," I whispered. "Can we . . . ?"

"Yeah, hang on." He slipped one arm beneath me. I hooked my ankles behind his hips and he moved us farther up the bed. He made me feel as light as a feather. After a moment, he turned his attention back to me. I shivered as we slid together and clamped my hands against his lower back.

"Just a—"

"I know." While he waited for me to acclimate, he painted my shoulder with openmouthed kisses. The rough scrape of his five o'clock shadow against my collarbone made me gasp, but it almost felt good.

I eased the pressure on his back and said, "Okay."

And then we began to move.

For a few delirious moments, I wondered why I ever bothered with anyone but him. I liked the sight, the feel, the taste, and the sound of him in bed. I liked how we knew just enough about each other as lovers to be comfortable and move in sync, but not so much that I wasn't strung tight with anticipation every time he tried something new. I liked that I could predict that even though he would hop out of bed just moments after we were done, I knew he'd come back right away and kiss me and ask if I was all right.

And, I reminded myself, it was for all of those reasons that I wanted him around when my relationships went bad. He was my port in a storm, and I couldn't imagine losing that. I also knew that he hadn't really let anyone into his heart since Meghan, and I didn't ever want to be a placeholder. As the Sorbet Girl, I was singular, and that was just fine with me.

His promise was good. By the time we lay in a contented

heap, waiting for our heart rates to return from the stratosphere, T.J. was nothing but an unfortunate bump in the road.

"I—" Matt started to speak, but stopped to swallow hard and let out a forceful breath. "Did we fix it all?"

"Yes." I turned my face into his cheek and gave him a gentle bite. He squeezed my ribs, making me jump, and laughed.

"I'll be right back." He slunk out of bed without letting in too much cold air and I burrowed deeper into the capsule of body heat we'd created. I listened to the sounds of running water and let my eyes drift shut.

"Come here for your stupid spooning," he said with exaggerated distaste when he returned to bed.

"Shut up," I said, but slipped happily into the space he made for me.

"So, I know you're all kinky now, but . . . don't hit me in the family jewels, okay?"

I laughed. "Fuck you, Matt."

"I'm not touchin' that one."

I elbowed him halfheartedly, but I wasn't mad. I was amused as hell, actually, and that was part of the magic of Matt. He knew I'd be ready to find the T.J. thing funny after we'd so successfully overwritten the memory.

We drifted in a drowsy haze for a while, sharing space and letting our breathing settle into synchronization. "Thanks for being here," I said.

"Yeah, of course."

The weight of his arm felt good across my waist. He always put off heat like a generator, which felt amazing as my body cooled. "He was kind of . . . soft," I confessed suddenly.

Matt snickered. "I thought that's why he wanted you to hit him."

"No, I mean, like, pudgy."

"Oh." He paused, trying to determine my point. "Okay."

"He just seemed so nice."

"I thought you didn't like nice," he said immediately.

"Of course I like nice."

"But not *too* nice," he reminded me. "You told me I was too nice a million times."

"Well, maybe I've changed my mind about nice guys. Maybe I just want someone intelligent, funny, and yeah, nice. Someone who likes me, isn't a pervert, and happens to be fantastic in bed."

"Just happens," he echoed, laughing. "It's good that you have realistic requirements."

"I'm sure there are plenty of guys like that. I just have to find one." Suddenly, I was too warm and I had to toss the comforter away from my shoulders. The cool air helped a little, but my nerves continued to send signals of discomfort. Like an all-over itchiness. I wriggled a little and tried to shake off the feeling.

Matt slid one hand down my arm and threaded our fingers together. "Well, I can tell you one thing—all guys are a little bit perverted."

"I can handle a little bit. But, I never want to need props, reinforcements, or a protein shake for sex."

He laughed, chest vibrating against me. The itchy feeling receded. Weird.

"Okay, what about the famous lingerie collection? That's a prop," he said.

I considered, pursing my lips. "Fine. I don't want to need a safe word."

He laughed again, harder this time. "New rule: no safe words."

"That's too broad, counselor. Nothing *requiring* a safe word."

"Deal." His body shifted against mine. "Of course, there's always the possibility that this will be the last time, you know."

"I know." It was always a possibility. The weird, itchy feeling came back. "God, what is wrong with me? I feel like I'm going to crawl out of my skin."

"You look okay," he said, but the room was dim.

"Maybe I'm allergic to something. Maybe I should take a shower."

"Yeah, go 'head." He peeled his body away from mine to let me up.

I got out of bed, simultaneously feeling better and worse when the cool air hit me.

"Are you okay?" he asked.

"I don't know. I'm just—I feel jittery." I grabbed clean pajamas from the dresser and headed for the bathroom. When I had the water running, I heard a tap on the door.

"Joss?"

I opened the door. "Yeah?"

"Seriously, are you okay?" He looked genuinely concerned.

The electricity jangling through me settled a bit as I looked at him. I didn't want to worry him. "I'm okay, really. I probably just need to cool off or something."

"See? Spooning is bad for you."

I picked up a hand towel and swatted him in the face, right on his grinning mouth. "Oh, shush."

"You want any help in there? I could scrub you down with the toilet brush." Matt smirked.

"Gee, our first shower together and already you're offering the toilet brush?" I put on false doe eyes. "You're such a romantic."

"I have never once claimed to be a romantic," he reminded me.

"No kidding." I stepped away from the gap in the door and got into the steaming shower. Already the feelings were going away, but I figured I might as well give myself a rinse. I couldn't imagine what had caused the weird sensations, but a shower wouldn't hurt.

"Was that a no on the toilet brush?" Matt called over the sound of the water.

I laughed, quiet enough that he couldn't hear me. "That was a no."

"Suit yourself."

I heard the door latch shut, then a few minutes later open again. "Where do you keep your clean sheets?" he asked.

"What?" I opened one end of the curtain to look at him.

"Clean sheets? Where are they?"

"Why?"

"I'm going to change the sheets, just in case that was the problem."

"Really?" I blinked, trying to process the kindness. "Uh, in the trunk at the foot of the bed."

"Is that what those things are for?" he asked. "I've always wondered."

"That's what it's for in my house."

He nodded. "Okay, I'll take care of it."

"Thanks, Matty." I made a kissy face at him. "You're the best."

He very deliberately looked through the curtain at my wet body. "I'm sure you can make it up to me."

Which sucked all the romance right out of his gesture. That was Matt.

I turned my back to the spray as he left, letting the water beat away the last of my unease. Next up on my agenda: finding a guy who would know when to keep his mouth shut and let me pretend he wasn't a lecher at heart.

"I still don't see how T.J. is relevant to anything."

Matt tilted his head from side to side. "He is and he isn't. I just . . . sort of realized something around that time."

"What?"

"That we aren't as . . . unaffected by all of this as we should be."

I tightened my arms around myself. "I don't think I understand."

He sighed. "This isn't as clean as it should be."

"What isn't?"

"This"—he moved his hand in the space between us—"us. It's too blurry. Sometimes we're more than friends, and in between, I don't know what the hell we are anymore."

I tried to make a dismissive sound, but there was a lump in my throat. "We're friends, Matty. You know that."

"The point is, it's not so easy to separate stuff anymore." He shook his head. "Not that it ever really was."

Despite the chill in the air, my spine broke out in sweat. Did he know? Had he seen it on my face? *Cover, cover, cover!* "We can do it. We just have to concentrate."

"No, we can't. And besides, that's my point. It shouldn't be so hard to behave."

"It's not." I looked away from him. "We do a great job of being friends."

"Yeah, tell that to Christine and Josh."

I scowled at him. "She was a crazy person."

"And what about him?"

I was convinced he could hear my thoughts and my hammering heart. "He was—he was . . ." What? A casualty? An innocent bystander? *A really good, decent guy who I ditched for* you, *Matt. For you.*

ONE YEAR EARLIER . . . THIRD YEAR OUT OF COLLEGE

It is a fact that a single girl cannot get a date during the holidays. Men are all convinced that women are trying to get a date for New Year's Eve, someone to spend Christmas with, and possibly even introduce to their families. Mostly, they're right, which makes it almost impossible for a single girl without those motives to get a simple dinner date from early November until January 2.

So I was decidedly single in December when Matt and I met for brunch. It was just the two of us that Sunday morning, and the venue was one of our favorites. A bar in the hipster part of town—or as close to hipster as Milwaukee gets anyway—it was a cobbled together collection of storefronts with all the original brickwork exposed. It always wore the stale smell of old cigarettes and spilled beer, but the food was good and their Bloody Mary was the best in town for Sunday brunch.

We'd already ordered our drinks when Matt ran off to the bathroom. The waitress returned and set the mounded glasses on the table. The garnish outweighed the drinks by a long shot, but that was the fun of it.

"There you go . . ." she drawled as she eased away from the glasses. Triumphant, she straightened and looked at me. "And I'll come back for your orders when your boyfriend gets back."

I didn't bother to correct her. "No, that's okay, I know what he wants."

"Oh!" She pulled her pad out, and I ordered Matt's usual cholesterol fest, and my only-slightly-better-for-you favorite.

Matt arrived as I was finishing.

"I ordered for you," I said.

"How did you know what I wanted?" he challenged.

"Because you have the same thing every time we come here."

He grinned. "I should change my order just to annoy you."

"Then you wouldn't get to eat your precious breakfast burrito."

"Good point." Matt tweezed the shrimp from the edge of his glass. "You are a woman of infinite wisdom, Alvin."

The waitress laughed. "Is there anything else I can get for you guys?"

"Did she tell you I want the potatoes on the side?" he asked.

"Of course, I did. *And* the Cajun sour cream."

"She did." The waitress smiled. "She knows you by heart."

"She'd like to think so," he said, making a face at me.

"No thinking involved—I know so."

The waitress laughed again as she started to walk away. "You guys are adorable together."

I only had her back to glare at, but I gave it my all until she rounded a corner. When I turned back to Matt, he was munching one of the mozzarella whips from his drink. "I'm going to find you a girlfriend," I declared.

He narrowed his eyes at me. "No, thank you."

"But I've been a student of the Mystery of Matt Lehrer for six years. I've watched you pick the wrong women time and time again. Surely, I can do better."

"This has Bad Plan written all over it."

"No, it'll be fun!" I was really warming to the idea. "I'm sure I can find you the perfect woman."

"What do you know about the perfect woman?"

I leaned back from the table, putting on airs of being offended. "Besides the fact that I am one?"

"Yeah, right. Besides that." He fished an olive out of his drink and popped it in.

"Come on, Matty. Don't you want to have someone special in your life?"

"I have lots of special someones in my life," he said. "A mom, a dad, my brother . . . oh, and Dewey. Don't forget Dewey." He grinned.

"You're being a punk."

"Why do you care so much?" he asked.

"I don't." I went after my own olive with a miniature plastic sword. "I just want to help you."

He stretched his mouth into an "I hate to ask this but . . ." grimace. "Can you not?"

I stuck my tongue out at him.

"Joss, if I wanted a girlfriend, I would have a girlfriend."

"So what *do* you want?"

He shrugged. "I'll know it when I see it."

"That's very helpful."

"I'm not trying to be helpful." He raised his glass to his lips, but not before I saw his smile.

I shoved his chair with my feet, succeeding in sending my chair backward and failing to move his at all. "I'm trying to get you laid here, Matthew."

He choked on his drink. Hard. His hand came up as he coughed, preventing the spray of tomato juice from hitting me in the face, but giving him a nice even splatter pattern across his shirt and the tabletop.

I tried to apologize and offer napkins, but I was giggling. We both knew I was responsible.

"Do you wait until I've got something in my mouth before you say things like that?"

I giggled, tried to sober myself, but broke down again. "I'll pay for dry cleaning."

He plucked at one of his buttonholes. "I don't do dry cleaning."

"I'll wash it, then."

He considered that for a moment, unbuttoned his shirt and shrugged it off before wadding it up and throwing it across the table at me. I caught it, but not before a wet patch of sleeve slapped my chin.

"Eww."

"Serves you right." Inspecting his revealed T-shirt, he found some damp spots and a few stains at the top where his buttons had been undone. "Great."

"If you throw that one at me, I think they will probably throw *us* out."

"Helping me like that, I'm sure you'll find me my future bride in no time."

I flinched at the unexpected reference to marriage. "I—I didn't say I was going to marry you off."

He smiled slowly. "Well, whatever your evil plan is."

I shook my head, regrouping. "Does that mean you're going to let me?"

"If you promise to stop ruining my shirts, then sure, go ahead and try."

I clapped my hands and wiggled in my seat. "Yay!"

"You're still washing my shirt."

For the first time since I was eighteen, I decided to spend New Year's Eve in Milwaukee. Nellie's boyfriend had a friend in a band and we could all get VIP wristbands to the show. Nellie secured an extra one for me, hoping I would have a date to bring along. I didn't, because no one in their right mind goes on a first date on New Year's Eve. So after some serious cajoling, I got Matt to take the place of my date. He was supposed to be at a party hosted by some law school friends. Supposedly much classier than my offerings, but as I rationally pointed out to him, Matt was not exactly classy himself. Further, who wanted to spend New Year's Eve with a bunch of lawyers, which was a point he couldn't really argue with. He did, however, reserve the right to leave if things sucked. In turn, I reserved the right to follow him right out the door if things were really bad.

Arriving was surprisingly fun. Cruising past the line of non-VIPs to flash our wristbands, we felt like celebrities. On a very small, Midwestern, local-band scale. We divided forces to accomplish all the required tasks: Nellie and Jason were to elbow their way through the crowd to hold a place for us at one of the tables near the stage. Matt and I were to procure refreshments for the group.

It was a long wait at the bar, and people passing by kept jostling me into Matt. I don't know if it's a function of being the size of a twelve-year-old boy or just a certain *je ne sai quoi* about me, but people always seem to squeeze past me in crowded situations. In the rough approximation that was the next line over, I spotted another smallish girl being tossed on the human tide and made a commiserating face at her.

"I don't know why I bother!" she shouted to me.

"No kidding," I shouted back.

Matt turned to see why I was yelling. I stood on my toes to get closer to his ear and said, "A fellow chipmunk in danger of being trampled."

He looked in the direction of my head nod and smiled at the girl. "She's cute."

"If you like small woodland creatures, sure." I grinned.

"Which I do." He elbowed me lightly.

"You're not supposed to admit that in public."

He laughed and we edged a little closer to the harried bartenders. Our line picked up speed over the next several customers and soon we found ourselves bellied up to the bar. Waiting for our drinks took another interminable period, during which I continued to be the number one person to squeeze by. Then, with two cups each in hand, we started on the treacherous path back to Nellie and Jason.

I squeezed past my fellow small girl and shouted, "Good luck!"

"Thanks!"

I'd only lost about a quarter of a beer total by the time we made it to the small area defended by our friends. I handed one cup to Nellie and steadied myself on her shoulder to scoot onto a stool. The music hadn't started yet, so the seats were stable. The minute the standing crowds started gyrating to the beat, the tables would most likely be the outermost ring of the dance floor. I took the moment of stillness to slurp a few ounces from the top of my beer.

A few minutes later, I noticed the girl from the line making her unsteady way down the aisle toward us. She mounted a bar stool between some large guys just a few feet away from me. I indicated her to Matt, who leaned forward to poke her in the back. She turned, startled, and caught sight of me.

"You survived!" I said.

"You, too!"

"And now we won't be able to see a thing!" I said, pointing as a guy came to stand directly in front of me. He appeared to be with her group, and had to be six foot two.

She laughed. "I know! I'm like a cocktail shrimp among lobsters!"

I glanced to my right and left. "It's more like a shrimp among crawfish over here!"

"Hey!" Matt elbowed me again. He never failed to be sensitive about his five-foot-ten-inch height.

The line girl laughed as the crowd went wild for the arrival of the band, and then her attention was diverted to the stage. The stools began their persistent vibration at the mercy of the nearby amps and I decided to fight hoarseness by not talking for a while.

During the lull between songs, Matt leaned close and said, "She really is cute."

"Oo-ooh!" I sang. "Matty's got a cru-ush!"

He just rolled his eyes.

I waited until he decided to brave the men's room, then poked the girl in the back again. She turned, looking surprised by the third contact.

"My friend thinks you're cute!" I said.

"Him?" She pointed at the empty spot beside me.

"Yeah."

"I thought that was your boyfriend!"

"No! Just a friend!"

"Oh!"

"Sorry, just thought I'd tell you!"

"Oh . . . okay!"

I turned my attention back to the stage and caught Nellie giving me a sour look.

"What?"

"Are you seriously trying to get Matt a date with that girl?"

"So?" I asked, confused.

"You are mentally ill," she said, shaking her head.

It was my turn for an eye roll.

When Matt returned from the bathroom, the line girl turned around and smiled at him. "I'm Christine!" she shouted.

He grinned. "Matt!"

"Nice to meet you!" She wobbled on her stool and turned forward to regain her balance.

"See? I told you I could get you a girl," I said in his ear.

"Yeah, nice screening process."

"I still did it. I am an awesome wingman."

"We'll see."

He bought her a beer, and she repaid him with her phone number at the end of the concert. And that was how Matt met Crazy Christine.

I'd heard the grocery store was a good place to meet guys, but I usually considered it an acceptable place to go when I was looking my worst. So, I was in my scrubs, just stopping in for a few essentials on my way home from work when I met Josh. I was covered in dog hair, with my hair held in a twist by a pencil and my glasses on. I'd forgotten I was wearing them when I got out of the car—I only used them for driving these days, and restricted them to that use since they made me look like a nerd. I cannot understand how some people look sophisticated and urbane in glasses. I have always looked like the girl who doesn't get a date to prom.

Josh was behind me in line at the deli. I didn't even notice him, distracted as I was by my serious deliberations between oven-roasted and smoked turkey breast. Dewey loved turkey with a passion bordering on zealotry. I intended to make my own sandwiches, but I knew he'd beg for a scrap or two the moment I walked through the door and I was wondering which flavor he'd prefer.

"You're a vet." The voice behind me startled me into spinning around, wide-eyed.

"What?"

"Scrubs and animal fur. You've got to be a vet."

"Oh. Um . . . I'm a vet tech, actually."

"I knew it."

"Very impressive. Most people assume I'm a nurse."

"I'm a dog lover," he said, immediately winning my heart. The quickest way to a vet tech's heart is through her animals.

"Do you have dogs?"

"Two."

My heart pitter-patted. "Really? What kind?"

"A German shorthaired pointer, and a Chesapeake Bay retriever."

"Aww," I crooned. "What are their names?"

"Luke and Bo."

I felt my eyebrows go up before I could stop them. "Like *The Dukes of Hazzard*?"

He let out an embarrassed laugh. "Yeah, I know. It was this thing with my brother . . ."

"I should have known." I wished I didn't have my glasses on. Or a pencil in my hair. Or my hairy scrubs.

"I'm Josh," he said, holding out his hand.

"Joss," I replied, shaking his hand.

"No, it's Josh. As in Joshua."

"Yeah, and I'm Joss. As in Jocelyn."

"Oh." He flushed and rubbed the back of his neck. "Right. Sorry."

"Number eighty-seven!" called the deli worker.

"That's me," I said, holding up my little pull tab. I placed my order, deciding on the smoked variety of turkey for the day, and received my little packet of meat with a tiny flash of anticipation: I knew Dewey would love it, and I loved that stupid cat.

"I guess you're up," I said to Josh as I turned to go.

"Guess so."

I smiled and started to walk away, but he put one hand on my elbow. "Can I take you to dinner sometime?"

My first instinct was to reach up and apologetically pat my disheveled hair and glasses, but I fought the urge. "That would be nice."

"Number eighty-eight!"

I wrote my phone number on the back of a business card I found in my purse and handed it to Josh just after he accepted his packets of honey ham and Swiss cheese.

"Joss," he read. "I'll call you."

"Okay."

And that was how I met Innocent Bystander Josh.

He called me two days later, and we made a date for the following Friday. It was a nice conversation, and I could hear the chesty bark of one of his dogs in the background. The sound triggered all the mushy animal-loving buttons in my body and I was really looking forward to the date. We talked until I got a call interrupt from none other than Matt, and Josh excused himself to go run with his dogs.

I clicked over to my new call and greeted Matt with, "I think I'm in love."

"What the hell are you talking about?"

"I met a dog lover at the grocery store and I'm going to marry him."

This was greeted with silence.

"Hello?"

"I heard you."

"And?"

"I think you're full of shit."

I laughed. "Yeah, maybe. But I am going on a date with him."

"Great."

"Wait, what did you call for?" I asked.

"Oh, right. Do you think it's too soon to bring Christine to Gavin's birthday thing?"

"Why?"

"You're a girl. Do you think she's going to think I'm too serious if I bring her around to meet my friends right away?"

"I wouldn't worry about it. She already met me, right?"

"Oh, yeah. My wingman."

"Exactly. So, I'll see you on Saturday?"

Matt's law school friend Gavin, who had a disturbingly nice apartment on the lake, celebrated his birthday like it was Mardi Gras instead of the middle of January. He reserved the community room on the top floor of the building, and gave all the neighbors immediately below the room gift certificates for dinner out. He came from money and knew how to use it. Inexplicably, he'd taken a shine to me through Matt—also a strange bedfellow for

Gavin—and I'd gotten my own invite to the party, with instructions to attend come hell or high water. He'd declared the theme Early Summer, and was celebrating with tropical drinks, tacky palm tree decor, and a beach-attire dress code.

When I'd heard it was on the top floor of a building, I was ready to make excuses not to go, but Matt assured me I would survive. It wasn't a high-rise building, and the windows didn't go all the way to the floor—a major no-no as far as I was concerned. Who knew when the windows would suddenly disappear and I could plummet to my death? Fear of heights is not rational.

So I went, and he was right, it wasn't that high relative to the rest of the buildings nearby. Still, I was into my second therapeutic mojito when Matt arrived with Christine and I ran over to greet them. I flung my arms around Matt's neck and gave him a kiss on the cheek.

"Hi! You made it! Hi, Christine! It's nice to see you again!"

"Simmer down, Alvin," Matt said, unwrapping my arms and laughing.

"Hi, Joss," Christine said, looking a little startled.

"Come on, Gavin's got mojitos!"

In retrospect, my mental filter may have been loosened by the rum, and it's possible I spent a little too much time trying to "sell" Matt to Christine. In fact, it would be fair to say that I gushed about how wonderful he was, and how great it was that she was with him. Some of my ebullience translated into a lot of touching of Matt. I put my arms around his waist a lot and trailed my hands over his shoulders when I was standing near his chair. I was determined that my matchmaking abilities would prove worthy.

Finally, Matt knocked my hand off his shoulder and gave me a small head shake. When Christine wasn't looking, he whispered to me. "Back off, Cujo. Are you trying to scare her off?"

I saluted him. "Gotcha. Can do."

He laughed and pinched my waist before turning his attention back to Christine, who was regarding me with a squint. I didn't have time to consider the implications, however. My drink was empty.

The next week, I had my first date with Josh. I met him at a new steakhouse in town and we had a pleasant getting-to-know-you period while we sat at the bar waiting for our table to be ready.

"So, tell me about your dogs," I said.

He grinned and reached for his pocket. "I have some pictures if you want to see."

"Of course, I do!"

He produced his cell phone and played with it for a few moments, looking for photos. At last, he handed it to me. "Just swipe right to see the rest."

"Oh, they're great!" I'd learned from work that single guys didn't appreciate hearing that their dogs were "cute" or "adorable."

"Yeah, they're good boys."

I arrowed my way through a few more shots of the dogs. Sleeping, sitting in the back of a pickup truck, in a field . . . Then I came to the first shot of Josh in hunters' camouflage with Bo and Luke at proud attention and a brace of pheasant in his hand.

"Oh . . . you went hunting with them?" I asked, heart sinking.

"Mmm hmm, they love it. Bo's a hell of a pointer, and Luke can flush like nobody's business."

"Oh." I couldn't stand hunting.

"You don't like that, do you?" he asked as I handed the phone back to him.

I tried a half-smile and gave a simple, "Oh, I don't know." As tempting as it was to mount my anti-hunting soapbox, I decided to keep my cool and learn more about Josh. Luckily, we were called to our table then, and the conversation moved into safer territory.

He didn't forget, though. When our waitress left the table with our orders, he tapped this fork on the tabletop nervously. "Look, I don't want you to think I'm a big sport hunter or anything. My dogs came from purebred hunting stock—my uncle breeds them, actually. He had me up to his place to check out Luke for possible studding . . ." He grinned with embarrassment. "Anyway, the dogs liked it, but, uh . . . it's not really my thing."

I was relieved. "It's okay if it is."

He smiled. "No, it's not. I can see it by your face."

I blushed. "Okay, yeah, not a fan."

"Tell me what you are a fan of." He tilted his head. "Besides oven-roasted turkey and keeping office supplies in your hair, that is."

Oh, I like this guy.

He was from Minnesota, loved Monty Python movies, and thought red hair was adorable. By dessert, we were laughing over dog stories, quoting *The Meaning of Life,* and delighted to agree on cheesecake for a shared finale to an entirely pleasant evening. He picked up the tab and threatened to knock my wallet out of my hand if I attempted to contribute. We walked out to the parking lot together and spent too long standing in the cold beside my car. My nose was running when we kissed, but he didn't say anything about it.

It was a good kiss. A kiss that made me consider violating my agreement with myself to leave him in the parking lot. I liked this guy. A lot. Enough that I was already steeling myself for the inevitable "I'll call you sometime." No way was I going to get lucky enough to be in the right place at the right time for once.

Instead, he asked, "So, can I see you again?"

"I'd like that."

"I'll call you tomorrow." He kissed me again—runny nose and all—and I thought of Matt. Because I intended to call him and tell him I'd successfully matched us both in a matter of weeks.

I didn't have to call him. He'd already left me a message, I discovered when I got in my car and checked my phone. I called him, eager to gloat.

He answered the phone mid-conversation. "I've got to break up with Christine."

"What? Why? I thought she was so great!"

He made a snort-slash-scoff sound.

"No, Matty, you can't do this! I just had the greatest date of my life. We were going to double-date." I put my fingers on the wheel. Still too cold. I tucked my hand under my thigh.

"Yeah, *that* wouldn't be awkward."

"Never mind that now, you're going to ruin it anyway. Ruin a perfectly good relationship with a perfectly good girl."

"She is not perfectly good, Joss, or should I say anti-wingman?"

I laughed. "All right, all right. Tell me your big whiny baby story."

"I'm pretty sure she's nuts. Like *Fatal Attraction* nuts."

"What, did she boil your rabbit or something?"

He laughed. "No, not yet. But if I had one, she might."

"What happened?"

"She's a too-much-too-soon girl."

"She didn't tell you she loved you, did she?" I asked. They'd met three weeks earlier.

"No," he said, but his tone was hesitant. "Not in so many words."

"Tell me."

"She's just making so many plans . . . She's talking about whose parents we're going to spend Christmas with."

"Oh!" It was January. She was planning for the end of the year already? "That's, um, presumptuous."

"Exactly."

"Maybe she just really likes you?" I suggested.

"She wants to get a cat."

"So? I have a cat."

"She wants *us* to get a cat. *Together.*"

"You have to break up with her."

"And you are aware that this is all your fault?"

"I will only admit that I introduced you. I can't be held responsible for her being crazy."

"I would never have talked to her if it wasn't for you."

This was true. "I will consider taking a small portion of the blame."

He sighed. "I'm gonna call her."

"Good luck."

CHAPTER TWENTY-ONE

ONE YEAR EARLIER . . . THIRD
YEAR OUT OF COLLEGE

Christine turned out to be hard to shake. When Matt called her with the breakup news, she cried and promised to change and made a general scene. He reinforced his position that he didn't really want to see her anymore, and thought he'd done a thorough enough job, but she called back the next day. Like nothing had happened. Talked about what their plans were for the weekend. Matt was flummoxed. He'd never encountered her particular brand of crazy before, and he didn't know what to do about it.

They broke up every day for a week. He tried the phone. He tried email. He tried not answering her calls. But Christine didn't seem to understand the words he was saying.

"What are you exactly saying?" I asked him when he called me on Wednesday.

"I say, 'I don't think we should see each other anymore.' You'd think that would work."

"Maybe she's interpreting the 'don't think' part as you not being decided or something."

"Maybe she's just crazy."

"Could be."

"I'd like to remind you this is your fault. Your taste in women sucks."

I laughed. "Well, excuse me for not having good taste in heterosexual women."

"I'm not even gonna touch that one."

"So, what are you going to try next?"

He blew out a sigh. "I have no idea. How do you convince a delusional crazy woman of something she doesn't want to believe?"

"Does she have a rabbit you could boil?"

"Wow, I never thought I'd hear you suggest pet abuse."

"Desperate times call for desperate measures."

"Maybe I'll just tell her I hate her family."

"Have you met them?"

"No."

I nodded, even though he couldn't see me. "Well, good luck with that, then."

He groaned. "You owe me for this."

Normally, a threat like that from him made my stomach go all liquidy with anticipation. This time was no exception, but I pressed the heel of my hand into my abdomen, remembering Josh and our upcoming date. "I gotta go," I told Matt.

When he called me on Thursday, he sounded more desperate. And more annoyed.

"She says she doesn't want me to see you anymore."

I could barely make sense of the words. "I'm sorry, what?"

"She said she sees the way we are together, and you must be the reason I can't commit to her."

I didn't even know what to say. My stomach clenched and my ears got hot.

"Joss?"

"Yeah, I'm here." I sank onto the arm of my couch and scratched at a sudden itch behind one knee.

"How the hell am I going to get rid of this nut job?" he demanded.

The itch spread down my calf and I nearly toppled from the couch as I reached down to chase it. "Maybe you could change your phone number."

"She knows where I live, genius."

"Well, why the hell would you bring her to your house?"

"I didn't know she was crazy at the time."

"Maybe you can get her to break up with you."

"Doubtful."

"Think about it."

He sighed again. "This is your fault."

"Yeah, I know." The itch migrated to my other leg. "Ugh, Matty, I gotta go. I have to wash off the fur."

"From anyone else, that would sound downright disturbing."

"Gotta love me," I said distractedly, already stripping off my scrub pants as I headed for the bedroom.

"Your charm almost makes up for the fact that you saddled me with a crazy woman."

I tossed the phone to the bed and hauled my Hello Kitty scrub top over my head. That felt a little better and I sighed as I picked the phone up. "Look, I'm sorry I didn't set you up with your dream girl."

"You'll just have to make it up to me, I guess."

"You'll have to break up with her before I do a damn thing," I said. "You know the rules."

"I'm trying, doesn't that count?"

"No." I carried the phone into the bathroom and turned on the shower. "Besides, I've got a date with Josh. You might be on your own with this one."

"The grocery store guy? Please."

If I was a dog, I would have flattened my ears at that point. "Thanks for the vote of confidence."

"Joss, come on, I didn't mean anything by it."

"Then why did you say it? I really like this guy. Just because you're all pissed off at Crazy Christine doesn't mean you should be a jerk to me."

"All right, all right. Don't get your panties in a twist."

"Actually, Matt, I'm not wearing any." And then I hung up on him.

The next day I had a series of text messages from Matt.

I've decided you should break up with her for me.
She's planning a weekend trip to Chicago for us.
I have a plan and you're helping me.

I called him, but got no answer. I left a voice mail. "I have a date with Josh tonight, so whatever evil plot you've cooked up is going to have to wait."

The return message arrived while I was in the shower. "Fuck your date with Josh, I need your help. You owe me. Please, Joss, I don't know what else to do."

I returned the call with my hackles up out of principle more than any remaining anger. I'd never heard him so genuinely at a loss, and it made me soften toward him. To my surprise, he didn't answer again. "I can't imagine why you think I owe you after you were such an ass to me last night. Tell you what, I'm going out with Josh. Call me if she's wielding a knife or something. Wait. Scratch that. Call 911 if she's armed. Good luck. Bye, Matty." Not completely softened, I guess.

The next call from Matt came just after I'd arrived at the restaurant to meet Josh. I didn't answer. Then, I muted my phone and ignored a volley of text messages while Josh and I worked our way through cocktails and appetizers.

Before our main course was served, I decided to make a quick bathroom run, and out of habit, I checked my messages.

She's gonna kill me in my sleep and it'll be on ur head.
I need u to come to my house at 9.
Please Joss. Tell me ur gonna meet me.
Hello?
<poke>

I dialed his number.

"Damn it, Joss, it's about damn time!"

"I'm on a date, Matt!"

"You can ditch."

"I'm not ditching him in the middle of a date. My food hasn't even arrived. I'm calling you from the bathroom!" I whispered, earning a curious look from a woman at the sink.

"I finally figured out how to get rid of her," he said, ignoring me. "I'm gonna convince her that I'm going back to you."

"Back to me?" I repeated.

"She's convinced that you're my ex-girlfriend, and that you want me back."

I bridged my forehead with one hand and turned into the tiled corner near the hand dryer to avoid more furtive glances from Sink Woman. "So, what does this have to do with me leaving in the middle of my date?"

"She left me a message that she's coming over tonight. I told her not to, but she's coming. I want you to be here. As proof."

"More like as your bodyguard, you big chicken!" I hissed, my voice echoing off the wall. I glanced at the woman at the sink, who was taking a suspiciously long time drying her hands on a paper towel.

"Alvin, just do this for me. I can't keep breaking up with this girl. She's a fruit loop and I don't speak crazy!"

"What makes you think I do?"

"I need your help," he whined. It was not an attractive sound, and I wrinkled my nose.

"I can't just ditch Josh."

He huffed, then tried a new tone of voice. "This is Sorbet, Joss. You owe me."

"How is this Sorbet? There's nothing about helping you break up with a crazy girl in the rules." I finally turned to the woman, still laboring over her hand drying and said, "Do you need something?"

She startled and shook her head, making a beeline for the door.

"New rule."

"Oh, no, buddy. No new rules to get me to walk out on a date. Besides, you know the deal: the relationship has to be over for Sorbet."

"I've been trying to make it over for a week!" he said. I could hear from his tone of voice that he was searching, desperate for the thing that would make me cooperate. "Okay, no new rules. Old rules. I'm allowed one violation."

"No way. You can't choose your violation while I'm in the middle of a date."

"Why not?"

"I like this guy!"

"Have you slept with him yet?"

"No."

"Then you're not in a relationship."

"Sex does not define a relationship," I said, squeezing my eyes shut to avoid my reflection.

"Joss, come on! I don't know what else to do."

"I can't believe you'd even ask me to ditch Josh. He's really nice, and he could be, like, *the* guy. What do you think he'd say if I told him I had to go so I could pretend to be another guy's girlfriend?"

"He might think it was funny. Maybe he'd give you a ride. You don't know until you ask."

"Yeah, I'm sure he'd just love it if I asked for a ride to go have Sorbet Sex with you." My voice was still echoing off the tile when the door opened and another woman came in to use the bathroom.

"Who said anything about having sex with me?" he asked, with a smirk so obvious I could hear it.

I blushed and dropped my voice to a whisper. "Don't tell me you weren't thinking it."

"Of course, I was thinking it, and obviously you were, too."

"Come on, Matty . . ."

"Alex."

I knew he had me. At least, I knew I was going to let him have me.

I sighed. "All right, all right."

"Thank you," he exhaled, relieved. "Thank you, thank you, thank you!"

"What am I gonna say to Josh?"

"The truth?"

"Um, no."

"Family emergency?"

"That's so trite."

"Don't say anything," he suggested, and I imagined the shrug that accompanied the words.

"What?"

"Just walk out."

"I can't do that! That's horrible."

"Why do you care? You don't even like this guy."

"Yes I do." I propped my forearm on the wall to rest my head on.

"But you like me better."

I shifted my shoulders, trying to ease the pressure of my clothes against my back. They'd gained at least twenty pounds during this conversation. "Don't push me."

"Seniority?" he tried.

"You've got to be kidding me."

"Come on, Joss. Live a little."

"Live a little?" I repeated. "This is hardly on anyone's a-thousand-and-one-things-to-do-before-I-die list!"

"Come on, it'll be a great story."

"Matt!"

"Part of you wants to do it."

And part of me did. I so rarely did anything truly awful. I didn't even speed . . . much. It would be a horrible, thrilling thing to do. Like shoplifting. "This is a terrible idea. I'm going to hell for this."

"Well, save me a seat when you get there."

I hesitated, looking at myself in the mirror. The stressed out look of my eyes and mouth didn't go well with the light, date-night makeup and the sparkly clip that held back my hair at one temple. I closed my eyes against the image and exhaled loudly into the phone. "If I'm gonna do this, you're staying on the phone with me."

"I will."

My heart was hammering as I walked out of the bathroom. I glanced back at the dining room, and then down the hall toward the kitchen. Josh was sitting with his back to the bathroom and I could skirt through the bar to leave. I took a deep breath and whispered, "I hate you," into the phone.

"Stop stalling and go."

I ducked my head and strode confidently through the bar, not risking a backward glance as I was briefly exposed in the entry. I had to stop long enough to retrieve my coat from the coatroom. Josh would have no reason to look in that direction, but my heart was in my throat anyway. I opened the door and walked in triple-time to the parking lot, barely breathing until I thumbed the UNLOCK button on my key fob.

"You are gonna owe me so big for this one."

"Big-time," he agreed.

"You have no idea . . ."

"They'll build a statue in your honor someday, Jocelyn Kiel."

I rolled my eyes, but couldn't hold back a grin. "All right. I'll see you in a few minutes."

My nerves made my foot heavy on the gas pedal and I was at Matt's place less than ten minutes later. I banged on his door repeatedly until he came down to open it for me.

"I can't believe you made me do that!"

He tilted his head. "Come on, it was kind of fun."

"I am a horrible person."

"You're not."

"Yes, I am." The illicit thrill of walking out was gone and I felt awful.

"It was a second date. You didn't leave him at the altar."

"And now I'll never be able to."

"Oh, you didn't want to marry some guy you met in a grocery store anyway."

I frowned at him.

"Look, you could have made something up and gotten a rain check from him. You walked out"—he spread his hands—"obviously, you don't like him that much."

"I was listening to your stupid advice!" I shouted.

"Why the hell did you start doing that?" His voice wasn't as loud as mine, but it wasn't his usual low, unflappable tone.

I clenched my jaw. "I can't believe I just did that. I wrecked things with a perfectly good guy because *you* can't handle your girlfriend."

"Who *you* set me up with."

"I must be some kind of masochist." I looked at my watch. "And he's gone by now, I'm sure, so I can't even go back."

"What would you say anyway?" Matt clasped his hands below his chin and batted his eyes. "Sorry, there was a puddle in the bathroom and I slipped, hitting my head on the sink. I've only just come to this very moment."

A startled bark of laughter burst from my mouth. I pressed my lips together and tried to maintain my anger, but my feet took me into the tiny vestibule at the bottom of the stairs anyway. "I should have told him there was an emergency."

"I told you that. You said it was trite." He crossed his arms.

"This is still your fault." I took my coat off and hung it on one of the pegs on the wall.

"Okay, fine. It's my fault, are you happy?"

"No, I'm an idiot."

He stayed silent.

"Why am I doing this?" I asked. "Why did I do this horrible thing to this great guy?"

"Don't examine your motives right now, there's a crazy woman on her way to my apartment."

"You really know how to make a girl want to stick around."

"Just go upstairs, please." He threw the dead bolt and gestured for me to precede him.

"Does she know I'm going to be here?"

"I told her I was going back to you. She said she wanted to come over to discuss it. I told her not to. Then, I didn't answer her last call, but she left a message saying she was coming over. She says we need to talk."

"So, how do you want to play this?" I asked. I didn't want to think too hard about what it said about me, but I'd decided to stick around. Might as well get down to logistics for the disaster in the making.

"I don't know. Just back me up about our fictional former relationship."

"You owe me so big . . ." I gave him an arch look when I got to the top of the stairs. "He's already called me four times."

"What did you say?"

"I didn't answer."

"Cold." He grinned.

"Hey, this was all your idea. You don't have a leg to stand on."

"Mea culpa."

"God damn lawyer," I muttered, loud enough that he'd hear.

Matt grinned. He was in law school for lack of another direction in life. He had no intention of being an attorney and loved lawyer jokes.

There was a loud pounding on the door below and we glanced at each other.

"Showtime," Matt muttered, headed for the stairs.

After my reprehensible escape from dinner, I should have been doing something considerably more karma-building than this, but as long as I was already here, I was inspired to take on the role. "Wait!" I said, catching him by the back of his shirt.

"What?" He turned.

I set to work on his shirt, opening the top four or five buttons before it was loose enough to pull over his head, followed by his T-shirt. He was left in nothing but his jeans. "Okay, go."

"What is on your devious mind?" he wondered aloud as the pounding resumed on the door.

"Get the door before she breaks it down." I pointed a finger at the stairs and gave him my sternest look. He didn't seem impressed, instead stroking his thumb along one side of my jaw before he walked to the door.

As soon as he headed down the stairs, I darted down the hall to his bedroom. It was dark in the room, but I knew my way around well enough. I stripped down to my panties, leaving my clothes in a pile on the floor and whipped the blanket off the sloppily made bed. Then I pulled the top sheet free and wrapped it around myself toga-style. I dragged it down the hall with me, ruffling my free hand through my hair and taking a moment to smear my mascara before I stepped through the mullioned door at the top of the stairs.

"Matty, who's at the door? Come back to bed."

He glanced over his shoulder and took in my appearance with only the barest hint of surprise.

"What's going on?" Christine demanded, anger making her small features take on the look of Tinker Bell.

"What's she doing here?" I asked.

"I knew it!" she shouted, shoving past Matt to storm up the stairs. "I knew you were after him!"

"Me? He broke up with you," I said.

Matt hurried up the stairs, trying to get around Christine, but she had one hand slammed against the wall on each side of the stairs. "No, he didn't!" she snarled.

"Yes, he did, you fruit loop," I said, amused to hear Matt's term come out of my mouth. "Haven't you been listening?"

She turned. "Matt, how could you do this to me?" she said, chin quivering. "Everything was going so well!"

His eyes widened. I could read his thoughts loud and clear: *Are you fucking kidding me?* He schooled his features before speaking. "I'm sorry, Christine. I just can't say no to her."

And then she did the last thing I expected. She wheeled around and hit me. An openhanded slap to my left cheek. I had never been hit before and several thoughts crossed my mind simultaneously. First, I felt a detached fascination. Second, the stinging pain that shot through my cheek and made my eyes water amazed me. Third, I felt an immediate desire to hit her back.

"Hey!" Matt said, making me realize that less than a second had passed. He shoved past her to put himself protectively between us. "What do you think you're doing?"

"You crazy bitch," I gasped, covering my cheek.

"I hate you!" she screamed, trying to reach around Matt to get another swipe at me. I darted backward, catching my heels in the trailing sheet and nearly falling. I caught the edge of the doorframe with the tips of one outstretched hand.

"Get out, Christine. Now," Matt said in a tone that offered no room for argument.

"I don't ever want to see you again," she said.

"Thank God. Get out," he repeated.

"You can keep your precious whore, you . . . you . . . jerk!" She made an about-face, thundered down the stairs, and slammed the door.

"God, Joss, are you okay?" Matt asked me.

I didn't hesitate—I punched him in the shoulder. "She fucking hit me!"

"You just hit me!"

"You owe me even bigger now," I said, taking my hand away from my hot cheek. He winced, looking at my face with concern.

"I'm so sorry."

"You better be!" I slugged him in the shoulder again. He had the decency not to rub the spot.

"Let's get you some ice."

I shook my head and pressed my fingers into my cheek. "Don't. It's not that bad."

"I'm really sorry."

"I can't believe she slapped me!"

"Me neither."

From a distance, we heard the sound of squealing tires. I braced for the sound of an impact, fearing that Crazy Christine was going to total my car in revenge. None came. I heard her race down the service drive, engine roaring in protest.

"Holy crap. She's seriously insane," I said, dabbing at my cheek again.

"I told you," he said. "Rabbit-boiling crazy. But, I swear, I didn't think she would get violent. I'm really sorry, Jossie."

"New rule. You're not allowed to get me bitch-slapped anymore."

"Deal."

"God damn, that really hurt!" I said in amazement. "I had no idea it would hurt that much."

Matt grinned. "You should have hit her back."

"I'm not having a naked cat fight for you, pal. I think I've done quite enough for you tonight." I hitched the sheet tighter to my body.

"You're naked under there?"

"Almost."

His eyes moved down, as if he was praying for the sudden onset of X-ray vision.

"Matt!" I protested, more out of form than any real indignation. "You've already convinced me to disappear in the middle of my date *and* gotten me slapped in the face by a crazy woman. Are you seriously gonna suggest I should have sex with you on top of all that?"

He made a thoughtful face. "It sounds worse when you say it all out loud."

"No kidding."

"Then, I guess you should go get dressed."

"Nope." I dragged the sheet to the couch and flopped down in front of the TV. He'd left it on mute, showing a hockey game. There was time on the clock, but I didn't know how much of the game was left. I didn't know who was playing—hell, I didn't even like hockey, but I was in the mood to be a pain in the ass. Matt had earned a little of that.

"Why not?"

"I'm gonna sit here with you knowing full well that I have nothing but a thong on under this sheet and you're just gonna have to deal with it."

"Is this supposed to be some sort of payback for tonight?"

"You got it."

He sat across from me, in the room's one chair and watched me rather than the game. I studiously avoided his eyes and tucked my feet up beneath me, leaning on the arm for a better view of the television. Knowing he was watching, I let the tight wrap of the sheet loosen, slowly revealing more of my back until it was pooled around my hips, but still covered my breasts. The Red Wings were pulling their goalie in a desperate bid for victory when Matt spoke.

"Are you trying to seduce me or something?"

"Shhh . . . the game's almost over."

Matt stood and came to my side of the room. He knelt on the couch behind me and braced his hands around my torso so that he could lean close enough to kiss my right shoulder.

"What are you doing?" I asked, turning to look back at him.

"Invoking the conflict rule. You're pissed at me, and I get to make it up to you." He brushed my hair aside to kiss the back of my neck. My eyes fluttered closed.

"I'm not pissed at you," I said.

"Seems like you are."

I shifted slightly onto one hip to get a better look at him. "I just can't believe an evening that started with a nice dinner date ended with me getting slapped in the face. Literally."

He skimmed his fingertips over my offended cheek. "It doesn't have to end that way."

"It sounds like *you're* trying to seduce *me*, O Person Who Is at Fault for This Whole Mess."

"Maybe." He leaned closer and kissed my willing lips.

I turned more and slid my hands over his still-bare shoulders. "Why are you doing that?"

"I told you. I need to make it up to you. It's my fault you got slapped."

I kissed him, and felt the sheet slip down to near indecency. "It's my fault you met her in the first place."

"That's true," he agreed, kissing my cheek in a trail toward my ear.

"But it's not my fault you're such a little man-tramp that you had to bring her back to your house as soon as you could get her out of her clothes." My eyes slipped shut as he passed my ear and worked his way down my throat with soft, wet kisses. He laughed against my neck, breath tickling me into goose bumps.

"You're right, that was my fault."

"And it's your fault that I blew my chance with Josh."

He stopped kissing my collarbone for a second, and I heard hesitation in his voice when he agreed, "Also true." I was willing to take it.

"And you're the one who came up with this stupid plan."

"I never told you to take your clothes off and come traipsing out here looking like lust in human form."

I smiled. "It seemed like a good idea at the time."

He straightened up to grin at me, then kissed me again, letting his carefully balanced weight descend onto me. "So, are you mad at me, or not?"

I didn't answer at first, in favor of savoring the warm contact with Matt. He was radiating heat, as usual. "Not," I decided.

"So, we don't need to resolve any conflict?" he said into my hair.

"Wait, then, yes. I am mad."

"Okay, good."

There wasn't much clothing between us, but the sheet was something of a nuisance and it wasn't long before we were both struggling against it. "You're laying on it—" I gasped, trying to pull a section free from my legs.

"Fuck it, the couch is too small anyway." He picked me up, sheet and all. I made transporting us to the bedroom difficult by refusing to stop kissing him. "Joss, I can't see," he said, pulling away.

"Sorry, sorry." I turned my face into his shoulder, trying to clear his vision.

He dropped me onto the bed, hard enough to knock the breath from my lungs, and grabbed the end of the sheet. It took two or three tugs to pull it free, and I got a bit of a rug burn on my back from the last pull, but I didn't care. I stripped off my last scrap of clothing while Matt did the same and then he was on top of me.

Our skin stuck together like window clings as we lay together that night. Outside the cocoon of blankets we'd created, February was hard at work cooling the bedroom to a goose-pimply sixty-something. Beneath the sheets, though, we could have thawed a Thanksgiving turkey. The tip of my nose, exposed to the elements, was frosty and I pushed it against Matt's cheek.

"One more new rule," I said. "Next time, we're going to my place. My heater works."

"I may have to break up with someone just so I can sleep at your place."

I smiled, eyes heavy with sleep. "Maybe we should just start fighting a lot."

"Set me up again, and I don't think we'll have a problem with that."

"All right, all right, point taken." I pinched him. "You're on your own."

"Sounds good to me."

CHAPTER TWENTY-TWO

NOW

"Okay, fine, so that was kind of . . . messy," I admitted. "But, we've been fine since then."

"How many second dates have you been on since you walked out on Josh?"

I frowned. "I don't know."

"How many *dates* have you been on? Period."

"Jesus, Matt, it's not like I keep a logbook."

"All right, sorry. I just . . ." He sighed. "I think it's gotten to the point where we can't do this anymore."

The room seemed to tilt wildly and I slapped my hands down on the cushions. I blinked and the world was steady again. Physically anyway. "What do you mean?"

"I don't think we can keep up this . . . *thing* much longer."

I wanted to cry, but I shoved my forearm into my stomach and got out a whisper. "Is this about the new girl?"

"Yes and no."

"Would you just tell me the story already? You're starting to freak me out."

Matt shifted into the corner of the couch, bringing one knee up so we were facing each other, one cushion between us. "So, there's this girl at school, like I said. Tara."

"Right."

"And she's cute." He shrugged and shifted his gaze to a point somewhere behind me. "She's blond and pretty, and she seems smart. So, I should like her."

"So, what's the problem?"

He looked down and found a loose thread on his jeans to pull at. "The problem is that when I look at her, I look for what's wrong. I look for the reason we're gonna break up."

"I think that's normal. I always think the same thing. *How long is this gonna last? Is it worth it?* I think everybody does that."

"Yeah, but it's always worth it because I know you'll be there at the end." His expression was impossible to read and I began to feel nervous.

"What does that even mean?"

He shifted again, rising to his feet and pacing to the desk. I had to twist to follow his path. He perched on the corner of it and crossed his arms. "I'm willing to be an ass and break up with Tara, because I know you'll be there when I do. And I'm starting to hate that about myself. I keep dating all these stupid girls because I know I can get out of it and you'll still be there."

I blinked, feeling like the sofa was suddenly less steady in the room. "So . . . what? The deal's off?"

"I think it has to be."

"I don't understand where this is coming from. Why now? Did I do something wrong?"

"No! Joss . . ." He pushed off the desk and walked past the fireplace, stopping to drum his fingers against the back of the armchair. "It's just that ever since my dad died, I've been kind of . . . I don't know, lost? Maybe that's it. I've been thinking about what's important, and I don't want to waste Tara's time. Or mine, anymore."

I swallowed around the lump in my throat, willing myself not to cry. "I get it. This whole thing is kind of silly, I guess." I tried to smile. "It was bound to end sometime, right?"

He looked relieved. "Right. I think we're getting too old for the game."

"Okay." I nodded and stood up, unable to make eye contact. "I'm sorry I dragged it on for so long."

"You?" His tone was one of shock, and I looked up. "This is my fault. I should have said something before. I should have said something after my father's funeral."

I gave him a little half-smile, still not able to look in his eyes. "I don't think I would have believed you, then. You were so upset."

"You're probably right."

CHAPTER TWENTY-THREE

SIX WEEKS AGO

I was in my underwear when the call came. It was early in the morning, before I even left for work, and I answered out of curiosity more than anything. I didn't recognize the number, and the display on my phone told me it was out of state.

"Jocelyn?"

"Yes?" The voice was vaguely familiar, but I couldn't place it.

"Hey, this is Tom Lehrer. Matt's brother? We've met a few times . . ." Tom lived in Nevada and I couldn't imagine why he was calling.

"Yeah, of course. I remember. How did—why—what can I do for you?"

"Well, look, Matt would kill me for calling you, but, um . . . our dad died early this morning."

I dropped my toothbrush, already loaded with paste into the sink. "Oh my God! What happened?" Their dad was young, and healthy as far as I knew.

"It was a heart attack."

"Shit. Oh God, Tom, I'm so sorry!" I sank to the small rug on the bathroom floor and let Dewey crawl into my lap. His needle claws made me jump as he got settled.

"Thanks. The reason I'm calling is Matt's taking the whole thing pretty hard. He's . . . uh . . . I don't think he's thinking straight. I remembered your name and I got your number out of the alumni directory. I hope that's okay."

"Yeah, of course. Where are you now?"

"I'm at the airport in Nevada. I'm on my way home. That's why I'm calling. I don't know if my mom can handle all this alone."

"Where are they?"

"St. Mary's up in Mequon. Do you think—?"

"I'm on my way."

I called in sick to work, and scrambled into clothes. Dewey yowled in protest as I rushed for the front door. I backtracked long enough to dump kibble into his bowl, and then I was gone. All I could think of was getting to Matt. The hospital was pretty far away, and I had to use all my willpower not to press the pedal to the floor. I still made it in record time and asked for John Lehrer's room at the information desk.

The elevator ride was excruciatingly slow. I wished I'd taken the stairs, and stood too close to the doors so I could squeeze through the minute they opened. My heart thudded in my ears as I found my way to the assigned room and knocked gently.

"Come in." I recognized Matt's mom by her voice.

I pushed open the door and peeked around the curtain. John was motionless in the bed, with the waxy look that only the dead possess. It was clear that the staff had cleaned him up a bit and given the family some private time. I'd never understood the practice myself, but I knew people wanted to say their goodbyes in their own way. I pulled my eyes from his still form and focused on the two people huddled on the vinyl love seat on the far side of the room. Matt's mom, Linda, was puffy eyed and had a vacant expression. I couldn't see Matt's face. He was slumped forward, head in his hands and rocking just slightly. Linda had one hand on his back, patting him rhythmically.

"Matt?" I whispered and he startled.

Linda looked at me, recognition dawning in her eyes. "How did . . . ?" she wondered.

"I'm sorry," I breathed. "Tom called me. He's on his way."

"Joss . . ." Matt looked up. His eyes were red and wet. My heart hurt—physically ached—to look at him.

"I'm sorry," I said again. "I probably shouldn't have come."

He stood then and lurched at me. I barely stood my ground as he wrapped his arms around me and broke into fresh tears.

"I'm sorry," I repeated, words muffled by his shoulder.

"You're here," he said. "You came."

"Of course."

"Thank you."

All that long day, I stayed with Matt, holding on to him whenever he seemed to need it, and trying to make myself useful to the family. I picked up Tom from the airport when he arrived a few hours later. He seemed to be the final straw for Linda, who broke down at last. The grief was terrible, thick and heavy in the room. I wanted to pull them all into my lap and hum lullabies. Scratch behind their ears and murmur affection like I did with frightened animals at work. Instead, I brought them sandwiches, and made phone calls and shared their sadness.

Tom had been right about Matt. He was out of his mind with grief. Alternating between blank stares and painful tears, he was barely present in the room with the rest of the family. I was scared for him. Scared he wouldn't be able to pull himself together. He must have looked as awful to the professionals, because one of the doctors offered him a prescription for a sleeping pill. He shook his head, but I took the paper and tucked it into my pocket.

"I don't need that."

"I didn't say you did." I slipped my arm around his shoulders and pressed my lips against his head. "But when a doctor offers you the good stuff, you don't say no."

He didn't even smile. That was the worst of it. He had no sense of humor. I leaned in close to whisper in his ear. "You gotta at least fake it, Matty. Your mom can't worry about you today, okay?"

He winced and nodded. His participation didn't improve much, but it was enough for the stunned Linda to release a little of her worry for him.

When the arrangements were settled for the day, when John's body was moved to the morgue, when Linda's sister Janice was en route from Arizona, when the last close friend had left for the day, when Tom was ready to take Linda home, it came down to me to take care of Matt. I didn't mind. I wanted to make sure he was okay, and being the one on watch was the easiest way to do that. He didn't question me when I followed his car back to the east side and parked in my usual spot. He waited for me at the door, eyes blank with faraway thoughts, and didn't protest when I took the key from his hand and let us into his apartment.

"I'm gonna stay with you tonight," I informed him and he nodded.

I left him on the couch with ESPN playing for background noise and slipped down the hall to use my phone out of his earshot. My first call went to Nellie; I asked her to check in on Dewey.

"How's he doing?" she asked, referring to Matt.

"God, Nell, he's in bad shape."

"Poor kid."

Matt's bed was unmade, the comforter thrown back in his haste to get out of bed so many hours ago. I straightened it as I talked, just for something to do. "I'm going to stay with him tonight. Maybe tomorrow. I'm worried about him."

"Why don't I bring Dewey to my house until you're ready for him?"

"That would be great." I laughed. "Maybe I should bring Matt to my place. Dewey would molest him into happiness."

She snickered. "That'll be Plan B. Is there anything I can do?"

"I don't even know what I'm supposed to do." Tears slipped down my cheeks for the first time in hours. I'd held fast to my own feelings while Matt and his family cried, but seeing him in so much pain was killing me.

"You're already doing it."

"This sucks," I whispered. "I have no right to be crying."

"You have every right, you idiot."

I perched on the bed, on the side that was always mine. "Crying won't help him."

"All he needs right now is someone who loves him to be there." She paused. "And I know you love him . . . in your own fucked up way."

Scrubbing my eyes a little too hard, I exhaled. "Please don't lecture me right now."

"Lecture? I wouldn't dream of it."

"Sure." I heard a sound from the living room. "I should go."

"Okay. Don't worry about the fur ball. I've got him handled. Give Matt a hug for me."

"Will do. Thanks, Nell."

I tiptoed to the living room, but Matt had just knocked the remote to the floor. He was looking past it, as if it had only dented his consciousness.

"You okay?" I asked.

He nodded.

"Are you hungry?"

He shook his head.

I chewed the inside of my cheek while I thought of what to do next. I wanted to wrap myself around him and absorb some of the hurt from his body. "If I get some food, will you eat?"

"Okay."

I called for pizza delivery, and then called in sick to work for the following day before settling on the end of the couch. He was four feet away, but I felt a wall between us.

"Matty . . ." I reached across the chasm to touch his leg. "You still in there?"

"Yeah." He leaned over until his head rested in my lap, curling one arm across my hips. I felt the heat of his face through my jeans. I touched the inside of my wrist to his forehead. He was hot to the touch, but not feverish. Still, I shifted my perpetually cool fingers to his skin.

"What can I do?" I asked.

"Nothing."

I folded myself over him, cheek coming to rest on his waist. We stayed that way until the doorbell announced the arrival of pizza.

Matt didn't eat much, but more than I'd expected. Finally, knowing he'd been up since four in the morning, I took him by the hand and led him to bed.

I could have slept on the couch, but the idea was insane to me. I was here for Matt, and I was going to be as close as possible if he needed me. I stripped down to my underwear and borrowed a T-shirt from Matt's dresser before sliding into bed with him and pulling him tight against me.

"Matt, I'm so, so sorry," I whispered.

"I wish I'd known the last time I saw him was going to be the last time." His tone was flat, dull.

"I know." I kissed the top of his head.

"I wish I'd made it there before he died this morning."

"I know."

He started to cry again, and in the dark, I couldn't resist joining him. I didn't know his father well, although he had always been very nice when I'd seen him. I cried for Matt, who had never seemed so very far away before. His body was present, but his mind seemed lost. I pulled him closer, as if proximity was the cure for his wandering thoughts.

He tilted his head to find my lips and kissed me. His lips felt tight, stiff. Not soft and teasing like I'd come to expect. Normally, I felt promise from him. That night, I couldn't be sure what he was thinking. Did he want this? Would he regret it? I set my fingertips against his jaw and rubbed my toes along his shin, hoping he'd understand I was consenting, but letting him lead. Tears slipped in crooked paths toward my ears, joined by his. His mouth went rough, but I didn't care. At least he was present like that.

I played Follow the Leader—mirroring his actions—but ready to stop if he decided it was too much.

He didn't.

The sex was brief but eager. We were both covered in sweat and tears when it was done, and panting out the kind of hard breaths that feel as though they will never return to normal.

I clung to his shoulders, feeling overworked muscles protest against the sprint they'd endured. My thighs shook and it was hard to keep them wide around his hips.

"I'm sorry, Joss," he gasped. "I shouldn't—" It was the first time we'd ever had sex without discussing it beforehand.

"Don't be. It's fine."

"I'm sorry," he said again.

"Shh." I scrunched my fingers into the back of his hair and kissed his cheek. "Don't." I was happy I'd given him even a second of relief.

"Thank you."

*   *   *

I stayed with Matt for a week. Even after I went back to work on Thursday, I returned to his house in the evenings. The funeral was scheduled for Saturday to give all of the out-of-town relatives time to convene.

Every night, I climbed into bed with him, wondering if he would tell me he didn't need me there anymore, but he didn't. After the first night, we only shared the space, sleeping side by side, but not sleeping together. That was a first for us, and I was surprised at how natural it felt.

On the other hand, it was Matt. My Matt. I would have done a lot more for him if he'd asked me to. He was one of the closest friends I'd ever had. The only one I had a habit of sleeping with, but still—a friend above all else.

The day of the funeral, I was ready to step into the background, and let the Lehrers focus on each other. Then, Linda saw me and gave me a lung-crushing hug. "Thank you for taking care of my baby," she said.

I couldn't help smiling at the idea of Matt being her baby. "Of course."

"He's lucky to have you." She gave me one final squeeze before releasing me.

"I feel the same way."

Matt took my hand as he passed by to give his mom a hug. He didn't let go, turning me into a human kite as he first hugged his mother, then his aunt and other relatives I didn't recognize.

Funerals, especially for the young—and John had only been fifty-eight—are such an awkward mix of joyous reunion and terrible sadness. He still had so many living friends and relatives who came to celebrate his life and the unexpected tragedy of his death. All around me I could hear exclamations of surprise as the mourners found friends they didn't expect to see. Bursts of laughter, followed by guilty glances at the family.

The Lehrers didn't seem to mind. On the contrary, Matt, Linda, and Tom looked brighter than I'd seen them. Before the service began, Matt even smiled as friends arrived. No million-watt, used-car-salesman grin, but a real smile. It was a start.

The last person he spoke to before he had to report for pall-bearer duty was a great-aunt on his mother's side. She offered condolences, of course, but couldn't resist appraising Matt with astonishment.

"The last time I saw you, you were graduating high school, and look at you now." She smiled at him, shaking her head as if to say, "Where has the time gone?" Then she turned to me. "And this must be your girlfriend?" He was holding my hand again, as if I was his anchor to reality.

"Uhh—" Without thinking, I deferred to Matt with my eyes.

His great-aunt caught the movement. "Oh, Matthew, you should know better than to keep a girl guessing."

"No, no." I jumped to his defense with no earthly idea of what I meant to say next.

"I wouldn't dare." Matt gave my hand enough of a tug to bring me tight to his side. "This is Joss-elyn," he said, the second and third syllables of my name an afterthought.

"You know only two percent of the world has red hair." She patted her own hair, now faded to a peachy color. I smiled at her.

"It's lovely to meet you," I said, clasping her right hand with my left. Matt still had hold of my other hand, and I couldn't do much else.

"Keep an eye on him," she said. "He used to climb the trees in my yard. All the way to the top."

"He does it in my yard, too," I whispered.

She laughed, a trilling, delighted sound, and gave my hand a squeeze. Then she turned her eyes to Matt. "Keep ahold of this one, she's a rare creature."

Matt smiled. "I know."

Linda approached and caught the woman's elbow. They excused themselves.

"So, I'm your girlfriend now?" I teased.

He released my hand. "I do not have the energy to explain just what you are to my mother's elderly aunt."

"Oh, come on, I'm sure she'd be cool with it."

"Just do me a favor, and don't disillusion anyone over the age of sixty today."

He sounded so casual and . . . normal I almost burst into tears. "You got it," I said, "and I'll throw in under-eighteens as a bonus."

He smiled at me, a genuine smile that made my heart beat faster, fueled by relief. "You know what? I think it would be best if you just didn't disillusion *any*one."

I snapped off a two-finger salute with my free hand. "Done."

"And don't salute me anymore today either."

I saluted him again for good measure. "Don't push your luck."

That earned me a medium-sized grin, which quickly faded when his brother leaned close to speak in his ear.

"We're being called to the back," Matt told me a second later.

"Okay, I'll see you after." I stood on my toes to give him a hug. "I—I—" I bit back my own words. I'd nearly dropped in an easy *Love you, Matty,* but suddenly that felt like a heavy thing to tell him. As if the words themselves would add to the weight on his shoulders as he carried his father's coffin with his brother and four other men. Instead, I kissed him on the cheek.

Tension settled over the church when the funeral service began. Everyone waited to see if the tone would be one of tragedy or celebration. The first two pews were reserved for immediate family. I probably could have taken a space there, but I didn't feel it was my place. I sat beside Jessie just two rows back, and immediately wished I was close enough to touch Matt's shoulder if I needed to. Instead, I had to settle for curling my fingers around the edge of the pew. Jessie slipped her arm through mine, and gave me a little squeeze.

I watched the back of Matt's head for some sign that he was okay. It was, as always, just the back of his head. I should have ignored my instincts and sat in the family's row. I hated being away from him during the service. He'd been my responsibility for days, and now, at the crucial moment, I was out of reach. Jessie's hand on my knee made me realize I was vibrating with anxiety.

"Are you okay?" Jessie whispered.

"Fine." I fixed a smile on my face and glanced at her. "Too much coffee."

She nodded, as if she agreed, but kept her hand on my knee as the priest began to speak.

As the service progressed, my nerves eased a bit. Matt seemed fine, as far as I could tell. I still found myself tilting my head, trying to see anything but his dark hair and the edge of one ear. I don't know what I expected him to do—sob uncontrollably? Run from the church? Turn suddenly and search the crowd for me? He sat very still, as if watching a play. Eventually, I eased my vigilance and shifted a portion of my attention to the proceedings.

Matt always told me he'd gotten his sense of humor from his dad, and listening to his friends eulogize him I believed it. One of the speakers, John's best friend, even ran a slideshow of photos featuring John Photoshopped into famous historic events. The tension in the room melted as people laughed.

By the time we filed out of the church to the wide hall they called The Gathering Space, the emotional climate of the crowd had gone from solemn to celebratory. Laughter began to seem more appropriate and the guilty glances less so.

After a cookies-and-coffee type reception in the church basement, Jessie, her boyfriend, Evan, and a few other college friends made plans to go out for dinner.

"You're coming, right?" Jessie asked.

"Um . . ." I did a quick scan of the room looking for Matt. "I have to make sure Matt—"

"She's coming." Matt's voice startled me from behind.

I turned. "No, no, I can stay."

"You've done enough, Joss. Please. Go with them."

"Come with us," Evan echoed.

And I wanted to. What I really wanted was for Matt to come along; for this to be nothing but an impromptu reunion with friends. But, I knew Matt had to stay, and I knew I should stop mothering him to death.

"Okay, sure," I said. "Where are we going?"

Dinner with friends put me in a good mood, and it was hard to tamp it down as I rang Matt's bell. I'd left a lot of stuff at his apartment over the last week, and some of it I needed to get through the night. More than that, I wanted to check on him. He didn't answer, so I tried the door, which he'd been leaving open for me all week. It was unlocked and I let myself into the entry.

"Matt?" I called.

There was no answer.

"Matty? Are you home?" I slipped off my high heels and padded up the stairs in stocking feet. The living room was dark, so I checked the bedroom, pulling off my jewelry as I walked. It was empty as well. I'd seen his car in the driveway, but maybe he went off with someone else. *His brother?* I left my jewelry in a tidy pile on the dresser and walked back to the living room.

"Matt?" I went into the kitchen, flipped on the light, and screamed. Matt sat on the kitchen floor with his back against the refrigerator. "Oh my God, you scared me!" I gasped. "What are you doing?"

He shook his head. "I don't know."

"Didn't you hear me calling you?"

"Yeah. Sorry."

"Are you all right?" I lowered myself to the floor, awkward in my pencil skirt.

"Yeah . . ." He sighed.

"Matt, you're starting to scare me a little."

He blinked heavily and looked at me. "Why?"

"I'm worried about you. You seem . . . If I didn't know you better, I'd think you were going to kill yourself."

His eyes widened. "I'm not gonna off myself, Joss. Jeez. Give me some credit."

"I said 'if I didn't know you better,'" I reminded him. "You're just so . . . down."

"I know. I'm sorry. This has just been really hard."

I covered his hand with mine. "I'm sure."

"Fuck." He sighed.

"What are you doing in here?"

"I came in to get some water." He picked up an empty glass from the floor nearby. "It just seemed like a good place to sit for a few minutes."

"Do I want to know how long ago that was?" I asked.

"Probably not."

"Do you still need some water?"

"Yeah . . . I never made it that far."

I took the glass from him and got up to fill it from the sink. After sliding back to the floor, I offered it to him and he took a long drink.

"Thanks."

"Do you need anything else?"

"I just . . . I miss him. It's not like I even saw him every day, but I miss him. I miss knowing he's there if I need him."

"Your mom is still here."

"I know." He nodded. "But my dad was like this . . . rock. This *thing* that was always there when I needed it . . . I don't know."

"I'm sorry."

"Yeah, me, too."

I propped my back against the counter opposite him. "It was a really nice funeral."

Unexpectedly, he started to cry again.

"Oh, jeez, Matty, I'm sorry! I didn't mean to upset you."

He covered his eyes with one hand. "Fuck! I'm so sick of crying. I'm like a fucking Miss America contestant."

I laughed. "No, you're not."

He drew his knees up to meet his elbows and clamped his hands over the back of his head. "Why is this bothering me so much?"

"Because it's your dad, Matty! Jesus. Cut yourself some slack."

His head came up and he knocked it softly against the refrigerator door a few times. "I just want to stop thinking about this for a little while. I want to have a normal thought. Just one."

"You need to sweep," I said, scanning the floor now that I had a good perspective on it.

"What?"

"It's a normal thought," I said. "I'm trying to help."

"Who gives a fuck about sweeping?" he said without venom.

"Obviously not you."

That made him laugh softly.

"See?"

"I think I'm going to quit school," he said.

"What?" It was my turn for confusion.

"It just seems so pointless. I don't even want to be a lawyer. What am I doing?"

"Avoiding the real world for a while?" I suggested. "Getting a graduate degree that will make you a very desirable job applicant."

"Exactly. What's the point?"

I chewed my lip. "I don't think you should decide right now."

"Why not? Shouldn't the death of my father make me reevaluate my life?"

"Yeah, maybe, but maybe not right away."

He bumped his head on the refrigerator once more and tilted back to look at the ceiling. "Yeah, maybe."

"Just don't do anything irreversible right now. Give yourself some options."

"So, reversible stuff is still on the table?"

I narrowed my eyes. "What do you mean?"

"Specifically?" He looked at me. "I'm thinking of getting hammered."

I nodded slowly. "That's an option."

"Seems like a pretty great one."

"It always seems like a great idea at first. But think about tomorrow."

"Which totally defeats the purpose of getting hammered."

"Anything else? Some kind of sport on TV that might amuse you?"

He sighed, then smiled to himself. "Nothing I should mention in present company."

I made a show of looking over one shoulder, then the other. "I'm sorry, have we met? What precisely do you think is out of bounds?"

"You've done so much for me, Joss. I can't ask you to do anything else."

"You don't have to ask. I'm offering. That makes it okay."

He reached out and ran one hand up my shin. "I think what I'd ask for is too much. I already took it from you once."

"No, you didn't. I'm declaring an exception for the circumstances. And I'll gladly give it again if it will make you feel better. Even for a few minutes."

He answered by moving his hand over my knee and sneaking it under my skirt as he skimmed over my thigh. I was grateful for the tacit consent; I was in the market for a little comfort myself. Scooting closer, I balanced myself with one hand on his chest to kiss him.

We never made it off the kitchen floor that time. I didn't even make it out of all of my clothes. I knocked over his glass of water and we both got wet, but it wasn't enough to stop us. I liked the upright position, because it let me keep his lips in close proximity. My knees ached from the tile floor, and no amount of shifting alleviated it. He stretched up to rummage in a drawer and came back with an oven mitt and a towel. He offered them to me and I tucked them under my knees with a giggle. He grinned at me, and I felt a thrill in my stomach. I hadn't seen such easy happiness on his face in days.

The kitchen was less than pristine when we were done, with my underwear sitting in a puddle half under the refrigerator and Matt's suit pants shoved under the edge of the cabinets, where cobwebs lived. When I stood, water dripped from my skirt and ran down my bare legs.

"I'm gonna need to take these to the dry cleaner," he observed, retrieving his dusty pants.

"Yeah. I think we might need a mop, too."

He shrugged. "It'll dry."

I unzipped my skirt and stepped out of it, letting my shirt do all the work of covering my rear end. "You seem . . . a little better," I observed.

"I think so."

"Good."

He put an arm around me, making an abstract imprint of cobwebs and dust all over me. "Thank you, Joss. For everything."

"Of course."

"Will you stay?"

Relief uncoiled in my chest, and I nodded. "It's in my contract."

He winced for a flash before he cast his eyes to the floor. "Right."

CHAPTER TWENTY-FOUR

SIX WEEKS AGO

Going home the day after the funeral felt . . . flat. The rooms were too quiet, the carpet too soft in comparison to the echo of Matt's hardwood floors. Dewey made a beeline for one of his secret hideouts the minute we crossed the threshold, leaving me with a three-inch scratch down one arm. A reminder I should not leave him in someone else's care for six days. Cats. I walked through the apartment in a halfhearted attempt to find him, but mostly because I didn't have anything else to do.

When I flicked the wall switch in the bathroom, I got a flare of white light and a popping sound before the room was plunged back into darkness. I would have to climb on the counter in the dark little room to change the lightbulb.

So, I burst into tears.

And it seemed like such a good idea I gave in to it, sinking to my knees and then to my forearms. Head down on the floor, I cried. The kind of tears that dripped off my nose, and sobs that made my ribs hurt. I must have been making a lot of noise, because Dewey came to investigate, sniffing at my fingers where they covered the back of my head. I flicked my hand at him, but couldn't form any words to scold him away.

"Mrroww?" he said, rolling the *r*'s as if he'd picked up a foreign accent at Nellie's house.

I lifted my head and looked at him. "What?"

His only answer was to saunter a few feet away, sit primly, and wrap his tail around his feet.

"What?" I sniffed hard, but ultimately had to wipe my runny nose on the back of my hand. "I get to cry whenever I feel like it," I told him.

He walked his front feet out until he was positioned like a Sphinx, then lowered his lids as though I bored him.

"God, don't look at me like that." Whether it had been his plan, I couldn't say, but he'd successfully interrupted my crying jag. Now I was left with a throbbing head and the same feeling of lonely flatness I'd had before the tears. "It was nice, okay? It was nice to be with someone—it was nice to be with Matt."

Dewey opened his eyes at the mention of his favorite person.

"He's not here," I said, and my chest buckled again. Only one little choking sob escaped before I controlled myself that time. "I should just mail you to him," I told the cat. "Better yet, I should have just brought you along and left you there with your boyfriend." My right knee was on the tile side of the bathroom threshold, and it finally lodged a complaint loud enough to make me shift positions. I sat with my back to the wall and hugged my knees.

What on earth had changed in less than a week to make me feel like an orphan in my own, beloved apartment? I felt like I'd been dumped. Maybe it was just an emotional freak-out after days of being strong for Matt. Maybe, like some kind of trained animal, I'd started investing in Matt during our cohabitation. Close quarters were enough of an imitation of a relationship for me, and now I was on my own again and it hurt. Could I really be so pathetic that I was mourning the loss of a relationship that never existed? Apparently.

"*Mrow,*" Dewey agreed.

"I have to get ahold of myself." I pressed the heels of my hands into my eyebrows. "I can't do this."

But all that day I missed him. I kept listening for him in another room, starting to speak to him before I remembered he wasn't there. When I curled up on my couch with a magazine, I missed the feel of his hip pressed to mine and resting my head on his shoulder. And when I slipped into bed that night, shivering at the chill of the sheets, I missed his radiator warmth and the feel of his chest under my hand. The familiar scent of my own fabric softener seemed too clean. I wanted his customary kiss at my hairline as we settled ourselves. The ritual, oh God, how I wanted the ritual of sharing bedtime with him.

Instead, I got Dewey. Leaping onto the bed to stare at me, he kept a careful distance. I was still being punished.

"You're in his spot," I told him.

Dewey purred.

The backs of my eyes burned, and I considered crying again. It wouldn't change anything, though. I snuck one hand out from the blankets and scratched Dewey's cheek. His purring amplified. One of the best things about animals is they can't tell your secrets. Dewey was the keeper of plenty of mine. So, I confessed one more. "I think I have a crush on your boyfriend."

This would pass, I assumed, as I got further from the emotionally draining week. People could develop a passing attraction to someone, even a close friend. It was simply a waxing phase of my affection for a friend, right? All I had to do was wait it out. It would wane. Surely it would take no more than a month. If the moon could do it in a month, so could I.

The moon, however, wasn't constantly confronted with Matt Lehrer. I found myself thinking about him too much. Sitting across from him at our weekly brunch, whether we were alone or with friends, I looked at his mouth too often and the ghosts of his hands on my body were everywhere. Beneath the table, I pressed my palm to my inner thigh and remembered. It was maddening.

Nothing but a passing crush, I assured myself time and again as weeks turned into a full month. It was late April by then, nearly the end of Matt's semester. He hadn't made a decision about staying in school yet, but he also hadn't gotten a piercing or a tattoo, so apparently permanent choices were still on hold. He did, however, take a clipper to his own head. His hair, always a classic collegiate short-on-the-sides-shaggy-on-top, was reduced to a touchable half-inch all around. I loved to skim my palms over it, which did nothing to ease my desire to be close to him.

Nor did his continued grieving process. He was doing remarkably well, talking about his dad, and admitting if he had to go, Matt was glad he'd gone quickly. But he was still near to sadness most of the time, and I loved watching him find himself again, and loved being there for him when he needed me. None of which made it easy to squelch my inappropriate feelings for him.

I couldn't focus on anything. I wasn't hungry, but I stood in front of my open refrigerator for long minutes. I flipped through television channels without seeing any of the programs. I picked up the phone dozens of times, but couldn't think of anyone I should call.

Over an anesthetized Norfolk terrier in serious need of dental work, I blurted it all out to Nellie.

"I think I might have *feelings* for Matt." As soon as the words were out of my mouth, I hated the sound of them. *Feelings? Ick.*

"You're an idiot." Nellie's eyes flicked up to give me a withering look before she went back to the terrier's molars. I was glad I couldn't see the smirk no doubt hiding behind her surgical mask.

"What?" I demanded. "Why?"

"Of course, you're in love with Matt."

"I didn't say I was *in love* with him."

"Well, whatever you need to tell yourself to sleep at night." She straightened up and bent back, letting loose a cascade of pops from her spine.

"Nellie, I'm serious. I need help. I need input."

"You need the kind of help that only professionals can offer, sweetie."

"Could you at least pretend to focus?"

She sighed. "What do you want me to say? Of course, you do."

"What's that supposed to mean?"

"Please. Do not play me for a fool."

"It's not like that with us." I spared a glance for the heart monitor. The dog was doing well. I patted his little haunch.

"You're the ones who got sex all mixed up in things. You had to know this would happen one day."

My legs were starting to ache from standing. We'd been doing dentals all day. I flicked my heels up backward unintentionally kicking myself in the butt. "We were working just fine before this. What am I going to do?"

"You were not fine. You guys were like an episode of *Jerry Springer* waiting to happen. Seriously, what did you think was going to happen when one of you got married? Would you still get together every time the other one breaks up with someone?"

"Of course not!" I said. "I'm sure by the time one of us got married, the other one would have a serious relationship, too. There would never be a need for Sorbet again."

"Ri-ight," she drawled. "I'm sure everything will work out just peachy. And I'm sure your future husband won't have any problem with you hanging out with Matt. I mean, you guys are friends, right? The fact that you've been booty-calling each other for eight years is totally cool. Who wouldn't be okay with that?"

"Seven years," I protested feebly.

"Oh, well, that's fine, then." She gestured for me to reposition the dog before continuing, her tone shifting from sarcasm to genuine curiosity. "So, how are you going to tell him?"

"I'm not a hundred percent sure I should tell him."

"Oh my God, why not?" she hollered. Never a quiet person, Nellie bordered on television evangelist volume when she was worked up.

"Well, what if he doesn't feel the same way? How could we be friends after I wrecked everything? And then I'm out a friend, *and* my Sorbet Guy, and where does that leave me?"

"In the self-help section of your local bookstore where you belong," she declared. "Where do you come up with this shit, Joss? I swear, you're looking for a reason to start collecting cats and embrace your spinsterhood."

I backhanded her shoulder. "I knew I shouldn't have told you."

"So, your plan is what? Not tell him and wait for him to fall madly in love with someone else? Sounds perfect!"

I blew out a long sigh. "I guess you're right."

"I think we should start all future conversations on this subject with you saying those words. Scratch that, let's start *all* future conversations with you saying those words."

I laughed. "It's too bad you have such crippling self-esteem issues, Nellie."

"I know . . ." She made a theatrical sound of tragedy. "So, now that we've established that you're stupid and you obviously have to tell him, what are you going to do?"

"I don't know." I scratched our little canine patient's throat as Nellie started cleaning up, the dental procedure was complete.

"Maybe you should just call him," she suggested.

"I'm not telling him over the phone!" I was positive about that anyway.

"You're probably right." She sounded disappointed. "So, what are you going to do?"

"I'm not sure."

"Maybe you should go to his place and wait for him in bed," she suggested with a laugh.

"I don't need to confuse the issue with sex, thank you very much."

Her sound of indignant shock was priceless. "Oh my God! You are going to be struck down by a huge-ass lightning bolt for that! You are the biggest hypocrite in the history of the world!"

"Nellie . . ."

"I cannot believe you just said those words! Seriously, that was, like, politician-worthy. You're like one of those born-again virgins who gets all high and mighty—"

"All right! You've made your point."

She shook her head. "Oh, I'm just getting started."

"What do I need to do to stop this?"

"Just keep telling me I'm right."

"And how many times am I going to have to tell you that you are right before I hear the end of this?"

"Hmm . . ." She sounded like she was giving it some genuine thought. "I think thirty thousand might be in the neighborhood, but we'll have to see when we get there."

"Great. I'm gonna have laryngitis."

"I'll accept it in the form of written lines, as well."

"That's considerate of you."

"Okay, but seriously, what are you going to do? How are you going to tell him?" Her mercurial mood had moved on to voyeuristic enthusiasm.

"I truly don't know."

To say I obsessed about what to do wouldn't be out of line. Should I tell Matt I felt more than I should? What were the consequences? Was I going to get past this crush? And should I just wait to find out? What was the use of confessing to something transient? What if it wasn't transient? Could I really pretend everything was normal between us?

What if he started seeing someone else? The thought tied my stomach in knots. Even if some new girl wasn't the girl he wanted to spend the rest of his life with, I wasn't sure I could stand to see him with anyone else.

But what if my confession ruined everything? What if he couldn't handle my change of heart? What if he couldn't even handle being my friend after I told him?

I wanted to crawl under the reception desk and block out every sound and drop of light. Work was a struggle—the animals could sense my tension, and responded with more fear than usual. I tried to calm myself for them, but they weren't fooled. I got puked on twice and peed on more times than I could count. The day passed excruciatingly slowly.

The idea of not having Matt in my life was . . . awful. Yes, I'd intermittently shared my bed with him, but there was so much more to us than that. We'd spent hours talking about our lives, our families, and our pasts. He knew me better than most. He was certainly on the short list of people who I still talk to who know what I look like naked.

How could I risk that just because I was confusing sex with a relationship?

But on the other hand, how could I not? How could I just sit back and wait for him to meet the love of his life?

I needed to figure out my own head before I tried to figure out his.

When my mind got to the point where I could no longer sleep, I knew I had to do something. Without pen and paper to organize my thoughts, I'd be lost forever in a snowstorm of jumbled ideas. As each thought passed through my consciousness, it left a wake of emotions that I could scarcely get ahold of before the next thought carried in a different set.

I started the list at work, feeling guilty and foolish the whole time. Committing them to writing made my feelings so much more real. More dangerous.

Pros of Falling for Matt

1. He's one of my best friends.
2. He's smart and funny.
3. He thinks I'm funny, even when I'm not.
4. He's easy to talk to.
5. He's good in bed.
6. He's actually the best I've ever had in bed.
7. He likes my underwear.

Cons of Falling for Matt

1. He's one of my best friends.
2. If we don't make it, I'll lose my Sorbet Guy.
3. He puts ketchup on his eggs.
4. He's too nice.
5. He can't even fake being romantic.
6. *If we don't make it, I'll lose Matt.*

I stopped the Pros list at seven items, afraid to make it too much longer than the Cons. I folded the note and put it in the back pocket of my pants, returning to my day with a little less chaos in my brain. My fingers sought out the shape of the folded paper several times an hour—I was convinced it would slip out to be discovered by someone I work with. Nellie would be bad enough, but if one of the vets found it I would be mortified.

At home, I attempted to avoid it for several hours with laundry, dishes, and an hour of reality television. The list was heavy in my pocket, it seemed to suck all the energy out of whatever room I left it in. A miniature black hole.

Dewey seemed to know it had something to do with Matt, and insisted on sitting on it when I unfolded it on my coffee table. I frowned at him and pushed him away.

"Go sit somewhere else!"

"Mrrr!" he snarked, and curled himself into a shape that resembled something like a meat loaf—still sitting on the paper.

"I'm working on that," I said, tugging the list free and settling it on my lap.

Dewey did his bungee-cat routine and bounced onto the couch, wrinkling the paper and putting one claw through it as he climbed on top of me.

"What?!" I demanded. "Why are you obsessing?"

He purred and made his eyes into slits.

"You're impossible," I told him and freed the paper once again. I elbowed Dewey into a somewhat placated heap beside me, then leaned forward to stare at my dual lists once more.

By the time I was ready for bed, the lists were longer.

Pros of Falling for Matt	Cons of Falling for Matt
8. My cat is in love with him.	7. He has terrible taste in women.
9. My family loves him.	8. If we break up, I'll lose Matt.
10. We have so much in common.	9. If we break up, I'll lose Matt.
11. He kisses my hair before he falls asleep.	10. If we break up, I'll lose Matt.
12. The way he kisses, period.	11. If we break up, I'll lose Matt.
13. He knows almost everything there is to know about me.	12. If we break up, I'll lose Matt.

All night, I tossed and turned. I knew I'd repeated myself in the cons, but the idea of losing him carried more weight than any other argument I could have come up with. More than that, though, I knew I'd repeated myself so that the truth wouldn't be so obvious.

I had to tell him.

He straightened up. "But, I've been thinking about it for a long time, Joss. I mean, it's not like I'd just throw away seven years on a whim."

"No . . . no, I get that . . ." I sighed. "I just didn't really see this coming, I guess."

"Seriously?" Matt looked incredulous. "Crap." He laughed. "I'm really sorry."

"I'm just—" *Dying inside.* "Adjusting."

He nodded.

As much as it killed me, I wanted to put him out of his misery. And I had to put myself out of my misery or I was going to devolve into a sobbing mess right in front of him. "You don't have to worry, Matt. I'm not gonna make this . . . like, difficult for you."

He looked at me with obvious confusion. "What are you talking about?"

I was seconds from crying. I had to get out. I stretched up on tiptoes and kissed his cheek, careful to keep my eyes downcast. He could not see me cry. "I'm gonna go. I—I'll—I guess I'll talk to you later."

"Joss, wait." He caught my wrist, but didn't restrain me as I pulled away. "Joss—"

"Bye." I snatched up my shoulder bag as I rushed for the door.

"Joss."

"I'll talk to you later, maybe."

He tried once more as I ran down the wood stairs, nearly losing my footing three times. "Joss!"

I ignored him. I didn't need him to make me feel better. Nothing was going to make me feel better. I needed to get away. I jammed my feet into my shoes and threw open the door, letting the screen door slam behind me.

Seconds later, my phone started ringing.

I let it go to voice mail.

I made it to my car before the first keening sob escaped my throat. I put one numb hand over my chest and gave in. He didn't want me. I'd come so close to telling him I saw more than friendship in him, and he didn't want me. He wanted Tara. My sobs came out in big, barking bursts, making my head pulse and my teeth rattle.

Hurt throbbed in my heart. I pressed harder with my hand, wishing I could reach inside and make it stop. Stop beating, stop hurting, stop pushing hot, embarrassed blood through my face. And still the tears came. My throat burned, my vision blurred, and I had to pull over. In the deserted parking lot of a dentist's office, I let gravity pull me down to the passenger seat and drew my feet up. Hunched in a protective ball, I ignored the emergency brake where it bit into my side and bawled like a baby.

There was nothing cathartic about my tears. They just served as fuel for my heartache. I shook, I cried, I wailed, I clenched my fists, I considered throwing up. Ultimately, I ran out of energy and tears, and lay in a wilted heap across the front seats of my car. And what had I gained through this fit? A headache, a stuffy nose, a sore throat, and no relief from the awful, hollow pain in my chest.

He didn't want me. He wanted away from me, in fact.

I closed my eyes and let out a noisy exhalation. Thank God, I hadn't told him anything. What if I'd managed to keep my courage and admitted my feelings? He would have been nice about it, I knew. He was nice about God damned everything. But it would have amounted to the same thing—he would have turned me down. He didn't want his Sorbet Girl anymore.

I gave myself a few more minutes of wallowing before I hauled myself up and started the car. Home was as good a place as any, I supposed, when no place was good enough.

When I let myself in, Dewey came out from one of his hiding places and sat down a few feet from me. As if cats weren't superior enough on a daily basis, he somehow managed to look downright condescending.

"What's your beef?" I snapped.

"Mrow."

"Don't tell me you're on his side." But, of course, he would be. In Dewey's world, priorities were:

1. *Turkey*
2. *Matt*
3. *A clean litter box*
4. *Me*

"Traitor," I said.

The clock informed me that it was nine forty-five. I knew I could call Nellie, or Jessie, or my sister, but I didn't even know what I'd say. What I really wanted was a time machine to take me forward a few days, weeks, or maybe months. Far enough that I would have figured out how to live through this.

I carried my bag to the bedroom and pulled out the clean underwear I'd thrown in, just in case I ended up back at Matt's place for the night. It seemed like an indictment of sorts, and I shoved it back in the bag for later consideration.

Bed was deeply appealing, but I knew sleep would be a long time coming. So, I did something I'd never done before. I went to the medicine cabinet and looked for a pharmaceutical solution. It felt shady as I was doing it. Escapist and chickenshit. But, I was at a complete mental roadblock. This was worse than any breakup I'd ever been through. I had no idea what to do, and no idea who could help me.

NyQuil. Jackpot.

I took double the adult dose and changed into my pajamas. Dewey, never a complete traitor if it meant altering his own comfort, jumped on the bed with me and curled up behind my knees. I stared at the pillow on the other side of the bed. It was still in the condition I'd left it last time I changed the sheets. That gave me a sudden rush of loneliness and I reached out to slap my hand into it, making a dent like someone else's head would leave.

I brought my knees up closer to my chest and tucked my fists tight to my body. The room was cold, the sheets felt colder, and I was terribly alone.

Come on, NyQuil.

The hangover that greeted me in the morning was plenty of punishment for my rash decision to abuse cold medicine. My head was foggy, on top of being just as hollow and lost as it had been the night before. Getting out of bed seemed like a chore.

I dragged myself to the bathroom and splashed water on my face. It was unfortunate my bathroom cabinet didn't contain any kind of antidote to cold medicine fog.

I checked my phone when I got back to the bedroom and there was a voice mail waiting for me.

It wasn't Matt.

The message was from Nellie. "What the hell are you doing?

I've called you, like, ten zillion times. If you're trapped under something heavy, I'm going to be pissed at you. Did you talk to Matt? Call me! Also, I wanna go out tonight. Call me."

I decided to have coffee before the inevitable return call, but it didn't help. So I called anyway.

"Oh my God, you're alive!" she greeted me.

"Hi, Nell."

"Ooh, somebody's crabby today. Did you get my messages? I only called you a hundred times."

"Yeah." I poured another cup of coffee.

She finally seemed to catch on to my bad attitude. "Did you talk to Matt? What happened?"

Fresh tears threatened to spill, so I tipped my head back, blinking at the ceiling. "He doesn't want to see me anymore."

"What!" It wasn't a question. "Are you kidding? Wait—what happened?"

I told her as quickly as I could. Newspaper-like reporting made it easier.

"Why would he do that?"

"I don't know." I pulled my knees up and hugged them tight.

"Did you tell him? About how you've been feeling, I mean."

"No." I sighed. "Thank God."

"So—wait. You didn't even tell him, and he *still* doesn't want to see you anymore?"

"Well, he said we can't keep having Sorbet Sex anyway. I don't know what he was thinking as far as being friends goes. I guess it doesn't matter. He's talking about moving away."

"Moving away?"

I told her about his idea for a fresh start, realizing for the first time we hadn't finished that conversation. I didn't know if he was serious about it, or just spitballing. I couldn't decide how to feel about it either way. If he was leaving, perhaps that was better for me after all. If he wanted me out of his life, there would be no easier way. But the idea filled my stomach with grit and acid.

"Do you think he was just saying that?" Nellie wanted to know.

"For what?"

"I don't know, to make you think he was only breaking up with you because he was moving far away? To make you think now might be the time to tell him you're in love with him?"

I winced and fought back immediately. "A, we're not dating so he didn't break up with me, and B, I never said I was in love with him."

"A, shut up, and B, you didn't have to."

There was a pause from her end long enough that I thought I'd lost the connection.

"Nellie?"

"I'm here."

"Are you going to say anything?"

"I've decided he wanted you to say something first. He was just testing the waters."

"Why would he do that?" I tried to lift my coffee cup again and tipped it over instead. There wasn't much left, but the spill made me want to cry. Again. I dug my fingernails into my palm and fought to stay quiet.

"Matt is not exactly known for his bravery in relationships, Jocelyn."

I opened my eyes. "What?"

"He's a relationship wuss. A nice guy with a fear of commitment, which is about the worst combination possible."

"But, I thought you liked Matt." I went to get some paper towels for my spilled coffee.

"I did. I do. That doesn't change the fact that he's too nice to tell a crazy girl to take a hike, and that's just for starters."

My instinct was to come to his defense. Christine had been truly nuts. That was hardly his fault. But I had a feeling she wouldn't take kindly to anything pro-Matt from me at the moment. Not to mention how pathetic it would make me feel. I kept quiet, which was fine with Nellie. She was still rolling.

"I also didn't like the idea that he was using my girl. That would be you, dummy. And it was *not cool* of him to take this long to break it off."

My cleaning up process slowed to a stop. "So, wait—you're in favor of him calling it off?"

"Obviously."

"You *enjoy* me feeling like the world's biggest idiot?"

"Yes. And no. I think he's bluffing is all."

"Nellie, don't do this to me. I can't have sick little hopes about him bluffing. I got lucky last night. I got out of this whole screwed up situation without him finding out about . . . about my stupid little feelings. If he wants to run away to California, let him. Hell, let him go to Australia."

"Okay, first of all, I wish I had a recording of you admitting this whole thing was screwed up from the beginning—"

"Nellie."

"Okay, okay, cheap shot. Second of all, you're a worse bluffer than he is. You don't want him to leave."

I didn't. But I wasn't going to get what I wanted, obviously. He might as well be out of my state as well as out of my reach. "I don't care if he does."

"Liar."

"Whose side are you on?" I demanded.

"Same side I'm always on, baby. The side of truth and beauty."

My fingers clenched around the phone. She could be so infuriating. "You are completely useless to me," I told her. "You were supposed to be on my side."

"You know what your problem is?" she asked, blithely ignoring my comments.

I sighed. "No, but I bet you're going to tell me."

"Your problem is you're an idiot."

"Excuse me?"

"You're an idiot for not telling him you love him and living happily ever after."

"I don't love him, I don't care if he moves to Tibet, and I don't want to talk about this anymore."

I didn't want to talk about it. I had to do something about it.

So, I got dressed for battle. The only pair of jeans that made me look like I had anything but a fourteen-year-old boy's ass, and a satin top that ordinarily made me feel like a million bucks. That night, I only got up to maybe a thousand, but it was an improvement over the dollar-fifty or so I felt like in my faded Badgers T-shirt and penguin-print pajama pants.

I went out on foot. My apartment was a few blocks from the nearest bar, but I had every intention of being over the legal driving limit within an hour of arriving, so why bother moving the car? I was early, for the bar world, and there were plenty of empty seats at the bar. I put my bag on the adjacent seat so I could pretend I was meeting someone.

There were two bartenders behind the bar, a busty blond girl and a tall, very muscular guy. The guy took two ambling steps toward me.

"Can I get you something?"

"Something strong."

He smirked a little. "How 'bout a vodka cranberry?"

I tilted my head and set my jaw. "Look, I walked here because

I have every intention of being over-served. Can you please not patronize me?"

His smirk melted into a true smile. "I've got something for you."

"If you bring me a cosmopolitan, you will officially be on my shit list."

He laughed out loud. "You got it."

I propped my elbows on the bar top and laced my fingers together behind my neck while he worked. *Coping through alcohol—always a great idea!* I thought, but I wasn't going to stop now.

The bartender returned and presented me with a tall glass, full of ice and a reddish-purple liquid. "This is going to go down easy," he said, "but this thing is no joke."

"What do you call it?" I asked.

"I learned it from a buddy down in Arizona, but I don't remember what he called it."

I took a sip. It was fruity and sweet with the nose-itching undercurrent of alcohol. Very drinkable. I hummed my approval. "It's good."

"What's your name?" he asked.

"Jocelyn," I said. "But everyone calls me Joss."

He nodded and looked beyond me for a moment. "We'll call it a Jossmopolitan."

"Ick. Please don't."

"Do you want to be over-served tonight, or what?"

"Right." I made a zipping motion across my lips.

"Well, then, I'm Matt and I'll be your over-server."

I'm quite certain I failed to hide my shock. *Of course, you are.* It figured.

"You okay?" he asked.

"I will be." I lifted my glass in acknowledgment.

* * *

The Jossmopolitan was everything he promised. When I finished my first, I took a walk to the bathroom on wobbly legs and looked at my reflection through bleary eyes. "What are you doing?" I asked the blurry girl in the mirror. She didn't answer.

So, I went back to my seat and waited for Bartender Matt to finish tapping out beers. When he looked my way, I knocked on the bar twice and he laughed.

"You are *not* drinking another one of those," he said.

"*Au contraire.*" I lifted one eyebrow. Drinking makes me think I not only can, but should speak foreign languages.

"I'll get you something else, but one's your limit for Jossmopolitans, you got it?"

"Well, then"—I rapped the bar again—"dealer's choice."

He set up a lowball glass in front of me and tipped an ounce of cherry flavored vodka over the ice inside. "You know, normally I make it a policy not to ask about people's problems, but I'm curious what's got you hittin' the sauce tonight."

Before I'd arrived, I had planned to lie if anyone asked me. But Bartender Matt's cocktail had punched a hole in my mental filter. "I just got dumped."

"I figured." He topped off the glass with tonic water and set a lime wedge on top of the ice. "How long were you with him . . . or was it a her?"

I laughed. "Him. And we weren't really together."

Bartender Matt pushed the glass at me. "Interesting."

"Long story." I took a sip. The tonic water was bitter compared to the sweetness of my last drink, but I liked it. "The dealer has good taste," I said.

"Thank you."

A forty-something man eased up to the bar, and Bartender

Matt turned his attention to the new customer. I sipped my drink and looked around. The crowd was thin for a Saturday night and I checked the time. Nine-fifteen. I really had showed up early. People would filter in over the next hour until finally there was a line at the door, I suspected.

Down the bar, a guy about my age smiled at me. I tried to smile back, but suddenly the idea of a one-night stand was loathsome. My salivary glands kicked into overdrive as nausea passed through me like a ghost. What was I doing? Did I seriously think I could just ease the loss of Matt with a random stranger? I should have known better. I didn't have the stomach to go through with a cheap one-night stand when I was eighteen, and I didn't have it at twenty-six.

I swiveled forward and picked up my drink. I would finish and go home before I did something stupid.

Bartender Matt returned, spreading his hands wide on the bar. "Slow down there, heartbreak, you're gonna fall off your stool."

"That would be a fitting end."

He left to serve a few more newcomers, and I finished my vodka tonic. But when I caught his attention to get my tab, he came back with another drink.

"I can't," I said, pushing the glass away.

"What happened to being over-served?"

"Bad idea. This whole plan was a bad idea."

"Do me a favor and taste this—" He pushed the glass back at me. "And it'll be on the house."

I shrugged and took a sip. It was light and lemony, and barely tasted of alcohol. I supposed I could tolerate one more.

The next time Bartender Matt came around, he leaned on his forearms and smiled at me. "I get off at ten. You wanna hang around and have another drink with me?"

I wasn't sure what I wanted to do. I'd had enough to drink that my worries seemed distant and faded. I *should* stop and go home, start chugging water and hope my hangover wouldn't be too deadly. But a night of solo crying wasn't terribly appealing. I pushed my hair behind my ears and nodded. "Yeah, sure."

"That's a deal."

I waited for his shift to end, nursing my lemony drink and forcibly avoiding all thoughts of the other Matt. My Matt. I was mostly successful.

Then, when he logged out of the register, Bartender Matt gestured for me to follow him to the end of the bar. There was a sizable crowd to navigate by then, and he beat me there by a full minute. At the end, there was a clear space where the cocktail waitresses came in and out with their trays. There weren't any stools open, but Matt got a couple of beers with no wait.

"Why are you off so early?" I asked. "People are just getting here."

"I'm the new kid," he said. "I get the dinner shift."

"That sucks."

He shrugged. "I get to hang out and drink for free all night."

"Classy."

He laughed.

We sipped our beers and talked for a while. I found out he had just been let go as a tight-end from the Arizona Cardinals. He'd never even gotten to play—he'd been injured during training. So, he'd come home to Milwaukee to figure out what to do next. I wasn't enough of a football fan to know if he was telling the truth, but he did look big enough to be a pro. I told him a little about myself, leaving out the details of my recent not-dumping.

All the while, my head was getting foggier and the room less stable. I wanted to sit down so badly I found myself looking at the floor for a clear spot.

"I think I have to go home while I can still stand," I said. "Sorry."

"You want a ride?"

"No, don't leave, it's only a few blocks." My ankles were in a conspiracy against me, however, as one of them took that moment to wobble and knock me off my wedge sandals. "Ow! Shit!" I grabbed the bar for support and tried to bring my injured ankle up to my other hand. I couldn't do it without falling, though, so I let my foot drop and settled on sucking air through my teeth.

"Let me drive you home. You're going to fall off the curb if I let you walk."

I couldn't say no.

Bartender Matt insisted on walking me into my apartment. It didn't take much effort on his part, I really was having trouble walking by then. He eased me onto my couch and pulled my feet into his lap to unbuckle my sandals for me.

"You don't have to do that," I said.

"Hey, I've brought you this far." He let my sandals drop to the floor with a *thunk*. "So, have you been sufficiently over-served?"

I nodded, and the room nodded with me. "More than sufficiently, I think."

"How drunk are you?" His fingertips caressed my ankle.

"Just enough," I said. "I know what I'm doing if that's what you're asking."

"So, if I . . . ?" He trailed off as he bent over and kissed me.

"That would be fine with me," I said when he pulled back.

The couch was adrift on a sea of my own drunkenness as we kissed, and I had to stretch one hand down to touch the floor to be certain it was there, and not moving. It didn't seem to be, so I let go and set sail once more.

Matt—the wrong Matt—shifted to put me on top and slipped his hand under my shirt. I tried to focus on the feel of his fingers on my skin and the warmth of his lips, but it was all wrong and I knew it. I wanted to cry.

He opened the clasp on my bra and I pulled back. "Do you do this a lot?"

"Do what?"

"Get girls drunk and talk your way into their pants?"

He grinned. "You're direct, aren't you?"

"That's not an answer."

"Do you really want one?" he asked and cupped my breast. His thumb flicked over my nipple and heat dripped into my pelvis.

"I don't know . . ." I had to think, but it was so hard. My brain was so muzzy and my body had turned traitor. "Maybe not."

"Think about it," Bartender Matt advised before pulling my shirt off.

I didn't. I didn't think about anything; I just gave in to my body's urging.

Thud. Thud.

When the knocks at the door startled us, I was down to my panties.

"Who's that?" he asked.

"I don't know?"

"*Joss?*" It was Matt.

"Oh my God," I gasped.

"Who is it?" Bartender Matt asked.

"Um, um . . ." I was on my feet and trying to struggle into my jeans.

"Joss?" Matt called again. *"Are you home?"*

"Just a minute!" I called.

"Damn it," Bartender Matt muttered.

I made a dash for my bedroom, stumbling into the walls twice, and pulled my bathrobe over my bare torso. When I walked through the living room again, Bartender Matt was working his shirt on, and although his pants were still open, he was sitting down. It would do.

I opened the door.

Matt took a step back when he saw me. His eyes were red-rimmed and his face was pale. "You're okay," he said, as if he was expecting otherwise.

"Yeah, I'm fine." I kept the door at about an eighteen-inch crack. My heart was hammering.

"You weren't answering your phone. I saw your car in the parking lot . . ." He gestured helplessly. "I just wanted to make sure you're okay."

I looked over my shoulder to see Bartender Matt getting his shoes on. "I'm fine."

"Look, you left so quickly last night. I think we need to talk."

I didn't want Matt to see Bartender Matt. I either had to get Bartender Matt to psychically determine he should hide in a closet, or I had to get my Matt to leave. My choice was obvious. "You don't want to see me anymore, and you're moving to California—what's to talk about?"

He winced. "You're mad."

"I'm not mad. This isn't a good time."

"You're very mad," he amended. "Please, can I just come in and talk to you? I think you misunderstood me."

"Joss?" Bartender Matt spoke up, and startled Matt and me into looking at him. "I'm gonna go."

Matt looked at him, then me, then him again. "Who are you?"

"Matt," Bartender Matt said, holding out his hand.

Matt turned his eyes back to me, ignoring the proffered hand. I cocked my head defiantly. "What?"

"Matt," Matt said, keeping his eyes on me as he belatedly shook hands with Bartender Matt.

Now they were both staring at me. I didn't say anything.

Bartender Matt shook his head and put up hands of surrender. "Well, this is gonna be a real shitshow, I'm sure. So . . . I'm gonna go."

Matt stepped back and made a sweeping gesture for him to leave.

"You don't have to go," I said.

"I really do. I don't want any part of this voodoo exorcism, or whatever it is you're doing here." He slid in the small space between me and the doorframe, and nodded at Matt. "Take it easy, man."

Matt watched him disappear into the stairwell and looked back at me. At my bathrobe, more accurately. "I should go."

Panic welled up in my throat. "Are you really moving?"

He looked at me like I didn't speak English. "I've got some job applications out. We'll see. I applied to transfer to Tulane, too. I have to go to New Orleans for an interview next week."

My chin started to quiver. "Oh."

"Is that it?"

I looked down at the floor, realizing that the whole world was still in motion as far as my brain was concerned. A sudden wave of nausea crashed through my stomach, and the acrid taste of all those mixed alcohols crept up my throat. "I think I should go lay down."

"Are you drunk?"

So, so drunk. "A little."

Due to staring at the floor, I could only see his feet shuffle. I had no idea what he was thinking. "Did you—?" He cut himself off. "Never mind. I'm gonna go."

"'Kay," I said.

He walked out of my limited field of vision and I closed my eyes. "Joss—"

I lifted my head and found two Matts. I blinked hard, and then there was only the one.

"What?" I asked.

He opened his mouth, then shook his head. "Nothing."

"Right." I nodded. "Nothing."

His eyes darkened. "What the hell were you doing with that guy?"

"What do you think I was doing?" I snapped.

"Looking for another drunk frat guy, huh?"

I flinched and went into full wounded animal mode. "Fuck you. I sprained my ankle and he gave me a ride home."

"You and your God damned damsel in distress fetish." His hands flexed and curled at his sides.

"Excuse me for knowing what I like."

"You have no idea what you like," he said. "You think love is flowers and sappy greeting cards and fucking carriage rides. Well, I've got news for you, Joss, that's just what guys do to get girls in bed."

"You have no idea what love is," I said. "You don't have a romantic bone in your body."

"Like you know. You think you want romance, but look at you—" He pounded his fist once against the wall. "You think you want it, but you don't."

I pulled the door open hard enough to bounce it against the wall. "Excuse me?"

"If you had any clue what love was, you wouldn't need flowers and your fucking knight in shining armor assholes. You're not their type." He threw his hands up.

I crossed my arms, which challenged my balance quite a bit. "And I suppose you think you know what I need?"

"Yeah, I think I do."

"Well, enlighten me, *sensei*!" I clasped my hands in front of my chest.

"You—" He cut himself off again, holding up a flattened hand between us. "You know what? You're drunk, and I'm not having this conversation with you."

"Fine by me." I scrabbled my hand against the door until I found the edge. "Have a great night." I almost closed the door, but at the last moment, decided on a final, cheap shot. "Scratch that. Have a great life. Get me your new address, okay? Maybe I'll send you a fucking Christmas card." Then I slammed the door.

And then I slid down the wall and buried my face in my fuzzy robe so he wouldn't hear me sobbing.

My hangover was born at three in the morning, and it was immortal. No amount of hydration, coffee, greasy food, or vitamin B could quell it. I began to suspect it was a hangover of the soul when it was still there—pulsing in my temples, churning in my stomach, stripping my mouth of moisture—a week later. Alcohol was a mild poison when it came down to it, guilt, disappointment, and a broken heart were far more potent.

Every day that went by was another day that made reconciliation less likely. We should have been talking to each other. But we weren't. It felt strange and awful to be estranged from someone who meant the world to me. He was always there if I needed him. Even if it was for something stupid, like getting my Christmas decorations out of the storage locker in my basement, or coming over so I could order a pizza without feeling like a pig.

He would be in New Orleans, I realized at one point. If I'd had any courage, I might have been there with him. If he'd wanted me to, that is. Was there even a chance he might have seen me as more than his future ex–Sorbet Girl if I'd only told him I saw him as more than a part-time booty call?

When no one was looking at work, my eyes leaked tears. The sound of my footsteps tapped out accusations as I walked: *You. Hurt. Him. You. Lost. Your. Chance. You. Stu-pid. Girl.* At night I lay awake, turning over our last conversation until it didn't resemble a human interaction so much as a term paper after a harsh teacher had corrected it.

I applied to Tulane—I don't want to leave law school, I just have to get away from you.

Looking for another drunk frat guy, huh?—You haven't changed at all, and I've outgrown you.

You think love is flowers and sappy greeting cards and fucking carriage rides—You immature little girl.

Well, I've got news for you, Joss, that's just what guys do to get girls in bed—Girls like you, Jocelyn Kiel. Girls just like you.

The truth was there in the subtext. He thought I was an immature idiot, and I could hardly blame him. I'd labeled myself childish when I'd made the pros and cons list. How could I argue with both of us?

Not that he was one to talk. The only person that he'd ever been in love with that I could even think of was Meghan, and that was probably just a matter of duration. He didn't know anything about true love.

Which was what exactly?

The question stayed with me as days passed. I prompted myself so many times: Love is . . . Love is . . . Often, the only completions came from quotes I'd heard throughout my life:

Love is patient, love is kind—1 Corinthians 13:4

Love means never having to say you're sorry—Love Story

The stuff of wedding vows and Hollywood. But what was it really?

Love was knowing someone, truly knowing him, and still wanting to be with him. Love was caring so much about another person that you willingly put his needs before your own. Love was sharing passion, history, trust. All of that, plus a fearless belief that life is better with your love than without. That everything that comes next will be made easier, happier, richer by his inclusion.

I'd become an ad hoc philosopher. I was centimeters from the truth, and the only thing that separated me from it was my own stubbornness.

Love was coming to my apartment on a Tuesday night so I could decorate for Christmas. Love was calling in sick to work so I could get to the hospital when his father died. Love was the best kisses I'd ever had in my life, and the lazy, sleepy talks we had in bed.

Love was Matt, and I was wrong not to see it before. I would be a fool not to tell him. We were already as distant as we'd ever been, what risk was there in putting myself on the line? None, really. He was slipping through my fingers, and I would never forgive myself if I did not tell him the truth before he was completely out of reach.

So, what's a girl to do on the morning after she realizes she's in love with someone? If my life was a movie, it would have been the point when I got dressed up in something girly and made a mad dash to my love's side to declare my feelings and we'd kiss and live happily ever after.

My life was not a movie.

I woke up feeling like a lukewarm cup of death after a broken night of sleep. I got dressed in my least-favorite scrubs, since everything else was still in the laundry. I drove to work in a sloppy rainstorm that flooded the storm sewers and drilled through my shirt with needle-like determination. I got puked on by a poodle named Francie within the first hour of work.

I drank coffee to keep my eyes propped open and watched the

clock. Although my mind was clear and the ache had gone from my chest, the day did not seem any less monotonous than the preceding weeks. Because it is one thing to admit to yourself that you love someone. But it is entirely another to admit it to that someone. And after that, you have to figure out what you're both going to do about it.

In the past, I'd told only a few guys that I loved them. It had been a straightforward process: start seeing someone, become exclusive, realize I loved him, and tell him. With Matt, I had clearly gone a long and circuitous way around the normal process. It was something of an advantage to know how I felt going in, but it was also terrifying. Was it possible that the act of dating him could make me not love him? I hadn't considered the possibility until that morning. What if I loved him, and we became a couple, and I learned about a million little quirks that would send me screaming for the hills?

I tried to imagine what he might be hiding; what idiosyncrasies could I have missed over the years? I already knew he watched way more sports than I could stand, but that was true of every guy I'd ever known, much less dated. I knew he ate ketchup on his scrambled eggs, which, despite being akin to eating a plate of garbage in my opinion, was hardly a deal-breaker. I ruminated on the subject all day, trying to come up with something about Matt that I could tolerate as a friend, but would certainly drive me mad as a girlfriend.

My list was short and limited to things that annoyed me about men in general, rather than Matt in particular. It included: leaving the toilet seat up, a considerable gap between our standards for housekeeping, and a tendency to snore if he slept on his back.

From there, my focus moved on to listing my own idiosyncrasies. Which of my tiny compulsions would be the one to drive Matt to leave me? My reality TV habit? My inability to cook chicken? The high cost of maintaining the infamous lingerie collection?

At the end of the day, I was forced to involve Nellie again. She'd gone out on a call with one of the vets. Dr. Srivastava was the only one who did it, and Nellie loved to go to the far-flung purebred breeders' compounds where Dr. S was the vet on retainer. She'd been gone all day. I nearly jumped her when she returned—I couldn't be alone with my thoughts any longer.

"Hey, girly-girl, how was your day?" she greeted me.

"Francie puked on me," I said in a conversational tone.

"I got bitten by a cat," she replied.

"You win."

"I know."

"Did it break the skin?" Cat bites were awful.

"Yeah." Nellie sighed and held up her right arm. Just below the wrist, she wore loosely taped gauze, stained with dried blood. "Antibiotics."

I winced. "Ooh, ouch."

"Hurts like a sonofabitch," she agreed.

She'd be back at work the next day, though. I would have bet on it. It takes more than a bite to get a true animal lover to leave the business. I'd been bitten half a dozen times myself, and had the scars to prove it. Animals are terrified at the vet; it's not personal.

"Sorry, Nell."

"I'll live." Her tone said the matter was trivial. "Now, tell me about something more interesting than poodle puke."

I was ready. I hooked my arm through hers and dragged her into the cramped supply closet. "I'm in love with Matt."

She tipped her head back to look down her nose at me. "When did you figure this out?"

"Last night."

"You're an idiot."

"What?" I demanded. "Why?"

"I can't believe it took you that long."

I gaped at her for a second before shaking myself back to the present. "I swear to God, I will never figure out how your mind works."

"At least you'll never say I'm predictable."

"Never mind that." I swatted that line of thought away, knocking my hand into a stack of boxed gloves. We both tensed for the collapse, but it steadied. I turned my attention back to Nellie. "Is he going to love me back?"

"He'd better."

"I'm serious, Nell. Have I completely screwed this up already?"

She steepled her fingers in front of her mouth and took a centering breath. Then she put one hand on each of my shoulders and stared straight into my eyes. "I'm going to tell you something right now, and I need you to know that I'm saying this out of love. Got it?"

I had a sinking feeling I wasn't going to like this. "Yeah . . ."

"Okay. Here it is: *Talk. To. Matt.* I cannot answer any more questions about this. You have to take responsibility for your own happiness. Tell him. Make it happen. And if it doesn't work, then you're allowed to come back to me and cry, okay?"

Take responsibility for your own happiness . . .

Those were some words to live by, if ever I'd heard them.

I had to stop wondering what if. I had to do something. Anything.

Perhaps I needed to do it like pulling off a bandage. As I drove away from the clinic, the sound of rain drumming on the roof of my Honda would normally have been a sufficient excuse for me not to call Matt. I was busy feeling like a brand-new girl, however, so I speed-dialed him, shocked when the call went straight to voice mail.

Even with my damn-the-cannons attitude, I didn't think a confession of love was voice mail material. Nor was I willing to hang up without leaving a message. I decided to go simple.

"Hi. It's me. Listen, I know we left things badly last time we talked. If you're willing, I'd like to try again. Please call me."

Just that baby step made me feel lighter. *Maybe,* I thought, *I can have this whole thing resolved by the end of the day.*

Of course, that depended on Matt calling me back. Which he didn't.

I didn't know if he was out of town or ignoring me, but I figured I could give him a couple of days to adjust.

At least, I hoped I could.

Despite my best efforts to be brave and confident, I still had to be alone with my thoughts as I lay in bed, waiting for sleep. Dewey was there, of course, offering feline moral support in the form of purring loudly and kneading my stomach until I groaned. I thought about Nellie's advice, and the last words Matt and I had spoken to each other.

Take responsibility for your own happiness.

You and your God damned damsel in distress fetish.

They amounted to the same thing. I counted on someone else to make me feel special, wanted . . . loved. And *that* was what made me childish. That was why I kept Matt shoehorned into the tiny box I'd created for him. He counted on me to know who I was and what I wanted, which I clearly didn't. Hadn't. Now it was starting to come clear.

Who was I? Just me. A little more insecure than I'd imagined myself to be, but ready to admit it for the first time. A work in progress.

Dewey flopped over in his sleep and twitched against my thigh. I furrowed my hand through his downy chest. One thing was certain—I wanted Matt and I had to take a shot at getting him.

Giving Matt time to adjust got me nowhere. He never called me back. As tempting as it was to turn tail and run, I knew I had to be brave. I had to take responsibility. So I called him again.

"Matty, it's Joss. I—I miss you. I'm sorry for the things I said. Please call me. Before you leave, at least. I just want us to be okay. Even if I never see you again."

And while I waited for him to reply, I had to make plans for Jessie's wedding. My plan was simple—take the train to Chicago and count on the kindness of one of my college friends to put me up for the night. It could backfire, for sure, but I didn't think it would. Worst-case scenario, I could pull an all-nighter and get the first train home in the morning.

With only two days to go before the trip, I called Matt one more time.

"Hey, it's me again. Here's the deal: You don't have to talk to me, but if you could at least let me know if you're still coming to Jessie and Evan's wedding, I'd appreciate it. And if you are, can we agree to be civil? Please, Matty. I hope I mean enough—*meant* enough to you, at some point—to get an answer to this."

The next day I got a text message: *Yes, yes, and yes.*

And I promptly burst into tears.

I was relieved that he responded, angry that he'd obviously chosen not to respond to my other messages, and nearly shaking with anticipation. I wanted to see him so badly. And what exactly did he mean by all those yeses? I tried to remember exactly what I'd said to him. I recalled asking about the wedding, and whether or not we could be civil. Was the last yes supposed to tell me that I'd meant something to him? Did I still?

For the third time since our argument, I drove to his apartment. The house was dark and his car wasn't in the service drive. As it hadn't been every time I'd come by. I didn't know where he was spending his time, and with him not answering his phone, I had no way to find out. I was starting to feel like a stalker, and I vowed not to stop by again without an invitation.

I was late for the wedding. I'd had two options for departure times on the train, and I'd obviously made the wrong choice. That meant slipping in the side entrance of the chapel and waiting for a good moment to take a seat.

I paused to take off my shoes—I am not a quiet walker in heels—and stuff them in my voluminous shoulder bag before I opened the big exterior door. The processional was in progress, with only a few members of the wedding party left to make their entrance. I'd known Jessie's bridal party was all relatives, but I hadn't expected them to look so alike. It was immediately obvious who was related to Jessie and who to Evan.

Jessie looked amazing. Her white dress rustled softly as she moved forward with her hand tucked in the crook of her father's elbow. Her cheeks were flushed with excitement and her eyes blazed. She couldn't wait to get to the end of the aisle.

The door I'd come in snicked shut, and Jessie glanced my way. When she saw me, her face lit up and she waved.

I waved back and whispered, "You're so beautiful!"

"You're late," she mouthed, but grinned.

Just then, the prelude died down and the whole building seemed to hold its breath. The string quartet struck up the traditional bridal march, and all of Jessie's focus lasered in on Evan.

"Let's take a walk," her dad said softly.

When they were out of sight, I snuck through the side door and tiptoed up the aisle until I found a good spot. Everyone was still standing for the bride's entrance, so I was able to join the crowd without attracting too much attention.

The officiant told the crowd to sit and I was finally able to look around a bit. I recognized a number of people from college and we exchanged tiny, excited waves. Then, I leaned forward to check the rest of my pew and saw Matt.

He looked different to me, even as my eyes took in the familiar shape of his face, the dark brown of his eyes and even the look in his eyes—he was in his own world. The difference was in the way I let myself feel about his familiarity. It was like the first time I wore my glasses: I couldn't believe how much detail I'd never known existed. I saw that Matt could be everything I wanted. I saw that if he let me, I could fall harder than I'd ever fallen before.

He blinked and saw me. My heart took off like a sprinter at the starting gun.

I mouthed, "Hi," and smiled a tiny smile.

He didn't smile, but mouthed, "Hi."

There were six people between us, and I would have gladly seen them all evaporate for a chance to slide down and touch him. But he looked to the head of the chapel, reminding me why I was there, and I had to follow suit. I chewed the inside of my cheek, concentrating on the wedding.

The ceremony was short—thank God. I hate the ones that trick you into going to a church service, then drag it out with lots of musical interludes for the unity candle and all that. Under the circumstances, I wouldn't have survived a long wedding. I needed to see Matt. He kept his eyes trained away from me as everyone stood and waited for the ushers to dismiss each row.

The day was expectedly gorgeous: sunny, breezy, and warm without being hot. The very reason that people get married in June. I took a deep breath of fresh air before doing the obligatory hugging and squealing with all my girlfriends. Seeing old friends is like slipping on comfy pajamas; I can never remember why I don't do it more often. I lost track of Matt as he drifted to the people he knew, and I had a feeling he was careful to keep it that way.

But after the tiny bubbles escorted the wedding party to their limo, and the families with children hurried off before their kids exploded with boredom, the crowd had thinned down to out-of-town friends with two hours to kill until cocktails began at the reception hall. That included me—and Matt. I caught up to him at the edge of the wide pathway leading away from the chapel.

"Can I talk to you?" I asked.

"Now?" His face was neutral, but his eyes betrayed him. He was hurt. Still.

"Yes, now."

Someone grabbed my hand and whirled me around. It was Kerry. "Are you coming?" she asked.

"Where?"

"We're all going out for a drink—it'll be great!"

"Where are we going?"

"Don't know! But we're right by the Magnificent Mile for the reception, we can find something—no problem." She grinned behind me. "You're coming, Matt?"

"Definitely," he said. "Let's go."

He got away from me again as everyone started dividing up into carpools and agreeing on a meeting spot. Someone produced an iPhone and found the name of a bar on Michigan Avenue. Then Matt was gone, and I ended up in the back of Kerry's car. We had to park a few blocks away from our destination, at Kerry's hotel.

As soon as we rounded the corner onto Michigan, the quality of the sound changed. It was a man-made cavern of skyscrapers filled with artificial darkness and the echoes of traffic bouncing off the concrete and glass structures all around us. I hitched my bag higher on my shoulder, wishing for the tenth time I'd been able to leave it in a hotel room. Not that I had one to leave it in.

"That's the John Hancock building, right?" Kerry's boyfriend, Mitch, asked, pointing at the tapering black monster a few blocks away. My knees went watery at the sight of it. Of all the panic-inducing heights around me, it was by far the most terrifying.

"Ugh, no thank you."

"Sweetie, that's where we're going," Kerry said.

"What?"

"The Signature Lounge. It's in there." She pointed at the Hancock building.

I stopped dead. "I'm not going."

"Oh, come on, you'll be fine."

"I can't!" I wailed.

"It's a *building*, Joss," Kerry said. "Just don't look at the windows."

I thought of Matt. "How high up is it?"

"I don't know," she said. "Probably not very high."

I followed them, totally prepared to bail at the last minute if necessary. We found everyone waiting in the lobby. The chorus of greetings when they spotted us made me feel like Norm on *Cheers* and I laughed.

"Is this everyone?" Annemarie's boyfriend, Kurt, asked, looking around.

Everyone agreed it was.

"This way to the top of the world," he pronounced and swept his arm to the elevators across the lobby.

"The top?" I asked. "How high?"

"Ninety-sixth floor!" Kurt announced with maniacal glee.

I shook my head and set my bag at my feet. "No. I can't. I'm afraid of heights."

"You're going to the reception, aren't you?" Annemarie asked.

"Yeah."

"It's on the eighty-third floor of the Aon Center," she said. "Didn't you know that?"

I most definitely did not. "I—I—I—I—" I stammered while cold sweat sprung to life all over my body and blood began to pound in my ears. "I can't!" Not that I could have stopped them, but the tears that rimmed my eyes embarrassed me. "I can't do it!"

The general reaction was laughter, which I'd come to expect after years of living with a phobia. "Don't be a baby," someone said. "We'll get you a drink as soon as we get up there," someone else promised. "You'll be fine."

"At least we're not going to the observation deck." Matt spoke for the first time. "It's open to the air." He raised an eyebrow at me. The crooked set of his mouth made it clear that he was enjoying my discomfort.

"Come on, Joss, don't be a pussy." The final, crass exhortation came from Kerry.

I glared at her.

"I told you she wouldn't do it," Matt said to the group, then headed for the elevators without a backward glance.

I wanted to stay on the ground. The very idea of being so high in the air made me nauseated. But, on the other hand . . . Matt.

I squeezed my eyes shut for a moment. "Okay, let's go. But I'm going to need a shot the minute we get up there."

The group cheered when I scooped up my shoulder bag and three people grabbed onto my arms, frog-marching me across the lobby with enthusiasm. My bag had mysteriously gained fifty pounds. It wanted me to stay on the ground. It was a wise bag with good ideas.

"You'll be fine," Kerry promised, squeezing my arm.

"You can do this, Joss." Geena squeezed the other.

I nodded and gasped, "I can do this."

Then, just as the elevator arrived, Matt announced, "You know, I think I want to see the observation deck after all. I'll meet you guys in a bit."

In the shuffle that followed, I ended up on the elevator, just inside the doors. Matt was still in the lobby.

Be responsible for your own happiness. I needed to get off the elevator. "Wait! I don't wanna go," I said, but the doors were already closing.

Matt stared at me through the closing gap, while Geena kept a fist curled around the wide strap of my bag and Kerry held me by the opposite elbow.

"Don't be such a chicken!" Kerry chided.

"No, I—" I started to protest, but I couldn't finish. The words died in my throat as the express elevator made a stomach-dropping move. My ears popped as the car shot up through the long shaft. A weird croak escaped my lips.

At last the elevator yo-yoed to a stop and the doors opened on a windowed lobby. All I could see was sky. I gasped and stumbled back into someone. Whoever it was caught me and tried to urge me forward, but I shook my head and groped for the wall.

All around me, my friends and a handful of strangers left the car with whistles and gasps of appreciation. As soon as they were all out, I stabbed the button for the ground floor. I had to get out of there. I had to get to Matt.

"Joss! Where are you going?"

"Oh, come on, at least have a drink!"

"It's perfectly safe." This last was accompanied by jumping on the part of Mitch.

"I'm sorry," I whispered.

The elevator descended even quicker than it had gone up. My ears popped three times and I clung to the thin metal rail that lined the walls. At least being alone, I was free to make whimpering sounds with my eyes squeezed tight and my legs shaking.

"One . . . two . . . .three . . . ." I panted each number to myself, trying the classic count-to-ten technique, but it was complete bullshit. As fast as the elevator was moving, the ride seemed to be lasting too long. Was I going to end up in some sub-sub-sub-basement? Had the cables snapped and I was in some hellish free fall?

Suddenly, the ride stopped, buckling my knees. I opened my eyes. The LED display read G with a star beside it. I was back on *terra firma*. The doors eased open and I burst out, sucking in sweet, street-level air. A small group was waiting for their turn to load and I got a few strange looks.

"'Scuse me," I said.

My breathing was still too fast as I looked around for the entrance to the observation deck. There was a queue made of black stanchions and retractable tape near a ticket booth. Apparently, I was going to pay for the privilege of facing my number one fear. Wasn't that just fantastic?

Okay, okay—one step at a time. Just buy the ticket. You can handle buying a ticket. "A ticket could be for anything," I mumbled as I forced myself forward on legs that seemed to be suddenly devoid of knees. After a quick search of my bag, the security guard determined I couldn't take the tower down with clean underwear and a tank top. I turned down the free multimedia tour, much to the confusion of the woman passing out the small screens on lanyards. And I walked past the photographer who had a green screen that I could only imagine produced trick shots of the horrifying scene at the top.

And then my chant was, *This is the line to go home, this is the line to get the hell out of this place* . . . It wasn't helping. My bra had shrunk three sizes, binding my ribs with every rushed breath. The line moved forward too quickly—there weren't enough tourists. How the hell had Matt gotten up so fast? Why couldn't the line be even fifteen minutes long? I could have found him in the crowd rather than submitting myself to torture. I was three people from the front of the line when I started to get dizzy. My turn was next—I had to get control of my breathing or I was going to pass out before I could even get on the elevator.

"Miss? Are you all right?" a strange woman asked me. She was wearing Bermuda shorts and a Day-Glo yellow T-shirt that read, *Wendy's Wandering Wenches.* I stared at the trio of W's. They were moving against that retina-injuring background. "Miss?" she repeated.

My lips twitched into a few random shapes before I managed to gasp out, "Fine."

She may have responded, but I'd gone deaf with panic by that point. The elevator doors were wide open, and my vision had narrowed to a crystal clear tunnel that turned the innocent door into yawning void of the Grand Canyon.

Ohgodohgodohgodohgodohgodohgod! MATT! Some small part of my mind was still in control. It shouted to be heard and did a hostile takeover of my motor functions. I rushed into the elevator and pressed my back against one of the corners, my bag pushed around to the front, keeping everyone else at arm's length. Still there wasn't enough air. I felt each vibration as the rest of the ticket holders got on board. The car was jangling in the shaft—it felt like the clapper of a bell as far as I was concerned.

I could hear my own panting from inside my head. Everything else seemed distant, like I was underwater. Then the doors closed.

The sound track in my head turned to static and endless chants of *ohgodohgodohgodohgodohgodohgod, ohshitohshitohshitohshitohshit- ohshit, nononononononononononononononononono, fuckfuckfuckfuck- fuckfuckfuck!* I was starting to see spots.

One of my sweaty hands slipped off the rail. I pressed it flat to the wall as my eyes clamped shut. Again my ears popped as we soared to the ninety-fourth floor. What the hell was I doing?

With a soft bong and a terrifying jerk, the elevator settled into its topmost perch. The doors opened and the last of my breath escaped me. The whole place was made of sky. Everywhere I looked—windows. Windows and the cursed clear day that height- ened visibility to its maximum. My eyes filled with tears.

"Are you getting off?" A blue-shirted employee looked in at me, his arm blocking the doors from closing.

I couldn't move.

"It's perfectly safe," he said.

I stayed frozen.

He tilted his head. "It's probably safer than the elevator." He pointed at the floor. "You do realize you're standing over an empty hole that goes about a thousand feet down?"

"Go to hell," I gasped, but got out of the elevator with my toes curled inside my shoes.

"Always works," he said.

A quartet of invisible giants was pressing on my chest from all sides. I tried to look around without seeing the windows, but it was impossible. The observation deck was glaringly white and filled with people wearing headphones. None of them were Matt.

He's not here. He left. He was lying just to get away from you. You came up here for nothing. He's not here. Whatthehellwhatthehellwhatthehell?

I found an interior wall to press my back to, breath now coming out in audible sobs. My vision was covered over in spots and my legs grew weaker with each second. I needed to sit down, but I couldn't move.

"Joss?" Matt's tone was pure wonder.

I turned my head with cogwheel movements.

"What are you doing up here?" he demanded.

"Trying not to throw up," I said. "Or faint."

His jaw clenched as he looked over his shoulder at the elevators. "You have to go."

"No, please!" I said it too loudly, but almost everyone had headphones. "I really need to talk to you."

"You need to go back down," he said. His eyes were dark—anger? My heart clutched in my chest.

"Please, Matt."

"Fine." He stretched out to grab my wrist and pulled me to the nearly empty queue of people waiting to go down again. Moving made me feel like I might slip through the glass and plummet to the ground. I knew it was insane, but I couldn't shake the image. I squeezed my eyes shut, colliding with him when he stopped. My bag thumped against my back and my eyes popped open. "You have until the elevator gets here to talk," he said.

"Really?" My voice cracked on the word.

He tilted his head back, eyes rolling. "Yes. Go."

All over my body my muscles received messages to sag or contract, my brain was a mess. I tried to catch my breath, but it was pointless. "I hate that you're not talking to me."

He sighed. "What is there to say?"

I tried to focus on his face, to not see the panorama through the windows. It helped a little. "You came to my apartment because you wanted to talk a few weeks ago. There's got to be something to say."

"Yeah, well, that was when I thought you'd be alone."

"I am." I hated the desperate sound of my voice and that my hands scrabbled at his shirt sleeves. "Are you?"

He nodded.

My panic was more manageable as long as I kept my eyes trained on him. I must have looked manic. "I have something to say, if you'll listen."

His mouth tightened into a line. "Yeah, fine."

"Okay." I took a deep breath, trying to control the shaking in my voice. "The thing is . . . I love you."

He stiffened and leaned away from me. "Love me like a friend?"

"No." My knees had gone watery again. "Love you, like, I'm in love with you. And I wanted you to know that before you move away."

His stiff posture broke and he looked up at the ceiling. "Are you kidding me?"

"No." I shook my head. Behind me, I heard the soft ding that announced the arrival of the elevator. Tingles raced up my spine. "I'm sorry if that's not what you want to hear, but I thought you should know the truth. I don't expect you to do anything about it . . ."

"Jocelyn—stop talking."

I flinched. Even with all the reactions I'd rehearsed in my mind, this one took me by surprise. "Sorry," I said again.

He shook his head with a clenched jaw that told me he was fighting to stay calm. Behind me, the queue shuffled toward the elevator. I heard the tiny sound of his knuckles popping as he curled his fingers in. He was perfectly still except for the rise and fall of his shoulders as he breathed oh-so deliberately.

My heart was a mad thing beating against its cage. "Matt . . . please . . . just look at me."

The moment his dark brown eyes, usually warm, lowered to mine I thought of a storm cloud. Tears burned my eyes. I had never imagined he would be angry.

Suddenly, he grabbed my shoulders and drove me back toward the open elevator. I stumbled, my mind an instant hurricane. I just needed another minute. "Wait, wait, wait!"

And then he was in the elevator with me, and still pushing me back and back until I was up against the wall and then his mouth was on mine and the other passengers on the elevator murmured indignantly. But it didn't matter because he was kissing me and it was Matt and the doors closed and my stomach dropped as we started the controlled fall into that thousand-foot well, but I didn't even think about it because Matt Lehrer was kissing me in broad daylight, in public and it was Matt and me against the wall and he was kissing me at last.

My hands were pinned at my sides, fingers splayed in a startle reflex. My heart threatened mutiny. He grew frustrated with trying to get a tight enough hold around my arms and my big leather bag, so he hooked his elbow behind my neck. His other hand found my waist. All the while, we shared the kind of kiss that I'd only seen in movies.

Distantly, I heard the uncomfortable shifting of feet and a few people cleared their throats. I didn't care. Matt was kissing the fear right out of me, and I didn't want him to stop for anything.

When at last he released me, he cupped my jaw in his hands and looked me in the eyes. "Don't you ever say you're sorry for that again, you got it?"

"Matty, what—?"

"I love you, too. That's what I was trying to tell you that night we had dinner. We can't keep up this Sorbet bullshit anymore because I fell in love with you."

The river of adrenaline flowing through my veins ran dry and I sagged against the wall. My bag slid down my arm and dropped to the floor. Tears spilled down my cheeks at last. "Really?"

He nodded. Someone in the elevator coughed again. I still didn't care.

"And I . . ." I mimed running with two fingers.

"Yeah."

"Oh God." I covered my face with one hand. My ears popped, but the sensation of the slow fall was all but gone. I couldn't feel anything but the places our bodies touched.

"Yeah."

"I'm sorry." My mind sorted through memories like a librarian on crack. "You weren't exactly up front about it!" I dug my fingers into his shoulders and gave him a little shake.

"I know, I'm sorry. When you ran off, I figured you weren't interested, but then I realized you probably thought—" He shook his head. "Never mind. It was a big cluster fuck."

The elevator announced our arrival on the ground floor with its soft electronic tone. The rest of the passengers crowded the door, and it occurred to me that we were probably the cause of their flight. I kept quiet long enough to get off the elevator and away from the outgoing tide of people. Then, I grabbed at his arm and he stopped.

"Are you really moving away?" I asked.

"Not without you." He kissed me again. One of those amazing Matt kisses that set me on fire. When he pulled back, he checked his watch. "Everyone is probably wondering where we are, but I seriously want to take you to bed right now if you'll let me," he said.

I considered. "I can live with that."

He grinned. "Let's get a cab."

In the back of a Chicago cab with a cracked vinyl seat and the sound of a Cubs game blaring from a boom box next to the driver, Matt and I made confessions and tried to keep our hands off each other, or at least keep our hands between first and second base.

"When did you know?" I asked.

"It was Jessie's wedding invitation," he said. "I just . . . it just made me think. I wondered if I was going to wait until your wedding invitation showed up in my mailbox to tell you how I feel."

"That's all it took?"

He kissed me for the length of a stoplight. "No, that was just the last straw. When did you know?"

"Not long after your dad died. But I didn't make up my mind to tell you until recently."

"Why not?"

"I was scared." I put my hand on his cheek. "You're one of the best friends I've ever had, Matt. If we screwed this up, I'd . . . I don't know if I could forgive myself."

He nodded. "I know. We're not exactly experts at relationships."

I laughed a little. "I'm not even sure we're amateurs."

He kissed me. "We'll learn."

"I was also worried that I wouldn't live up to your Sorbet Girl," I confessed.

"What?"

"I'm not perfect."

He burst into a loud laugh. "I know that."

"I'm serious, Matt. The lingerie, the perfectly smooth legs . . . I work my ass off for you because it doesn't happen very often. I wanted to be better than whoever it was that broke your heart or made you want to break hers. But, that's not the real me—not all the time anyway."

"I know that."

"I'm worried that you're in love with something that isn't real."

"Do you seriously think I only notice you when we're in bed? Give me a little credit here. I see you, Joss. I see you all the time."

I pinched the bridge of my nose in a weak attempt to hold back tears. His unexpected vehemence overwhelmed me.

"Does that help?" he asked. "Are you still scared?"

"I'm terrified," I confessed. "But I still want to do this. I still want to be with you, if you want to be with me." My nose itched with unshed tears.

The driver nosed into the curb and I beat Matt to the punch. There was a twenty-dollar bill tucked into my bra, which I passed up to the driver.

"Hey!" Matt protested. "I was gonna get that."

"Too slow." I took my change back from the cabbie and climbed out of the car. He was right behind me and he reached for my hand as we walked into the hotel. It gave me a private thrill that hand-holding had not given me since junior high. I couldn't hide my silly grin, and he noticed. "What?"

"Nothing." I lied out of self-preservation.

He led me toward the bank of elevators and I couldn't help groaning. "How high?" I asked.

"Second floor."

"Thank God."

In yet another elevator, he pressed me into the wall for a kiss again. I wrapped my arms around his neck, and focused all my attention on the feel of his mouth moving against mine. He really was the best kisser I'd ever known. The car jerked to a halt and buzzed loudly to announce our arrival on the second floor.

Matt carded his way into the room, then paused on the threshold. "I probably shouldn't be looking gift horses in the mouth and all, but . . . seriously, Joss, are you sure? 'Cause I really don't want to wake up tomorrow and find a Post-it note on my pillow."

"I would never do that!" I protested.

"It was a metaphor."

"I'm really sure. I want to be with you."

He smiled in relief and rubbed the back of my hand with his thumb.

"Besides, I always leave my Post-it notes on the bathroom mirror," I added, looking at him from the corners of my eyes.

"Right, I forgot." He grinned and let go of my hand to open the blackout shades. The room was small, worn, but clean, and it looked perfect to me. I dropped my bulging shoulder bag on one of the double beds while Matt emptied his pockets onto the desk.

Watching him move through his routine, I was struck once more by the combination of familiarity and newness. The lines of his body were the same, the vacant look in his eyes when he was doing something by rote was one I recognized from years of knowing him. But, I saw him with a distinct sense of ownership. Those lines, that look, that movement felt like it was part of my heart. I supposed it had been for a long time, but identifying it had been . . . enlightening. My own motives and actions from the last few years seemed clearer. I'd been positioning myself to be available to him as much as possible, even if I'd done it unconsciously. How utterly ridiculous not to see it before.

When he was done, he looked at me and smiled. "Hi," he said.

Nerves trickled through me, and I giggled. "Hi."

"You okay?" he asked.

"I'm—" I hesitated. *Go for broke.* "I'm nervous."

He laughed and took my hands in his. "Now this is the one part you shouldn't be nervous about."

I shivered. "It's good nervous. Like before a big game."

"I get it." He gathered me in and took a deep breath. "I've missed the smell of your shampoo."

I smiled. "I'm always available for smelling."

"When you stayed with me, after my dad died, you made my pillows smell like this." He buried his nose in my hair. "It stayed, even after you were gone. And the sheets smelled like . . . summer vacation."

"Coconut lime lotion," I said. "I've always thought it smelled like vacation, too."

He lifted my wrist to his nose. "Yeah, coconut . . . that's it." He pressed a kiss against the pulse point before releasing my hand and goose bumps thrilled up the back of my arm.

I went on tiptoe to kiss his lips, eager for more of him. It was heady, knowing that I wasn't gathering kisses to store in my memory; that I could have more for as long as he'd let me. There was no sense of the end being just around the corner. It made for a different kind of excitement.

His hands smoothed up and down my dress, lifting the skirt with each upward movement. I loosened his tie, unbuttoned his shirt, and pushed it down his shoulders until he had to let go of me to slip it off. The warmth of his body was easier to feel through the T-shirt he wore beneath, but it was still too much separation for me. I felt his abs contract in surprise when I skimmed my fingertips over his stomach and hoisted the T-shirt over his head.

"And now, my favorite part . . ." he murmured, drawing my zipper down slowly, "what is Joss wearing underneath her clothes?"

I lifted my arms over my head to make it easier for him. The dress came off easily, leaving me in one of my most indulgent buys, a red lace bra that fit so well it had been worth every extravagant penny.

"Oh my God, it's red," he breathed and looked heavenward for just a moment.

"Is that good?" I asked.

"That's good." Starting at the hollow where my collarbones met, he anointed my skin with his lips, steering me by the hips to the bed where he could finish the job after I was laid out on the blanket. Hovering above me, he was determined to make me squirm, it seemed, but I wanted my chance, too.

I pressed on his shoulder until he relented and lay on the bed, with me kneeling over him. My hair clung to what remained of my lip gloss and I tossed my head. Matt traced the shape of my body with his hands, looking mesmerized.

"I don't think I've ever seen you like this in sunlight," he mused. The yellow light of the afternoon sun blazed through the windows. The blackout drapes had given way to sheers that probably didn't obscure us from sight. Luckily, the glare from the sun was creating a mirror if anyone cared to look. He was right. We'd never been together before sundown. There was something honest about being naked in daylight, and I was glad we decided to risk the wrath of our friends.

I had to move to tug his pants off, and he took charge again, kissing my stomach and hips. I squirmed, unsure whether I wanted to escape the sensation or press closer and intensify it. I pushed at his waistband as best I could, but couldn't reach far. He rolled back with a grin and helped me get him down to his underwear.

"When did you switch to these?" I asked, slipping one fingertip under the waistband of his boxer briefs.

He shrugged. "I've got both. I don't know."

"You look kinda sexy."

He seemed pleased as he reached for me. "Come back up here."

I complied, fitting my body to his and taking up a fresh round of openmouthed kisses. Our pace was so much slower than usual, as if we both wanted to make this time different. I rolled my hips and shifted my legs between his, discovering new sensations with each move.

"I've always loved how you can't be still," he whispered.

"Really?"

"Yeah, it's like you can't help yourself."

"I'm just playing," I explained. "I love the way your skin feels against mine."

He found the clasp on my bra and set it loose, featherlight fingertips tracing the marks in my skin left by the elastic. He pulled each strap off my shoulders with such exquisite delicacy that I felt like the lace was a part of me. The tension building in my belly was tighter than any I could remember; I had never wanted someone more in my life.

I flattened my palms to the bed and pushed up enough to let my bra slip to my elbows. I freed my hands one at a time, then Matt hauled me up his body, high enough to kiss my freshly exposed skin. I was forced to brace myself above him while he used his lips and tongue to drive me to the brink of madness. The rest of my body was begging for contact and attention, attention I was reluctant to give if it meant I had to interrupt him.

In all the times we'd been together over the years, there had been little need for him to open his bag of tricks. The naughty thrill of Sorbet Sex had always been enough to get us both riled. The things he did to me that afternoon were enough to make me dizzy.

"You're driving me crazy," I panted.

"Good." He pushed my hips to the side and I rolled onto my back. He peeled the blanket back, and scooped me up to set me on the exposed sheets. For someone of such average size, he'd always been remarkably strong. I remembered how much it had surprised me the first time we'd been together as freshmen in college. When he had me settled to his satisfaction, I caught him by the upper arms and pulled him down to kiss me again. He dropped to one elbow, smiling against my mouth.

I could only reach his underwear with one hand, but I gave it an obvious shove in the direction of off, and looked him in the eyes. "I'm ready."

"Just a second." He pushed back to sit on his haunches and pressed his warm palms against my ribs. Moving down slowly, deliberately, he caught the elastic of my panties with nothing more than friction and rolled them down my hips. I rolled my hips a few times to help him free the scrap of black lace from my body. When he reached my ankles, I lifted my feet and he kissed the arch of one of them. "There's something I've always wanted to do . . ." he murmured and moved slowly up my body, leaving wet kisses on my knee and all along my inner thigh.

"Matt, please. . . ." I breathed. "I can't—I want you . . . please."

He paused just long enough to press his lips into the crease where my thigh met my body. His breath grazed over my most sensitive skin and I dug my fingernails into the sheets. Deep in my pelvis, the pleasure and naked wanting was akin to pain in its intensity. I needed him.

"Please," I repeated, tone sliding toward begging. "I want you—here, up here." I raked my fingernails through his hair, urging him to bring his mouth back to mine. "I want you inside me."

He made a low sound of approval and helped me get his boxer briefs off and on the floor with the rest of our clothes. The pause was almost more than I could stand. Then, he came back to me, and we slid together as easily as two long-lost puzzle pieces. I groaned at the relief that flooded me, and wrapped my arms around him. Every motion sent waves of pleasure through me, until I was dizzy with it.

The room faded as I focused on Matt's face and the sensation of our bodies moving together. He kissed me over and over, our breathing getting louder as we got closer to bliss. He slipped his hands beneath my hips, arching my back and altering the angle of our joining. I gasped at the change, quite suddenly on final approach for ecstasy. He recognized the sound of my breath.

"Take me with you," he said.

"I—I . . . uhhnng . . ." I became incoherent at the last moment, but clamped my thighs tight to his body and dug my fingernails into his back. I couldn't manage more than that, but it seemed to be enough for Matt. He forced me into an almost painful second peak with his last few thrusts and I made some unintelligible sound of delight. The room seemed to brighten, then fade like an explosion and my thighs fell slack.

In the aftermath, we panted and giggled at the involuntary jerks that occasionally rippled through me.

"I'm sorry." I snickered. "I'm not trying to do that."

"I know."

When he'd regained his breath, Matt excused himself to the bathroom and came back with a bottle of water. It wasn't cold, but when he offered it to me, I happily took a long drink.

He settled onto the bed again and ran his fingers through my hair. "You're amazing."

I smiled and rolled onto my stomach to reach for the water bottle again. "So are you."

"Your freckles really show in the sunlight," he observed, letting his hand drift over my back.

"I know." I wrinkled my nose.

"I don't know why you hate them so much. They're cute."

"It's part of the chipmunk thing. More cuteness."

"Well, I like them." He kissed me between the shoulder blades just before I rolled over again.

"Matty, are we really gonna do this?"

He tried and failed not to look concerned. "I thought that was the plan."

"Okay. Good." I got to my knees and straddled his lap. "'Cause I could really get used to having full access to you all the time."

He smiled. "Yeah?"

"Yeah. And I'll be really glad not to go on crappy dates anymore." I looped my arms around his neck.

"How soon should I expect you to bust out the ugly underwear?" he asked.

I burst into laughter. "Ooh, I don't know."

"How ugly are we talking about?"

"It's not ugly. It's just cotton and boring. I wear it to work."

"Dogs and cats don't appreciate French lingerie, huh?"

"Some of it's Italian. And no. Plus, I get peed and puked on . . . a lot."

"Right." He kissed me lightly, initiating a brief exchange of affection that ended with me on the bottom of a two-person pile, and our legs a tangled pretzel. "I guess we can tear up our contract."

I laughed. "Even the laminated one I keep in my safe deposit box?"

"Yeah, and have your assistant shred any copies you might have lying around."

"I'll send her a memo."

"Okay, good." He pressed his lips to a ticklish spot on my neck.

I squirmed as goose bumps popped up across my chest. "You're making me cold!" I scratched at the sheets, trying to catch hold of something to cover myself with.

"Mmm, that's no fun," he complained when I succeeded.

"Why not?"

He paused. "I can't come up with a reason other than wanting you to be naked."

"It's not good, but it's a reason."

"Maybe the novelty will wear off after a while."

"You've been seeing me naked since we were eighteen. There's no novelty left."

"Only intermittently."

"True."

He kissed me—another of his amazing kisses that made me wonder just how necessary oxygen really was for a person. "I love that you came to the observation deck today," he said.

Automatically, I got butterflies in my stomach. "Yeah?"

"I never thought you'd do it."

"So you *were* trying to get away from me!" I shoved at him without any success.

"I—" He exhaled, all traces of defensiveness disappearing. "Yes."

"Very mature, Matt."

"I was mad at you," he said.

"I know." I laid my hand on the side of his face. "Are you still?"

"No."

"And when I have my clothes on again, are you going to remember that you were mad?"

He just laughed, and kissed me, and laughed some more. "No. Promise. I love you, Joss."

"I love you, too."

Our lips came together in slow, simmering kisses. They tasted of promise rather than impermanence—a main course, and dessert, too. Which reminded me . . .

"How long do we have before the cocktail hour starts?"

Matt lifted his head and squinted at the clock. "It started fifteen minutes ago!"

My eyes flew wide. "Oops!"

He was already on his feet. "To be continued?"

I paused mid-scramble and smiled. "No end in sight."

CHAPTER TWENTY-NINE

AND NOW . . . ?

We had to hurry, but my hair and makeup might as well have been an advertisement for Afternoon Delight. I had to do repair work. Matt peeked in through the bathroom door. "Are you almost ready? We're so late."

"I can't get this damn earring in." I held out the offending jewelry and gave it, then him, a frustrated scowl.

"You can do it in the cab, come on." He disappeared from the door and I rolled my eyes.

But he was right, so I cupped the earring in one hand and scurried back into the hotel room. The bed was rumpled and my shoulder bag looked like it had gotten sick on the floor, but there was no time to do anything but grab my small purse from the mess still left inside. "Okay, I'm ready."

"You don't have shoes on."

I picked them up from the floor. "I'm not putting them on until I have to."

"Whatever." He opened the door and gestured for me to go first. We hurried down the hall to the elevator where Matt stabbed at the button repeatedly and I held my shoes between my knees while I tried once more to get my earring in. I almost had it when the elevator arrived, and had to waddle into the car to prevent losing my shoes or my chance for victory over the earring.

"Aha!" I exclaimed when it sank home. I looked in the mirrored panel in the back of the elevator and saw that my ear was bright pink from the effort. Hopefully the swelling would go down by the time we got there. I stepped into my shoes just as the doors opened on the lobby and I gave Matt a final look of triumph. "See? Totally ready to go."

He smiled, shaking his head.

We pushed through the revolving doors to the street and hailed a cab.

He reached for my hand and threaded our fingers together.

"So, how do you want to play this?" I asked.

"What do you mean?"

"People are going to want to know what happened to us." A quick check of my cell phone told me I'd ignored three phone calls from the group at the John Hancock building. I was sure Matt's would be the same.

"You can tell them the truth if you want." He looked at me from the corners of his eyes, not bothering to hide a smirk.

I held up a staying hand to my imaginary audience. "Sorry, everybody, urgent hotel sex situation."

The cabbie's eyes looked in the rearview mirror, so I gave him a wide-eyed blink.

Matt laughed. "Look, people, I can only go so long without getting Joss out of her clothes, and it had been a while."

The cabbie glanced at us in the mirror again, but I was laughing too hard to look innocent that time.

"Aon Center's to your left," the driver said, pulling to the right of the wide boulevard.

"We'll walk it," Matt said. We got out of the car and scurried across traffic hand in hand. The sidewalk was a full story above the crashing waterfalls in the entrance courtyard. As we reached the stairs that would take us down to that level, I spotted our friends hurrying toward us from the west.

"I guess we're not the only ones who are late," I said.

"Jocelyn Kiel, where the hell have you been?!" came Kerry's shout while they were still fifty yards away.

We waited for them to catch up, still holding hands. I had butterflies again, but they were the good pre-game kind. We were about to go public.

The interrogation began as soon as they were within earshot. "What the hell happened to you guys?"

"You losers ditched us!"

"You know when your phone rings, you're supposed to answer it, right?"

"You missed a kick-ass view!"

"Sorry, guys," I said. "We, uh—"

"Joss couldn't handle the heights," Matt cut in.

I elbowed him for giving me the blame.

"You still could have answered your phone," Annemarie said.

"Sorry."

"Well, whatever, we're late," Kurt said. "Let's go."

The group crowded down the stairs, and just before we went inside, I finally allowed myself to look up at the glass facade. My knees turned to water. The skyscraper reached eighty-three stories toward the clouds, and Jessie and Evan's reception was on the very top floor. I couldn't imagine standing that close to the sky. I was officially going to kick Jessie's butt for failing to mention this in all the times I'd asked her about wedding plans. Not that she would have cared—it was her wedding.

"I can't do it again," I whispered, gripping Matt's hand.

"You'll be fine," he assured me.

"Maybe I should just stay down here."

"Come on, you big wuss," he teased, giving me a tug toward the entrance.

I made a whimpering sound, but let him lead me through the

lobby. There was an attendant outside the elevator who seemed to take a malicious pleasure in using his key to activate the private elevator. When the doors opened, he grinned at us and said, "Next stop, top of the world."

"Why do they always say that?" I whimpered.

Matt laughed. "You can do it, Alvin."

The others were chattering, ignoring my oncoming panic attack. It was all back again—the pounding in my ears and chest, the lack of air, the prickling feelings all over my body. The doors closed and I turned my face into Matt's chest.

He kissed the top of my head and rubbed my back while my stomach sank into the region of my ankles. My curiosity got the better of me, and I had to peek at the readout in the corner of the elevator. The numbers were in the forties and climbing.

"I can't do this! I want to go back down! Don't make me get off the elevator!"

Matt took my face in his hands and kissed me soundly for the rest of the ride.

The silence among the other passengers was deafening. The elevator opened on the eighty-third floor, and I allowed Matt to nudge me into the lobby.

"So, uh"—Geena pointed at Matt and me with one swiveling finger—"what's going on here?"

"We're . . . together," Matt said.

"Shut up!"

"This isn't, like . . ." Kerry made an uncertain gesture and face to match.

"No." I shook my head. "It's . . . real."

A slow smile spread across Kerry's face. "I knew you couldn't keep it up."

* * *

By the time we were seated for dinner, I was already convinced that I'd never been to a more spectacular wedding. The club was luxurious, and if I kept my eyes away from the windows, the interior was lush enough that I could pretend I wasn't nearly a thousand feet from the ground. The freely flowing champagne helped keep my nerves at a dull undercurrent. Even the table settings were the most elegant I'd seen.

We listened to the toasts and watched as a flurry of servers hit the floor with the first course. Our table was populated entirely by friends from college, and we were by far the loudest group in the room. The evening was filled with so much laughter that I had to reapply mascara after the video.

When the salad plates had been cleared, the servers returned with small plates.

"That doesn't look like dinner," Nate groused. "I'm hungry!"

"Maybe it's just really small," Geena said with a grin.

Our servers arrived to set down the chilled plates and Matt and I locked eyes. It was a sorbet course. I laughed and quickly covered my mouth.

"Is this dessert?" Mitch wanted to know.

"It's the sorbet course, you idiot," Kurt said.

"Why are we eating ice cream before dinner?"

"Haven't you ever had a sorbet course?" Kerry asked.

"It's supposed to clear your palate," Matt said.

"All right." Nate shrugged and dug into the small pink scoop of sorbet on his plate. "Not bad."

I picked up my spoon, but hesitated. I knew it was stupid, but it seemed wrong to eat it. Looking at Matt, I saw that he wasn't eating either.

"It's ridiculous not to eat this, right?" I said in a low voice.

"Right," he agreed, but didn't touch his spoon.

I watched everyone else eat, still holding my spoon, until at last Matt reached over and took it from my hand. He set it on the edge of the plate in the international symbol for "I'm done," and did the same with his own.

"I don't care if it's stupid; I'm not eating it," he said.

I smiled and leaned close to kiss him. "Me either."

He sat back in his chair with a contented sigh. "Good."

"I mean, people can go their entire lives without ever having sorbet again, right?" I asked.

"I intend to."

ACKNOWLEDGMENTS

Endless thanks to the Ballantine team, but most especially Junessa Viloria whose enthusiasm for this book has been a ray of sunshine from day one. And to Laura Bradford, the agent with the mostest, for championing my little misfit story.

Squees, and whipcracks to the Wednesday night crew. Hugs as always to Jessica Souders for unerring support. And retroactive thanks to everyone who read this story the first time around. You know who you are, WTFers.

Thanks to my Classmates, and the Binders for talent, support, and knowing more than me. And my shocked, humbled gratitude to all the amazing readers and book bloggers out there whose contagious excitement has bowled me over.

Love and gratitude as always to my family. I couldn't do this without you.

Although many of the locations in this book are real, I have taken some liberties with their geography and characteristics. College campuses in particular are subject to frequent change and I had to pick a point in time to set this story. Don't throw things at me.

© SHANNON WUCHERER

ELLIE CAHILL is the much easier to pronounce super secret identity of Liz Czukas. Liz is an author of books for teenager-type people, but *When Joss Met Matt* is Ellie's first novel. Both Liz and Ellie can be found at lizczukas.com. Off-line they are probably writing another book or fangirling over television dramas, and most likely eating chocolate chip cookies at the same time, too.

elliecahill.com
Facebook.com/EllieCahill
@Ellie_Cahill